NO SAFE HAVEN

ANGELA MOODY

ISBN: 1514643677
ISBN-13: 978-1514643679
Library of Congress Control Number: 2016901919
CreateSpace Independent Publishing Platform,
North Charleston, SC

DEDICATION

I dedicate this book to my mother and father. Thank you for always believing in me. I love you.

ACKNOWLEDGMENTS

I couldn't have written this book without the help of too many to name here. I do want to thank my wonderful family for putting up with me while I undertook this journey. Your love and support means everything to me. The same goes for my fantastic critique partners. You ladies pulled things out of me I didn't know existed and you did it with love and good humor. Thank you so much, Audrey, Deb, Julie F, Julie K, and most of all, thank you Monica. To Deirdre Lockhart, of Brilliant Cut Editing, the most wonderful and gifted editor anyone could ask for. You took a diamond in the rough and made it sparkle.

Prologue

July 4, 1893
Selinsgrove, PA

Tillie Alleman sat back in her new Adirondack chair, chewing the last of her watermelon slice and watching her family enjoy their picnic.

Her husband, Horace, strolled through the garden, talking with their son, Harry, a serious nineteen-year-old, starting his second year of college in September. Harry's interest in law pleased his father. From the tilt of their heads and low murmur of their voices, surely, they discussed appropriate college classes, law schools, and which type of law to pursue as they ambled through the gardens.

Seventeen-year-old Mary and thirteen-year-old Annie sat on the picnic blanket nearby, a Godey's Ladies Book between them.

"I can't wait until I can wear long skirts." Annie fingered her sister's flowered lawn dress. "Ma says when I turn fifteen I may."

Mary leaned in close. "She made me wait until fifteen as well." She glanced back at their mother. "How old were you, Ma, when you started wearing long skirts?"

Tillie rose and joined them on the picnic blanket. "I was fifteen as well."

Annie's face fell.

Tillie placed a gentle hand on Annie's knee. "It's an appropriate age for girls to start with long skirts."

Mary leaned into Annie and wrapped her arm around her sister's shoulder. "Don't be in too much of a hurry to be a lady, Annie. Then it becomes inappropriate to run, skip, or jump."

Tillie arched a brow. "Mary." She leaned forward. "I do hope you behave like a proper young lady at the academy."

"Of course, Mother." Mary sang. She sat back and lowered her eyes to the blanket for a moment. She looked at Tillie. "I have excellent grades and no demerits for improper dress or deportment. But, sometimes, I would love to jump into a mud puddle or run down the street, just because it feels good to do so."

Tillie opened her mouth to berate Mary for such an admission, but Horace and Harry joined them.

Harry dropped his lanky frame down across from Annie, causing the Godey's Ladies Book to slip off her lap.

"Harry!" Annie grabbed at it.

"What are you looking at, Mouse?" He tried to grab the magazine, but Mary and Tillie reached in to stop him.

"Harry, leave her be." Tillie swatted his arm. "And don't call her mouse."

"She is a mouse." He shrugged, ignoring her admonition, and then dropped onto his back and looked up at the sky beginning to change to early evening light. "So what did you all do for fun on the Fourth of July, when you were young?" He glanced at his parents, and then resumed staring at the sky.

"Who said we had fun on the Fourth of July?" Tillie teased.

Horace chuckled and Mary laughed. Harry grunted.

"Ma, would you tell us the story?" Annie closed the magazine and laid it on the blanket between her and Mary. "I just love hearing the story. Would you tell it, please?"

"Oh." Tillie wrapped her arm around Annie's shoulder. She pressed her cheek to the top of her daughter's head. "You've heard that story a thousand times."

Harry shifted and leaned on an elbow. "We don't care. We love the story. Please tell it."

"Yes, Ma, please," Mary joined in. She readjusted her skirts and pulled her knees up, making herself more comfortable.

Horace chuckled, pulled his pipe out of his shirt pocket, and clenched it between his teeth. He reached into his trouser pocket and removed a pouch of tobacco. "I don't believe you have much choice, my dear." He tamped tobacco into the bowl and lit it with great big puffs.

The scent of applewood pipe smoke curled around them and wafted away on the evening breeze. The smell of her family. Just as the metallic scent of animal blood and lemon verbena were the smells of her childhood.

"Oh, dear." An amused grin tugged at her lips. "How can I refuse these faces?" She glanced at the remains of their picnic feast. "We should clean up first, and then," she looked at Annie, "I suppose I can tell the story."

Horace blew pipe smoke into the air. "We can clean up after." He grinned and bit into his pipe stem.

Tillie shot him a look of love and amusement. He loved the story as much as their children did. "Very well." She pushed off with one arm and raised her hip off the ground. With her free hand, she pulled her skirts out in front of her so they wouldn't bunch and tighten about her legs. Then, when she was comfortable, she peered off to the west. The sun was gone now, but the heat lingered, and in the half-light of the remaining day, she gathered her thoughts. "I can't believe thirty years have come and gone since," she began. "I was just a girl when the Confederate soldiers marched into Gettysburg and changed my life forever."

“The hand of our God was upon us, and He delivered us from the hand of the enemy.” - Ezra 8:22

PART ONE

GETTYSBURG

Chapter 1

Monday, June 22, 1863

Nothing ever happened in Gettysburg. Fifteen-year-old Tillie Pierce gripped the front step railing and hoisted herself up. She braced her hips against the wood and leaned as far over as she dared without falling. She didn't want to miss the goings-on at the Diamond, the town square.

Traffic increased along the cobbled stones of Baltimore Street. Farmers with empty wagons bumped along, negotiating the narrow roadway shared with gentlemen on horseback shouting and pushing their way through traffic, intent on reaching their destination. Men and women dashed across the street, weaving in and out as the teamsters whistled and shouted to horses and pedestrians alike. Young couples strolled toward Evergreen Cemetery.

Tillie set her feet on the stoop, as a proper young lady ought.

Waning sunlight bathed the brick houses' rooftops across the street. A gentle breeze rustled the three linden trees in front of the house, and the evening sky deepened.

On Tillie's left, Mr. Codori's wagon appeared on Breckenridge Street.

Her eyes widened as he attempted to force his way into the traffic on Baltimore Street, causing a jam. His horses reared and whinnied. Mr. Codori stood and shouted at the man with whom he almost collided. The man shook his fist. A crowd gathered. When she was sure no one saw her, she hoisted herself up on the railing again, straining to see over the tangle to discover when the men might begin their evening spectacle.

Father said the Rebs would never get this far north, so why the codgers tramped the streets in the town's defense went beyond her comprehension.

The traffic jam sorted itself out, and the crowd dispersed. An uneven stomp caught her attention. Hoisting herself up again, she peered north, toward the Diamond where the tops of pickaxes and pitchforks stabbed the sky as the men marched into a slope in the road. They bobbed into view again when they topped the rise near Middle Street. Tillie dropped to her feet and braced her elbows on the railing. She snorted, rolling her eyes at the gray-haired lawyers, doctors, farmers, and businessmen shuffling down Baltimore Street, in defense of the town. The front door opened, and Father emerged. She straightened up as he put his arm around her in a gentle squeeze.

She wrinkled her nose, suppressing a gag at the metallic scent of animal blood still clinging to him. "Finished for the day?"

"Yes." He kissed the top of her head, releasing her. "Mr. Codori was my last customer."

Thank goodness. She stepped to the side, turned her face away, and forced a cough. She covered her mouth, using the gesture to squeeze her nostrils together, then dropped her hand and glanced at him through her lashes. He faced the street as the men marched by. Should she tell him about Mr. Codori? No. Father didn't like tattletales. She slipped her arm through his and put on a bright smile. Together they viewed the parade.

Father smiled, waving off the greetings and entreaties to join them.

The old men playing soldier reminded Tillie of her brothers, James and William, one in the Army of the Potomac, the other in the Army of the Cumberland. Gone to the army more than a year ago, she wrote to them without fail every week, and initially she got regular letters back each month. She received her last letter from James in March and William in April. Their recent silence scared her. Her heart lurched even now. She prayed for them nightly, although she didn't think her prayers carried much weight. "What do you think James and William are doing right now?"

"I'm sure they're safe, my dear. No doubt they're too busy to write, is all."

"It's just…they haven't written in so long." She winced. Even to her ears, she sounded childish.

"If Mr. Buehler had any news, he'd tell us straight away. There's nothing to fear. The boys are in God's hands."

She didn't dare say his words offered little comfort. Having them home to touch, to talk to—that would be comforting.

Instead, she focused on the sorry looking group marching in the street. They acted nothing like the men of the Union Army, just old men playing soldier with pitchforks, pickaxes, shovels, and the occasional rusty Revolutionary War musket. How did they think Rebel soldiers would find them daunting? She didn't.

"They'd be taken prisoner." She pointed her chin at the men.

Mr. Kendlehart, the Borough Council President, couldn't march and handle his ancient gun. His brow furrowed. He fumbled at the mechanisms, causing the men around him to duck while the barrel of the weapon swung to and fro. He stopped midstride, and Mr. Fahenstock crashed into him.

Tillie burst out laughing. "There they go, the great knights of Gettysburg!"

"Don't mock, Tillie." Father frowned. "They're your elders. Be respectful."

"Yes, Father." Warmth crept up her face, but… "Still, don't you think they're being silly? The war is in Virginia. Not here."

He gave a slight shrug and kept his eyes on the men filing past. "No. I don't think so." The men disappeared over the brow of Cemetery Ridge. He turned and opened the door.

"Then why aren't you in the Home Guard?"

He held the door for a second, then with careful deliberation, pulled it closed and faced her. "Because. While I don't think they're being silly, I do think they're overreacting. The Rebs won't maneuver their entire army over the Mason-Dixon Line."

"So why do they think we need a Home Guard? What possible good can they do?" Tillie studied Father.

He shoved his hands into his pockets. "It doesn't do any good. But they believe they're contributing to our security. That's why I don't ridicule them." He pointed to her. "And neither shall you."

She lowered her head in acquiescence. Why would they want to take a small, even ridiculous, part in the war to feel important? As businessmen and members of the Borough Town Council, they loomed large to her. Why should they need to prove anything? She raised her eyes to Father. "Can I ask another question?"

"May I ask another question." A sly smile curved his lips.

"May I ask another question?"

"You just did." He crossed his arms and gave her a teasing glance.

"What?"

"You may."

"Oh." Tillie giggled and relaxed as he chuckled.

"The other day I read in the newspaper that folks in Waynesboro saw Confederate infantry and cavalry all over the place. Almost four thousand troops. Would the Rebs need so many men to raid a few farms?"

"Don't fret, child. Perhaps they're stragglers, like last year. The newspapers exaggerate to sell their papers. That's how they stay in business." He patted her shoulder. "Now come. Your mother says supper is ready."

Tillie walked through the sitting room to the kitchen. To the right a long table stood with six chairs around it, one at each end for Father and Mother, and two on each side. When the boys were home, they sat on one side, and the girls on the other. Maggie had the table almost set. Along the back wall, in the center, the door to the backyard and butcher shop stood open to catch any breezes willing to waft into the room. On the other side of the room, Mother worked at the stove, transferring fried potatoes into a serving dish.

Beside her, a set of shelves held white bone china. Gay pansies and peonies painted the center of each dish. The same design stamped the center of each cup, as well as serving bowls and platters. Crocks of jams, sauces, and jellies, as well as Tillie's favorite, strawberry-rhubarb pie, for dessert waited closer to arms' reach. Her stomach grumbled. "What can I do to help, Mother?"

"There you are." Mother's deep-brown eyes pierced her with a where-have-you-been stare as she handed her a plate of cold ham.

Like a storm cloud hanging over the house, George Sandoe, her sister Maggie's beau, occupied William's seat, the chair next to Mother's. Here for supper again. Ever since Christmas. Tillie curled her lip as Maggie laid a hand on his shoulder while placing a dish in front of him. Maggie lit up like a firefly every time he showed up.

Tillie rolled her eyes. "Hello, George. Aren't your parents expecting you home soon?" She plopped the ham down and dropped into her seat across from him.

"Hello, Tillie." He matched her sarcastic tone. "Nice to see you again as always."

Mother inclined her head toward George. "Tillie, how rude. You owe him an apology."

"Oh, it's all right, Mrs. Pierce. It was sweet of her to inquire after my parents." He winked at Tillie.

Father entered the kitchen carrying the family Bible. "Glad you could join us today, George." He shook George's hand before settling in his chair.

Sam Wade, Father's twelve-year-old apprentice, slipped into the seat next to Father, Maggie's normal chair, and copied his every move. Tillie eyed Sam. Maggie should be sitting there, and George should go home.

Mother placed the potatoes, and Maggie carried a steaming bowl of green beans and a plate of bread. At the smell of potatoes, fried with onions, Tillie's mouth watered. She couldn't wait to eat, but first…

Father opened the Bible and read from Galatians, chapter four. She lowered her head and closed her eyes, intending thoughtful meditation on the Word.

Perhaps after school tomorrow, she might take a ride on Lady up Culp's Hill and look for ripe berries. She stifled a yawn behind clenched teeth and tightened jaw muscles. Could Lady make the trip without going lame, poor thing? I don't care what Father says. I don't want to say goodbye to her yet.

The Bible closed with a resounding bang.

Tillie jumped and jerked her head up, eyes wide.

Father's brown eyes focused on her. A tremor rippled through his jowls as he shook his head. "Welcome back, daughter. As usual, you listened close. Would you like to tell us about the passage?"

Her face and ears burned, and she stared at her lap. "I'm sorry."

Father sighed as he accepted a bowl of green beans from Maggie. "You worry me."

Tillie braced for a lecture and shot a quick, miserable glance toward George.

"I hear the Rebels are trying to get to Harrisburg." George placed a piece of bread on the edge of his plate. He passed the bread to Tillie.

She laid a slice on her plate, refusing to meet his eye as she chanced a peek at Father. His steady glare promised he would let it go for now. They had company, but his expression also told her George would go home.

"George says the Rebs are coming, and we should all be prepared." Maggie slid her hand through George's arm. "Isn't that right?"

"I don't believe it," Father said.

George covered her hand with his own, but kept his eyes on Father. "I think they are. I know how you feel, sir, but I respectfully disagree. All the indications show they're coming. The question isn't if, but when."

Tillie uttered an exaggerated lovelorn sigh and batted her lashes. She forced a high falsetto voice. "George says the Reb Army is coming, and he's going to be my knight in shining armor." She put her elbows on the table edge and laced her fingers together, placing them under her chin in an angelic air. "Oh, how chivalrous of you. Be still my fluttering heart."

George and Sam laughed, but Maggie tsked and glared at her.

Tillie laughed loud and long.

Mother reached over and, using her thumb and middle finger, flicked Tillie's elbow. "Get your elbows off the table."

At the same time, Father's voice boomed. "Tillie, don't be unkind. George was speaking to me. You're fifteen now and a young lady. Time to start acting like one." He chewed and frowned at her.

She quieted and lowered her gaze. Her face burned, and the spot on her elbow stung, but she resisted the urge to rub the area. She speared green beans with her fork and raised them to her mouth.

Father kept his eyes on her for a moment longer before returning to George. "I do disagree with you. Did you read the proclamation in the paper last week?" Father scooped a forkful of potatoes. "President Lincoln called for fifty thousand men from Pennsylvania. He won't let the Rebs get anywhere near Harrisburg. Hooker will stop them before they reach Maryland again."

Maryland. Antietam. The bloodiest day of the war took place a mere fifty miles away. Both armies might find their way to the Commonwealth. No. Father said it won't happen. That's that. Recalling Mr. Brady's photographs near Sharpsburg afterward, Tillie suppressed a shudder. The newspaper printed a few of them. Mother cried when she looked at them.

Father waved his fork around. "My guess is these are only raiders. A small band of men causing trouble in the hope of scaring the President into sending troops here, so the bulk of their army can do mischief somewhere else. Like Washington."

"I must disagree, Mr. Pierce, which is why…" George closed his hand over Maggie's. He faced her. "I'm joining up. I'm twenty-one now and time I did my part. I wanted to go earlier, but Mother became distraught over the idea. I think Father convinced her it's the right thing to do. Yesterday, Governor Curtin called for more men. I answered the call this afternoon. In three days, I go to Carlisle to join the Twenty-First Pennsylvania Volunteer Cavalry."

Tillie perked up. She'd get her sister back, all to herself.

Maggie's mouth hung agape. "Oh, Georrrr-ge." She drew out his name in a long dismayed whisper as tears filled her eyes. When he patted her hand, Maggie nodded, forced a smile, and blinked fast several times.

Everyone fell silent. Another of their young men leaving for parts unknown to do his duty for God and Country.

Throughout the conversation, Sam concentrated on his food, but now he sat upright. "You're gonna be a soldier, George? I wish I could go."

"Well, thank heaven you're far too young to march off to war young man." Mother's glare pinned him to his chair.

Undaunted, Sam continued, "Well, I hope they do come here. Our boys'll whup 'em good, won't they, Mr. Pierce? One Yankee can whup a dozen Johnny Rebs, right, sir?"

George chuckled.

Father ruffled the boy's hair. "Well, I'm not sure about that, Sam."

Tillie snorted and chewed some ham. Maggie and Mother exchanged amused glances.

"All right, everyone." Mother flicked a hand over the table. "No more of this Reb talk. Your food is getting cold."

* * * *

After dinner, the family gathered in the sitting room. White lace curtains behind green velvet drapes floated over the large bay window facing the street. A rosewood couch with emerald satin cushions rested in front of the window next to Father's chair. The doilies Tillie made last year when she learned to crochet still graced its arms. She'd been so proud. Now, she hated their childish design. She set up her books and slate at the worktable in the room's center. The cold brick fireplace stood like a sentinel on the wall nearest the kitchen entrance. Mother placed her chair on one side of the fireplace, Maggie's on the other. Mother rocked back and forth, knitting.

Before opening her books, Tillie leaned her head in her hand, watching Mother knit. "What're you working on?"

"I'm making a sweater for James. When I'm done, I'll make one for William. I finished the stockings Mrs. Winebrenner requested for the Union Relief League, and I want to get these done so I can send them in time for Christmas."

"Let me know when you've finished. I'm making a sash for their uniforms. I'll include them."

"What a wonderful idea." Mother's right foot tapped the ground, rocking her slightly.

Sam nudged Tillie's arm.

"What?"

"I don't know how to do these sums."

Tillie showed him, nodding when he got the first two correct. After two more interruptions, she taught him how to check his work. Several minutes later, he hissed in her ear. "Tillie."

She snapped her Latin text shut. "What?" She bit the word short and pursed her lips to squelch her irritation.

"Did I do these problems right?"

She pulled the slate close in the fading daylight. "Yes." She pushed the slate and the chalk pencil back.

He glanced at Mother. "I still don't get what readin' and cipherin' has to do with butcherin'."

"Mother's right. How will you charge for your services if you can't cipher? How will you put an advertisement in the paper if you want to run a special, like Father does sometimes, if you can't write?"

"It's hard."

"Stop whining. Of course, it's hard. That's what makes it worth doing." At his puckered brow and trembling lip, she softened her tone. "You know…" She leaned her head in close. "If you stop grumbling and fighting and learn how to read and write, you might become the most successful butcher in Gettysburg. Why, you could even be a lawyer if you wanted."

A spark of interest lit his blue eyes. His elaborate shrug said he doubted the truth of her words, but he returned to the book.

"Tillie." He nudged her arm once again. "Do you think if I get good enough at this learnin' stuff, I might make a lawyer and not a butcher?"

"Perhaps." She smiled. "This is America. You can be anything you want. You're apprenticed to Father to be a butcher, but I don't see why you couldn't be a lawyer someday." She tilted her head. "Are you saying you don't want to be a butcher? Father's quite a good one, and people come from all over for his skills."

"It ain't that." Sam ducked his head. "I'm glad to be anything my father ain't." Scarlet flowed up his neck and into his face and ears. He ran his index finger over the page of his book, refusing to meet her eyes.

"Your father's not so bad—"

Sam slashed his hand through the air. "He's a drunk and a thief! You know that. The whole town knows it."

She hadn't meant to patronize him. She returned to her studies.

"It's just..." Though almost inaudible, his voice held pain and longing. "Sometimes I wish your father was my father."

Tillie sat back, jaw slack and eyes wide. She waited for him to elaborate, but he didn't. What made Sam idolize Father?

James Pierce, fifty-five years old, sat with legs crossed, reading his newspaper. For the first time, she noted his thick head of dark-brown hair showed gray at the temples. His deep-brown eyes radiated kindness and warmth, and care lines crinkled his mouth and forehead. Unlike most men, he did not sport face whiskers. He said men looked messy and unkempt with them. His career as a butcher made Father a well-muscled man, though his midriff expanded from age and Mother's excellent cooking. He gave the newspaper a quick shake. His scarred hands turned the page, drawing her attention to his left middle finger—shorter than the rest, due to an accident in his youth, when a knife slipped and sliced off the tip. It lent his hand an odd shape, making Father unique. Pride warmed her heart over being born to him and Mother.

Tillie glanced at Sam again. A surge of compassion and renewed liking rose up in her breast. Anyone who held Father in such high esteem deserved her respect. She wanted to give him a hug, but couldn't embarrass either of them. She grabbed her Latin text and flipped to her lesson.

Maggie entered the house and settled next to the fireplace, across from Mother's rocking chair, before picking up her book. Mother's knitting needles clicked and flashed. Father's newspaper rustled when he turned the page. He gave the paper another shake and cleared his throat. The pages of Maggie's book swished every few minutes, and Sam's chalk pencil squeaked across the slate.

Daylight faded from the room. Father didn't allow lit candles or burning lamp oil in the summer. The newspaper crinkled as he folded and laid it next to his chair, a signal to the family. "Time for bed, everyone," he announced as he did each night.

Mother wound up her yarn and wrapped her project around her needles. Maggie placed a ribbon to mark her place. Tillie and Sam put away their studies.

Outside, two men on Baltimore Street sang "All Quiet Along The Potomac Tonight." She sighed, happy and contented, as she made her way upstairs. She plodded along, bringing up the rear. Now that George was leaving for the Army, perhaps things could go back to the way they used to be. On the heels of the thought, her conversation with Father entered her mind. Would the Rebs invade? Father said no—but what if?

Chapter 2

Somewhere at the back of the line, a drum beat a constant tattoo as faceless, legless blue-clad soldiers marched by in an endless loop....

Tillie mumbled, rolled over, and opened her eyes. Rain slashed the windowpanes. A brilliant flash of lightning illuminated the room, and thunder rumbled.

She groaned, pulling the covers over her head. Maybe the weather would clear before she left for school.

As if in warning, thunder cracked across the sky. She stretched and swung her feet to the floor. Wriggling her toes into the braided rug, she yawned and stretched again. She put on her school dress of brown muslin, washed her face, and combed and braided her chestnut tresses, while pretending the thunder was a Union Army cannon driving off the hated Rebels. Once dressed, she headed downstairs for breakfast. The aroma of bacon, frying potatoes, and coffee enveloped her. Tillie closed her eyes, inhaled in anticipation as her stomach growled. She entered the kitchen to find Mother working at the stove. Maggie stood near the back door churning the morning butter.

"Good morning." Moving to the shelf beside the stove, Tillie pulled down dishes to set the table. She squeezed around Mother cooking scrambled eggs.

Mother took a step to the side. "Good morning, Sunshine." She poured the eggs into the skillet and gave the potatoes a quick stir. "Did you sleep well?"

"I did. How about you?"

"Very well."

Tillie set the plates down and returned for silverware.

Mother stirred the eggs and slid the potatoes into a bowl. Her eyes went to the ceiling when another boom of thunder pealed across the sky. "Heavens, what a storm." She pushed the eggs about in the pan a few times before transferring them to a platter and passed it to Tillie. "I need you and Maggie to do something for me today, if the rain stops."

"All right." Tillie studied her.

"Go out to the garden and pick any vegetables ripe enough—peas, beans, anything. We'll pickle and preserve tomorrow."

"There won't be much. Are you sure?"

"Yes, I'm sure." Mother wiped her fingers on her bib apron before putting her hands on the hips of her blue gingham dress. She nodded for emphasis. "I talked with Mrs. Broadhead yesterday. She told me Mr. Broadhead would rather pick his vegetables green and burn the rest, than allow the Rebs to get so much as one bean."

Tillie studied her mother, surprised by her tone. "You think the Rebels are coming? Father says they're not."

Mother stepped close and rested one hand on Tillie's shoulder. With the other, she cupped Tillie's chin. She took a deep breath and let it out in a slow, measured exhale. "Yes, I do. Your father says no, and I pray he's right. But I'm not so certain. With the dubious successes of our Army thus far…" She took another deep breath and huffed. "Well, as I said, I pray he's right. Just in case, though, I want you to gather as much from the garden as you can, for I'm in agreement with Mr. Broadhead."

* * * *

Tillie dashed through the downpour to the barn behind the butcher shop. The door creaked on its hinges, and she breathed in the earthy, woody fragrance of hay mixed with the sharp tang of horse dung.

Lady thrust her nose over the stall door. She blew a greeting and tossed her head.

Tillie took hold of Lady's muzzle, sliding her palm across her velvety nose, and kissed her. "Good morning, my dear. How are you this rainy day?" She presented two sugar cubes.

Lady pushed at her palm as she gobbled them. She blinked, which Tillie took for thank you. She imagined a smile on the horse's face.

Tillie stroked her nose, reveling in her soft, yet prickly snout. "Perhaps this afternoon we can ride to Culp's Hill. Don't worry, girl. I won't overwork your bad leg. We'll rest as much as you need." Tillie kissed her again as thunder rumbled and rain drummed overhead. "I have to leave for school now, but this afternoon we'll spend time together after I help Maggie in the garden." She gave Lady's nose another stroke, blew the horse a kiss, and then ran back to the house.

* * * *

Tillie eyed the low dark clouds and clutched her cape close to her neck. She bent her head against the onslaught, pulling her hoops high off the ground to keep her dress dry.

"Child, put your skirts down. What would your mother say? And where's your umbrella?"

Mrs. Winebrenner, Mother's Union Relief League and church friend, stood next to her. She held an umbrella high and wore the expression of someone about to launch into a firm scolding. Her eyes traveled up and down Tillie.

"Good morning, Mrs. Winebrenner. I didn't think walking two blocks would be such a problem. I didn't mean to do this much damage. I still can't walk in the rain without getting my skirts dirty." Mother would hear about this, the old biddy-body.

Mrs. Winebrenner braced her hand on Tillie's shoulder and leaned forward. "A cross we all must bear, my dear." She spoke as though imparting the wisdom of the ages, patted Tillie's shoulder, and walked away.

If that woman told Mother about showing her ankles in public, then so be it. She needed to get to school.

Tillie gathered her skirts and ran. She got a few paces before her foot landed in an unseen puddle. Cold water splashed her leg. Gritting her teeth, she lifted her foot and turned it from side to side. "Oh, Mother's going to kill me." She bit her lip against the urge to cry, and easing her foot down, continued on her way, taking mincing steps and grimacing at the water squishing between her toes.

At the intersection of Middle and Washington Streets, she stopped to remove and examine her Sunday shoes. She wasn't supposed to wear them for every day, and she'd be punished if she ruined them. Tillie balanced on one foot and the toes of her other. She turned her shoe around and around, examining the damage, ignoring the traffic passing by. She gasped as cold, muddy water hit her neck and ran under her collar, soaking through to her dress. Worse yet, her shoe got a second dunking as a gob of muddy water splatted her hands. Tears filled her eyes. She blinked them down as she stared at Mr. McCreary's carriage making its way up Washington Street.

"Land sakes, Mr. McCreary!" Tillie glared and glanced around. Did anyone hear her use foul language?

Nellie Auginbaugh, strode past carrying an umbrella, heels clicking on the pavement. She didn't acknowledge Tillie standing in the street with one shoe off and one shoe on. She crossed Middle Street and continued to her destination. Tillie raised her eyes to the sky and said a silent thank you. She didn't need Mother confronting her about using bad language. She turned her attention back to her shoe. Her heart seized over the damage done. Standing in the rain like a duck in thunder didn't help matters.

Her feet numbed with cold, she arrived at Lady Eyster's Female Academy. The rain plastered her hair to her head. Strands stood loose from her braid. Her clothes stuck to her body, her hoops fell, and now her skirt hem dragged in the mud. She raised sorrowful eyes to the imposing, white two-story building. Why couldn't she go home? Things were only about to get worse.

As she stared at the building, its seven upstairs windows glared down at her, and the two baronial front doors mocked her. "Go away. You're not smart enough to enter these rooms." She drew a deep breath and, with a halting gait, climbed the four stone steps.

Tillie stepped inside and leaned against the door until it clicked closed. She stamped her feet, freeing the muck from her shoes, eased off her cloak, and hung it on a peg, before assessing the damage. The cloak received the worst of the carriage attack. Perhaps she would be all right before the day ended. Her hem dripped, leaving small puddles at her feet, and she scarcely resisted stamping a dismayed foot.

Girls' laughter and chatter drifted from behind the closed door. Good. Classes hadn't started yet. At least Mrs. Eyster wouldn't dock her for tardiness. She eased the classroom door open a sliver and peered through. No sign of her teacher.

Tillie slipped inside, passing the youngest girls, who congregated near the door. They gawked. She lifted her chin and ignored them. She walked by the next older grade who took seats beside the front windows. They pointed and snickered behind their hands. Tillie squared her shoulders, lifted her head high, met ten-year-olds' stares and dismissed twelve-year-olds' giggles and whispers. A trail of muddy water followed her squishing shoes across the room to her classmates at the back. Maybe the floor would open and swallow her whole.

Catherine Foster gaped. "Look at your skirt. Mrs. Eyster will dock you."

Beckie Weikert laughed and wagged her finger. "Madame Imperious will say a thing or two about your dress."

"Ugh, I know. Mr. McCreary dashed by in his carriage and splashed me from head to toe. And my shoes!" She inched up her hem and held out each foot for careful examination. Her friends murmured "oh dears" and "what are you going to dos?" as she twisted each foot right to left, before dropping her skirt.

Belle Stewart bent and swiped grime from the back of Tillie's skirt.

Mrs. Eyster entered the room.

Tillie clutched Belle, using her as a shield. Belle straightened up and broadened her shoulders.

"All right, ladies." Mrs. Eyster clapped her hands three times. "Come to order." The teacher's black skirts swirled around her feet. She walked, ramrod straight, into the room.

When Tillie first started attending the academy, she disliked her teacher. With Mother's help, Tillie learned to look past her strict formality to the lonely, childless widow. Her deeper understanding of her teacher softened her heart, and over time, Tillie hated to disappoint her.

That didn't mean she wanted another demerit for dress and deportment. She had enough of those. She moved to her desk, scrunching into a small a ball behind Belle.

"Miss Pierce!" The teacher's words cut through the air like a bayonet, slicing Tillie's heart.

The girls went silent.

"Your skirts are atrocious. You leave a trail wherever you go. A lady never lets her skirts get dirty like some ragamuffin orphan child." Mrs. Eyster's black skirts swirled again as she pivoted and stepped onto the raised dais where her desk waited. She plucked up a long wooden ferule.

Heart pounding hard and knees buckling, Tillie clutched Belle, fearing she might crumple to the floor in a fit of vapors. Belle patted Tillie's hand before moving to her seat.

"Yes, ma'am. I couldn't help it. Mr. McCreary splashed me in his carriage."

Mrs. Eyster's brows shot up. "Oh? Were you in his carriage when he splashed you?"

"N–no, ma'am." Tillie's brow crinkled.

Her teacher pursed her lips, the equivalent of her smile. "Why don't you try your sentence again?"

Tillie blinked. "While I was walking to school—in the rain—Mr. McCreary drove by me in his carriage and splashed me with muddy water."

Several younger girls giggled.

Mrs. Eyster raised the ferule, rapped her desk once, and the giggling stopped. She locked eyes with Tillie. "There, now that wasn't so difficult. Alas, I must dock your grade for dress and deportment. You may take your seat. We have a long day ahead of us." She flicked her hand toward the desk.

"Yes, ma'am," Tillie whispered. Her shoulders slumped, and she plodded to her seat.

"It is a rare thing indeed, Miss Pierce, when I get a pupil such as you."

"Ma'am?" Tillie tilted her head. What did she mean?

Mrs. Eyster offered a faint smile. "Take your seat. We have a long day ahead of us."

As Tillie settled in, Beckie reached out her hand. Tillie clasped it. A folded piece of paper pressed into her palm.

Slipping her hands below the desk, she opened the note to reveal a caricature of their teacher, eyes and tongue bulged out, her hair like lightning bolts. One of Beckie's favorite jokes about Mrs. Eyster tying her corset strings too tight. Tillie respected her teacher too much to find Beckie's nasty jokes funny. Yet she didn't dare stand up to Beckie's sense of humor. She glanced at Beckie's self-satisfied grin, tore up the note, and tucked it into her pocket.

* * * *

The brilliant late-afternoon sun glittered like diamonds on the wet grass. The rain moved east to Philadelphia, leaving the air smelling fresh and clean. Tillie needed to hurry home. But the world glimmered and beckoned her to revel in it. She raised her face to the sun's warmth and breathed deep the loamy wet-earth scent.

Someone tugged on her cloak. She opened her eyes as Beckie slipped her arm through Tillie's. Tillie raised her face to the sun again. "Do you ever wonder what our great-grandparents would say if they knew the country was at war with itself? After all, they fought to free us from England. Would they be dismayed to discover what they fought for could be destroyed so easily?"

Beckie laughed. "You think too much."

"Perhaps I do." Tillie stiffened. "But still, I'm curious. What would they think if they saw us, north fighting south, and possibly destroying what they fought so hard to build?"

"Well…" Beckie shrugged. "I assume, they'd call us silly ninnies."

Tillie bit her lip, familiar with Beckie's I-don't-care shrug.

Beckie brightened. "I got a letter from my beau, Mr. Kitzmiller. Did I tell you?"

"Another one? You told me you got one a week ago. What did he say? Did he give you news of James?"

"Oh. I did tell you he wrote. I got the letter last week. He says it'll be the last he can write for a while so not to worry. Seems the army is moving again." Beckie uttered a long dramatic sigh. "It's to be expected at this time of year I suppose. I do wish he were home, though. I'm almost eighteen. Time to get married."

Tillie resisted the urge to roll her eyes. So, no news of James. Why didn't Beckie ask after him? Four words, that's all. How. Is. James. Pierce. "Has Mr. Kitzmiller proposed?"

"No. And Papa says he would refuse permission anyway until the war is over. I detest this war!" Beckie stamped her foot on the pavement. Stones flew out from under her shoe.

Her friend's melodramatic declaration coupled with the angry line of her lip and lowered brow made Tillie want to laugh.

She bit her tongue and cleared her throat. "George Sandoe joined up, the Twenty-First Volunteers. He leaves in a few days. Maggie's heartbroken."

"Well it's about time." Beckie tossed her hair. "After three years there isn't a rush to go anymore. But Mr. Sandoe waited until the legal age to join the army while my George went a year ago at eighteen. So did William."

"William was nineteen." Tillie cringed. What a stupid thing to say.

"I stand corrected." Beckie raised her chin and affected to stare at a bird flying overhead.

Tillie kept her gaze fixed on the road. "At least he didn't hire a substitute." Why couldn't she think of something better to say? George could have paid three hundred dollars and avoided the war altogether. He wasn't a complete coward.

Lost in her thoughts, she didn't notice they were at the corner of Breckenridge Street until Beckie let go of her arm. "Well, here we are, Lawyers Row." Beckie laughed at her own joke.

Along this side of Washington Street half a dozen law offices lined up next door to each other, as if Pennsylvania College couldn't produce anything but lawyers.

"I'll see you tomorrow." Tillie frowned as Beckie walked away, skirts swaying back and forth like a pealing bell.

When Beckie disappeared over the brow of Cemetery Ridge, Tillie stepped into Washington Street. Mr. Garlach's wagon came from out of nowhere, veering left on Washington Street from Breckenridge. He missed colliding with her, but she had to scramble back to the curb to avoid his team of horses. As he passed, he glared at her over his shoulder.

She smiled and waved an apology.

The shrill whistle of the four o'clock train departing the station startled her. Mother would scold her for dillydallying if she didn't hurry home. Tillie quickened her step east onto Breckenridge.

Inside the Wade house, people shouted at each other. She glanced at the front door on her way by. Then she tsked and crossed the road, as though walking on the same side of the street would somehow taint her. No doubt, Ginny, whose real name was Mary Virginia, gave someone the dickens.

A few years ago, William showed interest in Ginny. James pulled him aside, calling her bossy, mean, and worse, unscrupulous and fast. Tillie asked James what he meant. His words cut her to the quick when her adored older brother turned on her. “Well, little pitchers have big ears. Mind your own business, Tillie.” It still stung when she remembered the encounter. To this day, she didn’t understand what he meant.

Everyone knew Ginny’s sympathies lay with the Confederate cause, in particular, one young man, Wesley Culp, who left to join the rebels. His family owned a farm south of town. What a scandal they created last year when Ginny and Wesley wanted to marry. The Culps refused because of the Wades’ low standing in town. Mr. Wade, Ginny and Sam’s father—a drunk and a thief—started a ten-year prison term a few months ago for something called rape. Soon after, Wes ran off to join the Confederate Army. Ginny took up with Johnston Skelly almost the same hour. He served in the Army of the Potomac.

Tillie didn’t like Sam, either, when he first came to live with them, painting him with the same brush as his family. Over time, though, he proved himself a quiet, thoughtful boy who did his chores with efficiency. Eager to please, he worked hard. His devotion to Father warmed her heart, and she developed a grudging respect and admiration for him. Now she thought of him as a sweet younger brother, though she’d never tell him so.

A broom whisked on the cobblestones, breaking her reverie.

Mr. Weaver, a tall black man with graying hair, swept the street near the corner of her house. His loose-fitting clothing gave the impression of an undernourished man.

“Good afternoon, Mr. Weaver.”

He bobbed his head, raised his hat, and flashed a smile. His white teeth shone against dark skin, and his thick, curly hair, flattened under the hat, made a puffy ring where the brim rested. “Good day to you, young miss. Where’re you off to?”

“Home.”

“That’s nice. Give my regards to your folks.” He pushed his broom toward the gutter.

“I will.” Tillie hopped over his dirt pile.

Maggie and George stood on the stoop, laughing and pointing toward the Diamond.

"Tillie, look." Maggie gestured up Baltimore Street.

A colored family labored toward them, backs bent under the weight of quilts and blankets bulging with clanking and pinging items.

"Mr. Weaver…?" Tillie nodded to the family. "What're they doing?"

Mr. Weaver joined them on the corner. He leaned on his broom and scowled as the family passed by.

The slim black woman goaded her two boys. "Fo de Lawd's sake, chiluns hurry up." They staggered under the weight. The woman stopped and readjusted her pack. She let go one hand to herd the boys.

Her yellow dress and turban contrasted beautifully against her dark skin. The children, dressed in dirty, white linen shirts, dark pants, and bare feet, each carried bulging patchwork quilts slung over one shoulder. Ahead of them, their father led a cow. The cow lowed a plaintive lament.

"They's runnin' to hide on Culp's Hill." Mr. Weaver sighed and shifted his feet. "Many of our folk do these days. Word is, if the Rebs come and catch the black folk, we gonna get sol' inta slavery."

"But you're free! They can't do that." Tillie studied him, brows creased. She crossed her arms. "It wouldn't be fair."

"Keep up," the woman badgered, giving each boy a gentle shove. "Y'all don't want them Rebs to kotch you and sell you to slave masters."

The boys plodded past the woman who readjusted her burden before hurrying to catch up with her husband. She kept up a constant stream of chatter at her children.

"Mmm hmm." Mr. Weaver stared after the family. "They can, and they will."

"I've heard of overreacting before, but that's ridiculous." Smiling, George shook his head.

"They're being silly, if you ask me." Maggie slipped her hand under his elbow. "The Rebs aren't coming here. Father said so. Even so, they don't have the right to take people who've never been slaves."

"You think so, miss?" Mr. Weaver gave them a hard glare. His brown eyes, so filled with warmth and friendliness moments ago, now blackened with rage. His brows lowered, and he gripped the broom handle so hard, his knuckles looked as though they might crack the skin. "You think they're ridiculous? Maybe because you ain't never been hunted before."

"Mr. Weaver, are you…?" Tillie's eyes widened, and her mouth fell agape.

He shot her a glare. "No, but my daddy was."

Maggie peeked at George. He stared at his feet.

Tillie bit her lip, shame washed over her. She had no business prying into the man's personal affairs.

Mr. Weaver fingered his hat brim. "Y'all have a fine day." Voice dripping with sarcasm, he gave them each a baleful glare, turned, and shuffled up Breckenridge Street, pushing his broom as he went.

Tillie, Maggie, and George stood in chastened silence as the family trundled down the street. After they disappeared over the brow of the hill, George turned to Maggie and put his hand on her arm. He whispered in her ear.

She smiled, and her eyelids lowered as his lips brushed against her hair, his blond head close to hers.

Tillie ran up the steps to the front door and entered the house, shutting out the sight of the lovebirds.

* * * *

Upstairs Tillie hung her school dress over the armoire door and changed into her everyday work dress before assessing the damage from her walk to school. The mud would brush out, so no harm done thank Heaven. The water stains would require laundering. She grabbed the cleaning brush and brushed hard a few strokes before giving up. She crumpled the dress in a wash pile, shoved her shoes far into the back of her armoire, and threw a shawl on top of them.

At her dressing table, she loosened her braids, brushed, and tidied her hair.

Mother always said a woman's hair was her crowning glory, so Tillie took pains to keep hers healthy. After one hundred strokes, she threw the hairbrush down and ran her fingers through the chestnut tresses, satisfied when the light caught and shone through the silky strands.

Chin in hand, she studied her reflection, tilting her head and assessing large, brown, almond-shaped eyes framed by long lashes. Father called them doe eyes.

She wrinkled and stretched her nose. Still, it receded into her face before reemerging like a small ball hanging above her full lips.

Voices drifted up from downstairs, and she glanced at the door. Father would reprimand her for shirking if she didn't head down soon. Tillie gathered up her hair again to braid, but couldn't resist twisting a bun and held it on the back of her head, imitating Mother. Containing her tresses with one hand, she tipped her head from side to side, evaluating the effect. She frowned and let go. The mass of brown curls splashed over her shoulders and cascaded down her back. She scowled at her reflection. "I'll never be as pretty as Mother or Maggie. Grandmother is right. With a face like mine, I need a nose like mine." She puckered her mouth, gathered up her hair, and fingers flying, braided it.

She slipped down the stairs and into the sitting room, expecting to find Maggie, Mother, and Father. She walked into an empty room. Her shoulders dropped, and she let out her breath. As she passed Father's chair, she spied the Gettysburg Compiler lying folded in half on the table beside his chair. The headline screamed: Rebels Reported In Chambersburg, Carlisle And York, Looting Rampant. Fingers shaking, she picked up the paper and read the article. Clearly, the editor had so small an opinion of the story, he didn't allot more than a few column inches. Still, fear spiked through her. Two thousand infantry. Twenty thousand cavalry. No mention of the Union boys and their whereabouts. However, President Lincoln fired General Hooker and put General Meade at the head of the Army of the Potomac.

Chambersburg, Carlisle and York…They made a U shape around Gettysburg. So close! She scanned the room, half-expecting Rebs to jump out of the corners. Then she put the paper down and tipped it just right, as if the action would make them go away.

Leaving it there, she walked into the kitchen. Maggie stood by the door, holding Tillie's apron. She almost told Maggie about the story, but no. If Father thought it important, he'd say something.

"Where's George?" Tillie took her apron from Maggie and dropped it over her head.

Maggie's far-off, vacant stare fixed on a spot on the wall.

Tillie tied her apron strings behind her back, while bending her knees, attempting to catch her sister's eye. "I assumed you two would be occupied for a while so I didn't hurry down."

Maggie glanced at her, picked up two baskets, handing one to Tillie. "I told him he needed to leave as soon as you got home. That's why we waited on the steps."

Tillie snugged her bonnet on, tying the bow under her chin. She grabbed the fruit basket Maggie held out. "Shall we?" She slipped past Maggie into the bright sunshine.

George stood at the butcher shop door. Father sat before his whetstone, drawing a blade across. The stone zinged and sparks flew around him, but he didn't try to get out of their way. Sam worked behind Father, taking down equipment and putting others away.

"He hasn't left yet. He's standing by Father's shop."

"Father wanted to cut him a choice piece of meat to take home to his family. He leaves Thursday morning for Carlisle. I won't see him tomorrow, since he has things to do to prepare to go and we have all of this to preserve." Maggie flicked her hand over the garden.

"Oh." Tillie focused on the task. "What about the fruit trees?" She glanced toward the apple and peach trees. Only green fruit dangled from their boughs. "The peaches will be ready in a couple of weeks, but the apples, of course, won't be ready until mid-August so we shouldn't worry about them. Do you agree?"

Her sister's attention remained on George, deep in conversation with Father.

"Maggie?" Tillie touched her sister's arm. The cotton sleeve, warmed by the sun, nestled softly under her hand.

Maggie started. "Whatever you want, Tillie." Her voice sounded vague and despondent. Tears welled in the corner of her eyes, spilling down the side of her nose.

"What's wrong?"

"I don't want George to go. I'm afraid," Maggie choked out.

"He'll be all right. I'm sure of it." The words rang false to Tillie even as she said them. Would George be all right? Foreboding washed over her. Her heart pounded, and her hands shook. She grasped her skirt and squeezed the fabric to still the tremors.

Maggie uttered a small laugh. "You know, for the longest time, I didn't think you liked George."

Tillie offered her sister a wry grin. "I like him, I guess. I will admit to jealousy."

"Why?"

"Because," she knelt in the dirt, "you don't like to do things with me anymore. We used to go up to Culp's Hill and pick berries and flowers, but now all you do is stay home and wait for George to visit."

Maggie sat next to her. "I'm sorry. I didn't know you felt that way. It's not so much I'm waiting around for George, but I'm grown up now. I wager in another year or so you'll feel the same way." Maggie took her hand. "No matter what, you're my sister and nothing can change that."

Tillie threw her arms around Maggie in a fierce hug. "I'm sorry, too. When George started coming around, I didn't like it. I didn't want him changing things." She pulled away and chuckled. "You know, sometimes I get so frustrated with the sameness of each day, I want to scream. Other times, I feel as if I'm balancing on the edge of a precipice. I can't explain it. I want things to change if only for some variety, but I also don't want anything to change."

"I understand." Maggie squeezed her hand. "It reminds me of those wooden tops Father made for the boys, remember?"

"Tell me."

"They had strings you wound around the top, and when James threw his on the floor, the top spun and spun before wobbling to a stop. But William's top always staggered around and crashed into the walls."

Tillie laughed. "I bet he got mad. He hates being second to James in anything."

"Including birth." Maggie chuckled.

Tillie inspected a tomato plant. The basil-like aroma filled her nostrils. She moved on. "Is that how you felt? Like William's top?"

"Most of the time. When I was scared and unsure I whirled in confusion. I was James's top when things went right." Maggie plucked two large green tomatoes. She set them into her basket. "You know, William's top is how we act when we take our eyes off God, or refuse to acknowledge Him. James's top is what happens when God comes first in our lives in all things."

Tillie scowled and let her fingers search the peapods and green beans as she considered Maggie's words. They worked in silence for a few minutes.

"So did George propose?"

Again, Maggie's eyes darted to the butcher shop. Tillie followed her gaze. George was gone.

"Maggie?"

"No, he didn't. To propose now would be foolhardy. He's not the only man to join the army, I know that, but I'm afraid something will happen to him."

The hair rose on the back of Tillie's neck. "Oh, don't think that way. He'll be fine, and once he comes home a brave soldier, he'll ask for your hand."

Maggie opened her mouth, but a strange expression crossed her face. She closed her mouth again and picked vegetables.

Tillie observed her sister and waited for what she might say.

Maggie dropped cucumbers into her basket. "You're right." Her lips twitched. "Besides, it's all in God's hands. I must be brave and give George to God."

Maggie picked more cucumbers and placed them into her basket while Tillie searched the peapods.

"Did you read the newspaper in the sitting room?" Maggie's voice sounded frightened.

Tillie closed her eyes, and her shoulders drooped. "Yes."

"Father doesn't think the Rebs will come." Maggie spoke above a whisper. "But what if they do?"

Tillie sat back and folded her hands in her lap. "Most of the time I believe him, but sometimes I'm not sure what to think." She plucked a baby peapod. "There's something in the air. I can't explain what, but I sense it. I'm teetering on that precipice, and I'm afraid of falling off." She twirled the peapod between her fingers. "I don't know what made me speak so, except George is leaving day after tomorrow. James and William are miss—gone." She dropped the pod into her basket. "I don't know about giving George—or James or William, for that matter—to God. I just hope the Rebs stay away."

"I agree." Maggie twisted a pitiful green tomato off the vine, topping off her basket. "I pray the Rebs don't come and all the men we love will come home safe."

Tillie nodded her agreement, but the headline loomed before her eyes: Rebels Reported In Chambersburg, Carlisle And York, Looting Rampant. The words screamed for her attention, along with two other words: They're coming.

Chapter 3

When Tillie arrived home from school, the smell of coriander, pepper, and vinegar assaulted her nostrils. She ran upstairs and changed into her everyday work dress, before joining Mother and Maggie in the kitchen.

They were already working to preserve the vegetables picked the day before. Tillie slipped her clean, white cotton apron over her head and tied the strings behind her back.

“Oh, good, you’re home.” Mother used her forearm to wipe sweat off her forehead. The pickling process, something they usually did in autumn’s cooler months, left the kitchen stifling. “Why don’t you start at the kitchen table? Maggie and I have things at the stove well in hand.”

“Yes, ma’am.” Tillie settled at the table. She washed green beans, soaked them in a salt brine, and then stuffed them into glass jars filled with vinegar and spices.

Once filled, Mother capped the jars and placed them in a boiling water bath. When she removed them, she set them aside and added more jars.

Tillie packed the cooled jars in a box and brought it to the dank basement, where she took her time storing them in the food cupboard. When the beans were all jarred, she started cutting up green tomatoes. The cucumbers became pickles and relishes.

Jars of relishes and jams overtook the cupboard beside the cook stove. The intense preserving and pickling kept them working with very little conversation, but an easy camaraderie saturated the steamy room.

Knife in hand, Tillie reached with her left hand to find the vegetables still waiting for preparation. She felt around the table and then glanced over. She saw nothing but stems and pieces of tomatoes, empty peapods, and green bean stems. She looked at Mother boxing up the last jars of relishes, then at Maggie wiping the counter near the stove. Tillie took a deep breath and rolled her head from shoulder to shoulder.

Mother pushed the box to the side, and then pressed her sleeve to her forehead, sweeping away stray hair. “Well, that's that.” She smiled at Tillie and Maggie. “Thank you, girls.”

“I can take Lady to Culp's Hill on Saturday to look for berries, if you'd like.” Tillie rose from the table and stretched her arms over her head. “She could use the exercise.”

“I should say yes, but right now, I'm too tired to agree.” Mother grabbed a rag from the counter and began wiping the table. “You girls gather up the pots and utensils, and we'll wash everything after supper.”

“Yes, Mother.” Tillie wiped her hands on her apron, and then gathered her utensils to take to the washbasin as Maggie put water in the kettle to boil.

Tillie decided she'd ride up to pick berries. Perhaps if she gathered enough, Mother would let her make a pie.

* * * *

Tillie skipped down the stairs. The vinegar smell still tainted her hands and hair, making her grimace.

As she stepped around the landing, she gripped the handrail to keep from tumbling down the last steps. George stood just inside the parlor room door dressed in Army blue. She descended the remaining stairs, stopping on the last step. Should she go in and say goodbye? They were probably discussing adult things. If she went in uninvited, Father would tell her to get ready for school. She descended intent on leaving the adults to themselves, when George raised a hand and waved her in.

“I've been waiting for you to come down.” He stood straight and tall in his new uniform. Snappy gold trim twirled down the front of the dark-blue wool coat, swirled around the hem, and encircled each cuff. His light-blue cavalry pants sported a bold yellow stripe down the outside of the leg. Knee-high shiny cavalryman's boots completed the uniform. He combed his blond hair down, and his blue eyes sparkled. He twisted his kepi in his hands.

Her heart lurched. He was handsome. She stumbled over her feet as her face heated.

George held out his hands, and as if in a daze, she walked to him. He placed a quick, brotherly peck on her cheek.

"I'm leaving for Carlisle to join my regiment." He squeezed her hands. "But I wanted to say goodbye to my second-best girl."

Tillie smiled, unable to look away. "Uh…M–Maggie's going to write you so many letters you won't have time to read them all, but would you like to receive a letter from me, once in a while?" She lifted her eyebrows, suggesting he might think the idea of letters from her ridiculous.

"I'd be devastated if you didn't write to me, thinking in some way I'd offended you. That would break my heart."

Her uplifted brows creased. He truly sounded sincere. As if to prove it, he gave her hands another gentle squeeze.

Her throat constricted. Did he sense her resentment? Did Maggie tell him about their garden conversation? His tender grip warmed her, and searching his eyes, she found no sign of bitterness.

Breaking eye contact, he released her hands.

Did her palms sweat? She resisted the urge to wipe her hands on her skirts, afraid he might think she disliked holding his hands. She clasped hers behind her back and ran a finger across each palm to check for moisture. "Where's your rifle?"

"I'll get arms once I reach my regiment in Carlisle."

"Oh."

An awkward silence filled the room. Did the adults want her to leave?

"Well, if you'll pardon me, I need to get ready for school. Goodbye, George. Take care of yourself."

"Goodbye, Tillie, and thank you. I'm glad we can be friends now."

Fresh heat shot up her neck and exploded across her cheeks. He did know. "I am too." She smiled, crossed the hall to the sitting room, and entered the kitchen to get breakfast.

* * * *

Maggie bore up well since George's departure an hour ago. She didn't put on a bit of the melodramatic behavior Tillie half-expected, no heavy sighs or hands thrown to her forehead in abject misery, accompanied by wails of displeasure. Not once did Tillie want to slap Maggie in front of Mother and Father. Tillie's bottom lip curled over her teeth to hide a smile, amused by the idea of such a scene. Rising from the breakfast table, she brought her bowl to the washbasin then paused when someone knocked on the kitchen door.

Mother's calico skirts rustled as she moved to answer the door. "Good morning, Mr. Garlach." She pulled the door wide. "Please come in."

"Thank you, Mrs. Pierce. Don't mind if I do."

The white-haired man shuffled in with a stooped-shouldered gait. "Good morning, young man." He ruffled Sam's brown curls as the boy hunched over his porridge bowl.

"Morning, sir." Sam shoved a large spoonful into his mouth.

"When are you going to give up this idea of butchering and come to me to learn the Lord's trade? Carpentry is where the real money is, boy, not in killing cows." Mr. Garlach nudged Sam's shoulder.

Sam's blue eyes sparkled as he shoveled another big spoonful of porridge into his mouth. He made exaggerated chewing motions.

Mr. Garlach turned to Father chuckling. "A diplomatic young man right there, James."

Father laughed and shook Mr. Garlach's hand. "Very diplomatic indeed."

Tillie lifted a cup and saucer from the shelf and carried it to the table.

"Good morning, young lady." He turned around with slow, shambling steps and gave her cheek a gentle pinch. "Nice to see you alive and well. You gave me quite a fright the other afternoon when you stepped in front of my wagon." He wagged a finger.

"I'm sorry, sir." She peeked at Mother. She hadn't told her parents about her close encounter with Mr. Garlach's wagon while walking home Tuesday.

Mother closed the door and cast a questioning glance her way.

Tillie smiled and flicked her fingers. He made it sound worse than necessary.

"Ah, no harm done." He reached to pinch her cheek again, but she turned to join Maggie at the sink to make the motion seem natural.

"Miss Maggie, good morning to you."

She returned the greeting.

Mr. Garlach pulled out a chair and sat.

Mother poured coffee and placed a plate of muffins on the table.

He slid a cup close. "I came by to tell you some news, in case you didn't know." Mr. Garlach's hand trembled from palsy as he closed his fingers around a muffin and dropped it onto a plate. "That new regiment, the Twenty-First Pennsylvania Emergency Volunteer Corps, is expected on the noon train." He broke his muffin into small chunks before popping a piece into his mouth.

"It'll be good to get some of our boys back." Father stirred cream into his coffee. "I can't reconcile myself with the news from Chambersburg. Rebels looting and threatening to burn the town if they don't get what they demand." He pursed his lips as he handed his guest the cream pitcher.

Mother joined them with her own cup of coffee. "Since the Twenty-First gathered up the last of our Gettysburg boys, the town feels deserted." She put her hand over her heart. "I declare, with all this talk of Rebel soldiers marauding the country, I'd like to feel safe again. How dreadful to believe they're so close—only twenty-five miles away."

Mr. Garlach nodded. "Mrs. Garlach agrees with you. I'm sure the Rebs will go back to wherever they came from as soon as they clap their eyes on our good Union boys." He popped another muffin chunk into his mouth and chewed as he added a splash of cream. Some spilled in the saucer.

Father gestured toward Maggie. "In fact, young George Sandoe left this morning to meet the regiment in Carlisle."

"I heard." Mr. Garlach turned in his chair. "It'll be nice to get your beau back, eh, Miss Maggie?" He gave her a wink.

"It certainly will." Maggie grinned, and her cheeks pinked. She resumed drying the dishes. Tillie pressed her shoulder against Maggie's, sharing in the amity.

So many questions to ask, but she dared not speak out in front of company. Would the Rebs run as soon as the Yanks showed up? She doubted it. Would the Yanks stand and fight? She doubted that too. According to Tuesday's headline, the Rebs were all around. The Yanks? Who knew? Why didn't they come? Was General Hooker at fault? The newspaper reported President Lincoln dismissed him for good, as he fired Burnside before him, and McClellan and McDowell before Burnside. Now, with General Meade in charge, would they fight on Northern soil? Would they stand?

Maggie nudged Tillie back to reality, her rag poised and unmoving on a dish while Maggie waited for another dish to dry.

"I couldn't agree more." Father nodded. "Our boys will be here this afternoon, and once they arrive, the rebels will see we mean business. The show of force won't go unnoticed."

Tillie leaned close and whispered to Maggie, "George might have saved himself the trouble of going to Carlisle if he'd known they were turning around and coming here."

Maggie sighed. "Poor George. He could have stayed with me." She sounded sympathetic, but her brown eyes sparkled at the mention of her beau's return.

* * * *

The school day started with math calculations as usual. Tillie rose when called on to solve the algebra equation on the board. She approached with a halting gait. Mrs. Eyster held out the chalk. Tillie closed her fingers around it as if she contemplated slipping her hand into a lion's mouth. Would it bite? Her hand shook as she stood close to the board. She whispered the question, desperate to ascertain the logic in it. Find the product of the polynomials P(x) = 2x 2 - 3x and Q(x) = 3x 2 + x - 5. She pressed the chalk to the board then used her index finger to wipe away its mark. She read the question again. Her throat tightened, and her heart pounded in her ears. Her eyes grew hot, and she blinked fast. She started to write her answer. The chalk squealed on the board. Tillie's hand froze, and then she wiped away what she wrote.

Mrs. Eyster let out an exasperated sigh. "Miss Pierce, sit down. I declare, young lady…." Whatever she declared, she chose not to say. The teacher wrote twenty more equations on the blackboard for her.

Tillie choked. If she couldn't do one, what made Mrs. Eyster think she could do twenty? She bent her head close to her slate to hide her face.

Beckie rose, sashayed to the board and with swift, sure motions, solved the equation that sent Tillie to her seat.

Tillie glared at Beckie's back. She crossed her arms and bit her lower lip. As Beckie returned to her seat, she threw a triumphant smile Tillie's way. Tillie turned her face away.

Mrs. Eyster called on Catherine Foster as a piercing train whistle shrieked across town. Desks creaked, and dresses rustled as all heads turned toward the window. Jenny McCreary rose from her seat and leaned on the windowsill.

Tillie couldn't see anything unusual on Washington Street. Wagons rumbled up and down. Pedestrians went about their business, though several people stopped and turned toward Chambersburg Street and the train station.

"Girls, it's only ten o'clock. Too early for the troop train." Mrs. Eyster tapped her ferule on the desk. "Focus, please."

The train whistle undermined her strict rules. Jenny McCreary sat back down, hunched over, staring out the window, with her chin in her palm. When Mrs. Eyster called on her for a history recitation, Jenny jerked and faced her teacher. She wobbled to her feet as her eyes darted around the room. Her face turned the color of beets, and she pulled at her fingers with frantic motions. "G-G-George W-W-Wash-wash-ing-t-t-ton w-was t-the…"

Mrs. Eyster sighed and made a sit-down gesture with her hand. Jenny sat, hard, and dropped her head on her desk.

Libby Hollinger leaned forward and patted her on the shoulder.

"All right, girls." Mrs. Eyster reached for her ferule. "Recitation is done. Clearly, we're making little headway. For those who completed your assignments, work on the new lessons on the board." She tapped the stick against the chalkboard next to the lessons as she spoke. "For those with extra assignments set, continue in your study."

Desktops creaked, and papers rustled as the girls began their tasks.

The noon train's imminent arrival hung over the classroom like a pregnant cloud. The girls settled into independent study, and the room grew so quiet, the din of activity outside came in through the open window.

At noon, the girls carried their lunches outdoors and sat in the late-June warmth. The younger girls played in the schoolyard while Tillie and her friends occupied the front steps.

Belle dusted sandwich crumbs off her hands. "I hope the train arrives soon." She crumpled the paper wrapping and stuffed it into her lunch tin. "I want to see my brother again."

Beckie crunched a carrot and tucked it into her cheek. "You saw him yesterday. How much can you miss him?"

Tillie slipped her arm around Belle's shoulder to show her support and soften the blow of Beckie's words. "I wish my brothers were in the Twenty-First so I could see them."

"Have you any word?" Belle offered Tillie a cookie.

"None." In private, Tillie'd long since confided her anxiety to Belle. She didn't want to contemplate a fatal wounding, but their silence terrified her. She bit into the cookie and chewed.

"I pray for them." Catherine grasped Tillie's hand. "Please tell your parents their sons are in my nightly prayers."

Tillie nodded. Sudden tears stung her eyes and she squeezed Catherine's hand.

Beckie faced the girls in the schoolyard playing Blind Man's Bluff. "I told you I'd ask Mr. Kitzmiller about James. I've about finished a letter. I'll post it tomorrow."

"Thank you." The conversation stuttered to a close. No one said so, but surely the girls also listened for the train.

"I wonder what's keeping them." Belle closed her lunch tin and brushed off her skirts. "Time to go inside."

* * * *

"All right, girls." Mrs. Eyster clapped her hands as the girls settled into their seats. "If this morning has shown us anything, it's that we're all a bit distracted today, for obvious reasons. Therefore, instead of our usual afternoon recitations, I'm going to do something most unusual." She glanced around the room. "Grade school girls work on your history lessons. Middle school girls I want you to work on your mathematics, and high school girls—Latin. We'll do independent study."

A flurry of chatter ensued as everyone retrieved the appropriate books. Tillie opened her Latin text and tried to settle in, but could she concentrate? Honestly? She began conjugating verbs, but her gaze slid off her page. Belle peeked at her through her lashes and offered a small smile. Tillie smiled back and returned to her text. Pretending to think, she glanced at Mrs. Eyster.

The teacher sat at her desk on the dais, staring out the window, as though waiting for a special friend long overdue. Almost as if she felt Tillie's eyes on her, she glanced her way.

Tillie smiled at her and went back to work.

Abigail Hicks raised her hand. "Mrs. Eyster?" Abigail lowered her hand when the headmistress acknowledged her. "Do you suppose the Rebels are still here? In Pennsylvania, I mean?"

The girls put down their pencils. Some closed their books.

Mrs. Eyster sighed. "Child, I'm sure I don't know. However, I am certain our boys will arrive soon."

"What happened to them?" Belle's voice cracked. "My brother is on that train."

Tillie reached across the aisle and clasped Belle's hand.

"Again, I don't know, Miss Stewart. Of one thing I am certain. We've accomplished no learning today. I suggest you girls take your lessons and go home."

Beckie whooped. Catherine and Belle grinned. Tillie opened her desk and grabbed her books and writing pad. Desktops opened and banged closed. Jenny, Libby, and Abigail giggled together.

Mrs. Eyster never let school out early. "Mind you return all the more promptly tomorrow." She lifted her hands and ensured her cultured tones rose above their exclamations. "We will have a lot to catch up on."

Beckie tucked her arm around Tillie's—a gesture Tillie realized, irritated her. Then Beckie threw her head back and spoke to the sky. "Thank goodness Abigail had the fortitude to ask the question. I feared I might go mad sitting another moment pretending to study when we don't know if all is well."

Tillie kicked at the pavement, resisting the urge to pull her arm free. "I wish we'd hear from James and William."

"I've said it before, and I'll say it again. You worry too much." Beckie tossed her hair, making her curls dance.

"You don't understand. You criticize George, but you don't have a brother in the army." Tillie bit her tongue. Why did she say that?

Beckie stopped and glared at Tillie. "My brother… is only…thirteen," Beckie hissed through gritted teeth. She released Tillie's arm and walked the rest of the way in sullen silence.

At the corner of Washington and Breckenridge Streets, Beckie strode off without a goodbye.

Tillie scowled and squelched the urge to call after her. When so many boys fought and died, what gave Beckie the right to criticize George and belittle her for worrying about her brothers? Why did she have to take Tillie's arm when they walked? Did she have difficulty staying upright?

Oh, Lord. Here I go again, being mean. She bit her tongue to quell the viper within, but too many times, Beckie made jokes at her expense, or slurred her with veiled insults. Above all, Tillie hated hearing she worried too much.

Am I being a silly ninny? Of course, Beckie didn't try to be mean. That was just who she was.

The courthouse clock chimed out twice, and Tillie froze. Dread shivered through her. She squeezed her eyes shut and pushed away horrible thoughts of death, and heaven knew what else, to the town boys…her brothers…George. The train should have arrived two hours ago. Something told her it wasn't coming.

Chapter 4

Tillie tucked one foot up on a chair rung as Maggie wandered from sitting room to kitchen and back again, wringing her hands and worrying aloud. Her laments grated on Tillie's nerves, but she clenched her teeth and, with effort, remained quiet.

"Where is the train?" Maggie implored. "Why don't they come? Where are they?" She drifted around the kitchen, tears shining in her eyes.

Mother rolled out a piecrust. She pursed her lips but said nothing.

"What if something happened?" Maggie marched up to her. "I know something terrible happened."

Mother stopped and swiped her hands down her apron. "Maggie, this does no good. You'll worry yourself into anemia."

Tillie sat at the kitchen table, one elbow on the edge, her chin resting in her palm, fingers curled against her cheek. Her open algebra text lay unstudied in front of her. "Trains are always late. Why is everyone behaving like silly ninnies because a train is late? It doesn't mean something is wrong."

Maggie turned a hurt expression and tear-filled eyes her way.

"I'm sorry." Tillie held out a hand. "Perhaps they were delayed for some reason." The words rang false, even to her, but she persisted. "Isn't that right, Father?" she said when he entered the kitchen from the back door.

"Isn't what right, dear?" He carried a towel with him, drying his hands.

"Trains are never on time. Why, Uncle Robert said the same thing last Christmas, remember? He understands such matters. He runs the station."

"Why don't I go to the Telegraph Office?" Father crumpled the cloth. "Hugh Buehler often gets news faster than the newspapers do. To be honest, I can't stand the anxiety either. I'll be back as soon as I can." He kissed Mother's cheek, grabbed his hat, and left.

"Oh, Maggie." Tillie faced her sister. "Remember the colored family from the other day?" Standing, she bent over at the waist, her hands at her right shoulder as if weighed down by a gigantic pack. She did a grotesque half step to the door and back. "Y'all don't want them slave kotchers to git ya, does ya?" She aped the mother's words, laughing.

Mother cut her short. "Tillie, how terrible! Have Father and I taught you nothing? The Coloreds in this community should be pitied and helped, not mocked."

"Really, Tillie, you can be crass sometimes." Maggie put on her superior older sister voice.

"I can be crass?" She straightened and scowled. "As I recall, you and George laughed as much as I did." She grabbed her chair and yanked it back, plopping down hard and crossing her arms over her bosom.

Opening her mouth as if to deny Tillie's accusation, Maggie glanced at Mother, then stuck her nose in the air. "Well, what if I did? I'm not amused anymore." She reddened as Mother glared at them.

"Enough, girls." Mother dropped the pastry roller and stepped away from the worktable. "You both know how your father and I feel about slavery, don't you?"

"Of course." They spoke in unison.

"Had I known that family went into hiding, I would have taken them in and kept them here until the danger passed." Mother's face flushed, and her brown eyes snapped. "We've done much for the cause of abolition, and prayed a long time for their freedom. Even so, I'm sure the Rebs don't care a fig about emancipation." Her eyes bore into Tillie. "If they catch the Negroes, they will sell them into slavery. Do you comprehend? Do you want that to happen?"

"No." Tillie dropped her gaze to the table. Her ears burned. Why did she always say and do the wrong thing at the wrong time? She jumped up, excused herself, and fled upstairs.

She lay across her bed staring at the ceiling. Mother's words hammered at her, and she strained to cast herself in the position of the colored folks. She imagined standing on a platform bound at the hands while men shouted out bids for her. She studied the creamy white complexion of her hand and arm. There, but for the grace of God, go I. The significance of those words exploded in her brain. Had she been born with dark skin…She didn't dare finish the thought. To be sold away from Father and Mother, Maggie and even Sam, and never see them again. Concern over her brothers didn't come close. The idea of such a loss made her want to cry.

Her thoughts drifted back to a hot August night when she was eight years old. Unable to sleep, she wandered out to the upstairs breezeway for fresh air. A full moon illuminated the back yard. A colored man slipped into Father's butcher shop and closed the door behind him. Mother went out with a blanket and some food. A short time later, she returned to the house empty-handed. At breakfast, Tillie asked about him, but Father rebuked her and told her never to speak of him. She never did and, since she never saw him again, forgot the incident. Until now.

Sadness overwhelmed her. Tears streamed from her eyes and into her hair. She cried for the family in hiding, and for James and William.

At a soft knock on the door, she rose to her elbows.

"May I come in?" Mother entered without waiting for assent.

Tillie sat up, using the hem of her skirt to wipe her eyes and nose.

"Tilliiieeee! For heaven's sake." Mother took a handkerchief from her apron pocket. "Use this."

Laughing through her tears, Tillie buried her face in the cloth.

"What's gotten into you, my dear?" Mother perched on the bed and caressed Tillie's head. "You aren't the same Matilda who lived here a few short months ago."

"I don't know, Mother. I don't feel like her either. I can't say or do the right thing anymore. I'm like a stranger even to me. Sometimes I look in the mirror, and I don't recognize myself. It's scary." She sniffled and hiccupped.

Mother pulled her into her arms and kissed the top of Tillie's brown head. "My baby's growing up."

"I didn't mean to offend you with my story. I thought you'd be amused. I wanted to lighten the moment and get Maggie's mind off George. Instead, I walked straight into my own folly."

Mother squeezed her. "Believe me, Tillie, I understand. You've hit a stage in life we all go through, where you feel as though nothing ever changes. But, before you know it, the entire world has gone awry and you can't keep up."

Fresh tears welled, and she covered her face with the handkerchief, pressing it hard into her eyes. "Does it ever go away?" The kerchief muffled her voice.

"Yes, and sooner than I would like, that's for certain." Mother gave Tillie one more squeeze, and then released her. "I'll ask Maggie to do your chores this afternoon. Why don't you stay up here for a while? Perhaps you can write to James and William, or read a book."

"Thank you, Mother. I'd like that."

* * * *

Tillie returned below stairs at the usual suppertime, not daring to remain upstairs when Father came home. He might think Mother punished her for something.

Mother delayed the meal until six o'clock. "Girls, come in and set the table."

"Should I set Father's place?"

"Yes, dear. If Father gets hungry, he'll find his way home."

"He always does," Tillie sang out.

Mother laughed.

They finished cleaning up supper when Father entered through the back door, red-faced and out of breath. "I'm sorry, Margaret. I didn't intend to be gone so long, but we had much to talk about." After pouring water into a basin, he washed his face and hands.

"What news, James?" Mother spun from the sink, hands sudsy and dripping water on the floor. "Not the boys?"

"No." He went to her and squeezed her arms. "Not our two boys. Calm your fears, my dear. I bring news of the train." Father's eyes shot to Maggie. His brow puckered, and a frown drew his mouth down, making his jowls hang low.

Tillie and Maggie exchanged glances.

"Speak out, James." Mother wiped her hands on her apron.

He let her arms go and walked to his seat. His head hung low, and he did not make eye contact.

Mother brought a dish of food and placed it in front of him. “They have a right to know what’s happening. They’re old enough to understand.”

“Yes, Father.” Maggie took a firm grip on the back of her chair with both hands, turning her knuckles white. “George is on that train. I’m entitled to hear what happened.” She lowered herself into her chair, her face set in a wary expression.

“I as well, Father.” Tillie’s voice shook, and she wrung the dishtowel.

“Very well.” He placed his arms flat on the table. Then he clasped his hands, twisting his wedding ring around. He harrumphed. “Well, first, the train didn’t come because it derailed between New Oxford and Gettysburg. They hit a cow.”

For a split second, complete silence filled the room. Then Tillie burst out laughing. “Imagine.” She snorted, almost unable to speak between peals of laughter. “Frightened of the Rebs because of a cow.” She gave in to hysterics, releasing her anxiety. She wrapped her arms around her abdomen and collapsed, guffawing at full volume.

Maggie pounded her fist, cheeks scarlet. “It isn’t funny, Tillie.” She gave her a withering glare. “George is on that train, and those boys might have been badly hurt.”

With some effort, Tillie calmed herself. She waved her cloth in front of her face, needing fresh air. She drew in a breath and chuckled a few more times before pushing the cloth against her lips to staunch the flow. Holding her breath, she exhaled in small measurements until calm and collected.

Father smiled, though no hint of humor shone in his eyes. “I can see your point of it, though. I must say, when I first learned of it, I had a mental image of a cow standing astraddle the railroad tracks, chewing her cud and daring the locomotive to do its worst.” Father’s gaze darted to Maggie again.

This time, Tillie snorted as a fresh surge overtook her. The laughter rushed again, but she glanced at her sister, who glared back, lips flat and jaw clenched.

Tillie pressed the towel to her face and coughed to bring her amusement under control. She fell silent, though occasional spasms still shook her body.

Father's smile disappeared. His eyes held Maggie's for a long time. He sighed. "George wasn't there, and luckily, no one got hurt. However, they won't be here until tomorrow morning."

"Why not?" Maggie's eyes widened, and fear reshaped her face. Her brows puckered.

Father kept his head down and spoke to the table. "They have to bring up a new train of course, and that will take time."

Tillie got the impression that Father's response was a deliberate misunderstanding of Maggie's question. Her brows creased and she watched him carefully as he spoke.

"The word is the Rebs are about ten miles north and west of here. It seems they clashed with our boys around Cashtown. More are near Carlisle. The general consensus is they're trying to swing around in an arc and get to Harrisburg."

"How interesting, but what has it to do with George?" Maggie persisted, glaring at Father.

Father closed his eyes as though in a moment of silent prayer. He cradled Maggie's hands in his and dropped his gaze to their clasped fingers. "My dear, I am so sorry to tell you this." He cleared his throat. "George was killed."

Tillie gasped.

"No!" Mother's hands flew over her mouth as though to stifle her cry of shock.

Maggie yanked free of his grasp. "You said he wasn't…on the train." Her voice choked as she squeezed out the last few words.

Father let her go. "He and two other men rode to Carlisle to join the regiment. They were a mile outside of that town when they ran into Confederate soldiers—skirmishers. George and his companions—Billy Lightner, and I don't know the name of the other man—weren't armed. They made a dash for it. Billy and the other man escaped unharmed, but George…" Father wiped tears from his eyes. "He lay beside a snake rail fence. They think his mount refused the jump, which allowed the Rebs to catch up and…" Father pinched his nostrils, drew a deep breath, and resumed. “They shot him in the back of the head. Locals found his body earlier today.”

“How can that be?” Maggie’s voice quavered. “He promised to return at Christmas. He said he would write to me every day. I gave him a hair ribbon as a token. He can’t be dead. He can’t be!” Her head swiveled between Mother and Father, desperation pleading in her eyes. “He can’t be!”

Mother went to Maggie and put her arms around her. Murmuring words only Maggie could hear, she guided her out of the kitchen and up the stairs.

Father pinched his nose again and knuckled an eye.

Silent, Tillie bit her lip against the grief and guilt threatening to overwhelm her. She peered at Father through watery eyes. “I’m sorry I laughed.”

He didn’t respond. He pushed his plate away untouched and covered her hand with his own warm one. He squeezed her knuckles hard, but she didn’t mind.

Mother reappeared, wiping her eyes with a corner of her apron. She sat and dropped her forehead in her hands.

“Will Maggie be all right?” Tillie’s voice clogged.

Mother flung herself out of her chair and ran from the room. She pounded up the stairs, sobbing. Their bedroom door slammed.

Father rose to his feet. He trudged up the steps after her.

Tillie picked up his dish and finished cleaning the kitchen.

Chapter 5

A cloud of sadness hung over the house. While Maggie remained upstairs, Tillie swept the kitchen floor and gathered up the dirt to throw away as Sam entered.

"Hey, Tillie." The kitchen door banged closed behind him. "Did you have a good supper? Ma's doing okay. She's mad at Ginny right now for wanting to stay at Georgia's house a… little….long…er…." His voice trailed off as the grin left his face, and his brows creased. "You look like you been crying. Is everything okay?"

"Father's in the parlor. He wants to talk to you." She spoke without pausing.

Sam's eyes widened. "Did I do something wrong? He knew it was my night to visit Ma."

She dumped the dirt and clenched her teeth against a wave of emotion. Standing with her back to him, she drew in a deep breath, and then let it out. When she could relax, she turned, but refused to look at him. "He's in the parlor." She marched past him and put the broom and dustpan away.

She finished cleaning the stove, when Sam ran sobbing, through the kitchen, and burst through the back door. Tillie moved to the kitchen window and watched him race to the butcher shop and slip inside. She stared at the can of stove blacking and the rag in her hand, put them down, and went outside. It seemed a long march to the butcher shop, a place she never liked going to, but she needed to know he was all right. When she reached the door, she didn't know what to do.

Should she knock? Should she leave him alone? She didn't want to intrude on his private mourning. Tillie shook her head to clear her thoughts and knocked. "Sam? It's me. Can I come in?"

She paused, but there was no answer. She knocked again, more insistent. "Sam, I know you're in here. I saw you. Let me in." As almost an afterthought, she added, "Please." Again, there was no answer, so she opened the door and entered.

The smell of congealed blood and animal parts made her stomach flip. She stifled a gag and glanced around, but in the growing dark, couldn't find him.

"Go away." His voice came from the back corner.

She closed the door and felt her way toward the sound of his voice. "No."

When her foot hit his toe, she stopped and sat next to him. "I'm sorry. I know you like George as much as the rest of us."

"The rest of us? You didn't like George. You were always mean to him."

A dagger of guilt sliced through her heart. She paused, measuring her words. "I'm truly sorry for that. I was jealous of the time he took from Maggie. It was wrong of me, I know, but now I realize I liked him. He was ever the gentleman to me. I wish I could tell him I'm sorry."

Sam sniffled. Though she couldn't see him in the gloom, from the rustled movements she had the impression he wiped his nose on his sleeve. She shifted a little.

"I liked George a lot." Sam's voice shook. "He treated me good."

"Well," Tillie said. "He treated you well." The words were out of her mouth before she could stop them. She bit her lower lip and squeezed her eyes shut. Stupid. "George liked you a lot, too." She tried to amend.

"Tillie?"

"Yes."

"Would you mind leaving me alone? I want to think."

She didn't move or speak. She couldn't think of anything appropriate to say. "Of course." She rose to her feet. "I'm sorry about what I just said. That was stupid. You're a nice boy, Sam. We all like you." She felt her way to the door. There, she stopped and again tried to think of something comforting. "Come inside when you're ready."

* * * *

She went in search of Father. Although she'd grown too old to sit in his lap, perhaps he would hold her close and cuddle her as he used to when she needed comfort.

She found him still in the parlor, the big family Bible open on his knees. She crossed the braided rug and stood next to him. The book was open to Psalm 23, his eyes closed, his lips moving.

Her hands curled into fists. Her body tensed, and she ground her teeth together. Father wouldn't make time for her until he finished praying. She turned to leave him to his prayers, but he clamped his hand on her wrist.

"Sit and pray with me." His head remained down, his eyes closed.

She studied him, noticing for the first time a round spot on top of his head.

"What good does prayer do, Father? It didn't stop George from being killed, did it? Pray for what?"

Father stared at her. His reddened eyes shone with unshed tears.

Her spine stiffened at the pity in his gaze. "Well?"

His jaw loosened, and tenderness smoothed the crinkles around his eyes. His gentle thumb stroked the back of her wrist. "Oh, daughter, prayer isn't about keeping people alive or not. He's going to judge us all when we die—yes, even you, someday. The wages of sin is death. The question is, will you be judged worthy of heaven or hell? That is what prayer does for us. It brings us to the Lord contrite and humble, so we can live in obedience and He can intercede for us in Paradise."

Tillie gave an exasperated cry and wrenched free. "I don't understand you, Father. Why would you worship a God who would condone such a terrible war? Why should I? A God who would let good people like George or perhaps even James or William die?" She backed away. "No. I don't think He cares about what happens to us. If He even exists." She clambered upstairs, hoping to escape her father's wrath.

* * * *

At the top of the stairs, she cringed from the weeping emanating from Maggie's bedroom. She inched open her sister's door. Maggie lay on her bed across the room, curled into a ball, sobbing into the pillow.

Tillie stepped inside and closed the door. Easing herself down on top of Maggie's Log Cabin quilt, she pressed up against Maggie's back and slipped her arm around her in a clumsy attempt at solace. Maggie rolled over and nestled her head on Tillie's shoulder, crying out her anguish while Tillie held her.

After an hour, Maggie's breathing changed, and she snored in exhausted slumber. Tillie eased off the bed and headed to her own room.

After changing into her nightdress and brushing her hair, she scrambled into bed. She lay wide-awake, listening to the crickets' comforting chirrup outside, thinking of George and all the times she'd been mean to him, either to his face or behind his back. She wanted to apologize and now she couldn't. The verse in James, chapter four came to her. She began to whisper, "Whereas ye know not what shall be on the morrow. For what is your life? It is even a vapor, which appeareth for a little time, and then vanisheth away."

Tillie kicked the covers off and lay spread eagle on her mattress. Sweat trickled down her neck and stuck her nightdress to her body. She slid the hem up her legs as far as she dare, and dangled her left leg over the side, swinging it to catch a breeze. Perhaps the breezeway would offer fresh air. She jumped out of bed. Halfway to the door she stopped and reconsidered. Father might be out there. She padded back and stared at the ceiling.

A distant short burst of thunder vied for her attention. Something about the length of the rumble nibbled at the corners of her mind, but she pushed it away, intent on thinking about death and George and Father.

She jumped out of bed, got down on her knees, and folded her hands in supplication. Closing her eyes, she tried to focus her thoughts. How should she pray? What should she ask? What good would prayer do? George would not return.

"Heavenly Father…if you're up there." She yanked her taut nightgown out from underneath her. "Lord, keep the Rebs away from here. Protect James and William, and keep Beckie's Mr. Kitzmiller safe from harm." She shifted her weight to relieve the pressure on first one knee, then the other. "God, make the war end soon. Thank you. Amen."

Her hands fell on the patchwork quilt adorning her bed, and she stared at the star pattern with unseeing eyes. Why was praying supposed to comfort her? She didn't feel comforted and couldn't comprehend why Mother, Father, and Maggie set such store by it. She huffed to her feet and climbed back into bed.

Lacing her fingers under her head, she resumed contemplation of her ceiling. Several quick muffled booms caught her attention. She turned to the window, waiting for a telltale sign of lightning. None. The storm must be further away than she thought.

Tillie threw back the covers, got up again, and went to her writing desk. Perhaps if she wrote to her brothers…

As she started to light her lamp, a loud boom shook the walls, a boom nothing like thunder. It reverberated through the air.

She froze. "What in the world?" Her voice came out in a frightened whisper.

Another muffled blast immediately followed the first. Sticking her head out the window, she leaned out as far as she dared and peered south toward Cemetery Hill. Below her, people popped out of their homes, peering in the same direction.

A full moon lit the landscape. In the distance, gray smoke rose in a drifting cloud behind South Mountain. A red light flashed. A few seconds later came a loud bang and crackling, popping sounds. She pulled in, rapping the back of her head on the window sash.

"Ouch!" Pressing her hand on her head, she bumped into her desk, scattering papers and knocking over her chair. She flew out of her room and raced down the hall, to her parents' bedroom door. Their soft voices whispered through from the other side.

She pounded her fists on her their door until Father snatched it open. He still wore his shirt, but without his cuffs and collar. "Ah, we were just discussing you. What's the matter?" His expression softened from stern parent to concerned father.

"Father, Mother, something's going on. I think I hear something." Her voice cracked high.

"Goodness gracious, child." Mother rose from her dressing table. She wore her nightdress and her hair tumbled down. She moved to the bed and slipped on her emerald green wrap. "Look at you! No wrap, no slippers, what's possessed you? It's thunder. I declare."

"Mother! Under a clear sky and a full moon? Something is going on south of here. I can hear the cannons." She ran to the window facing Baltimore Street and threw it open. "Listen!"

No one spoke. Another crumpf-boom reverberated through the air.

Father peered out. He shook his head. "I can't see anything from here. What do you say we go outside and take a gander?"

He went downstairs toward the front stoop. They followed him.

Neighbors, in various states of dress, milled around the street. Tillie's heart pounded harder as their nervous speculation and anxious questions swirled around her.

Mrs. Winebrenner stood in the road facing south. She pointed at something and spoke to Mrs. Buehler. Mother moved off to join her two friends and fellow Union Relief League associates.

Anna Garlach and her mother, Catherine, talked in low tones. "…I don't know, Ma. Perhaps another wildfire."

Tillie and Father joined them. Anna contemplated the orange sky, her arms crossed in front of her in a protective gesture. In the distance, cannon boomed again followed by the crackle of gunfire.

"What do you make of that, Mr. Pierce? Do you think it's another wildfire?" She greeted them.

Father stared toward the sound of the fighting. South Mountain glowed with orange lights. A cap of gray fog topped it. He didn't answer right away. "No. Sounds like some sort of battle. Those are campfires, Miss Garlach." He didn't take his eyes off the heights. "Perhaps they're fighting somewhere close to Taneytown. We better hope those fires belong to our boys, but if not, then pray as soon as the Twenty-First arrives, they can push them back into Maryland."

"Do we have reason to fear, Mr. Pierce?" Anna turned the upper half of her body to face him. "What if they aren't our Union boys and the Twenty-First doesn't get here tomorrow? I need to consider my parents. How do I keep them safe?"

"Don't you fret about me, dear." Mrs. Garlach put her hand on her daughter's arm, twisting her fingers into the white lace shawl draped over Anna's shoulders. "I survived Indian massacres as a child. A few unruly Rebs don't scare me." Mrs. Garlach nodded at Tillie and gave her a mischievous wink.

Tillie laughed.

"Yes, Mother, but that was a long time ago, and no offense meant, but you're not a girl anymore."

"I can hold my own, daughter. Don't be cheeky."

Tillie giggled again.

Father chuckled. "You're the last person I'd want to be up against in a desperate situation, Catherine."

Anna rolled her eyes and shook her head. She and Tillie exchanged amused glances. Tillie's eyes passed Anna to Mrs. Schriver, who walked up behind them.

Mrs. Schriver smiled as her eyes swept Tillie from top to bottom. "What are you doing outside in your nightclothes?"

Glancing down at herself, she wiggled her toes and tugged at her nightgown, then giggled, a high nervous twitter. She indicated the strange lights flickering in the distance. "What do you make of that?"

"I wouldn't worry. If they're ours, we have nothing to fear. If not, I doubt they'll get this far. The Twenty-First will stop them."

"That's what Father said. I hope so."

Father joined them. "I agree." He nodded to the glowing mountain. "This appears ominous, but if they're Rebs, our Army will get them."

Tillie hoped so, but a few days ago, citizens of Chambersburg ran to Gettysburg telling woeful tales of Rebel raiders looting and pillaging their livestock and produce. Poor Chambersburg, the adults commiserated. Why didn't they think the Rebs could show up here? She'd bet her life George didn't think he'd run into Rebs, either.

The adults grouped themselves to talk and laugh, no longer paying attention to the fighting just south of them. A line in one of her textbooks came to her, "they danced while Rome burned."

Feeling forgotten, she wandered back to her bedroom. Out of the mood for letter writing, she walked over and set her chair to rights. Tomorrow, after school, she promised, she'd compose a long missive to James and William, telling them all the happenings. She stared up at the glowing full moon. The moon didn't care a fig about the turmoil raging beneath its ethereal glow. Tillie leaned on the windowsill and watched the adults on the street while their laughter drifted up to her. Mother and Father joined in as the neighbors engaged in an impromptu party.

She glanced again at the full moon. Her heart skipped a beat, and she gasped. In the upper left hand section, a reddish tinge colored the orb. It hadn't been there before. Blood on the moon, her grandmother's voice sounded in her head. Goose bumps crawled from her scalp to her torso.

Tillie slammed her window closed. Mother always said things appeared more frightening in the dark. Everything would be different in daylight. "Lord, please let it be different in daylight."

Chapter 6

As she walked to school Friday morning, a train whistle shrieked through the air. Amidst cheering crowds, the tinkle of a martial tune carried on the morning breeze. The Twenty-First!

Tillie spun toward Carlisle Street, and her feet, rooting to the ground, somehow kept her from racing to join the crowd. She didn't dare. If Mother and Father found out, they'd punish her. She stood on the corner of Washington and High Streets, imagining the townsfolk welcoming the troops, the grand parade, and the musicians playing "Garry Owen". How much trouble would she get into if she ran down, for a minute or two?

A quick tug on her sleeve made her jump. Her face flushed. "You startled me."

Beckie grinned. "I can tell." She giggled, ending it with a long sigh. "I want to go too, but we need to get to school." She grasped Tillie's arm and turned her around.

"Do you think they'll push the Rebs back into Maryland?" Tillie glanced over her shoulder, one last longing gaze.

Beckie shrugged and pouted. "I don't know. If there is going to be a fight, I think they should have the good grace go somewhere else and leave us be."

Tillie's jaw dropped. "You don't want the Rebs to beat us do you?"

"I want the rebels to go back to Virginia, where they belong, and leave us alone. Let them set up their own government, if that's what they want. Just go away and let us live our lives."

Tillie moved the conversation off such a dangerous and traitorous subject. "Did you see the campfires on South Mountain last night? At first, I thought, wildfire. But it didn't behave like one. Do you remember the terrible fire in May at Emmitsburg? The sky glowed orange for hours."

Beckie nodded. "I remember. Everyone said the Rebs set fire to the town. Turned out to be arson, but the Rebs weren't anywhere near Emmitsburg."

Tillie pressed on. "Bright orange dots covered the mountain. Father said they were campfires, but whether Rebel or Yankee, he couldn't say."

"I don't know what the armies are going to do." Beckie's grip tightened on Tillie's elbow, and she almost pushed Tillie toward school. "But if we don't get moving, we will be late."

They walked in silence for a couple of paces. Tillie peeked at Beckie through her lashes. "Did…" Her throat tightened on a sudden surge of emotion. "Did you hear about George Sandoe?"

"I did. I'm sorry for Maggie. Don't worry so much, Tillie. I'm sure our boys will drive them away."

* * * *

After lunch, they sat in their respective seats, quietly studying their lessons and enjoying the summer breeze billowing the white lace curtains like graceful flags.

A distant, strained, frantic shout cut across the usual street noise. Clattering hoof beats rang on the cobbled street outside as the shouting became louder and more strident.

Tillie and the others turned toward the noise.

Mrs. Eyster rose and went to the window. She reached to lower the sash, but the girls jumped from their seats and joined her, crowding and jockeying for positions from which to see. The older students pushed the younger ones to the back, amid cries of "stop it" and "we were here first"—cries which went ignored.

A horse and rider galloped down the road at breakneck speed, his rider hunched over the animal's neck. They came from the northwest, from the direction of Pennsylvania College. He held his reins in one hand and waved his hat with big, frantic motions over his head, all the while shouting garbled words.

As he flew past the school, Tillie caught two words: Rebs coming.

Students and teacher ran out to the front porch as a second rider charged pell-mell around the corner of Chambersburg Street, not slowing while he made the right-hand turn. He charged toward them. "The rebels are coming! The rebels are coming!"

"Why, he sounds like John Revere." Catherine giggled.

Beckie pinched her. "Paul Revere, not John, for heaven's sake."

"I know." Catherine's face reddened. She scowled and rubbed her arm.

Mrs. Eyster gathered her skirts and ran down the front walk. Tillie gawked and the others gasped. They'd never seen her move at more than a sedate, ladylike walk, but now she flailed her hands to catch the man's attention.

He pulled his horse up short. The animal shied, its hooves missing her by mere inches. Several girls gasped again. Tillie's hands flew to her face as she cringed and sucked in her breath.

Mrs. Eyster reached for the bridle. "Sir, am I to understand the Confederates are coming here?" She stepped into the street, unconcerned about the horse.

"Yes, ma'am." He whipped off his hat and wiped the sweat from his brow. He glanced at the girls and spoke loud enough for them to hear. "We went out to scout their position. They're headed this way for sure. Now, if you'll excuse me, I must be on my way." He jerked the reins and jammed his spurs into the horse's flanks. Horse and rider swerved around her and resumed their mad dash down Washington Street.

Mrs. Eyster stared after him, a hand over her mouth. She gathered her skirts and sprinted back to her students.

Belle screamed and pointed toward the Lutheran Seminary. The massive three-story, red brick building with a high white cupola dominated the landscape about a mile away. A roiling dark mass appeared just below the crest of the hill, ominous in the bright sunshine.

Tillie's heart squeezed in her chest, and she struggled to draw breath. That couldn't be the Union Cavalry.

As if offering a challenge, a rider appeared, separated from the cloudy mass, alone on the hillcrest.

A chill rippled up Tillie's spine as the mass caught up to him and moved toward them. She clasped Belle's hand.

The girls murmured in low voices and glanced at each other, nervous fear contorting their faces. Then all eyes fixed on their teacher.

Mrs. Eyster's hand went from her mouth to her throat. Her fingers shook as they played with her lace collar. Keeping her eyes fixed on the cloud, she addressed her students. "Girls, run home! Fast as you can and stop for nothing!" Her voice trembled.

Tillie started to suggest Beckie come to her house, thinking it impossible for her to make the long three miles home in safety.

Beckie grinned, squeezed her hand, and took off running in the direction the soldier went.

The rest of the girls scattered as the dark mass drew to the end of Chambersburg Street.

A sharp prick of fear goaded Tillie. Lifting her skirts to her knees, she ran for her life. She lived two blocks from school, but no sooner reached the front door than a commotion clamored behind her. Confederate cavalrymen entered the Diamond and fanned out. She estimated at least one hundred men turned right onto Baltimore Street, headed straight for her.

She screamed, flung herself against the door, and leaped inside, slamming it closed. She sped into the sitting room.

"Tillie, you're home, and so early!" Mother came from the kitchen, her eyes wide. "What's the matter?"

"Mother, they're here!" Tillie's voice cracked, and she started to cry. She flew across the room and threw herself into Mother's arms.

"Who's here?"

"The Rebs."

Mother held her tight. "Don't weep, child. We'll be all right."

"Oh, Mother." Tillie hiccupped. "I'm so scared. I'm certain some of the girls didn't get home ahead of them. I barely got inside myself. What about Beckie? What'll happen to her if she doesn't make it home?"

"Calm yourself. She's a smart girl, and whatever else these Rebels think they are, they're still Americans. They know how to treat a young lady."

Bloodcurdling shrieks and popping crackles reverberated in the street.

Mother pushed Tillie aside and rushed to the front window. Leaning her legs against the arm of the couch, she eased up the green velvet curtain to peek out. Tillie followed, crowding close to Mother's skirts.

Gray and butternut clad men marched past the house, uttering an ululating screech and firing pistols into the air.

"That must be the Rebel Yell." Tillie's heart hammered, and her hands shook.

Mother didn't answer. She continued to hold the curtain against her cheek and watch.

More soldiers appeared, muskets and pistols over their heads, firing into the air, all the while whooping and hollering.

To a man, they looked as if they hadn't bathed in months. Their faces unshaven, some with beards down to their waists. A man raised his arm to fire his pistol, displaying a mass of hair pushing through a gaping hole in his underarm. What's more, he walked barefoot, as did many others. One even had a rope tied around his waist to keep his britches up.

They came into the packed street and fanned out, shouting and cursing as they pounded the butts of their rifles on doors, demanding entrance.

Across the road, half a dozen soldiers banged on Mrs. Buehler's front door. No one answered. One soldier stepped up and used the butt of his rifle on the door, while two others attempted to force the lock. Without warning, the door flew open from within, causing the picklock to pitch forward. Mrs. Buehler blocked the entrance, her arms against the doorjamb, skirts filling the doorway. The man with the rifle grabbed her shoulder to push her into the house, but Mrs. Buehler held her ground. She had a verbal exchange with the man, shook her head, and then glanced behind her. She turned to face the soldier and again refused him entrance. The sounds, though not the words, drifted to Tillie and Mother.

"Oh, Fanny, what are you doing? Be careful!" Mother gripped the windowsill, her knuckles white. "Lord, protect her and her family," she whispered in fervent prayer. Then she rushed to the front door, turned the lock, and returned to peek out from behind the curtain.

Mrs. Buehler glanced over her shoulder again, turned back to the intruders, and said something. She smiled, lowered her arms and stepped aside, made a sweeping gesture. The Rebels pushed their way inside.

"Mother, what're they doing?"

"I don't know." Mother's voice shook, her words coming out clipped and urgent.

Hundreds more, dirty, ragged men swarmed the street, whooping and shouting, cursing and firing into the air.

"Gracious!" Tillie's ears burned at their language. She glanced at Mother, eyes wide and mouth agape, to see her reaction, but she seemed not to have heard, intent on the activity.

Maggie's heels clattered on the stairs. "Mother, what's going on?"

Tillie spun around. "The Rebs're here!" She almost screamed the words.

Maggie joined them at the window. She put her arm around Tillie's shoulder.

"Margaret." Father ran in from the back of the house, breathing hard. "I've sent Sam to hide Lady in the cemetery. I hope he got there in time."

"Oh, Father, do you think he made it?" Tillie clasped her hands tight. "What will happen if they take her? She belongs to me."

"Calm yourself, child. Lady is not a young horse. Most likely they'll not want her."

Fresh tears welled up, but she nodded, accepting his prediction. She glanced again at Mother, who all this time, acted as if she didn't hear any of them. She continued peering out the window at the enemy teeming on the street.

Four men advanced toward their front stoop. Maggie made a sound in her throat, and Tillie clung to her.

Cheering erupted, and the men broke off, veering in the direction of the cemetery. They fired over their heads and shouted in celebration.

Mother moved to the side window. "No, James. He didn't make it. Here he comes, along with the other boys." She gasped and shot up straight. "James, those men are pointing their guns on the boys. They've taken him prisoner. We'll see about that!" She ran for the front door, threw off the lock, and flung it wide.

"Margaret!" Father charged after her. "Get back in the house."

Mother sped out the door to the pavement, waving to the Confederate soldier leading the young boys and their horses up Baltimore Street.

"Please, sir." She waved at the officer sitting on a tired, emaciated bay.

Was it he who challenged the girls at school?

"What do you want, ma'am?" His filthy butternut jacket hung above pants so worn, his knee almost showed through the fabric. His matted hair, coated with too many layers of dust to discern its actual color, peeked out from his dirty gray Hardy hat. Blue eyes shone beneath its brim.

"Please." She pointed to Sam. "You don't want that boy. He's our apprentice. He lives with us. He's only twelve years old."

"No." He signaled, and a soldier pushed Sam toward the curb. "We don't want him. We will take the horse."

Sam relinquished Lady's reins and ran to Mother.

Mother slipped a protective arm around his shoulders.

Sam's two sisters, Georgia McLean and Ginny Wade, stood on the opposite curb, watching.

"Mrs. Pierce," Ginny's voice rang loud across the street. "If those Rebs take our Sam, I don't know what I'll do with you folks!"

His arms went around Mother's waist as though seeking her protection. Mother held him tight against her as she stared, wide-eyed at them.

The officer turned, considered the two young women, and then glanced down at Mother. He lowered his face and tried to hide a barely suppressed grin.

Ginny shook her fist. "If we must explain to our mother what happened to her son, you'll be sorry!"

Georgia glared at them, arms crossed, in full support of her sister.

Johnny Reb hid his grin behind a gloved hand and ahemed.

"Not to worry, Ginny," Mother called. "They only wanted the horse. Sam is quite safe."

"She'll get us into trouble, yet." Maggie stared at the two women, her voice full of angry, hurt surprise.

Tillie gasped. "How dare she? If she's so concerned about her brother, why didn't she protect him instead of making Mother do it? Southern sympathizer!" She clenched her teeth and balled her hands into fists.

"Leave be." Maggie grasped Tillie's elbow. "For Sam's sake."

Again, Ginny's voice rang out, loud and clear. "He's your responsibility now, and if any harm comes to him, I'll see you pay."

The soldiers watched the exchange like a crowd watching a tennis match. They cheered and egged the women on.

"Now, Ginny…" Father held up a hand palm out in supplication.

Tillie didn't wait for his reply. Nobody talked to her mother that way! She opened her mouth, to launch into a vicious attack, but Maggie pinched her. Hard.

"Ooooouuuuch!" She scowled and rubbed her arm.

Her sister shook her head and, with a glance, indicated Sam. Tillie followed her gaze. He hung his head, and tears ran down his cheeks. It seemed as though he tried to burrow into Mother's embrace, hoping to hide and escape the hostilities. Her heart went out to him. What must it feel like to be part of such a contentious, disagreeable family?

Georgia shouted at Father. He chose to ignore her.

The Rebels catcalled and egged on the two women again, hoping for more.

Letting her breath out in a huff, Tillie continued to rub her arm. "Oh, what do I care what Ginny Wade thinks?"

Eying the Reb holding the reins of her beloved friend, Tillie approached. She moved on wooden legs, intent on stopping him from taking Lady. "Please, sir, give me back my horse. Please don't take her away!" Her body shook, and desperation quaked in her voice. But she couldn't help it.

He leered at her, leaning so close his nose almost touched hers.

She stepped back, eyes wide.

His red hair—wild, filthy, and probably filled with lice—hung in his face. His thick, matted beard came to his chest, and crumbs of meals past hid in it. Cold blue eyes bore into hers. She gagged when he puffed his foul breath into her face.

"Sissy, what're you crying about? Git in the house and mind your own business!"

His breath touched her cheek. She retreated another step. Someone caught her by the elbows and drew her backward.

The soldiers moved away up Baltimore Street with their prizes. Dirty Beard yanked Lady's reins. The horse tossed her head, but followed without protest. She didn't even look back.

Tillie collapsed onto the pavement, sobbing. Father took her by the shoulders and walked her inside to the sitting room.

"Now, Tillie." Mother used a reasonable tone. "You're more frightened by the events of the day than upset over the loss of the horse. Calm down, child."

Sam stood at Tillie's side, patting her shoulder.

Father paced in front of her. "So foolish, Matilda. We don't know what these Rebels will do. Perhaps they'll mark us for this. We all must be more discreet."

Maggie knelt next to her. "I understand how you feel." She laid a soft hand on Tillie's arm. "I know what it means to lose someone you care about, even a horse."

Tillie threw off Sam's hand and jerked away from her sister. "Oh, I wish I was a boy! I would've told that dirty Reb what I think of him!"

"Matilda Jane Pierce, that's quite enough!" Mother's hands went to her hips, and her brow lowered. "The horse is gone, and most likely, there's nothing more we can do. Crying won't help things. Now stop acting like a child half your age. Count your blessings she's all they took." Mother's eyes darted to Sam. She took a deep breath, softened her tone. "Go upstairs. Wash your face and change your dress, then come down and help me get supper."

"Yes, ma'am." Tillie wiped her nose, cowed and hurt by Mother's scolding. She stayed in her room for a half hour, indulging in self-pity. She needed to get her displeasure out of her system before she got into more trouble. When ready, she put a smile on her face she didn't feel and rejoined her family.

* * * *

Tillie entered the kitchen as Mother answered a knock at the door. Four Confederate soldiers, among them Dirty Beard, stood on the back stoop.

They removed their hats like penitents. Dirty Beard didn't own a hat. Instead, he laced his fingers in front of him.

"Ma'am, might we get something to eat?" The leader's Southern drawl sounded so polite… It was hard to comprehend that, just an hour ago, they walked away with Tillie's most prized possession.

Father jumped from the table and ran out of the room. His feet pounded on the treads as he disappeared upstairs.

"Oh, yes." Her voice shook with anger. "You should ask for food, after you steal our horse and frighten our daughter half to death." She glared at Dirty Beard, blocking the door with her body as Mrs. Buehler had done.

Father returned holding a Revolutionary War musket.

Tillie's eyes widened. She started to ask what he meant to do with a gun that didn't work, but he put a finger to his lips and gave her a stern, be-quiet glare.

"Now, ma'am…" The leader changed his tone. Menace now laced his words. "We can ask for food, or we can force our way in and help ourselves. Which would you prefer?"

Mother sighed, and her shoulders slumped. She pulled the door wide, gesturing to the table. "You may sit down."

Tillie put the dishes down and waved at Father to hide the gun. He stepped into the sitting room and propped the musket against the wall, out of sight, but within easy reach. The rest of the family backed away as, like a pack of ravenous dogs, the hungry soldiers attacked the food.

Tillie went to Father and clasped his arm.

The men grabbed everything they could. They spilled the apple butter as they spread it on their bread. Pickle juice puddled on the tablecloth as they stuck dirty fingers into the crock, scooping the pickles onto their plates. They passed crocks back and forth, knocking them over. The contents dirtied the table and the floor as the fiends shoved food into their mouths in huge quantities, joking while they ate.

Dirty Beard licked his finger and used it to pick up crumbs, which he put in his mouth.

Tillie couldn't stand it any longer. She turned her back as the vulgar men gobbled their meal, spitting half-chewed bits while they talked and ate.

A glance passed between Mother and Father across the room, a silent communication.

Father took a seat. "Tell me." He directed his question to the one who asked to come in. "To whom would I speak regarding the return of our horse?"

"Well, sir." The soldier sat back in his chair, clasped his hands behind his head, and said in his peculiar drawl. "You ain't gonna get your horse back."

Their malicious laughter made Tillie's skin crawl, and a prick of fear stabbed her heart.

He raised his voice above the din. "However."

His men fell silent.

"However, if you must plead your case, I suggest you come with us and speak to Colonel White."

Father and Mother exchanged wary glances. Mother shook her head. He nodded and waited for the men to finish their meal. The soldiers, in no particular hurry to leave, lounged at the table and enjoyed several cups of "real coffee". They demanded Mother make more when the pot ran dry. She complied.

When they rose, Father went with them.

* * * *

Tillie wriggled in her seat, tucking her booted feet beneath her. She held Mr. Emerson's book of essays open in her lap, but she barely glanced at the pages. In the gray light of twilight, Sam sat on the front stoop whittling. From her vantage point on the sitting room sofa, she pretended to read, but she kept her eye on him. Every so often, he raised his head and looked toward the Diamond. She sat up straight, but when he returned to whittling, she relaxed again. Daylight almost completely left the sky when Sam entered the house and stopped inside the sitting room door. "Mr. Pierce is coming."

Mother put down her knitting. "Thank you, Sam." Turning to the girls, she gestured toward the kitchen. "Father will be hungry. I'll fix him some dinner."

"Sam." Tillie gave him a hopeful glance and closed her book. "Is Lady with him?"

"No, he's alone."

Father entered and paused in the doorway as though gathering his thoughts. He stepped inside the sitting room. The muscle in his jaw twitched, and his brows knotted at the center of his forehead. He laid a shaking hand on Sam's shoulder. "Sam, be a good boy, please, and close up the shop for me. Hide anything of value, all the tools, everything sharp. I'll be out to help you."

He studied Father's face, nodded, and clomped out the back door.

Father stared after the boy, a strange mixture of love and bewilderment in his expression.

"Where's your mother?" He didn't take his eyes off the path Sam took.

"She's in the kitchen getting you something to eat." Maggie set aside her mending. "Is something wrong, Father?"

"Girls, come into the kitchen. I must tell you something." He trudged forward as if he were going to his hanging.

The girls seated themselves as Mother placed a plate and a cup of coffee in front of him. She too sat down, her jaw tense and chin jutted forward.

He stared at his food for a long time, and then pushed the dish away. He looked at each woman. When his eye fell on Tillie, he sighed. "I'm sorry, my dear. We won't get Lady back. It would seem the Confederate Army is so desperate for horses, that even an old, lame mare will fill the bill."

Tillie nodded. She squeezed her eyes tight to stop tears from escaping.

"I sent Sam outside so I could talk free. It would break my heart to speak in front of him." Father pulled his coffee cup close and wrapped his hands around the mug. "When we got to the Confederate camp, the soldiers took me to see Colonel White. He allowed me to present my entire case, so I told him about the horse. I said she's old and lame. She won't be any use to them. When I finished, he said he understood me to be a black abolitionist; so black, in fact, I turned black in front of him. I'll admit he scared me…." His eyes glazed as he stared past his family. "He said he'd been informed my two sons serve in the

Union Army, and they probably stole more from the South than he took from me."

Mother straightened in her seat. She folded her hands together. An expression of determination and defiance crossed her face. "Who would say such a thing?" Her voice squeaked out, a frightened whisper.

Father took a sip of his coffee. "I asked him where he got his information. He said a young woman arrived earlier with a woeful tale of how we almost allowed her brother to be kidnaped by their troops, and only by her threats did we finally intervene for the boy."

"How dare she?" Tillie slammed her hand down. "Always the Southern sympathizer. No doubt, she did it to impress Wesley Culp. He's a Reb. He might appreciate a traitorous act from her. Everyone knows she wanted to marry him, but the Culps wouldn't allow it!"

"Tillie, control yourself." Mother gripped Tillie's arm.

"Enough!" Father's fist crashed down rattling the dishes. "You're angry about Lady, but there's nothing we can do. We must pray for our enemies. Much as you may think so, Ginny Wade isn't our enemy. Misguided, I'll admit, but not our enemy. Don't hate her. Pity her, and pray for her lack of Christian charity."

"No, sir." Sam stood inside the kitchen door. "Tillie's right. My sister is a filthy traitor, and I hope she gets what she deserves."

Chapter 7

Tillie pressed her nose and forehead flat to the windowpane, hoping for a glimpse of Lady. Perhaps her rider would pass the house. A Reb soldier passed right beneath the window. She ducked back, breathing hard.

"Tillie!" Mother's voice rang like a pistol shot.

Tillie yelped and knocked the lamp on the table next to her. As she made a grab, she bumped the base. It tilted toward the edge. Tillie's eyes widened, and she snatched with both hands, somehow managing to stop the fall before turning guilty eyes to her mother.

Mother's eyes darted from the lamp to Tillie. "Today is your lucky day. That was a wedding gift." She advanced on Tillie. "For the last time get away from those windows." Mother shook her finger. "If I must tell you again, I will confine you to your room for the rest of the day."

Tillie concentrated on the light as she suppressed a smile. What a perfect place to watch to her heart's content. "I'm sorry, Mother. Please can I go outside? I'll stay on the front steps. I want to see what's happening."

"Certainly not! Don't make me admonish you again, Matilda Jane." Mother pointed at her. "You have chores to do, young lady."

"Yes, Mother." As soon as Mother returned to the kitchen, Tillie took one last peek out the window. Lady cantered past the house, a huge man sitting atop her. Tillie sensed her struggle to bear his weight. He shouldn't make her canter. She can't. She'll be lame. Clamping her teeth down on her lip, she strained for another glimpse of her beloved horse.

Lady stumbled, and the rider yanked her reins. Tillie's body jerked as though she felt the pain as she bit back tears of rage. Poor Lady wouldn't last long.

Soon they were gone. She turned away to begin her chores.

* * * *

Tillie found herself condemned to dusting the parlor furniture. She knew better than to do a quick job. Mother would inspect her work, and if she didn't do it right the first time, she'd have to do it again. As she put the last touches of dusting wax on the table in the middle of the room, Father's voice rang out.

"Margaret, I'm leaving." Holding his hat, he approached the front door.

"When will you be back?" Mother's skirts rustled as she met him at the door.

"I can't say. General Early sent the Borough Council a requisition request. He gave us until tomorrow to come up with the items. I'm off to find out what's on it, and what we're to do. I might be gone a few hours or all day, depending on the mood of the men."

"Please, James, do be careful."

"Don't worry, my dear. I'll be the soul of caution."

Tillie buffed the table, pretending she wasn't watching and listening.

Mother slid her arms around Father's neck. They embraced and kissed. Father opened the door.

A piece of paper hanging from the knocker flapped. He tore it off and read aloud. "'General Gordon is pleased to report civilians and civilian property will not be harmed. We assure the townsfolk you may come and go as you please, within reason, and without fear of molestation by your Southern Conquerors. Signed, General John B. Gordon, CSA, General Jubal Early, CSA, Commanding.'" He crumpled the paper and threw the wad into the street.

Tillie's heart swelled over his act of defiance. Southern conquerors indeed! The Union boys'd show them when they arrived. In her imagination, the Yankee Army converged on Gettysburg, swords held high, guns at the ready, running at the Rebs and screaming with all their might, while the Confederates ran for their lives. She shivered at the thrill of the spectacle.

Father's voice intruded into her daydream, murmuring calming words to Mother, but he pitched his voice too low for Tillie to hear. He left, pulling the door closed behind him.

Mother bolted the door. She turned and locked eyes with Tillie. "Well, Nosy Nell, we need to put you to better use."

Under Mother's glare, Tillie's face flamed. She should tell Mother she didn't eavesdrop on purpose, but sensed Mother wasn't in a mood to listen.

"Come." Mother beckoned. "I have the perfect job for us."

Tillie followed Mother into the kitchen where Maggie took foodstuffs off the shelf and piled them on the table. Sam gathered the items into a box. Mother took Tillie down to the basement where a new set of shelves filled a small alcove near the back wall.

"Father and Sam made these for me over the past couple of days. He and Maggie are gathering all they can upstairs. I want you to stack the crocks and jars here, and once we're done, we'll hang a curtain. Those Rebs won't get any more from us, if I have anything to say on the subject."

"Yes, Mother." Tillie felt a weight lifted off her. Now, she had something important to do. She sank to the hard, dirt-packed floor before the shelves, the cold confronting her knees as she set the tallest crocks along a back row.

A half hour later, Maggie hovered over her and adjusted the sheet across the shelf, hiding the food. "This should be sufficient."

"I think so." Mother scanned the cellar with a critical eye. "If they come to the back door and see nothing to feed them upstairs, I'm certain they'll go away. I doubt they'll get close enough to come in through the basement entrance, but if they do," she indicated three cement steps leading to a pair of double doors, which opened to the backyard, "I don't think they'll find this shelf back in this dark corner."

"Do you think they might break in down here?" Sam stared at the doors, as if seeing a new menace he must guard against.

"At this point, your guess is as good as mine." Mother planted her hands on her hips, wrinkling blue calico. "A week ago I would have said they're misguided Americans, but from what I've seen lately…" She shook her head and pursed her lips.

Footsteps thudded down the stairs.

"Well, James, what did General Early want?" Mother asked, as he reached the bottom stair.

"That." Father waved a finger toward the curtain. "Along with whiskey, flour, meat, clothing, and fifty thousand dollars."

He sat on the last step, propped his elbows on his knees, and rubbed his hands over his face before dropping them into his lap. "Even if we possessed what he's asking for, I don't think we'd provide it, though no one came up with a satisfactory refusal."

"Well, I think if General Early realizes we don't, he will understand." Mother offered a reassuring smile.

Father chuckled. "You think so, my dear, if it makes you feel better, because tomorrow, David Kendlehart, Alexander Buehler, and I must go back and tell him no. Lucky for me, I'm not the Borough President. That's Kendlehart's job, so he needs to find a way to say no. My job is to appear angelic."

"No, James, not you." Mother gave an angry jerk to the curtain, adjusting an imaginary wrinkle in the fabric. "Why? What happens if this General Early becomes angry? He might take you prisoner!"

"No, dear, I don't think he will."

Mother huffed, but she didn't challenge him in front of the children.

"Oh, by the way." Father jerked his thumb over his shoulder. "Alex wanted me to tell you David got away with the postage stamps and his equipment. Fanny did a fantastic job stalling the Rebs until he escaped out the back."

Mother's face softened. "I'm glad. She acted incredibly brave."

The room fell into silent agreement.

"Father, why would they ask for whiskey?" Tillie asked.

He emitted a little cough, and then cleared his throat. "Well, because, my dear, soldiers drink whiskey. Never mind why." He shook his head. "Anyway, we need to return in the morning, and either hand over our goods to General Early, or say no."

"Why don't you do what they ask?" Maggie gestured to Mother. "Mother's right. Why aggravate them? Give them what they ask for. Perhaps they'll go away."

His expression changed from grim determination to sad sympathy. "Appeasement never works and is not our way. Also, I learned today, three weeks ago our bankers put most of their money on a train to Philadelphia for safekeeping." He twisted his wedding ring.

"Will you be arrested if you say no?" Tillie went to the steps and sat next to him. She took his arm in hers and leaned into him.

"It's anybody's guess what General Early will do. Given the fact I went and asked for Lady back, they're aware of me." He slipped an arm around her shoulders, giving her a gentle squeeze. He gazed around at the rest of his family. "Don't fret. We're right and they're wrong. I believe, if we deal honestly with these people, the Lord will take care of us. We will trust in Him."

Mother took a deep breath and let it out. "You're right, James. I'll pray General Early takes the news well."

"We all will," Maggie agreed.

* * * *

Tillie slumped at the sitting room table and tried to concentrate on the Bible lessons Father set for her in response to yesterday's outburst over Lady's theft. She didn't mind passing Sunday afternoons in the text of the sermon, but how unfair. She plodded through Psalm 4, and Matthew chapter five, verses twenty-one and twenty-two. Now she worked on Ephesians, chapter four, with special attention on verses twenty-five through chapter five, verse two. Father promised to review it with her when he returned home. Leafing through the passages, she sighed as she turned to chapter eighteen. She flipped her pencil between her fingers and beat a rapid tattoo on the pages.

"What's the matter, my dear?" Mother sat in her rocking chair, knitting.

"It's not fair I have to study the Bible. I said I'm sorry for getting angry."

"You don't sound terribly repentant in your apology, nor did you last night. I think studying these passages will be of benefit to you. I confess we've been lax with you. That's what comes of being the youngest child, I suppose. Well, we're correcting the problem now." Mother lowered her knitting and studied Tillie, who stared at the table. "Father will be unhappy with you if you don't study your lesson." With a deft movement, Mother wound the yarn around her left finger as she inserted the needle into her stitch.

"Well, I'm sick of hearing how I'm going to hell for a little outburst when the entire country is drowning in hate. Why can't I be angry because someone stole something from me, yet fellow countrymen can shoot and kill each other and no one does anything about that?" She bit her tongue, regretting the words. She refused to lift her face, but peered at Mother through lowered lashes.

Mother's chair and knitting needles froze. She dropped her project to her lap.

Tillie closed her eyes and groaned.

"God will hold us all accountable for our sin." Mother's voice sounded soft and gentle, but also hard as steel. "Don't think nothing is being done about the war. It is God's punishment for the unrepentant sin of slavery." Mother resumed her knitting and rocking. "As for your father and I, we hold you to a high standard of behavior because one day you will be required to account for your sin to God."

Tillie's eyes swept the table. Her index finger flipped the corner of the book, the pages riffled as she waited, heart pounding, for Mother to punish her impudence. Again, she peeked at Mother through her lashes.

Mother took a stitch. "Do your study, and while you do, I'll be praying for you. Rest assured, your father will hear about this."

Tillie closed her eyes, dismayed, and reopened the Bible.

Her pencil scratched across her paper. The pages rustled as she turned them.

Mother's rocker squeaked on every back motion. Her foot tapped against the floorboards, and her needles clicked through her project.

Tillie began to think she'd been studying the passages for a lifetime when the front door opened.

"Margaret, I'm home." Father called from the entrance.

"Finished so soon?" Mother rose and put her knitting down.

"No. There's another session this afternoon. I just need something quick to eat."

"Oh, dear." She rushed into the kitchen. "I didn't expect you home for lunch."

"Make me a sandwich, if you don't mind." He followed her.

With her parents distracted, Tillie gathered her things and slipped upstairs. She sat at her desk, pen scratching across paper.

Her hand froze as footsteps halted outside her bedroom door. Father entered. She refused to look at him.

"Matilda, I'm returning to the Borough Council now, but I want a word with you the minute I get back."

"Yes, Father." She couldn't remember the last time he called her Matilda. She chanced a peek over her shoulder to show him her docile manner.

His stern glare dismayed her.

Tillie turned around in her chair. She grabbed the knob on the backrest and squeezed with spasmodic motions. "I'm sorry, Father. I don't know what came over me."

He shook his head. "That's not going to work this time. I'll want to speak to you in the parlor right after supper tonight, no excuses."

"Yes, sir."

He trudged back downstairs, the bedroom door he'd closed behind him told her she consigned herself to an afternoon in her bedroom to think about her behavior. Tears filled her eyes. She returned to her letter and picked up her pen. Her hand shook, dripping ink on the page. She slammed her hand down on the paper, crumpled it up, and threw it across the room.

* * * *

When Father came home before dinnertime, Tillie remained upstairs, hoping to escape punishment.

"Matilda Jane!" he called from the bottom of the stairs. "You have chores to do."

She adjusted her skirts then went to her mirror and evaluated her appearance. With a shaking hand, she opened her bedroom door and, like a condemned man going to his death, walked to the stairs and descended. She entered the kitchen quietly, trying to make herself as small a target as possible. Her movements careful, she lowered the dishes and set the table.

Father sat in his seat, his Bible at his right elbow. "We didn't want to tell General Early no, but we also didn't want to tell him we sent everything to Philadelphia." He aimed most of his commentary at Sam, sitting next to him, his elbows on the table and chin in hand.

The boy listened, face enraptured. "What happened next?"

Father shook his head. "Well, we feared if he found out, he would become enraged and either burn the town to the ground or allow wholesale looting."

Mother took her seat. "I'm sure you all did the right thing, James. Samuel, get your elbows off the table."

Sam yanked his arms to his side as though afraid someone might swipe them out from under him.

Maggie sat, and Tillie slid into her place next to Mother.

Father opened the Bible to James and read from chapter one. He cast occasional glances at Tillie. "My Brethren, count it all joy when ye fall into diverse temptations, knowing this, that the trying of your faith worketh patience. But let patience have her perfect work, that ye may be perfect and entire, wanting nothing."

She eyed him. Did he send her a message?

"If any of you lack wisdom, let him ask of God, that giveth to all and it shall be given him. But let him ask in faith, nothing wavering. For he that wavereth is like a wave of the sea, driven with the wind and tossed."

Her scalp tingled, and her heart pounded with recognition. Her conversation with Maggie came back to her. What did she say? That's what happens when we take our eyes off God. Tillie bowed her head.

He finished reading, put the Bible away, and strode back into the room.

"What did you decide to do, Mr. Pierce?" Sam speared a potato.

Father picked up his fork and knife and cut his beef. "We did a lot of arguing and finger wagging, but no one came to a consensus about what to do or say. We needed to do something. Kendlehart quieted the committee down and said we wasted enough time. He, Buehler, and I went to talk to the general."

"What happened next?" Sam's elbows grazed the table. He shot a glance at Mother and snapped them to his sides again.

"Well, we left to go find General Early—he took over Moses McLean's house—much to his consternation." Father chuckled. "Imagine McLean forced to play host to a Confederate general and his staff. He's pretty peeved, but with a young family to care for, he can't very well say no." He took a bite of his beef and chewed while they waited for him to continue. He sipped his coffee and prepared to take another forkful.

"James, dear, please, go on with your story. What happened next?" Mother put a forkful of peas in her mouth.

Father eyebrows shot high in feigned surprise. He turned smiling eyes upon her. "Oh, yes, I'm sorry, my love. Well, the three of us approached and found the general standing outside McLean's house talking with some of his officers. We waited, as nervous as long-tailed cats in a room full of rocking chairs. After some time, he acknowledged us. I had no idea what Kendlehart would say, but Kendlehart's a genius." He scooped up some peas.

"Go on, Father, please. What happened next?" Maggie's dull monotone hit them all like a snowball to the face as she spooned some cucumbers onto her plate. She thumped the bowl down and blinked back tears. She picked up her napkin and dabbed at her nose and eyes.

Father glanced at her, brows creased. He swallowed and wiped his mouth. "Well, General Early acknowledged us, and Kendlehart says to him, 'We've come in response to your request for supplies. We regret to inform you it is impossible for Gettysburg to supply the requisitions you requested.' He stopped, and we all waited to see what he would say. Can anybody guess what General Early said?" He eyed them, a big smile crinkling his face. "He said the town appeared rather prosperous, and he didn't believe we were so destitute. Kendlehart insisted we told the truth. He even went so far as to say York is much more well-to-do. Buehler and I stood like perfect angels as he outright lied." He buttered his bread. "It's not an actual lie, as we don't physically have the supplies here, but still." He chuckled. "Kendlehart told him his men were welcome to peruse our shops, and if they found something worthy of buying, may make the required purchases, and not in Confederate script, only gold or greenbacks." He burst out laughing.

"I don't understand." Tillie's brows creased. She risked a comment and Father's renewed attention. "Why is that funny?"

"Because, his men must pay for their goods and our shop owners get to make some money off the Rebs." He chewed another piece of beef. "We're saying no, without appearing to say no. We won't give away our supplies. Our merchants will charge double to make up for the Confederate currency they will most likely receive. Now do you understand?"

Tillie nodded when the others smiled. "Yes." She still didn't get the humor.

"What did General Early say?" Sam's fork slipped from his fingers and clattered on his plate. He picked it up, turning red.

"Seems he agreed to our proposition."

Chapter 8

Tillie quaked as Father led her into the parlor. "Matilda Jane, your rebellion must stop. I don't understand what's gotten into you, child. You've never spoken to Mother or me the way you did the other night. First, your disgraceful outburst over Lady, and now, Mother tells me there's no point to Bible study. Explain yourself."

Tillie shifted. "I just—I..." Why did she always stammer so when he scolded her? She raised her shoulders to the level of her ears and dropped them. She fought back a surge of tears. She didn't like him unhappy with her. If only the floor would swallow her. "I'm sorry, Father. Sometimes I get frustrated because I don't understand how these things can happen."

"What don't you understand?"

She played with a crease of her skirt. "I don't see what good can come of war. Why do men do these things to one another?" Her heart hammered her chest, and her fingers shook as they fiddled with a pleat. Still, she rushed on. "I don't accept God wants us to kill each other and treat people so badly, yet we do. Why did George have to die? We all will someday, but why him? Why so young? Doesn't seem fair! Why does He let these things happen and not do something?" Her words came out in a rush, like a burst dam.

"Well." Father cleared his throat, adjusting himself in his seat. "Where do I start? How about we take them one at a time, shall we?"

She stared at him, wary. "I'm not in trouble?"

"No. Not when you express what's in your heart if you do so in a non-rebellious way as you've just done. When you misbehave, yes, you are."

Tillie released her breath in a huff of air, but suppressed a relieved smile. He wasn't mad at her.

"War is a terrible thing, you're right." He placed his elbows on his knees. "But some wars, like this one, are righteous. Even the Old Testament talks about war. Look at David and Goliath." He searched her eyes. "It's hard to see, in the midst of it, what good can come of hostilities. I think our country will come out the better for this particular one. I can't say how I know, because there's nothing to base my reasoning on." He took a deep breath. "I pray slavery will be abolished forever, and when free of that sin, we will become the God-fearing nation we can be." He took her hand in his scarred one.

Tillie studied his shortened finger.

"You're also right, God doesn't want us to fight each other, but that's what our sin does. We have free will, coupled with a state of sin that only faith in Jesus Christ can help us to overcome."

She whispered the words, mulling them over. "Is that why, even though I try so hard to be good and obey you and Mother, I still get in trouble for misbehaving? Because of my sinful state?" She turned frightened eyes to her father.

He took a long time to respond. He rubbed the top of her hand with his. She watched the play of his white cotton shirt across his broad shoulders and arms.

He sat back, releasing her hand. "Yes, but it's what's in your heart as well. For instance, every time you react with frustration when Sam asks for help with his studies, your sinful nature shows. You give willing assistance in the end, but always at first, you grumble and complain. Another example is the expression on your face when Ginny hollered over at us. I must confess shock over the hatred you displayed."

Tillie wrinkled her nose. "I don't like her. I don't know what happened between William and her, but I've not liked her ever since."

"What happened between them is William's affair, not yours. She wasn't right for him, and he cut off any further interest, lest she get the wrong idea. Her behavior over the entire matter was most unkind, but it doesn't concern you. Ginny needs our prayers, not our enmity."

"It does when she tries to get us—Mother—into trouble with the Rebs." Tillie heated up, more words rushing to her tongue.

"No, it doesn't." He cut her short and patted her hand. "That concerns your mother and me. Now, I thank you for being so willing to come to our defense, but it isn't necessary."

Tillie twisted her cotton skirt. "What about George?" Emotion choked her voice.

"A terrible tragedy, my dear. I'm grateful you're grieved about it. I had the impression you didn't like him much. He was a God-fearing man who's in heaven now. I'm as certain of that as I am sitting here talking to you."

"How do you know heaven and hell exist? You've never seen them. He hasn't come back and told us."

"Through faith. Remember, Hebrews eleven tells us 'faith is the substance of things hoped for, the evidence of things not seen.'"

Tillie's brow creased. She opened her mouth to ask another question, but someone pounded on the front door.

Father sat back. "Answer the door." His voice shook. He rose from his chair and tugged on the bottom of his waistcoat.

Tillie answered the door. Margaretta Kendlehart stood on the step, her hand raised to knock again.

A blonde-haired, blue-eyed girl, no older than fourteen, glanced around her as though afraid of being caught. "Hi, Tillie. Is your father home? My father wants me to deliver a message."

"Come in." Pulling the door wide, Tillie led their guest into the parlor. Father greeted Margaretta and helped her to a seat. Tillie left to find Mother.

"Mother, Margaretta Kendlehart is downstairs. She has a message for Father from Mr. Kendlehart."

Mother's eyes widened, and her brows came together in a scowl. She looked at the floor as though able to see through the floorboards to the parlor. Then she drew a deep breath through her nostrils. She rearranged her face and forced an encouraging smile. Replacing her pen in its holder, she picked up her papers and tapped them together against the desk before placing them to one side. Rising, she smoothed her dress.

Tillie breathed in the scent of lemon verbena surrounding her mother. She gave Mother a genuine smile.

Mother kissed Tillie's forehead, then went downstairs.

Should she follow, or did this not concern her? She followed. Maggie and Sam stood inside the sitting room door, listening to the conversation in the parlor. Tillie joined them.

"…Fears the rebels reconsidered the offer. General Early sent a courier to our house. My father instructed me to tell him he wasn't home. The man accepted that and rode away. Papa slipped away, fearing repercussions. We heard about what happened with your horse, so he told me to warn you."

The three of them exchanged glances. Maggie wrung her hands.

Sam lowered his chin to his chest. He crossed his arms and shifted his feet, widening his stance. "If my sister gets your father in trouble, I'll never forgive her."

Maggie slashed a hand through the air, shushing him.

"Thank you, my dear." Father's unconcerned tone soothed Tillie as he led Margaretta to the door. "Go home as quickly as you can. We don't want anyone to see you came here tonight."

"Yes, sir." The girl reached for the doorknob. "I do pray you'll be all right."

"We'll pray for your father's safety. Now, run on home. Try not to stir suspicion."

When the door closed behind her, Father glanced around at them.

Mother twirled and ran upstairs. He watched her go, frowning. Then he sighed and turned back to the three who waited for him to speak.

"Well, children." He stepped toward them.

Mother returned holding his valise, which she thumped to the floor. "You may need this. Fanny told me she prepared one for Mr. Buehler, ready in case. She didn't answer the door right away to give him time to slip out the back with his postage equipment. When you came back from your visit with Colonel White, I thought it a good idea, so I packed this for you."

Father shook his head.

"James, you must! If they come and take you away, what shall we do?" She picked up the bag and thrust it out to him. "You went and asked Colonel White for Lady. You were part of the delegation refusing to give General Early supplies. What if you're marked for arrest?"

Father took the valise from her hand and set it down. He led her into the sitting room, where he sat in his chair, pulling her down into his lap. He brought her hand to his lips and kissed her knuckles.

Mother rushed on, "I think you should disappear too. I can care for Sam and the girls. I want you to be safe."

"They may not remember my name. I never spoke to General Early. Kendlehart did all the talking." Father invited them all to stand around his chair. "No one came to the door except Margaretta. We don't want to overreact. Besides, I'm not the kind of man who abandons his family. I know why Buehler left; he's the postmaster. It's Federal property and worth a good deal of money to the Confederates if they get their hands on it. Young Hughes went into hiding with his telegraph equipment. That also belongs to the government, so I'm glad." He drew in a deep breath. "While we waited for General Early, I overheard the soldiers tell him they didn't get control of either the telegraph apparatus, or the postal operations, so they targeted them. I don't think Kendlehart had a real reason for running. I'm not saying anything against him. I'm saying I refuse to run."

"Yes, but what of Colonel White? What if he should supply your name?"

"I'll take that chance, Margaret. I've done nothing wrong. The Rebs have more important things to deal with than a man and his lame horse."

He sounded confident as he put his arms around his wife and held her close. Outside, hooves rang on the cobblestones.

His eyes darted to the window. Tillie's heart pounded in her chest. She caught the trepidation in his eyes, and a shiver raced up her spine. He glanced around and his gaze rested on Tillie. He smiled. She smiled back. If he showed bravery in the face of the unknown, she would too.

Father made eye contact with each member of his family. "I'm staying here, whatever happens." He kissed his wife. "Don't worry about me, my love. Let's concentrate on the children and keep them safe."

Mother offered a shaky smile. "You're right, dearest."

Father gave her a quick squeeze before he lifted her from his lap. He rose to his feet, kissed her forehead, and stepped into the hallway where he picked up his valise. He raised his arm to show them. "I'm going upstairs to unpack this and put my things away."

No one spoke as he disappeared from sight.

* * * *

Sunday morning dawned bright and hot. Church bells in every quadrant of Gettysburg pealed out, calling all believers to worship. Praying the intruders departed for good, Tillie and her family walked to the Methodist Church on Middle Street. Other neighbors also made their way to services.

On any other Sunday, people called out hellos and gathered in groups as they made their way to their respective churches, but not this morning. People left their houses, heads down, moving as fast as propriety allowed. Those who usually rode in from the surrounding countryside stayed away. Tillie walked behind Mother and Father, between Sam and Maggie. Father strode ahead, his head down.

Mother glanced at him several times as they moved along the street. "Is something bothering you, James?" She tucked her hand into his arm.

He patted her hand. "I can't get those poor people from York out of my mind. I feel guilty for telling the Rebs to go there. I had a twinge of conscience when Kendlehart mentioned the idea, but I kept my thoughts to myself. Now I wish I'd spoken up." He smiled at her concerned face. "We should never have foisted our problem on them." He shrugged.

"I see." Mother leaned into him, but said nothing more. They fell silent for a block.

"Sure is quiet today." Sam peered down the street. "It's…eerie."

"Sam's right." Maggie also scanned the area as if she expected a Reb to jump out of the bushes. "Everything feels strange and out of place. Almost as if the Rebels aren't gone, they're hiding."

"Come now." Mother smiled back at them. "You all have the jimjams now the Rebs are gone. A rousing church service will do us all a world of good."

Tillie doubted so, but walked on, shuffling her feet, feeling sorry for herself. After everything calmed down last night, Father resumed his conversation with her and set out an assignment for her to pay attention to the sermon and to write an essay. Then to do four new verses in the Bible. So unfair!

"I've been lax with you," he told her, echoing Mother's words, and left the room.

Now, as they walked to church, those words canted a rhythm in her head. I've been lax with you. I've been lax with you....

After they sang the opening hymn, Tillie seated herself and picked up a pew Bible prepared to do battle with the text.

Reverend Bergstrasser, hands clasped in front of him, climbed the podium with slow, deliberate steps and turned his solemn face to the congregation. "Please turn to Matthew, chapter ten." Even in giving instructions, he sounded stentorious.

Tillie sighed and opened the Bible.

After the reverend's opening remarks, she drifted off, back to Friday's exciting events. Her heart raced with the recollection. Now with the danger passed, she found the situation exhilarating. The only pain was the loss of Lady, and she prayed they didn't mistreat her.

Reverend Bergstrasser slammed his fist on the podium, and Tillie jumped. She shifted in her seat and glanced over to Father. He stared at her. Shifting again, she held the Bible close and turned her face to the preacher.

"This terrible war has seen much death and destruction." The reverend flung his face heavenward, arms outstretched. "And it seems the hostilities are about to visit our quiet corner of the world. Remember." He faced the congregation, slamming his fist again. The thud reverberated through the church and echoed off the walls.

Tillie's hand went to her throat as though to stifle an exclamation of surprise.

The reverend's face took on a dull red cast. His chest began heaving, and his words shot forth like cannonballs. "We-need-not-fear-death-if-we-have-life-for-we-will-have-life-everlasting-when-we-die."

What in the world did he mean, and how did one write an essay on this sort of nonsense? When you die, you die. If you have life and you die, you no longer have life, never mind everlasting life, so...Tillie sighed and clenched her fists.

"I beseech you to pay special attention to verse twenty-eight." Reverend Bergstrasser flipped a couple of pages of his Bible. "Read with me, please. 'And fear not them which kill the body, but are not able to kill the soul; but rather fear him which is able to destroy soul and body in hell.'"

Oh mercy. Tillie closed her eyes, shook her head, and gave up trying to comprehend.

The good reverend's voice intoned on, "These poor misguided men who came to our country thinking to make war on us, they do not understand they can kill our bodies, but they cannot damage our souls. Only our Heavenly Father can destroy our body and our soul in the pit of hell, reserved only for those who do not believe in Him. So fear not the Confederate Army." Reverend Bergstrasser shouted the words fear not, and Tillie jumped again.

She scowled and curled her hands into fists.

"God is in control of what will happen and not for us to know what the future holds. Attend to the state of your soul. If your faith is strong, all the Confederates can do is kill your body. They cannot damage your soul. If you are without faith the Confederates can kill your body, but Gooooooood will damn your soul."

Tillie ignored the rest of his words and read further down the passage. Her heart leaped into her throat at the words before her. "Whosoever therefore shall confess me before men, him will I confess also before my Father which is in heaven. But whosoever shall deny me before men, him I will also deny before my Father which is in heaven." Her pulse pounded so hard the rhythm echoed in her neck. Would God damn her soul? Would Christ deny her before God? She recalled a picture in the family Bible showing a rendition of hell. All kinds of weird creatures and humans fell into a pit of fire while Lucifer danced around the rim in triumph. Did that await her if she denied Christ before men? Despite the heat inside the church, goose bumps pimpled her arms as she shivered.

She came back around as the congregation rose for the closing hymn, "Am I A Soldier Of The Cross?" A popular song, but today, the words held special meaning as they pricked her conscience.

"Am I a soldier of the cross?
A follower of the Lamb,
And shall I fear to own His cause,
Or blush to speak His Name?"

Tillie cringed. All around her faces raised in worship as they sang.

"Must I be carried to the skies?
On flowery beds of ease,
While others fought to win the prize,
And sailed through bloody seas?"

She closed the hymnbook and placed it in the rack. Maggie gazed heavenward, full of rapture. Why didn't that ever happen to Tillie? What did it mean "to be carried to the skies on flowery beds of ease"? Could she fight to win the prize? Did she want to sail through bloody seas? Until a few months ago, she never questioned her parents' beliefs in God and eternity, but now…she bit back tears of utter sadness as a sense of desolation swept over her. She gripped the back of the pew, bent her head, and wiped her face, making it appear as though she removed a speck in her eye—or perhaps a log? She glanced at the rest of her family, but they conversed with friends. She went unnoticed.

Tillie filed out of the church silent, thinking.

Father shook hands with the reverend and praised him for his rousing sermon. Tillie murmured her thanks and bid him farewell.

As they descended the steps, Father slipped his hand through Mother's elbow. Then he led them back home. The Winebrenners joined them, chatting as they walked.

Mrs. Bergstrasser called out from her front step. "It appears they've left, do you think?"

"I hope so." Mother put her palms together as though in prayer. "What a dirty, filthy looking set! One can't tell them from the street!"

The women laughed.

Father jerked Mother's elbow, cutting her short. "Be careful! One is at our curbstone, right in front of us."

"Oh my." Mother spun toward him covering her mouth with her hand and hiding her face in his arm. "I didn't see him!"

A young boy, a few years older than Sam, knelt on one knee tying a shoe not worthy of the name. As he pulled the laces tight, the pink side of his foot showed between the separated sole and upper. In some spots, on his patched over breeches, his patches had patches. His pants may once have been a distinctive color, but no more. By contrast, he wore a brand-new, bright-red cotton shirt and a gray waistcoat two sizes too big for him. He tucked the shirt into his breeches, which still billowed over his waist as he bent to tie his shoe. The tails of the waistcoat trailed along the stones, and the boy pressed his arms to his sides to keep the folds out of the way.

The Rebs called what they did commandeering supplies. The storeowners called it theft. This young man procured for himself a new shirt. Why he didn't get a new pair of pants or shoes remained a mystery. As he finished tying his shoe, he rose to his feet and glanced about him.

Father gave a quick nod as if coming to a decision. He took a strong grip on Mother's elbow and stepped into the street. The rest of the family passed in front of the soldier and walked toward their home as if nothing happened.

He waited in polite silence.

As Tillie walked by, the handsome young man with ginger colored hair and sad, haunted blue eyes met her gaze. His gaunt face spoke of enduring hunger. For a split second, she wanted to invite him in for lunch. But images of Dirty Beard walking away with Lady sprang to her mind, and a wave of hatred surged through her.

His eyes met hers, and Tillie did her best to unleash a look full of hate. She narrowed her eyes and curled her lip. She stuck her nose in the air and turned away in what she hoped he'd take for a haughty move.

The boy smiled, dimples forming on his cheeks, and he continued to stare at her. He chuckled as she passed.

Tillie scowled.

Maggie hissed at the boy. She grabbed Tillie's elbow and yanked her toward the house. She allowed Maggie to drag her up the front steps, but she couldn't resist a glance back. He kept his gaze on her, a smile on his lips and interest bright in his blue eyes. When Tillie cast him another hateful glare, the boy put two fingers to his eyebrow and saluted, grinning wide. His teeth shone white in his dirt-streaked face. He bowed to her and sauntered up Baltimore Street, whistling "Dixie".

Once the door closed behind them, Mother let her breath out in a huff. "Well." She slapped her hands on her cheeks. "That will teach me to mind my manners and guard my tongue."

The family gaped at her and laughed. The danger passed. Mother smiled and blushed as she endured their good-natured teasing. She went into the kitchen to prepare the midday meal. Because of the Sabbath, she put out cold meat, bread, pickles, and jam.

After dinner, Tillie settled in at the sitting room table to spend time in the Bible reflecting upon the sermon. After a moment, she dipped her pen in the ink and wrote.

Dear Father:

Thank you for taking the time to talk to me the other night. I want to assure you I thought a lot about our conversation. You wanted me to write an essay, but a letter felt more appropriate. You caught me daydreaming in church, but I heard what I think is the most important part. According to Matthew 10, if I'm saved, then no matter what happens to me—by the Confederates or anyone else—they can only hurt my body, not my soul, and when I die, only my earthly body will suffer destruction. But, if I am not, my body will suffer destruction and God will damn my soul and I will burn in hell. I fear that, but I do not understand so many things, like how God can allow such terrible things as a civil war. You say He always uses these things for good. I say, why let them happen at all?

The hymn we sang this morning affected me the most. Am I a soldier of the Cross? I think not. Not yet. I realize I always adopted yours and Mother's beliefs as my own until recently. I can't say when I stopped doing so, and I'm sorry I did. I don't want either of you to be disappointed in me. Mother and Maggie say I'm at a stage where I'm starting to throw off childish ideas and adopt adult ones. Perhaps this is what is happening now.

George's death scared me. What happens to us when we die? That frightens me the most because, what if there's no heaven or a hell? I've never given the matter thought before.

I understand this is not what you or Mother are hoping to read, but I feel it's an honest assessment of the state of my soul. I'm a lost sheep, Father. If it's true the Lord searches out his lost sheep, He will find me. I, in turn, promise to commit myself to the search.

Pray for me. Your loving daughter,

Matilda Jane Pierce.

Tillie went upstairs to her parents' bedroom. She tiptoed across the empty room and placed the letter on her father's dresser. She tiptoed back out, hoping he wouldn't be too disappointed in her.

Chapter 9

The sun spilled over the hilltops, pouring its golden light across the landscape. Already the humidity smothered everything under a damp blanket.

Tillie rose from bed and dressed in her chemise and petticoats. Taking her brown muslin school dress from the armoire, she put it on, and then buttoned her bodice, her fingers clumsy and slow. Once done, she had to redo the entire thing when she found no corresponding buttonhole at the end.

Sitting at the dressing table, she picked up the brush, but her reflection showed a still crooked bodice, further up. What was wrong with her this morning? She threw the brush down, and with quick jerks, she started over. Partway through, her fingers stopped in mid-button.

She cocked her head and listened then crossed to the open window and stuck her head out.

Across the street, the red brick of the houses shimmered as if ready to melt in the heat. Doors and windows remained closed tight against the already oppressive day. The cobbled street below devoid of all traffic. The birds sang and twittered as cicadas sawed their high-pitched buzz. Even the crickets still chirped a noisy morning rhythm. The lack of human traffic on the street with its accompanying cacophony caught her attention. No wagons rumbled along the cobbles bringing produce into town. No carriages passed here and there. No clip-clop of hooves as riders made their way around town, intent upon their errands before the heat of the day set in. Neighbors stayed off the streets. No one called good morning to one another. Her heart pounded over the strangeness of the silence and the deserted streets. Where was everyone? Were the men still out fighting the fire?

Tillie shifted her gaze to the northeast, where black smoke still billowed. Late last night, Libby's father, Jacob Hollinger, roused the town when he rode in hard from his home on York Road, shouting something about the railroad bridge and

Confederates. When he caught his breath, he reported that the Confederates had set fire to the railroad bridge.

Acrid smoke reached her. She wrinkled her nose and withdrew from the window. She stared at the empty street, as if willing someone to appear and bring normalcy to her life. The street remained empty.

Tillie slammed the window closed. She moved her fingers down her bodice, feeling the buttons once again. She quickly fixed her braids and left her bedroom.

In the kitchen, Maggie turned out butter from the churn while Mother cooked.

"Good morning." The words left Tillie's lips without her usual enthusiasm. She squeezed around Mother as she reached to take the dishes down from their shelves. She waited for the usual morning banter, but Maggie glanced at her with puffy eyes while she rinsed the butter under cool water. Had she been weeping again?

Mother didn't answer either. She looked preoccupied as she stirred the potatoes around in the frying pan.

"Mother, is everything all right?" Tillie's brows came together, and she tilted her head. She started to reach out for her mother's arm, thought better of it, and withdrew her hand. Instead, she gripped the dishes tight to herself.

Still no answer. Maggie put the butter on the table and turned away, as though ignoring Tillie's concern.

Tillie's heart lurched. Did Father get hurt fighting the fire? Did a telegram arrive? In a flash, she saw her brothers' mutilated bodies lying on some battlefield. Worse yet, Father, lay flat on his back out by the railroad bridge, eyes staring sightless at the sky, arms splayed as though hung on the Cross. Tears filled her eyes, and her throat closed. Her heart pounded in her chest, and the sound resonated in her ears.

Mother's vacant stare stayed on the pan, and with mechanical motions, she moved the potatoes around as they blackened in the pan.

"Mother, are you all right?" This time, Tillie touched her mother's arm.

Mother came out of her reverie with a start. "What? Oh, yes, I'm fine. Everything is fine. Ahhhh!" She pushed the pan to the back of the stove. "I burned them." Her voice pitched with surprise. She stared at the offending potatoes, and then picked up the pan. "I was thinking… I don't want you to go to school today."

Tillie's mouth dropped open, and her eyes widened. "Why? I'll miss my lessons, and I'll have to work to catch up. The Rebs're gone now."

"Because, I say so, Tillie. That's why! I want you here today, so don't argue. I want you here in case something occurs. I want you to stay home and help Maggie and me around the house today. Can you do that? Is that so much to ask?"

Tillie opened her mouth, shocked by Mother's outburst, and wanting to protest. But Mother's dark frown stopped her. She bent her head in assent. "Yes, ma'am."

Mother turned back to the pan of blackened, smoking potatoes. She grabbed a spoon off the counter, scooped the potatoes out of the pan, and threw them away, all the while talking, though to Tillie or herself Tillie couldn't guess. "It's bad enough two of my children are gone and Lord knows if they're alive. I'm going to keep my other two safe if it's the last thing I do." She slammed the pan down on the stove. It rang with finality.

Tillie didn't know how she dared, but she had to ask. "Have you news of James or William?"

Mother picked up the saltshaker and salted the eggs. At Tillie's timid question, she banged the saltshaker down on the counter. "No! We've not heard from either of them in quite some time." Mother turned her back and resumed cooking.

Tillie stepped back as though struck across the face. Did Father show her the letter she wrote? Was Mother annoyed over its contents? She looked to Maggie, for guidance, but Maggie just shook her head—in warning or sympathy? Unsure, Tillie lowered her eyes. She still clutched the plates. Walking to the table, Tillie resisted the urge to slam down the dishes. She got silverware. Her hands shook as she tried to place the forks, and she kept dropping them. They clanged on the plates. Finally, she placed the silverware around the table and stepped back. She closed her eyes. Please, boys, write to us and let us know you're alive. Please be alive.

* * * *

Father returned home just after breakfast. Soot and sweat streaked his face, reminding Tillie of a minstrel performer. There was nothing funny in his appearance, though. He waved away questions and plodded straight upstairs to bed. He still slept, though noontime had come and gone.

Tillie chafed. She wanted to be at school with her friends, not home dusting furniture and sweeping floors. What was she missing? How far behind would this day put her? She got down on her hands and knees and took vicious swipes at the table legs. After a few minutes, she stopped her work and listened for sounds outside. The odor of smoke lingered in the air, but not as strong as this morning. Perhaps the wind shifted or the fire was cool enough to stop smoking. She opened the parlor windows airing the furnace-like house.

Mother came downstairs and found Tillie staring out the window, listening to the hum of cicadas in the trees.

Mother had donned her hoops and tied a cream colored bonnet under her chin. "Tillie, I have to go shopping. Would you care to join me? A little sunshine and fresh air might do us some good."

"I don't know. The street is so silent. Even the birds don't want to sing. It feels like everyone has gone to ground, like rabbits sensing a hawk overhead."

"It'll be fine. I just have to go to Fahenstock's for some flour and other supplies. We'll be back in two shakes of a lamb's tail."

Tillie was still piqued, but she heard the conciliatory tone in Mother's voice and met her halfway. "You're right. Fresh air would do me some good. Thank you." After putting away her cleaning supplies and removing her apron, she ran upstairs to don her hoops. A few moments later, she joined Mother at the front door. She reached for her bonnet and snugged it on.

Mother stopped with one hand on the doorknob, a rueful smile on her face. "I wish to apologize for snapping at you at breakfast. I confess I don't know what came over me. There's something in the air today. I can't explain it, but I feel it. I wanted you home with me just in case." She cocked her head and gave a small chuckle. "It was silly of me, I suppose, and now it looks as if you've lost an entire day of school."

"It's all right, Mother. I must say I feel it too, and I can't explain it either." Tillie shrugged. "It was rather novel to stay home today."

"I'm glad you feel that way." Mother smiled and stroked her cheek.

As they headed toward the center of town, she put her arm around Tillie's shoulders. "So, were you more upset about missing school or having to do housework?"

Tillie screwed up her face.

Mother laughed.

"A little of both, I guess." Tillie wrinkled her nose. "I like school, and I don't want to get behind. I have to admit I despise dusting and sweeping."

Mother gave her shoulders a squeeze. "I'll keep that in mind."

Their conversation stuttered to a stop as they approached Middle Street. Mrs. Fahenstock rushed out of their store, gathered her skirts, and hurried toward the Diamond. Tillie and Mother exchanged surprised looks and then quickened their pace.

Ten main roads converged at Gettysburg, and they all came together at the Diamond, where businesses of all kinds rose at the intersections. Groups of people hovered in their doorways, watching the action in the center of the square.

"Mrs. Fahenstock." Mother tapped the grocery storeowner on the arm.

The portly woman turned at Mother's voice. "I'd say good day, Mrs. Pierce, but I fear there's nothing good happening today."

"What's going on?" Mother waved her hand in the direction of the crowd. "What are they doing?"

About fifty colored people, mostly women and children, huddled together, ringed by armed Rebel soldiers. The women clutched their children close and wept loud, bitter wails. A few men positioned themselves in front of the women, as if trying to protect them with their bodies, even though they held their hands above their heads. The men kept silent. Their stoic expressions said they understood begging and tears were useless.

The Rebs formed shoulder to shoulder, their guns, with bayonets attached, jabbed at their prisoners from a dangerous and effective phalanx.

In the crowd the woman who badgered her children to hide out on Culp's Hill the week before, clutched her boys, tears streaming down her cheeks. They must have returned home believing the danger passed.

A stab of guilt pierced Tillie. This was what they feared and she'd laughed. No wonder Mr. Weaver was so contemptuous. Was he in the crowd? She scanned the men, women, and children. She didn't see him, but that didn't mean he wasn't there. Oh, poor Mr. Weaver. Why didn't someone do something?

Mr. Hicks watched from the doorway of his candy shop, arms crossed, scowling. Then he dropped his hands and went inside, closing the door. The We're Closed sign appeared in his window, and the shades came down.

At the Globe Inn on York Street, Charles Wills watched from his doorway, his hands shoved deep into his pockets, his son, John, next to him, leaned against the doorjamb.

By contrast, his brother, Mr. David Wills, shouted at a Reb, waving his arms in wild gesticulations. One of the Rebs said something back then took out his pistol and held it to Mr. Wills's forehead. The attorney took two steps backward. Mother drew a sharp intake of breath, and Tillie's hand flew to her heart. Mr. Wills stared at the soldier, as if challenging him to shoot. Then he stormed into his house.

"Mother, what's going on?"

"I don't know." Mother's gaze darted about, taking in the scene. To Tillie's horror, Mother walked up to a soldier and grabbed his arm. "What's the meaning of this?"

"Go away, lady. This don't concern you. We're taking this contraband South where they belong."

"Contraband? They are not contraband. They're people! You can't do such a thing. It's barbaric! You have no right! These people have lived here as long as I have. You have no right!" She reached in for one of the children.

The soldier knocked her backward with such force, she fell onto the pavement, striking the back of her head.

Tillie screamed and ran to her. "You leave my mother alone."

Mrs. Fahenstock knelt and cupped her palm on the back of Mother's head. She drew her hand away. No blood.

The soldier laughed. "You want the same, missy? Get your mother and get out of here. This ain't none of your business." He made as if to kick them to get them moving. Tillie cowered as she tried to protect Mother from a potential blow. Crying, she and Mrs. Fahenstock helped Mother to her feet, and together the three staggered away. Mother clung to Tillie.

At the store, Mrs. Fahenstock took Mother's arm and opened the door. "Come inside, Margaret, and set a store before going home."

"I'm fine, Caroline. I think Tillie and I can make it home all right." Taking a firm grip on Tillie's arm, Mother bid Mrs. Fahenstock a good day and slowly they made their way home.

They reached the corner of Middle Street and stopped as the Rebel soldiers marched their contraband out of town.

Townsfolk peered out of windows or watched in silence from open doorways.

Held at gunpoint like common criminals—instead of hardworking members of the Gettysburg community—the Negroes walked out of town wailing and clutching their children.

Would they ever return or see their homes again?

The family they had seen running to hide a few days ago stumbled past as a soldier used his musket to herd them along like animals.

Was there accusation and scorn in the woman's eyes? Tillie turned away.

* * * *

"Mother, what's wrong? You and Tillie have been upstairs crying all afternoon. What happened?" Maggie glanced between the two.

Mother and Tillie each picked at their food. Silent tears slid down Tillie's cheeks.

As though Maggie's voice finally roused a response in her, Mother shifted in her chair. She dropped her fork and put her hands over her face as fresh sobs shook her body.

Father got up and stopped behind her. Placing gentle hands on her shoulders, he patted her.

"They took those people." Mother wept.

"What people?" Maggie's eyes switched from Mother to Tillie. "Who did they take?"

"Several of the colored families who live about here." Tillie's emotion-clogged voice came out tight and strained. She cleared her throat and continued, "Mr. Weaver was right. The Rebs marched them away from the Diamond like common criminals. They called them contraband. Only Mr. Wills and Mother tried to stop them."

"Margaret, you did what?" Father said. "You didn't tell me that!"

Mother wiped her face on her apron and took up the story where Tillie left off. "Men, women, and children, James—at gunpoint." She stressed the word. "What would you have had me do? I couldn't just stand there and let them take innocent people—children—away into slavery." She used her napkin to wipe her eyes.

Tillie picked up the tale. "Other people stood by and stared or went inside and shut their doors so they wouldn't have to see." Tillie's voice rose as her emotions overtook her. "And the Rebs laughed. They laughed at us. One of them even pushed Mother down when she grabbed at his arm."

"That's disgusting." Maggie threw her fork down. "How dare they?"

"They dare because they can." Mother's voice choked. "Who is here to stop them?"

"I would have stopped them." Sam sat up. He stabbed his fork into a potato. "I would have told that dirty Reb to keep his hands off you." He turned his hate-filled face to Mother. "He wouldn't've got away with it if I'd been there."

Mother's eyes filled with fresh tears, and she smiled at him as they slid down her cheeks. "I thank you for the sentiment, dear, but I'm afraid they would have been too much even for you."

"Why don't they come?" Tillie spoke to the table. No one answered. Where was the Union Army? Why had they failed to arrive and protect them?

Father sat back down in his chair. "I went to the Scotts' to find out what's going on. Where the boys are, when they're coming." He shrugged as he resumed his seat. "I also wanted to find out where the Rebels had gotten themselves off to."

"What did Mr. Scott say?" Tillie asked.

"The older Mr. Scott says he has no idea. As you know, young Hugh took the telegraph machine and slipped away. Mr. Scott won't say where he went, even to friends. He doesn't want his son's whereabouts inadvertently revealed to the Rebs." Father shook his head. He took a deep breath. "While we all sat about yesterday, patting ourselves on the back and thinking the Rebs had left, they were busy burning railroad bridges and cutting the telegraph wires between here, Harrisburg, and Philadelphia. They have cut us off and rendered us silent."

Tillie stared at her father, uncomprehending, her fifteen-year-old mind still reeling from this afternoon. "Is that bad? Can't they fix it?"

"Who's 'they', Tillie? Who is going to fix anything?" Father exhaled and raised a hand in a gesture of apology. "After you and your mother returned home, I went upstreet to get the flour and other supplies. As you know, the Rebs have carried off most of what the town kept back, and there isn't much left with harvest still a month or so away." He placed his hands on the table and swirled his wedding ring. "There aren't any supplies. Fahenstock said the Rebs made off with everything not nailed down. Now, the supply trains can't get through. More importantly, the troop trains can't get through. It's bad."

Tillie studied her father's face, seeing for the first time the deep lines around his mouth and across his forehead. She sensed his anxiety, though he attempted to conceal it. It was too much for her to process. She sighed. "If you don't mind." Her fork tapped against her potato. "I'm not hungry. May I please be excused?" Fresh tears filled her eyes, and she tried in vain to blink them back.

Father studied her face. "You may."

Tillie picked up her dish and brought it to the sink, then slipped upstairs to her room. At her desk, the partially written letter to William sat waiting. Now was as good a time as any, but she wasn't in the mood.

She undressed and climbed into bed. She stopped weeping an hour later and lay wide-awake, thinking about the afternoon. Fear propelled her out of bed. She padded barefoot down the hall to Maggie's room.

Maggie opened the door to Tillie's knock as she tied her bathrobe around her waist. Maggie's four-poster bed was against the far wall. The blanket and sheet folded back in invitation.

On the wall next to the door, Maggie's armoire stood a door ajar. As she had done as a small child, Tillie crossed the room and climbed into her sister's bed. Maggie closed the door, removed her bathrobe, and slid in next to her. She held Tillie close.

Tillie tucked the top of her head under Maggie's chin. "Maggie?"

"Yes."

"I'm scared."

"So am I."

"What do you think will happen?"

"I don't know."

"Father's scared too. I saw it at supper."

After a long pause, Tillie glanced up to see if Maggie had drifted off.

Then in a low voice, Maggie answered, "Yes, he is. The whole town is frightened." She wriggled away to face Tillie. "Our boys will come. Don't fret. They will come, if for no other reason than to defend our homes and avenge those poor families—and George."

Moonlight washed the bedroom in a spectral glow. Maggie's creased brow and deep frown lent an air of defiance to her words. Perhaps all would be well after all. The Union Army would come and defend them. They had to. President Lincoln would never allow the Confederate Army to remain long in Union territory. Tillie wrapped her arms around Maggie's neck and gave her a hug.

"I love you, Maggie."

"I love you too."

Tillie rolled over onto her side away from Maggie and soon drifted into a fitful sleep.

Chapter 10

"Tillie! Maggie!" Sam's shout rang through the kitchen. "Where are you?"

"For goodness sake. Don't run in the house." Mother's words followed him as he bounded into the sitting room.

Tillie turned from dusting the mantelpiece, her mouth agape.

Sam's eyes shone, and his grin split his face. "They're here." He grasped her elbows and gave her a quick shake.

"Who's here?"

He released her and ran to the hallway, stopping at the foot of the stairs. He called up. "Maggie, you up there? Come down! The Yankees are here."

Tillie gasped. At last! She dropped her dusting rag and joined Sam.

Maggie appeared on the landing, a kerchief covering her hair and a feather duster in her hand. "Gracious, Sam, don't shout at me. I'm not a tavern wench." She untied her apron as she trotted downstairs.

He flapped both hands in a come-here gesture. "The Yankee Cavalry is here! They're riding up Washington Street now. Let's go watch!" Sam's breath came in short gasps.

From outside the open window cheering reached them.

"Oh, Mother, may we?" Tillie clasped her hands to her breast, her eyes wide and eager. She twirled to face Mother, coming from the kitchen.

"Please, Mrs. Pierce." Sam bent his knees and bounced back up.

"Yes, Mother, for a few minutes?" Maggie joined in.

Mother laughed. "So our boys have arrived at last." She nodded. "All right, but stay out of the way and don't go beyond Washington Street."

They jostled each other to get out the door. Hundreds of people lined the pavement on either side of the street as the three pushed their way along. They found a good vantage point at the corner of High Street, in front of Lady Eyster's Academy. Tillie craned her neck to peer above the crowd. The head mistress sat in a rocker on the porch. She waved, but the headmistress was looking the other way and didn't wave back.

The cavalry streamed up Washington in a column of three horses abreast. Their hooves clattered on the cobblestones, necks arched and tails held high. The men sat their mounts ramrod straight. They stared straight ahead and did not acknowledge the onlookers. They wore dark-blue woolen uniforms and black felt hats. The Black Hat Brigade. Tillie read all about them. Their fighting skills were renowned. The Rebs feared the Black Hats.

"Aren't they dashing?" A woman standing on the cub grasped her companion's arm.

"So brave and noble." Her friend waved a white handkerchief.

"I heard six thousand boys all told are marching." A portly man puffed out his chest and gave an emphatic nod.

His companion dismissed his information with a wave of his cigar clenched between his fingers. "Well, I hear Buford's in charge of this lot."

A waft of the foul smelling smoke hit the back of Tillie's throat. Coughing, she waved the smoke away and tried not to gag. Her eyes met Maggie's, and she mouthed the words six thousand. How many males over fifteen and under fifty escaped the army?

Her sister's hand clamped down on her shoulder. Alarmed by the stricken expression in her sister's eyes, Tillie let her grin slide away.

"What's wrong?" she shouted above the clamor.

"Where's Sam?" Maggie hollered in her ear as the noise rose. "Do you see him anywhere?"

Clattering hooves, mixed with cheering and hollering, as well as martial tunes played in the back of the line. Tillie barely heard her sister. She tilted her head, puzzled.

Maggie shouted the question again. They scanned the crowd. Sam huddled further down the road with his friends, Gates Fahenstock and Albertus McCreary.

Pointing him out, Tillie turned her attention back to the soldiers. She stepped near the curb and leaned out. Down

Washington Street flowed an endless river of blue and brown, and in the distance where the road dipped, a haze of dust revealed more men and horses riding toward town. In the other direction, those marching past her turned west on Chambersburg Street. Would they meet the Rebs or did they arrive too late?

Tillie grabbed Maggie's arm and hopped up and down, giggling. Caught up in the general mood of the occasion, she started singing "Our Union Forever," challenging Maggie with her eyes to join in. The others picked up the tune and sang along.

"A song for our Banner? The watchword recall
Which gave the Republic her station;"

The soldiers marched with more verve. Some raised their hats in salute while others smiled and waved. Many of them joined in the singing.

"United we stand, divided we fall!
It made and preserves us a nation!
The union of lakes, the union of lands, the union of States none can sever.
The union of hearts, the union of hands and the flag of the Union
Forever and ever! The flag of our Union forever!"

The crowd repeated the chorus as the soldiers raised their hats.

Across the road, Abigail Hicks and Jennie McCreary handed out flowers. What a wonderful idea. Why didn't she think of having bouquets on hand? Instead, Tillie sang at the top of her lungs, laughed and cheered and waved and thrilled to the spectacle of these gallant soldiers. Her heart and spirit lightened. If someone asked her, she might fly to Baltimore and back.

In the increasing heat of the day, sweat trickled from her hair down her neck. Her throat was parched. She tapped Maggie on the shoulder and pointed toward home. They bumped into Salome Myers, a pretty, twenty-one-year-old woman, whom James courted for a brief time before leaving for the Army.

"Hello, Sally." Maggie used her hand to shade her eyes. "What do you think of these soldiers? Isn't this exciting?" She sounded breathless, her eyes sparkling. "To think, they came at last. For George's sake, I hope they give those filthy Rebs the what-for." Her eyes slid to the parade of men.

Salome adjusted her parasol to shade the girls. "We've had no preaching." She sent the sisters an accusatory glance. "Reverend Isenberg skedaddled. Did you know that?" She skewered them with her eyes.

What did that have to do with the soldiers' arrival? Tillie spoke up. "Uh, we go to Middle Street Methodist. Reverend Bergstrasser."

"Well…" Salome leaned forward as though speaking of something confidential. When Tillie and Maggie moved in close, Salome continued, "Did you hear the Rebs stole some of the darkies and took them south with them? Can you imagine? Stealing people and forcing them into slavery? How cruel, just cruel." Sally drew her brows together. She straightened up. The lines on her face smoothed, and she pulled her shoulders back. "Mama and Papa hid our maid in the basement. She stayed hidden for a day and a half before they would let her out, but she's safe thank heaven. How would we get along without her?"

"We know," Tillie croaked. She longed for a glass of water. "Not about your maid. I'm pleased she's safe, but Mother and I saw what happened."

Salome's eyes went to the soldiers. Tillie followed her gaze.

The men rode by, smiling and waving to the crowds while the citizens continued singing.

"I hate all this excitement. I despise the reason for it. War only brings sadness." Salome faced the marching men for another moment more. She turned to Maggie and Tillie with such an abrupt motion, Tillie jumped.

"Well, I must go." Sally's bright tone signified another shift. "Good day to you both. Give my regards to your parents." She pushed past Tillie and disappeared into the crowd.

"I must say…" Maggie stared at the direction she'd gone, shaking her head. "I always feel one step behind her in a conversation. I can never determine when the turns are coming."

"It was all I could do, not to tell her what Mother did at the Diamond." Tillie shrugged. "Something about her always makes me want to go one better. I don't know why, but it's true." Tillie put her hand on Maggie's arm. "Come on, let's go home."

They walked for a few paces in silence, intent on working through the crowd. Maggie picked up the conversation. "Thank heaven James left off with her before he went away. I don't mean to sound unchristian, but I don't care for her much."

Tillie laughed. "I'm glad you said that. I don't either. You know," Tillie glanced back toward Washington Street, "with everything I've read in the papers, if someone told me two armies would meet here, I would have laughed." She stepped off the curb to go around a group headed in the opposite direction, before rejoining her sister. "After all, this is sleepy little Gettysburg, Pennsylvania. Nothing ever happens here."

* * * *

"Mr.-and-Mrs.-Pierce-guess-what-happened-to-me-this-morning?" Sam barged into the kitchen, the words spilling out of him, jolting Tillie.

Father squeezed Sam's arm. "Don't hold back, boy. Tell us what happened." Father laughed.

Mother passed the dinner bowls around.

They laughed at Sam's puzzled face, but joined in when he got the joke.

"We followed the boys to their encampment near Pennsylvania College. They invited us to help care for the horses, so we watered and brushed them." Sam took a quick bite of his bread, tucked the morsel into his cheek, and continued. "Some of the soldiers showed us their weapons and how they work, too. I even held a rifled musket today. They said if we get permission from our fathers, we can come back this afternoon and help some more." Sam took another quick bite, chewed, and swallowed. "Can I go back, sir?"

"Why, Sam Wade." Mother laid down her fork. "I distinctly remember telling you not to get too close to the soldiers."

"Yes, ma'am." He obviously tried to sound contrite. But his head bobbed up and down, and his blue eyes sparkled. "But they waved to us to come with them so I reckoned you wouldn't mind, since they invited us." He crinkled his forehead at Father. "May I go, sir? If I get my chores done early, may I go back to the camp with Gates and Bertie? Their parents said they can go."

Poor Sam worked so hard, a day off wouldn't hurt him. How unfair if Father said no.

Father scowled at the boy as he lowered his fork. "Did the soldiers invite you or are you telling me they did?" He held up a hand to emphasize his next words. "I'm not accusing you of lying, but I don't want you at the camp if they told you not to get in the way."

"No, sir." Sam's eyes opened wide. "I promise they invited us back. May I go?"

Father faced Mother with a what-do-you-think look.

"I don't object, but the decision is yours, dear." Mother speared a potato. "The boy gets so few distractions."

Tillie's eyes darted between Mother and Father as she bit off the end of her asparagus stalk. Good for you, Sam. Have fun.

Father nodded. "You may go. Forget the chores this once. I'll do them myself. See you mind them and stay out of their way."

"Yes, sir." Sam wriggled in his chair. "I will."

* * * *

Sam returned home for supper with two soldiers in tow. Both men removed their kepis.

"Mr. Pierce, this is Sergeant Woods and Corporal Morgan. I brought them home for supper."

Compared to the young Confederate who ogled her yesterday, these men appeared healthy and well fed, and so much more handsome for being Northern boys.

Corporal Morgan smiled at Tillie, and his even white teeth gleamed against his suntanned face.

"Corporal, what did you do to your hair?" Tillie pointed to his head. A distinct line ran around the edge of his hair, an exact match to the bill of his hat. Above the line, his hair was a lovely walnut brown, but below, a honey color.

His grin was warm and friendly. He straightened and put a hand over his heart, feigning hurt. "I worked hard for this hairstyle. Are you maligning my skills, perchance?"

She laughed. "Gracious no. Merely commenting on a most unusual style. I approve heartily."

Corporal Morgan drew his hand across his forehead and then flicked his fingers, as though shaking sweat away. "Thank goodness." His green eyes sparkled. "No, it comes from many days out in the elements, Miss Pierce."

She scanned him from top to bottom. His light-blue trousers with a bold yellow stripe down each side tucked into knee-high cavalrymen's boots, and the cloth clung to his muscular thighs. He reminded her of George. She pursed her lips and glanced at Maggie, who worked at the stove, her back to the men. Tillie readjusted her smile and turned to Sergeant Woods. A shorter, slimmer man than the corporal, he held a burlap sack in the crook of his arm.

Sergeant Woods appeared older than Corporal Morgan, though with their weather-beaten faces she couldn't tell.

Woods expression was more solemn, almost sad, and the haunted shadows in his eyes made him seem ancient. He smiled and gave a quick head bob for a hello.

"Please come in and join us for supper." Mother welcomed them. "I apologize for the slim fare, but the Rebs came almost daily and insisted we give them our food." She gestured at the meager spread. "However, you're welcome to share our meal."

Sergeant Wood stepped forward. "Then perhaps this might help alleviate some of your distress." He held out the burlap sack.

"Coffee!" Mother's eyes lit, and she buried her nose in the sack, inhaling the pungent aroma. "Oh, thank you, thank you so much. Let me make a pot now so it'll be ready after supper." She bustled to the stove.

Father chuckled at Mother's delight. "One of the first things the Rebs took was coffee. There's been none anywhere in town for the better part of a week now." He held out his hand.

"Thank you for welcoming us into your home." Sergeant Woods and Corporal Morgan shook hands with Father.

"Which cavalry unit are you boys with?" Father brought them to the table, inviting them to sit.

"We're with the First Corps, First Division of the U.S. Calvary, sir, commanded by General Buford."

"General Buford. I've read about him." Tillie put a bowl of stewed tomatoes down at the corporal's elbow. "He fought well at Antietam."

"Yes." Sergeant Woods's smile left his face. The same haunted look Tillie glimpsed earlier shadowed his eyes.

Her brow creased as she appraised first Corporal Morgan, then Sergeant Woods. "Did I say something wrong?"

Corporal Morgan frowned and laid a gentle hand on his companion's shoulder. "No, you didn't." He smiled. "Uh, the general is settin' up shop out near the college." He addressed Father. "He's having us spread out on that ridge of high ground there. He believes the Rebs went northwest toward Cashtown, so he wants to be ready for them. In all honesty, we're not entirely certain where they are."

Mother spun from the stove. Everyone turned at her sharp intake of breath.

"Whatever the case, ma'am," the corporal lifted his hands in a reassuring gesture, seeing her consternation, "we'll find 'em."

Mother finished with the coffee and claimed her place at the table.

Father read a passage from First Samuel, chapter seventeen. After reading the passage, he put the Bible away and returned to the table.

"David and Goliath." Sergeant Woods spooned the tomatoes onto his plate. "Is that how you judge the situation, Mr. Pierce? Are we David or Goliath?"

"Oh, David for sure." Corporal Morgan jumped into the conversation before Father got a chance to speak. He blushed and ducked his head to hide a chagrined smile. "I apologize, sir. I assure you my parents brought me up better than that. Three years in the Army does erode one's manners." He took the bowl of potatoes Maggie offered him.

"That's all right, corporal." Father placed some beans on his plate. "You expressed my thoughts well."

"We are the stronger side," Morgan went on, "they think they have God on their side, but we know we do." He scooped a large helping of mashed potatoes. "The more so because the infantry isn't far behind us." He passed the potatoes to Tillie. "I suspect they'll be here within a day or two and all will be well."

"Will there be fighting here?" Mother's voice diminished.

Corporal Morgan ate a forkful of potato. His jaw stiffened as he held the food in his mouth before swallowing hard. He turned to Mother with a deliberate, serious stare. "Hard to say, Mrs. Pierce, but most likely we'll fight somewhere near here."

Forks clattered on dinnerware as everyone absorbed the news.

* * * *

After supper, Tillie followed everyone into the parlor. Mother served the coffee with the fancy, company, silver coffeepot before settling herself in a chair.

"Sergeant Woods let me clean his carbine today." Sam sat on the floor near the sergeant's feet. His eyes gleamed with hero worship. "Didn't you, Sarge?"

Woods ruffled Sam's hair. "Yes I did, and a fine job he did, too."

Everyone ruffled Sam's hair. Tillie studied him, curious. Sam was easy to like. He didn't seem to mind when people did that.

Mother turned on Sam, breaking Tillie's reverie. "Why, Samuel Wade, you deliberately disobeyed. I told you not to get in the way."

Corporal Morgan and Sergeant Woods both rose to Sam's defense. They spoke over each other to reassure her.

"No, ma'am, he wasn't in the way. We enjoyed having him and his friends around." Sergeant Woods gave Mother a reassuring smile. He smiled at Sam and mouthed, "I'm sorry."

Sergeant Woods sat forward in his chair. "Mrs. Pierce." He laid his elbows on his knees and spoke in a slow, deliberate manner. "Young Sam here was a good boy and did what we asked him to do, right away and with good humor. To reward him, I offered to let him hold my carbine, and I showed him how to clean the stock and barrel. He did not ask, and he did not break any rules."

"No, he didn't," Corporal Morgan echoed.

"Well." Mother studied each man. She sat back and relaxed. "Since you say he behaved as a good boy, and you offered, I will not insult you, or Sam, by suggesting otherwise."

Tillie let her breath out. Thank goodness.

Sergeant Woods shifted as if about to rise and sat back again. "I must also beg your forgiveness for my behavior at the supper table." He dropped his gaze to the floor and held his palms out, at the general chorus of dismissal. "It's—well, you see—my brother and I fought at Antietam. He died there."

"Oh, sergeant, I'm so sorry." Tillie touched his arm in sympathy. "I didn't mean to be so thoughtless."

"You weren't thoughtless." He patted her hand. "How could you know? We've just met."

"Well, I feel bad nonetheless. I'm sorry for your loss."

Maggie left the room.

"Did I say something wrong?" Now he raised his eyebrows, an uncertain frown on his face.

Father sat forward and waved away his concern. "Her beau died a few days ago. He was on his way to his new unit when he was killed by a Rebel soldier."

"I'm so sorry," the sergeant whispered.

After a moment of awkward silence, conversation resumed and they talked like old friends catching up after years apart. The men stayed for another hour.

"We must be back by eight o'clock. General's orders." Sergeant Woods told them with regret. His slow, measured steps brought them to the front door. Corporal Morgan followed him.

"Thank you so much for the coffee." Mother grasped his hand in hers. "Such a wonderful treat."

"They took all your food?" Morgan shook his head. He fidgeted with the kepi in his hands. "The powers that be told us the Rebs didn't loot folks. Goes to show you, I guess."

"They appeared pretty hungry to me. I'm not surprised. But we'll manage." Mother shook the corporal's hand. "The Lord always provides."

"Yes, ma'am. He surely does." Morgan settled his kepi on his head. "Well, Mr. and Mrs. Pierce, thank you for a fine evening. Good night, Miss Pierce." He saluted Sam, who returned the gesture.

"Give our regards to the older Miss Pierce." Sarge shook hands with Father. "Good night, folks."

Tillie went to bed and stared at the ceiling, seeing Sergeant Wood's sad eyes and the corporal's infectious grin. Her eyes drifted closed as a vision took shape. She stood on the front porch in her best brown muslin school dress. In one hand, she held a white handkerchief, and in the other, a flower, which she held out to a man in a resplendent cavalryman's uniform, astride a black steed. Tillie sighed as he leaned down to kiss her goodbye. A smile twitched her lips. What a wonderful evening.

* * * *

Tillie bounded down the stairs for breakfast when the doorknocker rattled. Corporal Morgan and Sergeant Woods stood on the stoop with a huge wooden box propped between them.

"Sergeant, corporal, good morning. How wonderful to see you again."

"Good morning, Miss Tillie. Is your ma around?" Morgan panted, struggling to hold his end of the box and remove his cap. Sergeant Woods nodded a greeting.

"Please come in." Pulling the door wide, Tillie indicated the huge box. "What have you got in there?" She grinned. "I'll go find Mother. She's in the kitchen making breakfast. Are you hungry?"

The two of them manhandled the crate into the house, tilting it to get through the doorway. Big black letters burned into the side read: Official Property of the U.S. Government.

"What in heaven's name is all this? You two didn't do something illegal did you?" She giggled.

They put the crate down with a thump and straightened. Both men breathed hard from the exertion. "Your ma?" Sergeant Woods's eyes sparkled.

"Oh, yes. Sorry." Tillie twirled, belling her skirts, and strode to the kitchen.

"Mother, Corporal Morgan and Sergeant Woods are back with a huge box. They wanted me to come and get you." She turned to Sam eating his breakfast. "You might want to go get Father."

Sam nodded and bolted out the back door.

Tillie followed Mother back to the hall. The men bobbed their heads at Mother as she approached.

"What's this?" She wiped her hands on her apron. "What have you boys done?"

"Nothing illegal, ma'am, if that's what you're asking." Corporal Morgan twisted his cap in his hands, a grin on his face. "We took up a collection from our unit, and when General Buford heard what the Rebs did with your food, he wrote out a requisition slip to take to the quartermaster, so we brought you some supplies."

Father entered the hallway, still wearing his bloody leather apron and holding a crowbar. Tillie put a hand to her mouth and turned away as Sam joined Father, a hammer in his hand. Together they pried open the top of the box to reveal an enormous quantity of food—eggs, cheese, sacks of flour, coffee, sugar, rice, and beans.

Mother lifted out one of three rashers of bacon and gazed into their grinning faces. Her voice came out soft and heavy with emotion. "You boys must stay for breakfast." Using her apron, she wiped tears from her eyes.

* * * *

Tillie and Maggie ascended Culp's Hill, in the waning warmth of the day, scouting for wildflowers. At breakfast, Sergeant Woods and Corporal Morgan announced that much of the infantry had arrived during the night, and more were due in the next day or two.

"Thank you for coming with me." Tillie selected a handful of pink buttercups. "I hoped you'd keep me company. Some girls from school handed out flowers, and I wanted to do the same."

"I'm happy to. I think flowers are a wonderful idea. We can use our old ribbons to make pretty bouquets if you want." Maggie reached for a daisy.

"Good idea." Tillie plucked a daisy. "Imagine." She lifted the flower as an offering. "Handing a flower to a young, handsome officer and he pledge his undying devotion in return. How delightful!" She giggled.

"No!" Maggie almost yanked a flower out of the ground.

Tillie cocked her head. "Why not?"

"No more soldiers, not for me." A savage tone sliced through Maggie's voice as she reached for another daisy.

Did she mean George? A soldier for one day, for heaven's sake? And not an actual soldier, but a farmer. Tillie bit down hard on her tongue and turned her back to hide her burning cheeks. Her heart pounded out her shame for her cruelty and lack of compassion. Reaching for a black-eyed Susan, she pulled the stem until it snapped. She tossed the yellow flower into her bunch. They worked for the next quarter hour in silence.

They sat on a fallen log in the forest's cool darkness and organized their flowers. The lowering sun couldn't penetrate the thick trunks. They waved away clouds of gnats as they finished bundling flowers, tossing those already wilted. They descended the hill, stopping for a cool drink at Spangler's spring, a small creek winding around the base of the Culp's Hill.

As Tillie scooped water into her mouth, her words hung between them. She couldn't ignore it. "I'm sorry I said what I did about the soldiers, Maggie."

Maggie shrugged. "It's not your fault." She gave Tillie a quick smile. "I'm not upset. Come. Let's go home. The mosquitoes and gnats are becoming quite bold."

Tillie splashed cool water on her face. She let the droplets drip off her chin and run down her neck.

Once they left the cool of the woods, the heat assailed them again. Tillie gasped. "I wish we had Lady." The memory of her horse brought a sharp pang of sadness. Where was Lady? Did they mistreat her?

Maggie patted her shoulder. "I do too. It's a hot walk home."

They approached Baltimore Street as the sun slid behind Big Roundtop. Heat radiated off the red brick houses and the cobblestone street. Entering through the kitchen, Tillie and Maggie stopped at the washbasin to sluice their faces and wash their hands. Maggie went upstairs and returned a short time later with a handful of old hair ribbons. They settled at the sitting room table to make bouquets. Tillie rearranged her flowers, basking in the idyllic scene. Father read the newspaper, Mother knitted more socks, and Sam pored over his textbook. If only life might go on like this forever.

Chapter 11

Wednesday, July 1, 1863

Tillie's body rocked back and forth with Maggie's insistent hand on her shoulder. "Wake up, sleepy head. We're off to see the soldiers, remember?"

"I remember," Tillie mumbled into her pillow, her voice sleepy. "What time is it?"

"Time to get out of bed. I'll meet you downstairs. Hurry up." Maggie left the room.

Tillie rose and squinted at the window. The fiery red disc broke the horizon and glared with vicious intensity. Oh goody. Another hot, humid day. Tillie sighed and plodded to her armoire. She dressed in her pink checked calico and made the bed, then splashed cool water on her face before going downstairs.

Sam sat at the table, eating toast and jam.

"Good morning, girls." Father raised his coffee cup to his lips.

Mother placed a plate of toasted bread and some jam in front of them and then poured herself a cup of coffee. Tillie stared at her. They just received a huge box of food yesterday. What happened to the bacon and eggs?

She was just about to ask, when Mother inclined her head to the plate. "Just because we've been given it, doesn't mean we should squander it."

Tillie frowned at Father, but he chuckled and sipped his coffee. She wrinkled her nose, picked up her toast, and ate.

"Where're you all off to today?" Father crunched into his toast.

"We're going to welcome the soldiers again." Maggie spread butter and jam on her toast.

Tillie chimed in, "We have the flowers we picked on Culp's Hill last night. Other girls did that yesterday, and we didn't want to be empty-handed today."

Cheering erupted from the street. Tillie, Maggie, and Sam turned to Mother in silent appeal.

Father chuckled again.

Mother waved her hand as she began washing dishes.

Tillie bolted out the back door, Sam and Maggie at her heels as she flew down Breckenridge Street in time to see more of the cavalry passing up Washington Street, taking the same route as the day before.

Sam disappeared into the crowd.

Tillie grabbed Maggie's hand and pressed forward to find a thin place in the crowd—a difficult task with so many people packed tight on the curb. Some milled around, hoping for a gap in the pack. Tillie and Maggie moved up Washington Street, also looking for a hole in the wall of people. The dust rising off the road, and the odor of sweaty bodies, along with the tang of horses made Tillie sneeze. They finally came to a stop at the corner of Washington and West Middle Streets, one of the busiest intersections. Across the road, shops lined up, side by side, and shop owners, as well as their patrons, stood in the doorways or peered out the large front windows. On the floors above, their families hung out windows, waving and calling to the troops passing by. Tillie and Maggie stopped at the curb on the east side of the road to cheer and wave.

"We forgot the flowers!" Tillie whirled to Maggie with a disappointed frown.

"Oh, we left them on the sitting room table." Maggie shrugged, turned to Tillie, brows raised. "Do you want to go home and get them, or shall I?"

Tillie debated for a moment, and then shook her head. "I'm not going back for them now. I don't want to miss seeing the boys."

Someone in the crowd started singing. Tillie and Maggie joined in. The soldiers lifted their caps and acknowledged the crowd with grateful smiles. Sweat plastered their hair to their skulls and ran down their faces. Tillie sympathized with them for having to march in the intense heat dressed in dark-blue woolen uniforms.

First, the cavalry came through. The crowds waved and cheered. Some people whistled, sharp sounds that pierced through the rest of the noise. Then, for more than an hour, came long lines of wagons carrying supplies. The singing stopped and the cheering slowed, replaced by the whistles and shouts of the teamsters urging their animals onward.

A wagon passed. Men lay in hammocks strung across the interior. They stared out the back of the wagon, impassive and unmoving. Another passed and then another.

"Maggie, look." She pointed to the wagon carrying the sick and wounded. "I always assumed they went to a hospital in Washington or Philadelphia. Why would they come here?"

At least thirty more ambulance wagons passed by. Some already carried men, most did not. Tillie finally stopped counting. Then came the supply wagons. These carried the implements of battle aftermath, such as stretchers and coffins.

Tillie's heart lurched. She spun to Maggie—had she seen it too? Her sad frown and grieved eyes indicated she had.

"I'm ready to go home." Tillie grabbed her sister's arm to gain her attention.

"I was thinking the same thing." Maggie frowned as the wagons rumbled by. "I don't want to see this reminder. It's too painful."

They'd turned to leave when the thump-thump of marching men caught Tillie's attention. "Oh, wait." She stopped and waved. "Here comes the infantry."

Officers on horseback led each corps. The men came on, an unending line of soldiers in better physical condition than the Confederate infantry. Tillie recalled the desperate state of the Southern soldiers with their bare feet, shirts and jackets torn or patched in several places. Most of those men didn't have hats. After arriving in town, they procured headwear before most other things, food notwithstanding.

These Union soldiers, on the other hand, had shoes on their feet, hats on their heads, and packs on their backs bulging with supplies. Each man marched equipped with a rifle. A cartridge box hung at their side and rattled as they walked, creating a rhythmic clatter. The soldiers lifted their hats, waved, and smiled.

The townsfolk cheered and sang to the whump, whump of thousands of feet pounding on the road, punctuated by martial music somewhere at the back of the line. In the distance, the cobbles shimmered in wavy ribbons above the road.

At a short boom, Tillie glanced at the sky for the telltale sign of an oncoming storm, but the sun shone down out of a clear, deep blue summer sky. She turned in the direction of Pennsylvania College, near Seminary Ridge where another boom answered the first.

Townsfolk stopped cheering, and in the almost sudden silence, came a third distinct boom of cannon. The ground vibrated. It sounded nothing like thunder.

The soldiers fell silent. Their smiles disappeared. Some faces registered fear, others stoic resignation. Officers shouted at the men to pick up their pace. In the distance, the cannons grew louder. Gray smoke rose from behind the ridge as though trying to hide the activity there. People watching from their upstairs windows ducked inside and slammed the sashes down, as if a slim pane of glass might protect them.

Men pulled on their beards or tapped a finger against their noses. Women screamed and dispersed. People shouted at children and each other. The thud and clatter of thousands of marching men created a confused jumble.

"Maggie!" Tillie yelled above the din. Maggie didn't respond, and Tillie's heart pounded as she spun in every direction. "Maggie, where are you?" she called out as she tried to move against the throng.

People rushed past and buffeted her from side to side. They pushed her in the opposite direction she wanted to go.

More cannons fired in the distance almost deafening her. She shouted for Maggie again, but the din swallowed her voice.

"Maggie!" Tillie called above the screams and shouts of the men and women on the street as the crashes of the cannons died away. Her voice cracked, and a sudden image enveloped her. Something drastic happened to Maggie while she wasn't looking. What would Father and Mother say? She had stopped to watch the infantry enter town, and when she wasn't looking, a Reb abducted Maggie. He had hidden among the houses, attempting to escape the Yanks. Tears filled her eyes. Stop it! You're being ridiculous. Why would a Reb sneak all the way around the union army just to kidnap Maggie, of all people?

A man bumped Tillie from the side. She fell off the curb and stumbled into the side of a horse.

The rider steadied the animal and kept him from shying. At the same time, he grabbed her shoulder. "Miss, are you hurt?"

Tillie lifted a tear-streaked face to the stranger atop his horse. Kind blue eyes peered at her from a weather-beaten face, half masked by thick, dark whiskers. His gentle demeanor put her at ease. "No, I'm not hurt. Thank you."

"Then why the tears?"

"I'm scared."

"Then I suggest you head home right away. Do you live nearby?"

"Yes, sir, I do." She sniffed back her tears. "One street over, but I can't find my sister. I need to find my sister." Tillie's voice rose as the roar of cannons grew louder, now accompanied by the rattling crackle of gunfire.

The soldier turned his horse, and holding a pair of field glasses to his eyes, he took a long look in that direction. The smoke grew thicker and grayer by the minute.

She followed his gaze, but only saw dense smoke rising behind Seminary Ridge like a menacing fog. She put her hand on her forehead. Where did Maggie go? What happened to her? What should she do?

He faced her and lowered his field glasses. "Go home, miss." His tone was polite, but firm. "I'm sure your sister has already reached your house safely. Go home. Tell your family to go to the basement and stay there until the firing stops."

Tillie raised a hand to shade her eyes. A single star shone on his shoulder patch. "Thank you, general." She smiled. "You're probably correct. Good luck to you today."

He grasped the bill of his cap and inclined his head. "Thank you and good luck to you too." With that, he rode away, shouting encouragements to his men, herding them along.

Tillie ran home. A cannonball might land slap-dab on top of her head. Entering the house, Tillie found Maggie with the rest of the family in the sitting room.

Mother took two steps toward her. "Tillie, thank goodness you're home."

Tillie ignored her. "Why didn't you stay with me?" She glared at Maggie, her hands balled into fists. Heart pounding, she drew in short breaths.

"I thought you were with me." Maggie glanced at Mother and Father as though seeking support. "You said you wanted to go home so I went with you. I got through the crowd and realized you weren't beside me.... I tried to look for you, but I couldn't find you. I'm sorry." Maggie raised her hands as if to say, what more might I have done. "I assumed you'd figure out I'd gone home."

With a deep breath, Tillie unclenched her hands. She blinked, mollified. "It's all right." She drew in another deep breath and let it out. Her shoulders slumped. "It was my fault, really. I stopped when the foot soldiers arrived. I was frightened when I turned around and you weren't there." She gave Maggie a forgiving smile.

Tillie spun to Father. "I ran into a general—literally. Someone bumped me into the street, and I collided with his horse. I didn't get hurt." She showed her arms to demonstrate no scratches or bruises. "He said we should go to the basement and stay there until the firing stops."

"Sound advice." Father nodded. "We were discussing what to do when you came in. Why don't we collect some of our belongings and bring them downstairs with us?"

In the distance, another boom added an exclamation mark to Father's statement. He looked out the front window. "Quickly." He herded his family toward the stairs.

Tillie entered her room. What to take? She grabbed some paper and ink off her desk. James and William would be interested in what was happening. She started toward the door but turned back and gathered her schoolbooks and a novel as well. No telling how long they'd have to stay in the basement. She joined her family downstairs to wait out the coming storm.

As they settled on barrels and boxes stored in the basement, Mother surveyed the room. "Where's Sam?" She jumped from her barrel and started toward the stairs. Muffled cannon sounded in the distance. She stopped at the base, one foot poised to go up. Her eyes slid to Father, brows creased and lips pressed together. Her hand gripped the stair railing.

In the confusion, Tillie had forgotten him. Did Sam get hurt? Was he lying out in the battlefield dead? Had he joined in the fighting? She shook her head to clear the frightening thoughts. She needed to clamp down on her imagination today.

Father took Mother by the shoulders. "Perhaps he went to his mother's house to check on them." He led her back to her barrel. "Sam is a smart and resourceful young man. He'll be all right."

Mother said nothing. But she sat down, and her lips began to move in silent prayer.

Tillie lowered her head and closed her eyes. Dear Lord. The words ran over themselves in her head. Please keep Sam safe…please keep Sam safe…

They'd sat in the basement for about fifteen minutes when the cannon firing ceased. They waited, silent, but heard nothing.

After a while, Tillie's gaze lifted to the ceiling. Was the fighting over? Could they go up?

"It's been almost a half hour." Maggie shifted on her box. "They stopped firing fifteen minutes ago. Do you think it's over?" No one answered her question. Maggie arched a brow at Tillie.

Tillie shrugged. "The general said to stay down until the firing stops. That's all I know."

Mother lifted her hands and dropped them into her lap. "Well, I don't know what they thought would happen." She rose from her perch on the wooden barrel. "But I have a dinner to get on the table." She gathered her skirts and crossed to the stairs. She stopped and turned to Father. "Perhaps you should go look for Sam?"

"Of course. I'll go." Father followed her up the stairs.

Tillie's heart raced. Where had Sam gone? Had he been hurt? Had he stopped at his mother's house? She opened her mouth to ask if she should go to the Wades' to find out, but Mother cut her short.

"On second thought, no. Don't go out there. It might not be safe yet. I'm going to trust him to the Lord. I have to. I'm certain he's fine. It didn't sound like much of a fight anyway." She went upstairs.

Father chuckled. "You're right, of course. I must admit, I feel a bit foolish myself." He smiled at Tillie. "I'm sure the general meant well, but I too, have things to do."

Tillie and Maggie followed Mother to the kitchen and helped with the cooking. Sam arrived as they were putting the food on the table.

Mother's hands were on her hips before her next breath drawn. "Sam Wade, where have you been?" She picked up a bowl of sliced tomatoes from the counter. Then she carried them to the table and slammed them down. Tomato juice splattered the red-checked tablecloth.

"I was at the encampment." His eyes darted around the room, as if he'd fallen into some kind of trap and didn't know how to extricate himself.

"Didn't you hear the firing?" Maggie sat.

"Of course."

"Sit down, everyone." Father pulled out his chair, his Bible in one hand. "Let me read, and then we'll hear what he has to say."

When Father finished reading, Sam shoveled a forkful of beans into his mouth and chewed. He chased it down with a gulp of milk and set his glass down. "I was at the encampment with Gates and Bertie, brushing the horses, fetching water, and joking with the soldiers before the cannon started firing." He dropped a hot ear of corn on his plate and passed the bowl.

"You should have seen poor little Leander Warren." Sam laughed. "The minute the first cannon boomed out, Lee started screaming like a girl. He threw his hands over his ears and dropped into the hay. What a sissy. When the bugler called Boots and Saddles, that's the call to battle, Lee ran home lickety-split. I swear I never seen him run that fast."

"Don't swear, Sam." Mother lowered her brow and pressed her mouth tight. "It's 'I've never seen him run that fast.'" She pinned him with a stern look. "To that point, I hardly think you're being charitable of the feelings of a seven-year-old."

"Yes, ma'am." Sam frowned. He drew in a deep breath and let it out.

"Why didn't you run home, Sam?" Maggie passed him the bread.

"We, that is, Gates and Bertie and me—"

"Gates, Bertie, and I." Mother put her fork down and sat back. She dropped her hands into her lap. "I don't care for your language."

Sam blushed.

Father grinned and squeezed the back of Sam's neck.

Tillie laughed. "Take heart, Sam. Mother was frightened when you didn't come home. She's not really mad at you." Her heart went out to him. She hated their scolding too.

Mother's fierce gaze bore into Tillie. She stopped her fork halfway to her mouth. "Don't be impertinent, Tillie."

Sam smiled but tried to hide it by taking a drink of milk. He put the cup down. "Gates, Bertie, and I wanted to stay and see the fight. When the gun firing started, Gates asked Sarge what it was, and Sarge said rifle fire. Then he told us all to run home and don't stop until we get there." Sam's eyes sparkled.

Mother opened her mouth to scold Sam again.

"There's nothing to fear, Margaret." Father cut off whatever she intended to say. "The boy is unharmed and all's well that ends well." He gripped Sam's shoulder and then slapped him on the back.

Mother glared at Father, but said nothing more. She finished her meal in silence.

When dinner ended, Mother rose and, without a word, left the room. Father followed her. Maggie gathered supplies to bring to the basement.

Tillie cleared the table.

Sam crept up behind her. "Am I in a lot of trouble with your mother?"

Tillie gave him a sisterly peck on the cheek. "She was scared. We didn't know where you were or if you were safe or not. If we had to go look for you, we didn't know where to start."

Sam blushed. A pleased smile spread across his face, and his blue eyes lit. "She was afraid for me? No one's ever been afraid for me before."

Tillie grasped his elbow. "We all were."

Mother strode into the kitchen. "Tillie, tomorrow I'd like you to—"

Sam walked over, flung his arms around Mother's waist, and hugged her tight.

Mother held her arms out at her sides, eyes wide, mouth open. Then she wrapped her arms around the boy and leaned down, enfolding him in an embrace.

Tillie's throat clogged. She pursed her lips and blinked back tears.

Sam broke away, and his smile became a grin. "Thanks." He ran out the kitchen door.

Tillie turned back to washing dishes. She lifted her apron and wiped away tears. Behind her, Mother blew her nose.

The front door rattled with hard, insistent raps. Voices in the hall drifted back. Father came to the kitchen.

"Tillie. Margaret. Mrs. Schriver would like a word with us." He headed back to the hall.

"Mrs. Schriver." Mother grasped Mrs. Schriver's hands in greeting. "Please come into the parlor and sit down."

"No thank you, Mrs. Pierce." Mrs. Schriver smiled and shook her head. "I'm not here for a visit. I came to ask two favors of you."

"Of course." Mother stepped back.

"First, I'm going to my father's farm. I don't feel safe alone in the house with the girls. I came to ask if Mr. Pierce would look after my home for me while I'm gone."

"Certainly," Father said. "Think nothing of it."

"Thank you." She inclined her head toward Tillie. "I also wanted to ask permission to take Tillie with me."

Mother's mouth dropped open. She looked at Father. "What do you think, James? Should Tillie go with her?"

"I wouldn't ask, Mrs. Pierce, except I know Tillie and Beckie are good friends. They might enjoy spending the afternoon together. We'll be home by suppertime."

"I think it's a good idea, Margaret." Father walked over and put a hand on her shoulder. "If fighting does erupt again, it would get Tillie safely out of the way."

When Mother didn't respond, he addressed Tillie. "What say you, Tillie? Do you want to accompany Mrs. Schriver?"

"Well, if you and Mother don't object." Tillie shrugged her acquiescence. She preferred to stay home, but didn't want to hurt Mrs. Schriver's feelings by refusing. "I don't mind going with Mrs. Schriver. I can help with the girls."

"All right then." Mother lifted her hands in a gesture of surrender. "Go upstairs, get a clean dress, and put it in the basement. You can change into it when you get home."

Tillie went to gather her things. She emerged from the basement, kissed her parents, and said goodbye. Had she known what awaited her at the Weikerts, she might have refused.

Chapter 12

Tillie and Mrs. Schriver hurried Mollie and Sadie down a silent and deserted Baltimore Street. Every few seconds the air resounded with the pfoom, pfoom of distant cannon shots. Tillie's heart pounded, and her mouth went dry. The fighting hadn't stopped, but it did sound farther away. Perhaps the Confederates were yielding ground. It was strange that they couldn't hear it inside the house.

She had Mollie by the hand, and with each thud of the cannon, Tillie picked up her pace until she almost dragged the seven-year-old behind her.

They passed through the brick entrance gate of Evergreen Cemetery, cutting across diagonally, moving fast. Distant cannon blasts goaded them on.

"Mama, stop! I can't walk so fast." Five-year-old Sadie dug her heels into the ground and pulled back, like a donkey about to balk.

"I'm sorry, my dear. I want to get to Grandpapa's house." Mrs. Schriver kept hold of Sadie's hand. With the other, she reached over and patted the child's head. She slowed, however, and adopted a more sedate walk. Tillie did the same, though her stomach twisted and lurched. Cresting Cemetery Hill, they came upon Union soldiers placing cannon along the top of the ridge pointed toward the northwest. Tillie jerked to a surprised halt as groups of men positioned the big guns, while others sighted down the length of the barrels. More men placed large wooden cases at the base of each gun. Every team had a specific job to do, and they performed it with exquisite precision.

"They can't possibly think they'll fight here can they?" Tillie stared, awed as the men prepared the guns. "Mrs. Schriver, we shouldn't be here."

Men moved about the cemetery and pried loose gravestones, which they threw down on the ground.

"What are they doing?" Her voice rose to a horrified, angry pitch as the men threw down the gravestone of a young boy, a friend of William's, killed at Chancellorsville. She had attended his funeral. "They're vandalizing the graves!"

One man trotted up and down the line, shouting instructions and giving each gun a final check. He hurried over. "What are you women doing here?" He gestured at them with both arms, shouting above the din growing louder by the second. "Get out of here now!"

Mrs. Schriver pointed, indicating the direction they wanted to go. "If you please." Firm determination edged her words. "We want to go through the cemetery. My parents live on the other side."

"Go back the way you came, lady," the officer shouted at her. "You'll most likely get shot if you stay here."

"No!" Mrs. Schriver stamped her foot. "I'm going to my father's house." She glared at him. He glared back, and then shrugged. "Fine. It's your funeral." He started to turn away, but softened his tone while looking at the children's frightened faces. "Hurry up, then. Don't stop for anything. You're in great danger here. We expect the Rebels to shell us at any moment."

"Why are they destroying those headstones?" Tillie couldn't help it. They desecrated a beautiful cemetery, and her heart burned for the poor souls underneath them. "Tell them to stop it!"

"I'll tell them no such thing. I ordered it."

Her mouth dropped open, and her brows came together. "How dare you!"

The officer rolled his eyes. "Better to be wounded by one bullet than by hundreds of stone chips or sometimes both." He whipped his hat off and wiped his brow with his arm. He jammed his hat back on his head. "I don't have time to debate this with you, but I will say this: flying stone chips can blind and maim in ways bullets can't. Now, get out of here before I change my mind and send you back the way you came."

Tillie's eyes followed the direction the cannons pointed, northwest, toward Seminary Ridge. The Confederates had come over that same ridge Friday afternoon. A chill swept down her spine.

The large red building of the Lutheran Seminary stood sentinel as it always did, but around it, a confused battle raged. Men moved back and forth, and thick gray smoke rose from the ground like fog, obscuring the building's base and the surrounding troops. As they ran here and there, they created an eerie, confused specter, like men moving without lower legs. Every few minutes cannon boomed, and the shells burst in the air above them. The din rose and fell in mighty undulations.

They had run headlong into a battle. How stupid of them. A whimper rose in her throat, but she refused to let it escape. She clenched her jaw against the urge to cry as her breath came in short gasps.

Mrs. Schriver gathered Sadie close and started to run. Mollie cried after her mother, but Tillie gripped her hand so hard, the child couldn't break loose. Tillie stood riveted to the spot, unable to tear her gaze away from the fighting on Seminary Ridge. She was going to die, standing right here in the cemetery, because like a fool, she'd left home.

"Get out of here!" The officer shouted and shoved Tillie in the back, propelling her forward. That broke her spell, and she set off running across the cemetery, desperate to catch up to Mrs. Schriver. They ran toward Taneytown Road. There, below the crest of Cemetery Hill, the sound of the fighting diminished at once, almost as if there was no fighting at all. Tillie relaxed as the peaceful sounds of birds singing and cicadas buzzing calmed her frayed nerves a little.

The women shared the road with hundreds of soldiers and wagons heading toward town. With the rainstorms over the past week and the thousands of troops arriving daily, the road was now a quagmire of deep trenches. Mud collected around the hems of their dresses and sucked at their shoes. Soldiers heading in the opposite direction shouted to the women to get indoors.

Mrs. Schriver ignored them, so Tillie did too, though her heart said the same thing.

"Mama, stop, please!" Sadie yanked on her mother's hand. "I can't go anymore."

"I'm tired too," Mollie said. "I need to rest."

Mrs. Schriver acted as though she didn't hear, but without missing a step, she swooped Sadie into her arms. Mollie was too big for Tillie to carry, so she put one arm around her shoulders and held her hand.

"Well, we can't stop here." Tillie glanced around them. "We'd be run over for sure. Hold me tight, and I'll help you."

They stumbled and staggered but kept going, breathing hard.

The same wagons that entered Gettysburg that morning now overtook them. The last wagon, draped with black cloth over the canvas, had an honor guard of soldiers walking along beside and behind it. Inside the wagon, a dead man lay on a blood-soaked mattress. Someone had positioned one hand over the other on his abdomen. Thick black whiskers covered his kind, weather-beaten face. Wasn't he the general who warned her to go home? The men walking beside the wagon did not attempt to hide their grief.

Tillie got up the courage to ask the soldier nearest her who the man was.

"That's General Reynolds." The soldier removed his hat. "He got killed a few minutes ago." The soldier used his elbow to wipe his eyes. He replaced his hat. "He was a great general. We shall miss him."

Tillie politely ignored his tears. "He spoke to me on the street before noontime. He told me to go home and stay there until the fighting stopped." His words brought a rueful smile to her lips. She cast her eyes to the ground as the stupidity of her actions crashed down on her.

"I see you heeded his advice." A harsh tone rattled in his voice. He put his fingers to his hat brim, then picked up his pace, and rejoined the wagon carrying the general's body away.

Tillie's face warmed. She inhaled and let out a slow, measured breath.

Mrs. Schriver harrumphed.

Tillie ignored her. He was right. They shouldn't be out here. Tillie was out of breath and ready to stop and rest when they came to Widow Leicester's home, a small one-and-a-half storey farmhouse on the west side of Taneytown Road.

"We can stop here." Mrs. Schriver's words came in breathless gasps. "I know Mrs. Leicester well. She won't mind if we rest here a moment." Perspiration beaded her forehead and upper lip as she took a deep breath and licked her lips.

Tillie didn't respond, but plodded up the walk and sank onto the step, grateful for the chance to stop. A caisson laden with ammunition rumbled past, throwing up mud. She raised her arms and cringed from the mud splattering near her feet. She relaxed and sighed, then rubbed her hands over her face.

They'd made it roughly halfway between home and the Weikerts'. As far as the eye could see, thousands of wagons, horses, and soldiers headed toward town while the four of them struggled south to a safe haven.

A deafening roar engulfed them as the guns on Cemetery Ridge opened fire. The vibrations traveled through the earth and thrummed into her feet.

Sadie, Mollie, and Tillie threw their hands over their ears. Tillie cringed as a scream escaped her and went unheard in the roar of guns. Mollie threw herself to the ground, also screaming.

The roar grew louder and seemed to come closer. Tillie threw her arms over her head and curled up tight, bringing her knees to her forehead, trying to make herself as small a target as possible. She jumped from the step and ran to the gate. She grabbed hold of the top and yanked at it, but it wouldn't budge. She shook the gate and burst into fresh blinding tears as she fought with the opening. A frustrated scream escaped her. "I don't want to die out here. I don't want to die out here. Don't let me die out here. I want to go home."

Mrs. Schriver's arm reached over the top of the gate and, with a flick of her fingers, released the latch. Tillie yanked it open and tore through. She stopped short at the road. Too much traffic moved toward town. If she stepped out, a conveyance would run her down. She glanced back at Mrs. Schriver, who knelt in the mud and tried to console her children. They cried and clung to her.

Sadie hiccupped and then vomited on her mother.

Tillie blamed Mrs. Schriver for their predicament. They should have stayed home and gone into the basement. Before Mr. Schriver left for the Cavalry, he converted his basement into a tavern. Mrs. Schriver and the girls doubtless might have hidden there and the Rebs would never have known it. Why did they come out here? "Mrs. Schriver, what do we do? The girls can't go on, and we can't turn back. What do we do?" Tillie couldn't stem the wail of terror in her voice. Her question helped her push it down. She'd still have to deal with the situation. Better to stay calm, if possible, and deal with her emotions later.

"You there!" A soldier came out of the house and stalked toward them. He pointed a gauntleted finger at them. "You can't stay here. It's too dangerous."

"We don't want to stay here." Mrs. Schriver rose and shouted at him, red-faced. She waved at her girls in quick, furious gestures. "My girls cannot go any further. The mud's too thick to move, there's too much traffic, and they're frightened half to death." Her arm dropped over Sadie's shoulders in a protective embrace while Mollie clung to her skirts.

The soldier glanced at Mollie, who kept her face buried deep in the folds of fabric.

"We're trying to get to my parents' house just a mile or so down the road." Mrs. Schriver gestured in the direction they wanted to go as he knelt in the mud and reached to stroke the child's hair.

"Hush, my dear." His voice lowered kind and reassuring. "You'll be all right. I won't let any harm come to you, I promise."

Mollie turned her tear-streaked face and peered at him.

His face softened even more, and he smiled at her. He turned from Mollie to Sadie and then Tillie and Mrs. Schriver.

"You can't stay here," he repeated, his tone returning to one of authority. "The Rebels are expected to attack at any time. You're quite right. The road is a quagmire. Come with me." He marched toward the house.

The women followed him to the front porch.

"Wait here." He spread his hands indicating he meant the porch. "I'll find a ride to carry you the rest of the way." He stepped inside and closed the door.

Tillie and Mrs. Schriver looked at each other. "Well now, where did he go?" Mrs. Schriver removed a handkerchief from inside her left cuff and wiped her face. She grimaced at the vomit dripping off the end of her skirt. She lifted the fabric in her thumb and forefinger and shook it. She averted her face and held her handkerchief to her mouth.

"I'm sorry, Mama." Tears and fright clogged Sadie's voice.

"No worries, child." Mrs. Schriver stroked Sadie's hair. "No worries."

Tillie alternated between wanting to run home and dissolving into tears right where she stood. Instead, she sank onto the porch and put her head in her hands. A sob escaped her, and she let it but refused to allow any more. She wiped her eyes and nose on her sleeve.

The soldier reappeared from around the side of the building and jogged to the road. He stopped a covered conveyance as it lurched past. When the wagon stopped, the wheels sank to the hubs. The soldier talked with the driver. The driver shook his head. The soldier pointed toward the back of the wagon, then in the direction of the women.

The driver peered at them again, said something to the soldier, and shook his head again.

The soldier slammed his fist against the side of the wagon and then grinned at the women, gesturing for them to come.

The covered wagon was full of wounded men, groaning and crying out in pain. The soldier paid no attention as he lifted the children into the back. He placed Mollie inside and gave her curls a quick, affectionate tug. Then he lifted Sadie.

"Thank you, sir." She gazed at him, her eyes big, round, and blue.

The soldier pinched her cheek and smiled at her with warm affection. He removed his hat to say goodbye. "Your daughters remind me of my own little girls." His eyes misted. "My Patsy is this one's age." He indicated Mollie. "And my Laura is your age." He gestured to Sadie. "My wife is expecting our third." He added this piece of information with a wistful note.

"Where're you from?" Mrs. Schriver took his hand as she started to climb into the wagon.

"New York, ma'am." He straightened. "I'm Corporal Alfred Townsend of Middletown, New York at your service."

"Well, thank you, corporal, for all of your help. We appreciate it and will pray for your safety."

He helped Tillie climb into the wagon. She was still settling herself when the wagon lurched forward. The wounded soldiers cried out, and Mrs. Schriver grabbed hold of her children. Sadie uttered a short scream. Tillie almost fell off, snatched at the canvas side, and held tight. Corporal Townsend waved as they drove away.

Tillie lifted a hand in response. Would she see him again? Would he survive?

Chapter 13

The wagon bumped along, its spring-less wheels jolting the occupants at every rut. The wounded within begged for mercy.

Tillie tried not to look at the men, but her eye fell on one particular young man, lying in blood-soaked straw, his left arm severed at the elbow. The ragged bone stuck out of a gaping hole, the skin and muscle shredded and bleeding. Someone placed his forearm across his abdomen. Tillie swallowed hard and turned away. The open flesh reeked in the heat, and she tried to take shallow breaths to avoid the stench of blood and putrefaction, but couldn't help herself. The odor found its way into her cheeks and tingled on her tongue. She worked up saliva and swished it around to clean the taste from her mouth. Flies buzzed and crowded under the hot canvas wagon cover, adding their insult to the soldiers' injuries.

Behind her, a man whimpered and cried out. "Get them off me. Please get them off me."

She peered over her shoulder at him kicking his wounded leg covered with the black, crawling, biting pests. He began to sob.

She turned her back on him.

They even buzzed around her flying into her face and landing on her. She dared release an occasional hand to wave them away.

Despite her resolve, she stole another glance over her shoulder. Again, her eye fell on the now vacant stare of the young boy whose severed arm lay across his abdomen. His eyes in death accused her for her squeamishness. She snapped her head back to the front and swallowed hard, but couldn't hold back. Gripping the cover of the wagon, she leaned over and let her vomit splash into the muddy road, retching until nothing remained in her stomach. She rested her forehead on the rough canvas top. Her body shook, and despite the burn in her lungs, she tried not to take deep gasps of air. Instead, she wiped her mouth on her sleeve and steeled herself not to look behind her again.

After what seemed like an eternity, they stopped at the Weikerts'. Tillie jumped down almost before the wagon came to a complete halt. She turned to help Sadie off, using her as a distraction to keep from seeing the men.

"Hettie, girls!" Mrs. Weikert ran toward them, arms out.

The children sprinted to their grandparents, flinging themselves into their embrace.

Her grandfather lifted Mollie, tickling her face with his whiskers. The frightened girl squeezed his neck, hiding her face in his shoulder. He sobered and hugged her, crooning and consoling her. He turned to Mrs. Schriver. "You took quite a chance coming out here, daughter." He shifted Mollie to see around her. "You might have been terribly hurt." His gaze focused to the never-ending stream of troops.

"I didn't feel safe, Papa." She scowled, her face reddening from more than the heat. "The fighting came quite close to us. I feared for the girls and me." She glared at him, as though to say, don't judge me.

Her mother put her arm around her shoulders. "You did right."

Beckie, and her brother, ran out to greet them.

Tillie hugged her friend.

"Hello, Dan." She gave him a shy smile.

A long, lanky boy of thirteen with dark-brown hair and blue eyes bobbed his head at her. His face reddened. "Miss Tillie."

Mr. Weikert put Mollie down. "And how's your family, young lady?" He was a white-haired, blue-eyed, broad-shouldered man.

"They're fine, sir, and thank you for your hospitality."

He waved away her thanks. "Not at all."

The steady tramp-tramp of marching feet gave way to a low rumble punctuated by neighing horses.

The infantry moved to either side of the edges, as Union artillery charged headlong past them, as though they feared they might miss the battle. The road, torn up from so many wagons and columns of men, could not withstand another onslaught of caissons. The drivers guided their teams into the fields to avoid being stuck in the mud.

Mr. Weikert made a strangled noise as the heavy conveyances tore his wheat from the ground, crushing the stalks under their wheels.

A sudden blast ripped through the air. Everyone ducked and cringed. Sadie and Mollie screamed. Tillie clamped her hands over her ears. Her scream stuck in her throat.

A caisson exploded, hurtling pieces of shrapnel in different directions. The driver flew from his seat like a toy. He thudded into the wheat field, his shrieks of pain indicating where he landed. The wheat caught fire.

Without missing a beat, four soldiers stepped out of line. They found the wounded man, lifted him into their arms, and carried him to the house. No one did anything about the flames.

Tillie's stomach clenched. The blast destroyed his eyes and covered his body from head to toe in a black mass of gunpowder. She slapped her hands over her mouth and gagged.

Mr. Weikert reached down and cupped his hand over Mollie's face, turning her head into his leg.

Mrs. Weikert lifted Sadie and held the child's face against her shoulder. She kept her hand on the back of the child's head while the men approached.

"Take him indoors and put him in one of the bedrooms upstairs." Mrs. Weikert's voice choked, her eyes glued on the wounded man.

"We should all get inside." Mr. Weikert couldn't take his eyes off the caisson and his burning wheat field. "It is not safe out here."

"Oh dear." The soldier wept as they carried him by. Blood dribbled out the side of his mouth as he spoke. "I didn't read my Bible today. What will my poor wife and children say?"

Everyone followed the soldiers into the house as they took the wounded man upstairs and placed him on the bed. Tillie wandered along behind the men and stopped at the bedroom door. One of them patted the man's shoulder before leaving him to the family's ministrations.

Mrs. Weikert pushed past her, tearing up a linen sheet. She cleaned his wounds and bound his face. When finished, the woman sat by the bed. Every so often, she touched his hand in a reassuring way.

The man drifted off to sleep. Tillie went back outside to watch the soldiers tramp by the house. As they passed, she studied individual men. How many would remain when the fight ended? Who would return home after the war? She scowled and tried to find ways to brighten her spirits. Perhaps cheering the men on, as she did in town, might revive her.

Tillie waved, but they didn't wave back. They offered none of the jubilation of this morning. The fight had been joined, and these men, aware what they headed into, kept their peace. Most stared at the ground, rifles slung over one shoulder. Others focused their gazes straight ahead or on the back of the man in front of them. They marched, silent and tense, and moved with exhausted automation.

She dropped her arm. The sun beat down on her broiling her back. If she was hot, the boys must be in a bad way.

As if to confirm her suspicions, four men broke ranks and headed for the spring on the north side of the house. They dunked their heads and sluiced their faces in the cool water. Others dipped in kerchiefs and wrapped them around their foreheads or necks. They slaked their thirst before stepping back in formation.

She ran to the barn, grabbed a bucket hanging on a peg, and went to the house. "Do you have an old cup I can use?"

Beckie retrieved one from a cupboard and held it out.

At the spring, Tillie filled her bucket and carried the water back to the road, careful not to spill any. She set it down, dipped, and extended her hand. A soldier snatched the cup, draining the water.

"Hey," another called out. "Don't be greedy. Pass that cup right quick!"

The man who drank handed it back to her. Tillie refilled the cup. This time, the man passed it down the line. The last to drink threw it back to her, and it landed in the dirt at her feet. She wiped the rim, leaving a muddy streak on the front of her skirt matching the ring of mud at her hem.

The water seemed to ease their spirits. Even if they didn't get any, the fact she offered some helped them relax, and they began to tease and joke with her.

She dipped her cup in the bucket and scraped the bottom.

"Well that figures, no more water," one man bemoaned. His grin gave away his true feelings. Others groaned in mock dismay.

Were they angry? Tillie backed up a step. "Be patient, boys. I'll go get more." She ran back to the spring.

When she returned, the men who teased her were gone, but two men stepped out of line, dunked their kerchiefs into the bucket, squeezed out the excess water, and mopped their red, sweating faces. They soaked their cloths again and tied them around their necks.

"Would you like a drink?"

They nodded their thanks. They each drank deep, then the second man refilled the cup, walked over to a boy propped up between two other men, and held the water to his lips. Among the three of them, they got the semiconscious boy to swallow some.

The soldier came back and handed the cup to Tillie. "Many thanks for your kind service, miss." He tipped the bill of his cap and stepped back in line.

The sun continued to beat on her head. She paid it no heed, nor did she imbibe. The men needed the water more than she did.

At last, Big Roundtop cast its long shadow on her and the men marching by. The last of the men marched away. Tillie's head ached, and her stomach churned with queasy nausea. She tramped back to the barn and hung the bucket on its peg. A prodigious yawn escaped her as she walked across the yard. She wrinkled her nose, the effects of sunburn stinging her face. Her fingers explored her face where the sun burned her the most.

She released another deep yawn and stiffened. Did someone shout to her? She froze, listening hard. A voice shouted from beyond the barn. Tillie walked in the direction of the shout and encountered a young man coming toward her, his right hand cradled in his left. Behind him, several more soldiers arrived, some under their own power, others helped by comrades.

The soldier who hailed her lifted his uninjured hand and waved, grasped his right hand again holding the appendage close to his body. Picking up his pace, he trotted toward her. The sun slanted lower behind Big Roundtop, casting the mountain in black shadow.

She drew a deep breath. "I'm afraid there's no more water." She held her hands out. "The pump and the well both ran dry. I'm sorry."

"Well." He frowned. "I'm sorry also, but I'm not here for a drink of water. Our commanding officer sent us. He said this is to be the Fifth Corps field hospital."

"Oh, I see." She fingered her hair and played with the strands that fell out of her braid. He was handsome. She bit her lip and pointed to his hand. "Uh, does it hurt much? It looks dreadful."

"Oh, this is nothing, a minor wound. You'll see much worse than this, I wager."

She drew back. "Oh, I hope not!" An image of the wounded she rode in with rose up before her, and she shuddered.

Ambulances arrived. Horses neighed. The back flap of the wagons banged open, and the cries of the men emanated from within. The drivers jumped down from their seats, shouting orders.

"Was it bad?" She regarded the soldier as fear and sadness clenched her chest.

"It was bad." His voice sounded hard. "The fighting started around a place called McPherson's Ridge early this morning. We almost had them on the run, but they got up reinforcements and pushed us back through the town. I climbed a fence and tried to hide in a butcher shop. Fighting erupted in the street in front of the house, and I knew I couldn't stay. The family helped me. They hid me in the basement for a little while. I couldn't stand hiding like a rat, though, so I slipped out the back and made my way to Cemetery Hill. I joined a regiment and got shot in the hand."

The house…his description? Excitement shot through her. "This house you speak of. Did it sit on the corner of two streets? A red brick house with a mother, father, and sister?" She bounced on her toes and clasped her hands at her chest.

He nodded. “I believe so.” He stopped and seemed to consider the question. “Yes, the house was at an intersection and quite close to Cemetery Ridge where we gathered.” He raised his uninjured hand fingers outspread. “I spoke with the mother.” He lowered his pinkie finger. “I saw a sister.” Down went the ring finger. “And a brother.” He dropped his hand to his side. “I didn’t see the father, though. Why? Do you know them?”

“That’s my family,” Relief loosened her shoulders as a grin split her face. “I’m relieved they’re well.” Without warning, the smile left her face, and her eyes widened. She tried to ignore the lurch in her heart. “Wait! Did you say the Rebs are in control of the town and you didn’t see my father?”

“Yes, they are, but not for long. We’ll drive them away. Your family is fine. Don’t worry. Your father may have been in another part of the house. I only stayed a few minutes.”

She relaxed. “I hope so.” They stared at each other, lost for something more to say. Tillie shifted her weight. “Well.” She gestured to his hand. “I won’t keep you. You need to get your hand taken care of. Thank you for talking to me.”

The sun lowered well behind the heights to the west, about an hour from meeting the horizon. In the east, treetops glowed in the last of the sunlight. The sky made the subtle shift in blue signaling imminent twilight. If the soldier spoke true, the Rebs cut her off from home. Before she entered the house, her eyes followed the Taneytown Road toward home, her family now in enemy territory.

PART 2

THE BATTLE

Chapter 14

Jacob Weikert's 240-acre farm and large stone house occupied the west side of Taneytown Road. Across a small carriage lane, his stone and wood Dutch-style barn, common to the farmers of Pennsylvania, faced the house. West of the barn, a springhouse provided cool, clear water. A well stood on the barn's north side.

Tillie entered the summer kitchen. Beckie prepared biscuits at a waist high table. Mrs. Schriver and Mrs. Weikert flew about the room preparing the evening meal. Two uniformed men stirred beef broth at the cook stove.

The women made an issue of their presence by pushing past them to reach for things they needed. They punctuated their actions with heavy sighs and exaggerated excuse mes. One of the soldiers shot an apologetic look at the matron as he stepped aside to let her in.

At the aroma of the beef broth, Tillie's stomach growled loud and long. She put a hand over her abdomen and turned away as heat infused her face.

One of the men laughed. "I heard that." He banged his wooden spoon on the rim of the pot.

She giggled as she walked over to peer in. She inhaled. "Mmm, smells delicious."

"It's for the men. They'll need some broth soon." His face grew serious.

Her smile vanished. "Oh."

"Tillie, come away from there." Mrs. Weikert waved her toward Beckie. "They're busy. Help with the biscuits."

"Yes, ma'am." She smiled at the cook. "I'm sorry I bothered you."

He winked.

As she glanced at her hostess, a pang of uncertainty hit her, fearful she'd done something wrong, but the woman resumed cutting vegetables for dinner, giving her no heed.

Mrs. Weikert tied her salt and pepper hair into a severe chignon, which pulled the skin tight around her face. She returned Tillie's look, her stern blue eyes pinning her to the wall. When dealing with the woman, one did as told.

Tillie moved to the table where Beckie mixed biscuits. She took over kneading the dough while Beckie slipped a pan into the oven, then returned to begin a new batch.

They worked for the better part of an hour while Tillie's belly growled with insistence. Everyone stared at her. Helpless, embarrassed laughter bubbled up and overflowed.

The man cooking the broth laughed with her. "Sounds like you haven't eaten in a month."

"I don't understand why my stomach insists on shaming me so. I ate dinner this afternoon."

The cook laughed again as he stirred the pot while his companion sifted salt between his fingers. "You've been outdoors all day giving water to the men, right?"

"Yes." Tillie kneaded the dough, gathering and pushing.

"Well, fresh air and sunshine go a long way to inducing an appetite. It's good to see a girl hungry."

Beckie sighed. "Are you almost finished with that? I'd like to bake them sometime tonight."

"Oh. Sorry." Tillie formed a ball and handed the dough to her.

Beckie slapped her rolling pin down and with quick, hard movements, rolled and cut the dough. She arranged the biscuits on the baking pan before shoving them into the oven and slamming the door.

Tillie and the cook exchanged glances. He gave a one-shouldered shrug and returned to his tasks. Tillie studied Beckie's face, curious about her attitude. As Beckie prepared another round of dough, her mouth set in a hard line, and her eyebrows gathered in a sharp knot above her nose. Tillie shrugged away her worry. No doubt, Beckie was as hungry and tired as she. Tillie gathered more flour and began another batch.

The third pan came out of the oven, and with effort, she restrained an urge to pop a biscuit into her mouth. She was grateful for the willpower when the friendly soldier came over and gathered them into a basket while his companion carried the pot of broth.

After both men left the house, Mrs. Weikert let out a loud huff. "Finally." She put her hands on her hips and shook her head. "I didn't think they'd ever leave." She spun to her daughters. "Hettie, get the food. Beckie, call your brother and father in to eat. Quietly. Don't announce."

Mrs. Schriver approached a large closed and locked cupboard. She opened the doors and set out huge amounts of food. Tillie never beheld so much bounty at one time. Mother always prepared enough to satisfy everyone's appetite, but never cooked more than necessary. Her mouth watered, and her hunger pangs increased.

Out came an enormous platter, piled high with fried chicken, a bowl of gravy, two huge bowls—one of potatoes, the other vegetables—biscuits and jam, pitchers of milk and coffee. On a counter next to the table, Mrs. Weikert placed an apple pie and a chocolate cake. "Let us hope we aren't interrupted while we eat." She spoke to the room at large.

Mr. Weikert and Dan came inside. "They're taking down my fences and using them for firewood," Mr. Weikert shouted as he entered. "That…officer." He slammed the door shut, as though to make "that officer" disappear. His eyes fell on Tillie and the girls, and with effort, he calmed some. "He dares to tell me it's my patriotic duty to supply what the army needs while they're here." Mr. Weikert threw water on his face and washed his hands. He grabbed a towel and mopped his face, before slapping the towel next to the washbasin. "Patriotic duty," he spat, glaring at his wife. "They're destroying my farm, Sarah!"

Tillie lowered her face, clamping her lips between her teeth. Father would never display such anger in front of the family. Wishing she could go home and trying to be inconspicuous, she found a place to sit at the bench between Sadie and Mollie.

"Come and eat, Jacob." Mrs. Weikert took her place at one end of the table. She followed her husband with her eyes as he stormed over to the head, yanked his chair out, and sat.

Tillie focused on her plate while Mr. Weikert took his seat. She dared to steal a peek at him. A muscle in his cheek jumped, and a vein stood out on his temple. Her eyes refocused on her plate.

Mrs. Weikert picked up the bowl of mashed potatoes, scooped out a large spoonful, and passed them to Dan, signaling the entire family. They reached, grabbed, and filled their plates without waiting for anyone to pass anything. If an item passed by and they wanted some, they snatched it.

"Dig in, Tillie." Mr. Weikert set the bowl of green beans down. "Lest you find yourself with nothing to eat."

Tillie grabbed the bowl of green beans and spooned some on her plate. Taking her cue from the others, she snatched what she wanted from the bowls as they flew past. Then she folded her hands in her lap and waited for the blessing.

Mr. Weikert picked up his fork, leaned over his plate, and shoveled food into his mouth.

Tillie gaped. She'd never seen a man eat so much, so fast. A nudge jostled her left arm.

"Sorry." Five-year-old Sadie struggled to pour herself a glass of milk.

Tillie lifted the pitcher from her and poured a glass for Sadie and herself. She put the pitcher down and cut into the fried chicken. She closed her eyes and sighed. The outside crackled when she bit in, and gravy threatened to run down her chin. All propriety left her, and she too shoveled food into her mouth, devoted to filling the cavernous hole in her stomach.

After supper, the women cleaned up. Here, Tillie helped with confidence. She cleared the table and swept the floor. Mrs. Schriver took the leftovers and put them back into the cupboard.

The food cupboard, Mother called hers a pantry, stood against the north wall. Five shelves high, it held everything from jams and milk to cream, eggs, and butter. Father kept meat on his lowest shelves, and they didn't lock their pantry. Cool air entered from an intake pipe at the bottom. As the temperature warmed, the air rose and exited through an outlet pipe at the top, keeping the ambient air in the cupboard at least ten degrees cooler than the rest of the house, and allowing food to stay fresher longer than if left in the open.

Mrs. Schriver closed the doors, and Mrs. Weikert removed a key from her pocket and locked it. They returned to preparing biscuits for the soldiers.

Dan and Mr. Weikert clomped outside, leaving the cellar door open. The cool evening breeze drifted in, bringing sounds of a gathering army.

With a belly full of food, Tillie felt lethargy set in, but she had work still to do. She went to the door and peered out, to get a breath of air. The kitchen heat pushed at her back, but the breeze outside cooled her face and refreshed her.

A few feet in front of her Taneytown Road bustled. Wagon after wagon rumbled by, accompanied by teamsters' whistles and shouts, and horses' neighing and whinnying.

Beyond her vision in the front yard and on the other side of the barn, came the muted roar of hundreds of men.

Beckie joined her.

The two men returned. "Ma'am, may we come back in and make more broth? We promise to stay outta the way as best we can."

Mrs. Weikert continued kneading dough. "I'm finished with the cook stove for now."

"Mama, we're going outside." Beckie grabbed her shawl and flipped it over her shoulders.

"Close the door on your way out."

The girls shut the door and walked across the yard.

Beckie scanned the barnyard from one side to the other. "Why, there must be close to two hundred men sitting around."

Tillie followed Beckie's stare. Her eyes drawn to Big and Little Roundtops looming black in the fading silver of evening as the purple sky of darkness drew its cloak around them. Hundreds of campfires gleamed yellow orange in the coming darkness. Tillie redirected her attention to the lounging men. "At least that many." She took in the army at rest. "Look at the way they've arranged themselves."

"What do you mean?"

"Well, those men," she gestured toward a group of healthy men, "don't seem hurt at all, or at least not bad." She pointed to several campfires, well away from the barn, where whole and able men lounged in the grass, propped up on elbows or sitting upon logs, talking around the campfires. "But closer to the barn door." She indicated the men. "Those men are badly hurt. I'd wager the worst ones are inside."

"Do you want to go see?" Beckie sounded almost gleeful at the prospect of human suffering. Before Tillie could refuse, Beckie grabbed her arm and pulled her toward the barn.

They passed a group of lounging soldiers, discussing the outcome of the day's battle. One man threw a log on the fire as they talked of hard fighting and of their friends killed or wounded. The fire flared, illuminating his face. "I tell you." His fingers traveled around the bandage on his forehead. "I pert near didn't make it to Cemetery Ridge. I slipped through town and almost got caught a couple of times. I managed to hide well enough to avoid capture."

"It's a sorry thing." A second soldier, his left arm in a sling, stared at the fire. The empty sleeve of his coat hung at his side, and a hole winked in the fabric, just above the elbow. "That here in our own country the enemy has control of the town. If the rest of the army don't get here soon, we'll lose the battle, and maybe even the war." With his right hand, he threw a clumsy stick on the fire. Sparks flew upward. "Yes, sir."

Tillie and Beckie stopped behind him, listening.

"The Rebs captured quite a few from my unit. They hold the town tight as a tick, they do. Be a shame if we lose this fight, but I don't see how we can win. Bobby Lee is in charge over there, and they hold the town like we did at Fredericksburg."

A third soldier, who didn't appear wounded in any way, sat across from sling-arm and sighted the girls. "Good evening, ladies." He sat up from his reclining position, speaking with fake joviality, as though they talked of nothing more mundane than the weather.

Sling-arm peered over his shoulder.

"It's true then?" Tillie approached. "Do the Rebels control the town?"

"They do, miss, but not for long." The second soldier placed another piece of wood on the flames. "General Meade'll be here tomorrow, and we'll chase them away, you wait and see."

The other soldiers murmured, nodding in assent.

"General Meade." The bandaged soldier shook his head, his voice filled with disgust. Again, he played with the wrappings on his forehead. "Gotta ask yourself how long he'll last."

Some of the men punched him and hissed at him to be quiet.

"Don't fret, ladies." The third soldier put out his hands in a calming gesture. "There ain't a soldier among the entire Army of the Potomac'll let the Rebs keep the town. We'll win this battle if it takes all week."

Tillie and Beckie sat beside the men who made room for them among a chorus of hear-hears and huzzahs.

"What happened today?" Beckie moved her skirts away from the flames. She tucked her forearms into her lap and leaned forward.

"We went out to the railroad cut north and west of town."

"Out near the college," the first soldier said.

"They know that." The second soldier elbowed him.

"Anywaaaay." The speaker glowered at his companions. "We went out to the railroad cut and we found the Rebs, so we started shootin'."

"Just like that?" Tillie's stomach churned. "Like…fish in a barrel?" She pictured hundreds of men staring up at the enemy, hands above their heads, begging for mercy, then falling to the ground as the men on top of the railroad cut ignored their pleas and shot them dead. In her mind, the Rebs all fell in clean, graceful heaps.

"Well—yes, miss." Regret shone in his eyes. He turned away.

"They fought well, and we about had 'em when they got up reinforcements. By then, our commanders were either dead or wounded and we didn't have no leadership, so things kinda fell apart afterward. Someone sent word General Reynolds was dead and General Doubleday in charge."

"When you hear General Doubleday is in charge…" The head-bandaged soldier leaned toward her.

Tillie suppressed the urge to draw back. She held her breath as his body odor reached her nose.

"You may as well pack up your little dog and pony show and go home." The man waggled his finger, adding emphasis to his words.

"Guard your tongue." A soldier with a wounded hand threw a small stone at him.

"Yeah, be careful." The third man stared from across the flames. "You'll find yourself in a court-martial. Or worse."

"What's worse than court-martial?" Tillie's gaze circled the campfire.

No one answered her. Instead, Bandage Man continued his story. "We fought our way through the town, but there are so many narrow streets and just about every yard has a high stockade type fence. Weren't easy getting through. I needed to find a way through town where I wouldn't get stuck in the crowd. I made my way out of town to Cemetery Ridge where I got hit by a sniper." His fingers fumbled with his gauze again. "Just grazed me. Lucky for me. Some of the boys who tried to pass that way didn't survive." He stopped, his eyes growing vague.

"Very true." The second soldier stood, adjusted his pants, and sat back down. "Many of our boys are Reb prisoners now."

Silence fell on the group. The logs shifted. The fire crackled and sent sparks skyward. They floated up and winked out. Above, the stars blinked on as full darkness enveloped them.

The one who warned his companion to be quiet picked up a stick, tapping the end into his palm. "The Rebels have control of the town, but not for long."

"That's right." The third soldier smiled at the girls. "We'll drive them off sure enough."

Tillie and Beckie thanked the men and rose. They continued on to the barn, from where emanated the most heart-wrenching screams and cries.

On the straw-covered floor, hundreds of men lay in pools of blood. Some poor souls, in their delirium, called for loved ones. Some wept, unable to expend any more energy, their struggle for survival almost ended. Some prayed. Others lay still, perhaps having made peace with their God, and waited for death.

Two men shoved Tillie and Beckie aside as they entered the barn. They handled a litter carrying a wounded man.

Tillie's gorge rose in her throat as she sighted mangled muscle, bone, and skin. She turned away and by sheer strength of will, resisted putting her hands over her ears to shut out his screams. Rather than dump this man in the straw, they carried him to the back of the barn. The men dropped the litter to the floor and, careless of his pain, lifted him by his legs and under his arms, and plopped him on a table constructed of sawhorses and wooden planks. The two men picked up the litter and went back outside, shoulders hunched.

Tillie caught her breath as a gray-haired, heavyset surgeon, his eyes on the wound, groped around on the blood-soaked planks until his fingers landed on an instrument like the cooking utensil her mother used to pluck food out of a boiling pot of water. Even in the gloom of the poorly lit barn, the filth on the instrument was obvious. He adjusted the implement in his hand and gave it a quick shake, shedding some of the blood still dripping off the end. He picked off a piece of clinging straw, wiping his fingers on his bloody apron.

A medic stood at the wounded man's head, another at his feet. At a nod from the surgeon, the medic at the head pressed down hard on the man's shoulders. The man at the foot of the table grabbed the soldier's good foot and put his body weight into his arms to keep the leg immobilized. The surgeon seized the wounded foot and used the instrument to probe inside the wound. The soldier shrieked and screamed for mercy.

Tillie didn't know what the doctor probed for, but within a few seconds, he threw down the instrument and picked up a bone saw.

The solder threw up his hands. "No, no!" He struggled and fought the men holding him down.

The surgeon growled something to the medic at the head of the table. The medic released the patient, picked up a cloth and a small brown bottle. He put the cloth over the bottle and tipped. He jammed the cloth over the man's nose and mouth.

The poor soldier clutched at the medic's arm and tried to pry his hands away, fighting in earnest.

Tillie's hand pressed hard over her mouth, fighting back horror. Were they trying to suffocate him? Within an instant, the patient quieted. His hands dropped to the table, and his body went limp. If he was dead, why did the medic place a stick in his mouth? He returned to his original position of holding the man's shoulders down.

Tillie removed her hand from her mouth and drew in a ragged breath. She gazed at her fingers, surprised to discover them wet with tears.

Tillie shifted. Beckie's eyes shone too. Tillie turned back to the scene playing out in front of them. She couldn't make herself turn away.

The surgeon made three quick incisions in the leg above the wound. He folded back the skin, picked up the bone saw, swiping the blade across his bloody apron. Blood dripped from his fingertips as he took a firm grasp of the instrument and placed it on the leg. With one powerful push, he moved the implement across the soldier's leg, biting deep.

The man's body arched upward from the hips, and a bloodcurdling scream escaped him.

Beckie gagged and ran back to the house with Tillie right behind her. Beckie slammed the door as though to shut out the scenes of misery outside.

Mrs. Schriver and Mrs. Weikert spun around from their preparation of bread dough. "What's wrong?" Mrs. Weikert stepped away from the table.

Beckie ran to her.

The soldier who teased Tillie earlier stood at the stove, stirring the broth. "Ho and what goes here?" He sprinkled in some salt before taking a tasting sip.

"Oh, sir." She stifled sobs, letting out words in bursts. "We went to the barn. How terrible. They cut off a man's foot. How dare they?" She drew in a gasping breath. She wiped her eyes with her hands, but her tears flowed unchecked. She buried her face in the crook of her arm. "The poor man." She wailed into her sleeve. "Isn't there another way? Why must they make things worse for them?"

"Disgusting!" Beckie crossed her arms. "I hope never to see such sights again. I'm not going back outside." As if to emphasize her point, she started preparing more bread.

"It is most unfortunate." The cook lifted the pot off the stove and set it down. His companion gathered up the finished loaves. "But many times the docs don't have a choice. If they don't amputate, the soldier might develop infection." He regarded them both, as though imparting an important lecture. "Otherwise, they'll die, a much more agonizing and painful death."

"Mike is right." The second cook, a man with a ruddy complexion, dark hair, and dark eyes adjusted the loaves in his arms. "At first glance, one would think it cruel, but in the end, if a man can survive his wound, it's better to survive minus a foot, leg, or arm. Do you understand?"

"Yes." Beckie threw flour into a bowl and proceeded to mix the dough. "That doesn't mean I must see it."

Mike turned serious green eyes, eyebrows raised, toward Tillie.

"I understand." Tillie wiped her eyes and straightened her shoulders. "Thank you for telling me."

Mrs. Schriver opened the oven door. "If you wait a minute, another two loaves will come out of the oven." She shut the door and returned to the table.

The men sat to wait for the bread, telling stories to make the girls laugh. At first, Tillie resisted the urge to go along, but the humor of life in an army camp, as told by Mike and his companion, Bill, helped her overcome her fear and horror.

"I was a chef at Delmonico's before the war." Bill glanced at the pot of soup and the bread. "Now I make soup for wounded soldiers."

Tillie didn't know what Delmonico's was, but she accepted his comment without question.

A chaplain entered the kitchen, but no one paid close attention. He pulled Mrs. Weikert aside and spoke with her before sitting at the table. Mrs. Weikert brought him a cup of coffee and a plate of food.

The chaplain ate in silence, but glanced often in their direction as Mike and Bill teased and joked. The chaplain's frown and furrowed brow indicated his lack of amusement over their banter. A twinge of guilt assailed Tillie, but she ignored it.

Mike hitched his breath. "Oh, here's one I think you'll like." He put a hand on his chest, as though to calm himself, but he couldn't. After he regained control, he began. "Here goes. Two men carried one man on a stretcher. A shell crashed nearby, and all three men took off running."

The entire room erupted in laughter except for the priest.

Tillie wrapped her arms around her midsection and laughed deep belly laughs. This time, the tears pouring down her cheeks were from mirth. She turned at a hand on her shoulder.

The chaplain stared down hard at her. “Little girl, do all you can for these poor soldiers and the Lord will reward you.”

Tillie grinned up into his face, and with a snort, she burst out laughing. His dark, bushy eyebrows came together in a stern glare. She sobered.

“I beg your pardon, sir.” Heat rose up her neck and into her face. “I didn’t mean to laugh. Beckie and I went out to look at the wounded soldiers. We couldn’t bear the sight and started crying. These men told us funny stories to make us feel better. I didn’t mean to laugh at their circumstances. Truly I didn’t.”

The chaplain’s face softened. “Well.” He smiled. “It is better for you and the men if you’re cheerful.” He chucked her under the chin and turned to Mrs. Weikert. “Thank you for the food, madam. It was delicious.”

“You’re quite welcome, pastor…?”

“Father Corby, madam.” He put his hat on as he opened the door. He smiled at Tillie one more time. “Good night all, and God bless.” He left, closing the door behind him.

The room fell silent. Mrs. Schriver removed the two loaves from the oven. The cooks collected them, along with the pot of broth. They said good night and left the basement kitchen.

Beckie, Mrs. Schriver, and Mrs. Weikert cleaned up the bread-making activities. Mrs. Weikert banked the cook stove fire.

Mr. Weikert and Dan entered the house. Using a stick, Mr. Weikert lit candles and handed one to his wife and each of his children.

Upstairs, a clock chimed out twelve times. When did it get to be midnight? Tillie didn’t try to stifle a huge yawn as she followed the family to the bedrooms on the third floor.

“Beckie, show Tillie to your room.” Mrs. Weikert stopped at a bedroom door. “Hettie, I put the girls in your room. You can join them.” She yawned. “Oh my. It’s been a day. Good night all.” Mr. Weikert disappeared inside with her.

“Good night, Mr. and Mrs. Weikert.” Tillie also yawned, drawn in by Mrs. Weikert. She followed Beckie to her bedroom.

Beckie changed into a clean white nightgown and hopped into bed. "Are you almost ready?" She spoke through a huge yawn. "I'm exhausted, and I want to go to sleep. Hurry up and get into bed so I can turn out the lamp." Beckie flopped down, turning her back on Tillie.

Tillie took a deep breath, removed her dress and arranged it on the back of a chair, and crawled into bed in her chemise. She wanted to say a quick prayer for her family and the men fighting for her town. She fell asleep the minute her head touched the pillow.

Chapter 15

The cannons roared and belched smoke. Tillie spun in crazy circles, but couldn't escape. Deadly spurts of fire and thick, dense fog surrounded her. She sensed danger in the miasma, but couldn't find the source. She tried to run, tripping over things unseen in the blanket of dense fog engulfing and blinding her.

"Is this hell?" She froze, deciding not to escape, yet feeling like a human sacrifice. A medusa head slithered out of the mist. Its mouths yawned open, uttering faint booming sounds. The multi-headed creature shifted and became a writhing, bloody sea of dismembered bodies. Again, she tried to run, but couldn't shake her paralysis. Her gaze settled on one man lying on a table, arms outstretched, begging her for help. He stared at her with terror-filled eyes. Another man appeared standing at the table. Invisible from the waist down, he wore a bloodstained apron and in his bloody hands held a bone saw. More blood dripped from the deadly instrument as he cut the man to pieces. Tillie opened her mouth to scream. A staccato crackle issued forth instead. She tried to scramble away, but everywhere she turned, bodies surrounded her. From the dense smoke, a bloody hand clamped down on her shoulder.

Tillie jerked and flew upright. A small cry escaped her lips. Her eyes swept the room. Panic seized her.

"Wake up!" Beckie shook her. "Are you all right?"

"Yes." Tillie slumped and put a shaking hand over her eyes. "Yes. I'm all right."

Beckie lay back down. "Sounded like a bad dream." She yawned.

The pressure of a hand lingered. Her fingers found the spot. "Did you grab me?"

"Did I grab you?" Her friend barked a short laugh. "Yes. You thrashed around so, like a maniac. I almost fell off the bed."

"I was in some kind of pit with cannons. I tripped over dead bodies. One of them reached out and grabbed my shoulder."

"I did." Beckie sat up again. "We should get up. I've been hearing distant cannon and gunfire for the past few minutes."

The bedroom door reverberated in the frame when someone on the other side began pounding the wood. They squealed.

"Get up, girls, and come down to the basement. They're firing again," Mr. Weikert called through the closed door. A boom of cannon, followed by the staccato of gunfire emphasized his words.

Tillie shook her head to clear the cobwebs.

"Yes, Papa, right away." Beckie threw back the covers.

Tillie took her dress off the back of the chair. She held the garment up to the window and assessed it in the light of the sun, just appearing over Culp's Hill. Dried mud encircled the hem almost to the knee. Sweat stained the armpits, and dirt streaked the bodice.

Tillie peeked as Beckie, humming a little tune, opened the armoire and pulled out a fresh, pretty, pink dress. A good three to four inches taller than Tillie and wider as well, Beckie's dresses would hang on her slight frame, but she longed to wear something clean.

A rueful smile twisted Tillie's lips as she smoothed her filthy clothes. What would Mrs. Eyster say about her dress and deportment now? She opened her mouth to ask Beckie, but didn't get the chance.

"Hurry up, dear." Beckie moved to the bedroom door. "Papa doesn't hold meals for laggards."

"I'll be along in a moment."

Tillie washed her face and hands in the basin before examining her reflection in the mirror. She hadn't brushed her hair in two days. She thought to take down her braid and repair the damage, but Beckie's words echoed in her ear. Laggards. Tillie resented the implication. She worked as hard yesterday as everyone else did. She eyed the brush, but dared not use it without permission. Instead, she smoothed her hair as best as possible, tucking stray strands behind her ears. As she took a deep breath, her shoulders raised with her inhale and dropped with her exhale. She pursed her lips and went downstairs to help in the kitchen.

"Where are Dan and Mr. Weikert?" Tillie sat at the table as Mrs. Schriver placed a bowl of porridge and coffee in front of her.

"Trying to get some farm work done despite all these soldiers lounging about." Mrs. Weikert sipped some coffee.

Dan ran into the kitchen. "Pa says come outside, quick. More soldiers are coming. Thousands of them. They say they've been marching all night, from as far as Washington." The women dropped their spoons and cups and hurried to the front porch.

Union troops filed up Taneytown Road toward Cemetery Ridge, heads drooping with fatigue. They marched through the silver light of another hot, muggy morning. The rising sun separated from the horizon, glaring blood red. Red sun in morning, soldier take warning. The thought popped into Tillie's head with such force, she peeked around, wondering if someone spoke aloud.

Mr. Weikert joined them on the front porch. He put his arm around his wife's shoulders.

"Lord help us." Mrs. Weikert shook her head. "So many soldiers." Her arms tightened around her husband's waist. After several minutes, she broke away from her husband's embrace. "Well, I have work to do." She didn't take her eyes off the blue-clad men flowing past the house in a never-ending stream. "Standing here staring won't get it done." She headed inside.

Mr. Weikert tapped Dan on the shoulder. "Ma's right. We need to get to work repairing the pigsty."

"But, Pa." Dan raised his hands and shoulders in a helpless gesture. "How can we? They took all the fencing for their cook fires last night and now the pigs are gone." Nevertheless, he tromped after his father off the porch.

Whatever Mr. Weikert answered, his words were lost to distance and the steady tramp of soldiers in front of the house.

Tillie contemplated the burned-out wheat field across the road. She didn't want to be here, an unwilling witness to Mr. Weikert's troubles. Strangers should not view such a private matter.

She found chores to do in the kitchen and waited for an opportunity to ask about going home. She couldn't blurt out, "Mrs. Schriver, I want to go home," but she came close several times. As the morning wore on and she failed to broach the subject, she resigned herself to stay longer.

When she completed her small tasks, Tillie found work that didn't involve associating with Beckie. She didn't understand Beckie's resentment and didn't care either. Whatever the cause, avoiding her seemed wise.

"Sadie, for goodness sake, stay out of my way. I'm busy." Mrs. Schriver scolded as the youngster tried to climb under the table where her mother worked. Sadie grabbed at her mother's skirts. Mrs. Schriver yanked them out of the child's grasp. "Sadie, stop it, now."

That gave Tillie an idea. "Sadie and Mollie, do you want to come with me and give the boys water?"

"Yeah." The girls climbed from underneath the table and ran to Tillie, jumping up and down in front of her.

"Wonderful idea, Tillie. Thank you." Mrs. Schriver's face softened.

"You're welcome." Tillie grabbed the cup from the shelf and took the girls to the road. She ran and filled the bucket and lugged it back. When she returned, Mrs. Weikert offered each of the girls a cup. "There are a lot of men, and one cup won't do." She headed back to the house.

Sadie and Mollie dipped their cups in the bucket and held them up. Tillie did the same.

Today, the men were all business. They nodded their thanks and drank, too tired to speak.

"You look exhausted." Tillie offered them refilled cups. "Where did you come from?"

"Baltimore." He drank again. "We've been marching since midnight."

"Baltimore! But that's so far away." She dipped the cup back into the bucket and offered him more water, but he declined and stepped back into line.

The endless stream of men in blue trudged by without even glancing around. Regiment after regiment passed as the girls dipped their cups and held them out, dipped their cups and held them out. Mollie threw her cup into the bucket. "This isn't much fun. I'm going back inside."

Sadie took her cue from her older sister. She threw her cup down as well. "Me too." The girls clasped hands and walked back to the house. Tillie sighed and let them go. She picked up the bucket and strode to the spring.

* * * *

The final regiment passed. The cup dangled from Tillie's fingers as she gazed toward town. How did her family fare? Did the Rebs harm them somehow? Would they leave her orphaned? She wanted to gather her skirts about her knees and run for home. She'd never get through the soldiers. Please, God. Keep them safe. Please. The Weikerts were fine people, but she couldn't shake the feeling they didn't want her here, which left her uncomfortable and fearful of doing or saying the wrong thing.

A shrill whistle and good-natured shouting brought her back to reality. She turned as another stream of soldiers came toward her.

"Hey, missy, how about some water?"

"That's right." Another cajoled, taking off his kepi and using the crook of his arm to wipe the sweat from his brow. "What's a man got to do to get a drink around here?"

"Oh." Tillie dipped her cup. "Please forgive me."

The soldier closest to her drank. Others shouted at him not to hog all the water and to pass the cup right quick.

Tillie picked up the other two cups, filled them, and handed them over.

The first soldier drank and passed the cup to the man next to him. He winked at Tillie. "Sweetest tasting water I ever drank."

Heat crept up her neck and into her face. Handsome young men didn't tease her; they flirted with Maggie. She didn't know how to respond, so kept quiet, her eyes fixed on the pail. He dropped the cup in the water and left.

When the bucket emptied, she excused herself and sprinted back to the spring to get more water, but the spring ran dry. She ran to the well and hauled fresh water. After filling her bucket, she returned, but the first group of men were gone.

A train of twenty wagons, coming from town, turned into the barnyard and stopped. The drivers jumped down and hustled to the back to untie their loads. Orderlies emerged from the barn to unload empty pine boxes. They piled them near the fence and against the side of the barn. As one wagon emptied its load, another arrived and unloaded its supply of coffins.

"Well, boys, they're here," a ginger-haired solder called to his companions. "No telling how long before I get put in one of those."

"I'd consider myself lucky if I even get one," another joked to the laughter his companions. His dirt-streaked face made the whites of his eyes stand out. He leaned over and spat brown spittle onto the road.

"You're just a private. You don't deserve one." The soldier behind him, also filthy, and marching with one boot sole flapping loose, joined in to uproarious laughter.

Tillie found nothing funny in their remarks, but she kept her opinion to herself and offered water. Some men thanked her. Most did not. They threw the cups in her direction when through.

When the wagons departed, they left six hundred coffins stacked by the barn door. Did they think they would need so many?

The men gave her little time to think about the coffins as they asked for water. Tillie made another run to the well, wishing for a second bucket. When she came back, a soldier lay in the road, worn out from his march. Two of his friends tried to drag him to his feet. He got to his hands and knees, but no further. His shoulders collapsed. He hung his head like a beaten dog. His companions took him by the elbow to lift him to his feet, but he resisted.

"C'mon, buddy." One of his friends leaned down and grasped his elbow again. "Get up before the major finds you."

"He's coming now." The second companion glanced past the boy to a man riding a lathered horse toward them. "You need to get up."

"I can't," the boy wailed.

Tillie filled a cup and started toward him. The major rode up and reined his horse in front of her.

She stopped short. Water sloshed down her arm. Tillie glowered up at him, but he didn't acknowledge her. She stepped around the back of the horse.

The two soldiers straightened and saluted.

The major ignored them. He glared at the boy from his horse. "Get up, soldier."

The boy dropped to a prone position on the ground and rolled onto his back. He stared up at the officer with a blank face.

"I said get up, blast you!" The major snarled at the boy as he dismounted. He removed his sword from its scabbard and in two quick strides stood over him.

He wouldn't stab the boy, would he? The cup dropped from her hand as she clasped her throat, as though to strangle any sound.

Using the flat part of the blade, the officer struck the boy's prostrate body.

"I said get up." The sword winked in the sunlight as he swung the blade down again, slapping the poor boy on his arms, which he threw over his head, to protect himself.

"On your feet, lazy scum!" The officer brought the flat of the sword down again.

Tillie flinched from the thwack against the boy's torso.

The major hit him again. The blade whistled through the air and thwacked against the boy. Whistle, thwack. Whistle, thwack.

She lost count at a dozen. The boy's whimpers too much to bear. "Stop hitting him, and maybe he'll get up!" The strangled cry coming from her lips shocked her. She drew in a ragged breath, but held her ground and glared at the major. Didn't he realize the boy couldn't go on? No one could rise under such an assault.

The major turned and, for the first time, appeared aware of her presence. His breath came in short, hard puffs. His cold blue eyes traveled up and down her frame, and his nostrils flared. He turned back to the boy and gave him one more blow before sheathing his sword. "Laziness." He spat on the ground beside the prostrate soldier, before mounting his horse and riding away.

Tillie stared after him, mouth agape and eyes wide. She shook from fright and anger.

Several men fell out. One of the boy's companions hefted him into his arms.

"Take him to the house." Tillie lifted wide eyes to them, her voice barely above a whisper.

The soldier nodded once and headed to the house. The second placed a gentle hand on her shoulder and smiled into her horrified expression. "Don't fret." He squeezed her arm. "We'll mark that officer for this." He followed his companion to the house.

Mute with emotions she couldn't name, she watched him walk away. With halting movements, she bent and picked up the cup, running her fingers over the rim and brushing away the dirt. She wanted to cry for the boy and scream in rage at the officer. Instead, she sniffed back tears.

A hand reached out and took the cup. She raised her tear-streaked face to a man who dipped the cup into the bucket and savored a long, slow drink.

"What did he mean by marking him out?" She lowered her gaze, unable to look him in the eye.

The soldier drank some more and dropped the cup in the bucket. He wiped his mouth with the back of his hand. "Best you don't ask." He put his fingers to the brim of his cap and walked on.

Her mouth hung agape. She could not accept that men from the same army would kill each other for slights, real or imagined. Weren't they all on the same side? How many men killed each other in this way?

She trudged back to the well, confused and frightened. As she drew more water, the two men left the house and rejoined their comrades. She prayed they wouldn't find the officer.

Tillie carried the bucket back to the side of the road.

Three men on horseback rode up and stopped in front of her. A man with a round face and blue eyes, heavy with rings of fatigue, gazed down at her. A graying beard covered the lower half of his face. He removed his hat, revealing his balding head. Despite the dusty road, his immaculate uniform showed no sign he'd spent the night riding to Gettysburg.

"Miss, may I have a drink of water?" He extended his hand.

"Of course." She offered a brimming cup. "Please forgive my tin cup. It's a bit dirty."

"Certainly, that's all right."

The general drank. "Thank you kindly."

Tillie took the cup. She wanted to ask about the major, but didn't dare. "Would you like some more?"

"No, thank you."

Tillie asked the other two men if they wanted any water. They declined.

"Well, gentleman." The general shifted in his saddle. "We must be going." He nodded his thanks to Tillie, turned his horse, and headed toward Cemetery Ridge. The men marching up the road cheered.

Someone shouted, "Three cheers for General Meade." The men huzzahed and lifted their caps, waving them above their heads.

Turning back to the men, he saluted them before riding toward town, his two aides-de-camp right behind him.

"Excuse me." Tillie reached out a hand to gain the attention of a passing soldier. "Who did you say that man is?"

"General Meade."

* * * *

An hour passed while Tillie continued her water ministry. When the sun bore down overhead, she calculated the time near noon. Hot and thirsty, she ignored her needs in favor of the never-ending stream of blue marching to battle.

One of General Meade's aides rode back. He pulled his horse up short and removed his hat. Working by rote, she held the cup up to him when he stopped in front of her.

"No, thank you." He put his hand up, palm out. "The general wishes me to inform you that you need to get under cover now, miss. He thanks you kindly for your ministration of water, but he fears the situation is becoming dangerous." He rode away.

All around her the steady tramp, tramp of marching feet, the clanking of bullet pouches and eating utensils bouncing against men's bodies, mixed with the dust of the road from the dried mud, hanging at knee level. In the distance, men shouted and horses neighed. The low rumble of distant guns carried on the breeze. The sun shone from a clear, blue summer sky. She didn't sense imminent danger, but dropped the cups into the bucket and returned them to the barn. She hung the pail and proceeded across the farmyard. As she walked, the hair on her neck rose, and despite the heat, her skin goose pimpled. Remnants of her dream slipped through her consciousness. A feeling someone watched her make her way across the farmyard crept over her. She placed one foot in front of the other and steeled herself not to run.

Tillie entered the kitchen. "You'll never guess what happened to me just now."

Beckie stood at a waist high baking table, mixing dough, her hands squeezing and pushing. Flour streaked her nose and cheeks, and bread dough splotched her apron. "What happened to you?"

"Well," Tillie waved a hand toward the road, "three officers stopped at the gate, and one of them asked for a drink of water. General Meade!"

"How do you know? You've met the man before?"

Tillie stared at her. What had she done to deserve such a nasty response?

"Beckie." Mrs. Schriver's brows drew together. "What's the matter with you?"

Beckie shrugged and continued to knead the dough.

Tillie's gaze went from Beckie to Mrs. Schriver and back again. "Nooo." Her shoulders drooped. "The soldiers told me." None of the women reacted. She studied each woman in the room. "Should I be working in here?"

"There's no room for you, child." Mrs. Weikert slapped some dough into a loaf pan to bake. "Hettie and Beckie know what needs doing and what we keep where. You're better off doing what you're doing."

"General Meade told me to come inside. Is there another task I can do?"

They turned at a loud knock on the door. Three officers removed their hats when the women acknowledged them.

"Are you the lady of the house?" The leader entered the kitchen, stopping in front of Tillie.

She giggled.

"I am." Mrs. Weikert wiped her hands on her apron and stepped from behind the table. "What can I do for you?"

He turned to her and addressed her with a short bow. "If you please, ma'am." He gestured toward the staircase. "We'd like permission to go up to your roof and take a look around."

"Of course." Mrs. Weikert gestured to Tillie. "Take them upstairs and show them where the trap door is."

"Yes, ma'am."

They thanked Mrs. Weikert, and then followed Tillie to the highest level of the house.

On the third floor, she stopped below the trap door. She found the pole with which to grab the handle in Mr. and Mrs. Weikert's bedroom. When the door came down, a ladder slid from its mooring. The men scrambled to the roof, pulled out their field glasses, and turned in every direction.

Tillie stood at the base of the steps. One of them beckoned. "Would you like to join us?"

"Oh, may I?"

"Come on up."

She climbed the ladder, and when she grabbed their proffered hands, they lifted her to the roof. She held tight to their hands until she steadied herself enough to let go. Even so, her stomach lurched at the dizzying height.

"Don't look down." They laughed.

The soldier on her left handed her his field glasses. "Tell me what you see."

She accepted the glasses and put them to her eyes. "How astonishing!" She lowered the glasses and gazed at the field. She raised them again, took them away, and held them to her eyes again, marveling at the change in perspective. "It's as if I can almost reach out and touch things that are, in reality, so far away." She put her hand out as if expecting to touch the man galloping across a field more than a half mile away.

While the men chuckled over her wonderment, Tillie played with the glasses for a long time, fascinated. She trained the glasses on one group of men out near Mr. Codori's wheat field, adjacent to Mr. Weikert's property. Uniformed men filled the country for miles around. Horses and men hauled artillery pieces from one place to another as infantry support formed into a line. Men on horseback rode back and forth gesturing. "What are they doing?" She focused the glasses toward where men in blue formed up and adjusted their weapons.

"Well, they are forming up, preparing for battle." One of the observers held his glasses to his eyes and turned in the direction Tillie pointed.

Her smile disappeared, and she removed the glasses from her eyes. "Where are the Rebs?" She raised them again.

"That's what we came up here to ascertain." The officer stood next to her, his glasses trained on the trees, across Emmitsburg Road, on a low ridge to the west. "Can you detect movement behind those trees?" He faced her in the direction of the stand of trees on a low ridge about a mile away.

"That's Mr. Pitzer's property," she told them, as if imparting important information. "Mr. Pitzer won't like rebel soldiers in his woods."

"We don't either," they teased.

Heat crept up her neck and face. Chastising herself for saying something stupid, she focused the glasses in another direction. "And what are those men doing in Mr. Sherfy's peach orchard? Why are they out so far in front of the others?" She pointed northwest where Mr. Sherfy's property also bounded Mr. Weikert's beside the Emmitsburg Road. A solid, straight formation of Union soldiers had advanced from the wheat field and moved into the orchard, leaving a yawning gap on either side.

The two other men jumped at her question and turned toward the area she indicated. She handed her glasses back to the soldier who loaned them to her and stepped aside.

He put the glasses to his eyes and appraised the situation before sliding them in a special pouch at his hip.

"General Meade needs to hear about this," the leader muttered, his glasses glued to his eyes, as though unable to believe what he saw. He muttered under his breath. He returned his glasses to his pouch. A dark look passed between them.

Behind him, one man started down the steps. Halfway down he reached up for Tillie's hand and helped her down. The other two men waited at the top for her to get to the hallway. Tillie turned as the second man descended the ladder. Before descending himself, the third raised his glasses one more time and cast a last long stare toward the peach orchard. He swore.

Her cheeks burned, and she cast her gaze to the floor. She never meant to get those men into trouble.

Once they reached the kitchen, the men left without a word.

Mrs. Weikert handed Tillie a plate of bread and told her to take Sadie and Mollie outside and serve the bread to the wounded soldiers. Tillie wanted to remind Mrs. Weikert that General Meade told her to stay indoors, but she didn't dare. She accepted the plate with great reluctance and went outside.

Mollie walked over and held out a plate loaded with sliced bread and jam.

A soldier took a bite and drew in a deep breath. "Sweetest tasting bread I ever ate."

"Manna from Heaven." His companion took a bite and chewed, closing his eyes in mock ecstasy.

"It's Northern bread." Mollie's serious blue eyes met his. "That's why it tastes so good."

The men laughed and thanked her for the treat.

Tillie stared in the direction of the peach orchard, but a rise in the land blocked her view.

A sharp pop reverberated through the farmyard. Men scattered. Tillie glanced around, confused. Another pop. The man, who moments before thanked Mollie for the bread, fell dead, blood pouring from his temple, the half-eaten bread still in his fingers. Another pop, and a man standing by the barn dropped to the ground.

"Rebel sharpshooters!"

She heard a shout and spun first this way, then another, looking for the danger.

Someone seized her and almost threw her at the house. "Get inside and stay away from the windows. They're somewhere on that big mountain."

Tillie needed no further urging. She dropped the plate, grabbed Sadie and Mollie, and dragged them into the house.

The girls screamed and cried. Mrs. Schriver took them into her arms, comforting them as she scooted them under the worktable.

Tillie cowered in a corner of the kitchen, biting her knuckles as sobs racked her body.

As quick as the shooting started, the Rebs ceased their fire.

After some time, she managed to gain control of her terror. She swallowed her sobs, wiped her face, and crawled out of her corner.

Outside, everything fell quiet. She chanced a peek out the window. Her stomach clenched over the men felled by sharpshooters. Only the flies went near them.

As if tolling their doom, the afternoon breeze carried three faint bongs from the courthouse clock.

"Well." Mrs. Schriver settled the girls under the worktable and got back to bread making. "If that's the worst to happen today, let us all count our blessings." As soon as the words left her mouth, their world exploded.

Chapter 16

Tillie cowered back in her corner, squeezed into a tight ball, her head tucked into her knees, arms over her head. She wanted to marry, have children, but instead, someone would find her body among the broken bricks and plaster.

A shell exploded so close, the house gave a violent shudder. She pressed the side of her body against the wall and cringed. Upstairs, something crashed to the floor.

Mr. Weikert and his son flew into the basement as another missile whistled through the air. "They mean business now." Dan both laughed and shouted, terror and exhilaration fighting for control of his voice as he slammed the door behind him.

The windows rattled from the percussion of hundreds of cannon firing simultaneously.

Outside, artillery shells rained down with unrelenting ferocity. Another shell crashed so close, the wall at her back swayed from the impact. Pots, pans, and dishes smashed on the floor. She didn't want to die huddled in a corner of the Weikerts' basement kitchen. I want to go home. I want to go home. Tillie rocked back and forth to the rhythm of the words, too terrified to scream.

Mr. Weikert and Dan paced near the stairs. Another crash upstairs sent Dan's father running upstairs. He halted halfway up, seemed to change his mind, turned around, and came back down.

Mrs. Schriver crawled beneath the table with the girls, holding them and using her body and the table as a shield from falling objects.

Beckie ran to her father and cowered in his arms. She cried on his shoulder, her hands flat to her ears. He cradled her, one hand over her head in a protective gesture.

Mrs. Weikert continued kneading bread as if nothing happened. As she worked, tears coursed down her lined face.

After what felt like hours, the cannonading stopped. Tillie lifted her head and listened, her face awash with tears.

"Is it over?" Sadie peeked out from her mother's arms.

Everyone began to stir. "I think so." Mrs. Schriver climbed out from underneath the table and pushed to her feet.

Tillie rose and gazed about, dazed and confused. Her only thought of the bread she put in the oven seconds before the cannonading started. She lurched across the room on rubber legs. Her hand shook as she opened the door. The loaf continued to bake and brown as though nothing happened. She estimated another ten minutes and shut the stove door. "The bread should be ready—"

The kitchen door flew open and crashed against the wall. The women jumped and screamed. A lieutenant burst into the house. "Get out, all of you!" He made frantic gestures with his arms. "You must leave at once. Enemy artillery has moved into the peach orchard. We expect the shelling to start over at any minute. The shells will land on this house."

Mr. Weikert pushed Beckie off to her brother, who put his arm around her shoulder.

"No." He advanced a step toward the lieutenant. "We will not leave here."

"Sir, you must." The officer also stepped forward. "If only for the sake of those poor little girls." He gestured toward Mollie and Sadie still clinging to each other underneath the table.

Mr. Weikert turned to face his granddaughters. The hard lines on his face smoothed out. His piercing blue eyes softened, and he appeared to waver.

Tillie stared at the lieutenant, jaw agape. Did he mean for them to go out there? Did he want them to die? A smug smile tugged at the corners of his mouth, but he pressed his lips together until his features smoothed out. He again waved his arms in frantic haste. "Sir, this is not a request." He took another step forward when Mr. Weikert still made no move.

The farmer reddened, and the muscle in his cheek twitched. The vein rose in his forehead. "I've had it with your orders." His words hissed through gritted teeth. "You people demand the use of my barn and yard. Your wagons and artillery chewed up my land and destroyed my crops. You tore down all my fences, despite my best efforts to stop you. My pigs escaped. My cow is gone. My spring and well are dry. Your doctors want my house for a hospital, which I absolutely forbid. Now you tell me we must leave?" He pounded his fist on the table.

Tillie jumped. Mollie started to cry.

"No!" Mr. Weikert's shout reverberated through the basement.

The men glared at each other in a standoff.

The lieutenant spoke first. He lowered his voice and used a calm, authoritative tone, as if giving orders to his command. "This is not a request. You are hereby ordered to depart this house—now." He started for the door. As if to emphasize his words, a shell crashed behind the barn. Planks disintegrated as hay and body parts flew through the air.

Mr. Weikert blanched. He collected his family and herded them upstairs to the main level, and out the front door.

"Papa." Mrs. Schriver cried over the noise of the exploding shells, the crackle of gunfire, and men shouting and screaming. Her father didn't respond. She tapped him on the shoulder. He leaned in, and she said something Tillie didn't hear.

He nodded, and taking his wife by the hand, shouted something.

Tillie thought his mouth formed the words follow me.

He sprinted east across his fields. The rest followed as shells crashed and exploded around the house and barn, as if to chase them away.

They ran about a quarter of a mile when Mrs. Weikert stopped short. Her hand slipped from Mr. Weikert's as his forward momentum carried him on.

He turned back, a horrified, frightened expression contorting his face. Horror changed to stunned disbelief.

She stood stock-still. Everyone came to a halt. The crashing roar of battle subsided with the distance, easing their need to shout.

"What's the matter?" Mr. Weikert shouted anyway.

"Jacob, you need to go back. You must. I can't leave it."

"Go back? Are you mad? Go back for what?"

"My quilted petticoat!" Tears coursed down her face. "It's brand new. For winter. I haven't even worn it yet. You must go back before they tear it into bandages."

Mr. Weikert's breath came in short, hard gasps. He stared at his wife as the twitch began in his cheek muscle again.

Tillie gaped at Mrs. Weikert. How could she muster the nerve to send him back into danger for an article of clothing? Yet she stood in a field of wheat, demanding he do so. Would Mother require this of Father? Mother had sense enough to realize one could replace a petticoat, didn't she?

Mr. Weikert took a deep breath and exhaled. "Keep going and get to the Bushmans'." He pushed them in the direction of the Bushman farm. "I'll meet you there as soon as I can." He took off running back toward home.

A bullet to the head couldn't shock Tillie more.

As he ran back, a half-smile of triumph twisted Mrs. Weikert's lips.

What a terrible thing to do, you horrible woman. She turned away and started toward the Bushmans'.

Cutting across fields of ripening, undamaged wheat, they came upon a corps of Union soldiers in formation. The men relaxed in the summer sun as the battle raged three-quarters of a mile in their front. They did not impede the family as they moved between. Many opened a corridor for the women and Dan to run through, which they did, amid calls of "Hurry up," and "What the devil are you doing out here?" The rest ignored them.

As Tillie ran, a flash of light caught the corner of her eye. Toward town unusual lights glinted back and forth like fire in the sky arcing over the rooftops. She stopped and pointed. "What is that?"

"Oh, that." A soldier grinned at her, a glint of mischief in his eyes. "Why, that's the rebels burning the town to the ground with all the people."

Tillie screamed, pummeling his chest with her small fists while his companions laughed and cheered her on.

The man stepped back and grasped her wrists, keeping her at arm's length. "Whoa there, little lady. I was kidding." He held her tight with one hand while laughing. He dusted at his coat front as though she'd left fist prints.

"That was a stupid, terrible joke," she shrieked. Crying, she wriggled free a wrist and took another swing at him. She missed. "And you're a stupid, terrible man!"

The soldiers laughed.

"Shame on you." Beckie glared at them as she grabbed Tillie by the elbows and took off running, dragging her along.

Tillie cried the whole way, convinced the battle made her an orphan. She still sobbed when they reached the Bushmans' farm.

"For heaven's sake, your family is safe, stop being such a ninny," Beckie barked.

Tillie yanked her arm out of Beckie's grasp. "That's easy for you to say. You know what's happening with your family. I don't, so don't call me a ninny." Tillie's hands curled into fists. She clenched her teeth, her body stiff with fury, yet resisting the urge to hit Beckie.

She almost felt Maggie's hands, holding her back.

Mrs. Weikert knocked on the farmhouse door, lower lip quivering.

A Union sergeant answered. "Yes. What do you want?"

Mrs. Weikert's eyes bulged with fear, and her mouth worked in spasms. She shook her head and licked her lips. "They told us to come here." Her words came in short gasps as she tried to catch her breath. She wiped her upper lip with the back of her hand then gestured over her shoulder. "We live about a mile away. They told us to leave and come here."

"Who ordered you to come here?"

"The soldiers at our farm. They said to come here."

"I don't know why they told you that. Go back to where you came from, lady."

The soldier made to close the door. Mrs. Schriver put out her hand. The wood smacked against her palm. "Where are Mr. and Mrs. Bushman?"

"Who?"

"The people who live here. The Bushmans. Where are they?"

"I don't know, lady." The man adopted a bored tone, again, tried to shut the door.

Fingers curled around the edge of the door, which opened wider to reveal an officer. He stared at the sergeant until the man shrugged and walked away. He faced Tillie and the others. "Can I assist you?"

"Where is the family who lives on this farm?" Mrs. Schriver pointed back the way they came. "We live a mile across that field. The soldiers told us to leave and come here." She talked fast, using the same demanding tone as when they wanted to cross the cemetery.

"Now he says," she indicated the one who answered the door, "to go back the way we came. Why should we? Why can't we stay here?"

The soldier considered her questions. Regret shone in his eyes. He crossed his arms, almost in a defensive gesture. When his eyes fell on Tillie and her tear-streaked face, he stepped outside and closed the door. "Oh, my sweet, why the tears?"

Wiping her face, she told him what the soldiers said about the strange fires in the sky. She couldn't help letting out a sob of anguish. "My family lives there. What shall I do if the Rebs burn my house down?"

"I'm sorry they told you that." He put a gentle hand on her shoulder. "Those are signal flares, and they're ours. Besides, we have rules of war, the Rebs and us, and the first rule is to leave the civilians alone as much as we can."

Tillie stared at him. Did he speak true? "Thank you." She wiped her nose on her sleeve.

"You're quite welcome." He straightened and got back to business as his expression grew grim. He faced Mrs. Weikert. "However, madam, I am sorry. Sergeant Harris is right. You can't stay here."

"Why not?" She sounded as though she might dissolve into tears herself. "Don't you realize we've run a mile to get here because they told us to leave our house? Where are we to go?"

The officer pursed his lips. "You have to go back."

"I'm not going back." Beckie stamped her foot. "I refuse."

"Well, you must, and you must go now. We've received reports the Reb artillery has advanced out of some peach orchard and into a wheat field. Why even now, the First Minnesota is in a desperate situation trying to hold the Rebs. The fighting is close enough to your farm so the shells will miss you and land here."

An artillery shell whistled overhead and landed in the nearby field, exploding a tree on impact. The soldier flinched. The family acted as though nothing happened.

"We must go back?" Mrs. Weikert sounded almost petulant.

"I'm quite sorry. Yes." He reached behind him for the doorknob. "You must."

She sighed. "Very well." Her eyes flashed pure fury and hatred. Without a word, she gathered her skirts and ran as fast as her corseted, portly body would allow, back the way they came.

"Thank you ever so much." Mrs. Schriver sneered, grabbed her daughter's hands, and followed her mother with Beckie and Dan right behind her.

Tillie lingered. "Thank you for explaining about the signal flares."

"You're quite welcome, miss, and safe journey back."

Chapter 17

Back at the Weikerts', Tillie picked her way through the yard where hundreds more men, now clad in gray or butternut, lay scattered around on the ground.

Inside, Beckie's strident complaints carried, bemoaning a house full of wounded Yankees bleeding on the floors and carpets.

Judging from the argument, their flight had been nothing more than a ploy to get the family out, so they could turn the house into a hospital.

"I'm telling my father!" Beckie stormed out the kitchen door and stomped across the yard, looking for Mr. Weikert.

A soldier stood in the doorway, dressed in dark-blue army pants and a white shirt, sleeves rolled up to his elbows. He stared after her as she stomped off. He shook his head and went back inside. The wounded were in the house to stay. End of discussion. Even so, the barn and yard still overflowed with soldiers, awaiting some sort of care.

Tillie noted the color of the uniforms.

"You see right." An orderly stopped next to her.

She turned a questioning gaze to him.

"After you all left, we moved our boys into the house and put the Rebs in the barn. As many as would fit, that is."

Tillie tossed her head. "How kind of you."

He chuckled. "Not really." He missed her sarcasm. "But docs have their hypocritical oath. They said the heat and lack of shade killed more men than their actual wounds."

She smiled. "Don't you mean their Hippocratic oath?"

The orderly regarded her. "No. I meant hypocritical." He walked away.

Tillie lifted her skirts and picked her way across the yard, careful not to step on the men as she headed toward the basement door.

Mr. Weikert emerged on the front porch. Seeing their return, he stormed down the front porch steps and shoved the garment at his wife. "Don't you ever do that to me again." Fury rattled his voice. "I'm so pleased to know your petticoat means more to you than my safety! May you have many contented years wearing the blasted thing after I'm long dead."

"It didn't matter." She managed to sound both repentant and petulant. "They sent us away. They made us come back."

They stood nose to nose, his face the color of beets. The muscle in his jaw worked up and down.

Mrs. Weikert refused to meet her husband's eye. Instead, she folded the petticoat and laid it over her arm. Her fingers stroked the fabric, and she kept her eyes cast down.

Their children exchanged dark glances and went inside.

Tillie's face burned as she took particular care to study the men lying on the ground. She tiptoed around the Weikerts and followed Mrs. Schriver into the house, trying to recall a time when her parents argued in front of their children. Her memory failed her. Even the incident with the valise didn't qualify as an argument, just Mother expressing fear for Father's safety. Perhaps they never did. The conversation with her mother about picking vegetables came to her mind, and Tillie smiled. That must be how they did things.

She stepped into the basement and breathed in the yeasty aroma of bread baking. "Oh, no." She hurried over, expecting to find blackened loaves. Instead, when she flung open the oven door, a fresh loaf browned inside.

"We couldn't resist." Several men laughed at her delight. "We took the bread out before it burned and put a new one in. I must confess we enjoyed ourselves capitally." Appreciative laughter from the wounded surrounded her, and Tillie joined in.

Beckie, her mother, and sister entered the kitchen. Mrs. Weikert gave orders to her daughters, and they returned to work, picking up where they left off. She thrust the quilted petticoat into Tillie's hands. "Take this up to my room and put it away." She didn't say please.

Tillie did as ordered, and when she returned, the new loaf came out of the oven. The three women had the baking well in hand, so she sliced the bread and served. As she did so, she mopped an occasional sweaty brow or readjusted a bandage.

A group of soldiers entered carrying stacks of lumber, which they took to the back corner where Tillie hid during the artillery barrage. Mr. Weikert and Dan joined them, nodding, receiving instructions. Mr. Weikert went to another part of the basement, retrieved a toolbox, and returned. They set to work.

"So, Jacob, what took you so long today?"

He glanced at his wife. His expression betrayed annoyance.

Tillie marveled Mrs. Weikert had the nerve to bring it up.

"Well," he spoke to the wood rather than her. "After you scared the living daylights out of me, I came back to get your precious petticoat. It took me some time to find it. I started for the door." He cut a length of board. The sawed piece clunked on the floor. "As I reached the front door, I heard thumps and bangs and the strangest yelps coming from the stairway."

Mr. Weikert chuckled. "Imagine my surprise." He drew a lathe across the wood. The shaving curled off. "When the boy you bandaged up yesterday, Sarah, you remember the one who got blown up when Hettie and the girls arrived?"

She nodded.

Tillie frowned. With all that happened in the last day, she'd forgotten the poor man.

"Well…" Mr. Weikert ran his plane down the wood, curling off another shaving. He blew on the board. "He came tumbling head over heels down the stairs, frightened as a jackrabbit and blind as a bat with those bandages on his eyes, crying for mercy, certain the cannonballs would get him." Mr. Weikert laughed. "I'm sorry. It's not funny, but it is funny. I mean, now it's over I find the situation humorous." He choked back more laughter. "A soldier and I carried him back upstairs and into bed. He told me he would stay with him, and I presume he's still there. Someone should go check." Mr. Weikert worked on the coffin. He glanced up at the ceiling as if able to see both men through the levels of the house. He shook his head and laughed again as he worked on his rough wooden boxes. No one joined in.

Chapter 18

The afternoon wore on, and the heat intensified. Orderlies and nurses came and went through the basement kitchen. The door remained open to allow for better traffic flow.

With so many people crowded into the limited space, the walls closed in. Tillie broke out in a sudden sweat. She slipped out the door and walked across the barnyard half expecting a sharpshooter's bullet to find her.

The sun hung low behind Big Roundtop, coloring the sky a lurid orange. She stopped and listened to the crackle of gunfire, screams, and war whoops occurring unseen on the other side of Little Roundtop. So much violence and hatred. Why was there so much hate in the world? Why couldn't people learn to get along? She gave a sad shake of her head.

Ahead of her, two doctors stood inside the door talking and gesturing around the yard. She headed toward them to offer help.

"The temperature reached ninety-eight degrees today. If the fighting doesn't kill these men, the heat will." The first doctor swung his arm out, indicating the men in the exposed barnyard.

Hundreds lay in the dirt in the open. No trees, no shade, except those cast by the house and barn. All around her, men groaned and cried out.

Tillie stood aside and waited for them to finish their conversation.

The second doctor wiped his face with his sleeve and shrugged. "Can't do anything about the heat." His sad eyes took in the men as well. "It's all we can do in here with what we've got." Without warning, he turned on her. "Yes? What do you want?"

"I'm sorry." She took a step back, unprepared for his sudden assault. They had enough to do without her getting in the way. She almost turned to go back to the kitchen, but the exhaustion on his face stopped her. She straightened her shoulders. "I came to ask if I might be of some help." Her voice rose on the last word. A hopeful question.

Both doctors stared. The first pointed a blood-caked finger at her. "Aren't you the one who gave water to the men yesterday?"

"Yes."

"That would be a wonderful ministry for them. It's hot, and these men are desperate for some kind of respite. Water would be a godsend."

"Yes, sir." Disappointed by his request, she nevertheless wore a bright smile and got her bucket. The cup sat inside. She went to the pump and returned with water. The doctor walked with her. Those without abdominal wounds could have all the water they wanted. The poor unfortunate gut shot, could only have small drops of water on their tongue. Tillie's heart went out to them, but he was adamant. He left her and returned to his grisly task of amputating limbs.

****

Tillie didn't try to speak to these men. They were the enemy. She served her water in absent-minded silence. The Rebels held Gettysburg. What if they did mark Father and took advantage of him because of Lady or the requisitions? Scenes flashed in front of her: The Rebs mistreated Mother and Maggie. Father dragged off to prison, or worse. Sam forced to join the Reb army. As her imagination soared to new heights, a tug at her skirt brought her to reality.

"Miss, may I have a drink of water, please?"

"Hmm? Oh, sorry." Tillie got down on one knee and cradled the man's head before bringing the cup to his lips.

He smiled his thanks. She refused to smile back. Behind her, another man asked for water. Tillie gave him some. She glanced toward the Roundtops in front of her.

Big Roundtop, shaped like a large bread loaf, sloped down to a saddle before rising to form Little Roundtop, which rose to the north, like a smaller loaf. The rays of the lowering sun slanted between the heights, piercing the smoke drifting from the opposite side. The mountains glowed a lurid orange-gray as the battle roar intensified. A mass of gray-clad men moved through the saddle of the two, silhouetted against the light as they attempted to ascend the lower slope from the farmyard side.

A Union orderly sounded the alarm. "It's the Rebs. They're on this side of the Roundtops. They're coming across the fields. If they get to Taneytown Road, we'll be in danger!"

It didn't appear that way to her. If anything, they seemed to be attempting to scale Little Roundtop. Her brain told her to run to the house, but fear paralyzed her body as a crazy sense of déjà vu washed over her.

Shouts and bugles calling a charge came from the south side of the house. How did the Rebs get so close?

Tillie spun, expecting to see gray backs, guns raised, ready to kill them all. Instead, blue-coated men in ranks of four ran across the barnyard. A young boy in the first row, no older than sixteen or seventeen, held the battle flag and screamed, "First Pennsylvania!" The men roared and charged.

The First Pennsylvania? James! Tillie dropped the bucket, ignoring the wounded men's pleas. Raising her skirts, she hopped over men in her haste to find a place to observe as they ran by. She cleared the clot of men on the ground and stopped at the corner of the house.

The men of the First Pennsylvania Reserve advanced on the Rebels at Little Roundtop. Her heart skipped a beat as she scanned their faces. She didn't see James, but the men passed in front of her so fast, she couldn't be sure.

She cupped her hands around her mouth and hollered as loud as possible. "James Shaw Pierce!" A man turned his head in her direction. James? A flash of recognition hit her, but he didn't look like her brother. He seemed shorter and thinner than she remembered. Still, she knew him, but his identity remained elusive. Dismayed, she stared at their backs as they ran past at the double-quick.

As the men approached the lines, the Confederates fired on the Pennsylvania boys. A few fell, but undaunted they charged at the enemy. As the blue uniforms advanced, the gray retreated.

She tucked herself close to the corner of the house to observe the fight. Rebel soldiers tried to climb a stone fence near Little Roundtop, only to discover more Union soldiers hiding behind it. The Boys in Blue rose and fired at point-blank range, cutting the Rebs down. Tillie's body jerked as though their bullets struck her. Those able retreated between the two mountains and disappeared from sight.

* * * *

As twilight approached, more soldiers arrived at the farm with devastating wounds. Across the road, the new Confederate wounded lay in the fields and orchards further from the house.

Tillie nursed the men and tried to close her ears to their screams and pleas. After witnessing the devastating fight, she couldn't muster animosity. She decided to nurse them all as what they were: shattered men in desperate need of care.

She worked in the burned-out field across the road, giving water to the Confederate wounded and wiping their dirty, sweaty faces, wishing she could do more. As full darkness approached, the doctor who put her in charge of water came out to speak to her. "You need to go back inside the house now, miss." He took the dirty rag and bucket from her hand.

"But these men still need help."

"And they'll get it. You must go back inside. It's far too dark out here to see what you're doing."

"Then get me a lantern. For I'm determined to carry on my task here."

The doctor shook his head. "Can't do that, miss. I'm sorry." He let his eyes roam over the black hulk of Little Roundtop, backlit by fading daylight. Then he leveled those tired eyes on her. "Please, miss. I bet their guns are trained on us right now. The only thing keeping you alive is your skirts. In the complete dark all they'd see is a light, and they'd shoot."

She opened her mouth to protest.

"He's right, Miss Tillie," the rebel soldier she had been helping when the doctor arrived spoke up.

"Go back in the house, Miss Tillie," others implored. "Come back tomorrow."

"All right." She glanced around at the boys. "I'll go inside. Good night, boys. I'll come back in the morning." She scanned the men lying in the burned-out wheat field. How many would survive the night? She smiled at them as she pushed the thought away and returned to the house amid a chorus of good nights and God bless yous.

* * * *

Orderlies cut bread, spread butter and jam on the slices, and set them on plates, which Tillie took and served.

As she served the bread, her eye caught a young man in the back corner of the basement near a small storage room. He sat with his back against the wall, his legs spread out in front of him, crossed at the ankles. A wounded man lay with his head in the young man's lap, and the young man stroked his companion's forehead in an absent-minded manner.

She walked over, carrying the empty plate. She knelt. "Would you like some water?"

The soldier licked his lips as the man lying in his lap groaned. He glanced down at his companion and stroked his hair. The young man raised eyes so full of anguish, she had to touch his arm.

"What do you need?"

"Well, first, may I have some bread? I'm very hungry."

"Certainly." Tillie rose and approached the table. She grabbed two pieces of bread, spread butter and jam on them, and returned, offering him the plate so the crumbs wouldn't drop on his companion's face. He thanked her and ate the bread with slow deliberate motions, though he said he was hungry. She sat next to him and waited, her gaze drifting to the young man lying in his lap.

Dark-brown hair swept back off his face. His beard did nothing to hide the ashen appearance of a dying man. A hole in his coat near the shoulder left a bloody stain. The bullet that entered his shoulder and exited in a gaping wound at the base of his neck mangled one of the stars on his lapel. Tillie reached over and pulled away the bandage at his neck. She swallowed hard and recovered the wound.

When his companion finished eating, he passed her the plate. She set the dish by her foot. At each grunt or groan of pain, the captain stroked his forehead. "Would you do one more thing for me?"

"Of course." She shifted, expecting him to ask for water.

"Would you sit with the general for a moment while I step outside?"

"I will."

The soldier thanked her and eased himself out from under the man while Tillie exchanged places. She followed the young soldier with her eyes as he left the kitchen. What was it about men and their officers? Some exhibited absolute devotion like this young man, while others "marked them out." It must depend on the officer in question.

What happened to the major who beat the exhausted boy rather than help him? Was he dead now, killed by his own men or the enemy? Had this man been a good officer?

She glanced at the general and found him gazing up at her. His lips moved with an effort to speak. She smiled as he licked his lips and tried again. Tillie leaned close to hear him. "I'm sorry?"

"What's your name?" His voice came out as a raspy whisper.

"My name is Tillie." She stroked his forehead. "How do you do?" She chuckled at a sudden thought. "Today's my lucky day for meeting generals. This morning I met General Meade, and yesterday I met General Reynolds." She bit her lip. General Reynolds was dead. Did he know? Did he know the general? She turned away, hoping he wouldn't notice her cheeks aflame.

The general grunted again. His forehead shone with sweat. "General Reynolds—good friend." Pain contorted his features.

Using the corner of her apron, she wiped his face. "Where did you get wounded?"

"On that little mountain."

"Little Roundtop." Tillie supplied the name.

"Yes, Little Roundtop. Hit…helping place…artillery."

"Is it a bad injury?"

"Yes." He grunted, and his body stiffened. He relaxed and drew a deep, pained breath. "Pretty bad."

"Do you suffer much?"

"I do now. Perhaps in the morning…I'll feel better."

The general's companion returned, and Tillie switched with him, careful not to jog the general too much.

"Can I bring you some bread or water, general?"

He declined both with a shake of his head.

"Well, if there's anything I can do for you…?" She let the question hang, gazing at him, compassion and concern battling for control of her emotions.

His eyes met hers with an expression so earnest she got down on her knees and leaned in close again.

"Will you promise to come back in the morning and see me again?"

"Oh." Tillie slapped her hands on her knees. "Yes, indeed I will."

The general's lips twitched.

She glanced at his companion who nodded his thanks.

As she rose to leave, the general's voice came to her clear and loud. "Don't forget your promise, now."

She smiled at him. "I won't. I hope you're better in the morning." She waggled her fingers at him and left to help others.

****

Tillie went to Beckie's worktable and set the plate down. Mollie and Sadie walked around, also handing out plates of bread.

A yawn threatened, but Tillie inhaled through her nose and exhaled, releasing her yawn. "Can I help?"

"Fine time you did some work," Beckie snarled, kneading the dough with vicious strokes.

Tillie's eyes widened. Her mouth fell open. She skimmed the room, as though the source of Beckie's anger lurked in a corner somewhere. "Have I done something wrong?" She dumped a cup of flour on the table.

Beckie glared at her and gave the dough another violent push. "We stand here and bake bread until Kingdom come, and you prance about handing out water, like the queen of Sheba. You speak with every Tom, Dick, and Harry soldier here, and yet none of them speak to us. And we're doing more work than you are."

Tillie sucked in her breath. Her nostrils flared, and her jaw tightened. "You didn't want to talk to the soldiers anymore remember? You said so yourself." Tillie worked her dough. She inhaled and counted to ten, as Mother taught her. She tried again. "I'm sorry. You're tired. I'm tired. It's been a long day and doesn't seem as though it's going to end anytime soon." She locked eyes with Beckie. "But I'm going to continue talking with these men and caring for them, because I like to. If you choose to resent me, well, that's your decision."

Beckie glared and slapped her bread into a pan.

Tillie worked in silence. Her hands shook as she kneaded the dough, using the motions to calm herself down. Frightened by the intensity of her emotions. Beckie's ire came from exhaustion. Tillie didn't see hers did too. She reviewed the past day and a half, trying to recall if she'd done something so egregious the Weikerts would be angry with her. She offered to help in the kitchen on countless occasions, but Mrs. Weikert always sent her off with Mollie and Sadie as if she wanted Tillie out of the way. Not being content with the younger girls, Tillie went off and found other things to do.

Beckie sighed. "For as long as I live, may I never bake another loaf of bread," she muttered under her breath as she dipped her measuring cup into the flour barrel. Her cup scraped the bottom.

Tillie snorted and started to laugh. She bumped Beckie with her shoulder.

Beckie glared, angry surprise in her eyes. "Leave me alone." She moved away.

Tillie's laughter died. She sighed, sorry for her friend's anger. With a shake of her head, she gathered more flour into a pile and worked the dough, clenching her teeth as a wave of irritation and regret overtook her. She didn't want to be friends with Beckie anymore. A flash of insight blared through her: Beckie never liked her. Maggie was her friend, and Tillie was a tagalong. That's what Beckie used to call her until Maggie made her stop. Well, from now on, Tillie would treat her with respect, as propriety dictated, but no more. Tillie clamped her jaw against an urge to cry. Sorry she ever agreed to come to this place. She wanted to go home to people who loved her and made her feel safe.

Chapter 19

The fighting on Little Roundtop stuttered to a close around ten thirty that night. Within a half hour, a flood of wounded arrived, and a mad scramble ensued to find a place to put them.

The doctor from the farmyard, John Billings, now worked in the house, directing the triage.

Tillie turned one way, Doctor Billings the other, and they nearly collided with each other. "Come with me." He commandeered her and led her to the dining room upstairs.

A man waited for the surgeon, his left arm a shattered, mangled mess. The cuff dripped blood on the floor.

Tillie's heart pounded in her ears. She swallowed hard. Her shoes squished through puddles of drying blood. She approached the man who waited patiently for the surgeon. She forced a smile. "You'll be all right, soldier." Her salivary glands began to tingle, and her mouth filled with metallic tasting saliva.

He nodded and held out his right hand.

She glanced at his blood-covered fingers, slapped her own hand over her mouth, and fled.

Doctor Billings's voice followed her. "Well, I had hope for her."

* * * *

By the grace of God, she made it outside before her vomit splashed in the yard. What would Mrs. Weikert or Beckie say if she had a mishap on the floor? Tillie coughed and gagged a few more times, wiped her mouth on her sleeve, and let the tears flow down her cheeks. She leaned against the side of the house, her shoulder against the cold stone, face buried in her arm.

"Arrrrhhhh." She wept deep, bitter tears. "I want to go home. I don't want to be here. I want my mother." She raised a fist and pounded it against the stone. A jolt of pain shot down her arm, and she focused on it to calm herself. Still, she drew in deep, gulping breaths of air.

"Feel better?"

Tillie spun to her left to see Dan standing by the corner of the house, his deep blue eyes studying her face.

She spun away and used her apron to wipe her face and eyes. "Did you come out to laugh at me?"

"No, of course not. I was just coming back to the house, and I heard you crying." He stepped toward her. "I'm sorry I can't protect you. I'm sorry you have to see what you've seen. It isn't right. I would have protected you if I could."

Tillie half turned and studied his face. Was he making fun of her? Was he serious? He was only thirteen years old, only six months older than Sam. What did he know of protecting women?

"Thank you."

He took another step closer. "You shouldn't be out here in the dark. It isn't safe." Dan took hold of her elbow in a gentle grasp. "Come." He led her into the kitchen. "Good night." He offered her a solemn smile and moved to join his father making coffins, but his fingers lingered on her elbow before he left.

The kitchen, filled to capacity, could not hold one more person. Tillie dried her face, rinsed her mouth with some water, and plodded upstairs.

She reached the dining room, but couldn't bring herself to step over the threshold. A new man waited while Doctor Billings prepared to saw the man's foot off. The soldier clasped his hands together as though praying, but his constant thank yous made it clear he would rather go through the agony of amputation, than deal with the pain any longer.

Billings patted the man's shoulder, nodded at his medic, who jammed the cattle horn down over the patient's nose and mouth. Within minutes, the soldier became unconscious. The doctor went to work. When he finished, he beckoned Tillie into the room.

She walked with halting steps, uncertain and afraid he would chastise her.

"Feel better?" His eyes flicked in her direction as the orderlies dropped a new man in front of him.

"I'm sorry." Her body shook, and she suppressed an urge to cry. But her eyes filled with fresh tears.

"Happens to all of us the first time." He began examining the wound and didn't glance her way. "I remember in medical school seeing my first cadaver. My professor laughed as I ran out to empty my stomach. Thought he'd kick me out of med school."

Tillie stepped closer. "What happened?"

Doctor Billings shrugged. He took great care to pick the fabric out of the wound before extracting the bullet. "He pulled me aside after class and said I'd gone through the rite of passage of anyone called to this duty. He would've questioned my desire to be a doctor, had I responded any other way." Now he appraised her and smiled. "You've had your 'rite of passage'. Are you ready to get to work?"

Tillie wiped her nose and eyes. "Yes, sir."

* * * *

Morning sunshine streamed through the window, warming Tillie's face, and the change in light woke her. Opening her eyes, she yawned, stretched, and shot upright in bed as though blasted from a cannon. "Oh heavens, what time is it?" she asked Beckie, only to find her gone.

Tillie finally got to bed sometime around two in the morning, too tired to undress, and climbed into bed fully clothed. Beckie snored beside her.

Now, she flung back the covers, hopped out, and slipped on her shoes. She threw the bed covers up, and then raced down to General Weed, afraid he'd think she forgot him.

Mrs. Weikert and Mrs. Schriver put away the last of the breakfast dishes as Tillie entered the basement kitchen. Beckie worked at the table, preparing another round of bread.

"Good morning, Beckie." Tillie approached the table, irked, and determined to confront her. "Why didn't you wake me when you got up?"

"You were so deep asleep. I didn't want to bother you." Beckie made a show of pulling together her ingredients for bread making. She refused to meet Tillie's eyes.

There had to be more to Beckie's answer. She searched the girl's face, to no avail. Her body went lax as she gave up trying to understand.

Tillie started to ask Mrs. Schriver for food, but her neighbor closed the cupboard door with a bang. She reached into her apron pocket and produced a key to lock the cupboard. Beckie smirked as she began mixing the dough.

A plate of sliced bread waited for the soldiers. Still, she couldn't resist and ate a slice, chewing as she searched the room for General Weed. He and his companion still occupied the corner from last night. She started toward them, turned back, and grabbed the plate.

Mr. Weikert came in and crossed the room in front of Tillie. She stopped short to let him pass. He held the well pump handle in his left hand, which he placed on the floor behind some barrels stored underneath the stairway, out of sight to the casual observer.

Strange. Tillie followed him with her eyes as he walked past again, winked at her, and went to his wife. He whispered in her ear and left again.

Did anyone else find this odd? No one appeared to find it strange, so she went to visit General Weed and his companion.

The captain sat against the wall, head tipped back, eyes shut. General Weed lay still, his head in his companion's lap. His hands lay on his chest, fingers laced together, as though in peaceful repose.

Tillie started to sit down, hesitated not wanting to disturb either of them, but she promised and settled herself next to the captain. The general's still body made her wary. She leaned closer for a better look. General Weed wasn't asleep. Guilt pierced her heart as tears filled her eyes. He must've thought her a liar. Why did she oversleep? Why didn't Beckie wake her? Why did he die?

The captain sat still eyes open, watching her. "We've been waiting for you." He sounded groggy. His words held no condemnation, though she listened hard for it. "Do you know who this is?" He patted the general's chest.

"He told me his name is General Weed." Tillie set the plate of bread near the captain. She put her other hand over the general's heart. "I'm sorry I'm late." She spoke to him as though he heard.

"Yes." The captain ignored her comment. "This is the body of General Weed, a New York man. He got hit helping Captain Hazlet place artillery on the top of Little Roundtop. West Point Class of 1854." A sad smile played on the captain's lips as he gazed at the general. "He once told me he and J.E.B Stuart were best friends at West Point."

It surprised her to think generals had lives before the war. Like her parents, she tended to think they appeared, as they were, then disappeared again. "I'm sorry. I do hope he's greeting nearer and dearer faces than mine right now." She contemplated the captain. "You must have been quite intimate friends to pay such close attention. Are you related?"

The captain smiled. "No. I worked as his aide-de-camp, but he treated me like a younger brother." His eyes misted and he blinked. "I loved him like a brother." He adjusted his seat and stroked General Weed's forehead. "He died in the wee hours this morning. Before even the armies arose, I'd wager. The orderlies wanted to carry him away sooner, but I insisted we wait for you."

Tillie leaned over and placed a light kiss on the general's cold forehead. "Goodbye, General Weed. I am honored to have met you." She mustered up a slight grin. "Thank you for waiting for me. They can come and take him now, if they need to."

"You've been most kind to us." The captain took a slice of bread and chewed. "If I can do anything for you, please tell me, and I will carry it out posthaste."

Tillie thought of her family. How did they fare? If he found out… "There is something." She gave him her name and instructions on how to reach her home. "Would you tell them I'm safe?" Her throat constricted with a surge of emotion. She cleared her throat and forced herself to speak. "Would you come back and tell me if any harm befell them?"

"I shall consider it my sacred duty." The captain slapped his hand over his heart in dramatic fashion. "I'll go today, come back this evening and report." He took a second slice and ate.

Tillie smiled her thanks. Her gaze traveled to General Weed's body.

"What troubles you, my dear?" The captain laid a gentle hand on her arm.

She lowered her head embarrassed by her sudden emotion. "When I was little, I believed in God—at least I think I did. My parents are devout. We go to church every Sunday. But this summer, so much has happened I have a hard time believing a divine God directs everything." She broke off and gazed about the room. "The war never affected my family until last fall when my brothers left. James, my older brother, is with the First Pennsylvania Reserves, but when they arrived yesterday, I couldn't find him. I called out to him, but he wasn't there." Heat rushed to her eyes. Her words now came with soft, warm tears running down her cheeks. The idea of losing her brothers crushed her heart. "We've not had a word from him in several months. What if…?" She stopped, unable to give voice to her fear. "William is with General Grant out west, as far as we know, but we've not heard from him either. Just last week my sister's beau went off to join the Twenty-First Pennsylvania. Rebel sharpshooters shot and killed him on his way to meet his unit. He was unarmed, but they shot him anyway. Now, I don't believe in God. Worse yet, I don't even want to believe in God. I'm troubled."

"You're angry with God."

Tillie started and stared at him. "Angry with God? How can one be angry with God?"

"Well, you told me some pretty sad things. It's a guess, but sounds reasonable to me. Do you think it's possible you're angry for things like not hearing from, or seeing, your brothers? What about your sister's beau? Do you think that's God's fault?"

"Perhaps I do." Her voice finally came, almost too soft to hear. "I–I never thought of that. I think of being angry as stomping around and shouting at people." Her voice grew stronger. "I haven't done that."

"Haven't you?"

She turned hard eyes on him. "What do you mean?"

A smile tugged at the corners of his mouth. "Well, I've been sitting here, not able to do much more than observe. I see how you interact with that girl." He jutted his chin in Beckie's direction. "She gets under your skin, although you try not to show it, but I've seen the angry expression on your face sometimes. I don't think you're even aware…. But you get an expression, and Lord help the person you're upset with."

Tillie's mouth dropped open as the familiar warmth flushed her cheeks. "I didn't know."

"I know." He shifted his position and pressed his shoulder blades into the wall. "As you weren't aware of your feelings for her, I suspect you aren't aware of your anger with God."

Tillie stared off at the far wall, processing his words. He offered her too much to think about, but she promised herself to concentrate on it later. A new question struck her. "What I don't comprehend is how can God, if there is a God, allow so much horror and evil to exist? How can he allow men to be so destructive to one another? It doesn't make sense."

"Of course it does, if you think about it."

Tillie cocked her head.

"My dear." He took on the tone of someone about to embark on a Sunday school lesson. "When God created Adam and Eve in the Garden, he so loved Adam, He gave to him the one thing He did not give to the other animals."

"Free will." Tillie nodded and shrugged. "I know."

"You know." He raised two fingers and tapped the side of his head. "But you don't know." He tapped his chest, over his heart, and smiled. "Let me explain. God gave Adam free will. Adam used his free will to eat from the Tree of Knowledge. Therefore, God expelled them from the Garden of Eden."

She flicked an impatient hand. "Yes."

"As Adam used his free will to destroy the perfection and purity of the Garden, and impart to us his fallen sin nature, so we use our free will and fallen sin nature to destroy each other. It's the way of Man, but not the way of God, who knows this, as he knew Adam and Eve would destroy the Garden. He doesn't allow evil, but He will use it for His purposes, turning our evil to His good somehow."

She recalled the night she and Father talked in the parlor. This conversation sounded close to that one. Something nibbled at the corners of her mind. Something she felt she should understand, but what, eluded her. The more she tried to drag her thought to the foreground, the more elusive it became. She let go, knowing it might come back later.

"The Old Testament is full of war." The captain took another bite of bread.

She turned her attention back to him.

He nodded for emphasis. “David and Goliath. In First and Second Kings, First and Second Samuel, there were wars between countries, and in Judges, a civil war.”

Father’s words came back to her. Tillie smiled. “My father said the same thing to me a few nights ago. Am I correct you’re saying God condones war?” She regarded him. “Still, how can any of this be used for good?”

“Are you familiar with the term ‘a righteous war’?”

Tillie nodded. “My parents say this is a righteous war if it will condemn slavery for good.”

“I agree. If this country comes out more secure and unified than before, I say that’s a good thing. More important, if the Lord uses this war to scourge this country of the sin of slavery, hallelujah and amen. My point is, if God doesn’t fear war, why should you or I? General Weed—and General Reynolds, for that matter—both devout, Christian men, were not afraid of war and not afraid to die.”

The captain dusted the breadcrumbs from his fingers and pulled a small Bible from his breast pocket. He opened to a passage. “General Weed read this often. I believe the words gave him comfort. ‘Oh, death, where is thy victory? Oh, death, where is thy sting?’” He closed the book.

His stern expression made her think of Father.

“Faith is the assurance of things hoped for, the belief in things not seen,” she murmured, laying a palm over General Weed’s cold forehead.

“General Weed never doubted those words. If you do, then you dishonor his memory.”

Tillie sniffed and wiped her face with her apron.

“My dear.” He put his hand on hers. “Do not despair. For your brothers or for yourself. If these days of tribulation bring the faith of the Lord Jesus Christ into your heart, then don’t you think He turned this circumstance to good?”

Tillie laughed through her tears. “I never considered that.”

The captain placed the small book in her hand. He closed her fingers over it. “General Weed gave this to me before he passed. I’m giving it to you.”

“Oh, no.” She tried to push the Bible back into his hands. “I couldn’t. He gave it to you as a keepsake.”

"He gave it to me as a gift. It's mine to do with as I please. I have my own well-loved Bible. Besides, what good is the Word of God if we don't spread it around? Please, take this. To remember us by."

The words Holy Bible gleamed in beautiful golden calligraphy on the cover. She held the book to her heart. "Thank you. I'll treasure this always."

The captain signaled to three men standing by the kitchen table. "Don't treasure it. Read it." The men lifted the general's body off his lap and placed him on a litter. The captain eased his legs and bent his knees. He pushed off the floor with his hands. When he got to the kitchen door, he waved. "I'll visit your family today." He followed the orderlies outside.

* * * *

An officer stood outside the kitchen door waiting for them to carry the general's body out. He removed his hat, placed it over his heart, and bowed his head. When the entourage left, the man entered, tucking his hat under his arm. "Excuse me." He caught Tillie's eye. "Are you in charge of the well outside?"

Mrs. Weikert addressed him. "My husband is in charge of the well. What may we do for you?"

"Ma'am, I am First Lieutenant Ziba Graham of the 16th Michigan. I came to the field hospital to get a tooth removed. As I prepared to leave, I couldn't help notice the wounded men lying in the hot sun. They're thirsty, but there's no pump handle on the well. They asked me to inquire about it."

"I can't help you, lieutenant. That's my husband's concern, not mine." Mrs. Weikert turned her back on him. She tossed her next words over her shoulder. "I have enough to contend with, just keeping you men fed."

"Yes, ma'am." His face reddened, but he persisted. "Can you tell me where I might find your husband?"

"What can I do for you, lieutenant?" Mr. Weikert appeared like magic on the stairway to the upper floors, his arms crossed in front of him.

Tillie found herself standing between Mr. Weikert and the lieutenant. She retreated a step and cast about for something to occupy her. She couldn't go anywhere without crossing between them so she held her ground.

In the distance, artillery shells whirred through the sky. The conversation paused as everyone listened to the faint boom. A collective sigh of relief escaped them all.

"Sir, I am First Lieutenant Ziba Graham, 16th Michigan." He offered a jerky bow from his waist then explained how he came to be there. "The pump handle is missing from the well. Are you aware of that, sir?"

Mr. Weikert came down the last steps and stood in front of the barrels under the stairs. "No, I'm not." He planted his hands on his hips and shifted his feet, in a what-are-you-going-go-do-about-it stance.

Tillie drew in a sharp breath. "But you—." She stopped at the sight of Mr. Weikert's angry face and glanced at the lieutenant. When he stared at her, Tillie bowed her head and clamped her lips closed.

"Sir," Graham spoke in an exaggerated, reasonable tone. "Please state your name?" He slipped a small notebook out of his breast pocket and flipped the pages with his left thumb before poising a pencil over the open page.

Mr. Weikert glared at him. He crossed his arms again. "Weikert. W-E-I-K-E-R-T."

Lieutenant Graham wrote the name in the book and snapped it closed. He kept his eyes on Mr. Weikert as he slid the notebook back into his breast pocket. "Well, Mr. Weikert, I know for a fact you are aware of the pump handle. Several men told me they saw you remove it. Now, I suggest you retrieve it and put it back on the well. They'll die of thirst if they don't get water."

"What do I care?" Mr. Weikert's face turned dull red, and the vein in his forehead throbbed. His hands curled into fists at his sides. "Those men are the enemy, and I won't have my well pumped dry by Rebels who would only waste the water anyway."

"Sir." Lieutenant Graham's voice and eyes hardened. "I order you to replace the well crank now."

"No." Mr. Weikert moved to stand behind his wife.

Mrs. Weikert and Mrs. Schriver shifted so their bodies blocked Mr. Weikert from Lieutenant Graham.

Some soldiers snickered while others scowled. Lieutenant Graham's lip curled, and his eyes grew cold and contemptuous.

At this moment, Tillie disliked all the Weikerts.

An artillery shell whistled through the air and hit the chimney. The house shook and dishes rattled on the shelves. Something shattered upstairs.

Mr. Weikert blanched at the sound of bricks crashing to the ground and men screaming.

Only Lieutenant Graham acted unconcerned. He pulled his pistol out of its holster. "Sir, I order you to give up the well crank—now!" The lieutenant drew back the hammer and aimed the pistol between the women's shoulders, right at Mr. Weikert's forehead. "Don't make me shoot you in front of your womenfolk, sir."

Tillie's eyes widened. She exhaled in a slow, measured breath. Give him the crank. What did he gain from being obstinate? Rebel or Yank, they needed water.

The standoff lasted only a second or two. Mr. Weikert made an ugly sound, stomped to the stairs, and retrieved the well crank, which he thrust out to Lieutenant Graham with such force Tillie flinched, expecting Mr. Weikert to hit the man.

The lieutenant took the handle with solemn thanks. He nodded to each member of the family and left the house.

She ran to the cellar door.

Lieutenant Graham attached the pump handle, drew water, and gave it to the thirsty men. Before taking his leave, he posted two of the least wounded men, one with a bandage around his forehead and another with an arm in a sling, to guard the well.

She looked up at the blistering sun, then around the farmyard, heartsick. The yard, devoid of trees or shade of any kind, offered no respite. The men might as well lay in a desert, for all the comfort they received. They endured the flies and merciless, building heat while awaiting help from four surgeons who made their own men their first priority.

Tillie cocked her head trying to remember what today was. She began to count on her fingers. The soldiers came to town on Tuesday, the thirtieth. The first day of battle happened on Wednesday, the first, the same day she arrived at the Weikerts'. Yesterday, Thursday, the second, the army chased them away.

She smiled a tired smile. So today was Friday, July third. Tomorrow was the Fourth of July. Lord God, if you exist, don't let them fight tomorrow. Please let the fighting be over now, so we can enjoy our picnics and parades—and peace.

A movement caught the corner of her eye. She stepped outside for a better look. Across the small lane, Union soldiers moved about, placing cannons about three hundred yards or so from the barn. Behind the cannon, infantrymen lined up as if they expected another fight, this time right at their doorstep.

"They're setting up cannons on the other side of the dooryard." Tillie's heart lurched, and dread made her nauseous. She looked at Mr. Weikert through the open doorway.

Mr. Weikert swore. He joined her and looked where she pointed. His shoulders dropped, and his hands clenched and unclenched in spasms of unvented fury. The color drained from his face.

A sudden flash of insight struck Tillie so hard she gasped. In the last three days, this man lost everything he held dear, helpless before the onslaught. She tried to forgive him for the water.

"Tillie, go back inside and stay there." He spoke over his shoulder. "Don't come out for anything."

"Yes, sir." She headed inside as Mr. Weikert walked over to the men placing the cannon.

Mrs. Schriver joined Tillie at the door while her father and the soldier talked. When Tillie and Mrs. Schriver glanced at each other, Mrs. Schriver shrugged as if to say it was out of their hands. "Well, we have work to do." She returned to her chores.

Tillie walked among the wounded in the cellar, inquiring if she could do or get anything for anyone. A man lay on the floor near where General Weed had lain. Bandages covered his eyes. He gripped an envelope. Tillie knelt and placed her hand on his.

"Who's there?"

"My name is Tillie." She touched the envelope. "Would you like me to read your letter?"

"My friend brought it last night. It's from my wife."

Tillie slid the envelope from his grasp and unfolded the letter. A picture of two small children, a boy not much more than three and his older sister, perhaps five, fell on the man's chest.

She put it into his hand. He lifted the picture to his lips and kissed it.

Her voice choked as she read. When she finished, she folded the letter and put it back into the envelope. She slid the envelope into his hand again. He squeezed it tight.

"Thank you," he choked out.

She patted his hand. "Can I get you water or a slice of bread?"

Someone tapped her shoulder. "Miss, there are carriages waiting by the barn. Your father wants to find a place of safety. You're to come with me if you please."

Tillie scanned the kitchen. While she read to this man, the Weikerts disappeared, leaving her alone. "Is something going to happen?" She rose, unable to hide the fury roiling within her. She gave her poor messenger the full brunt of her glare. "Why didn't they tell me they were going? Did they think to leave me behind?"

His eyes widened, but he acted the gentleman. "Who knows?" He shrugged. "The rebels took a beating yesterday, that's for certain. Except for the shelling earlier, it's been pretty quiet this morning—probably because both sides are too hot and tired to fight anymore. But this thing doesn't feel over, so your father wants the family a safe distance away."

"He's not my father," she snapped, then relaxed. "I'm sorry." She touched his sleeve. "You couldn't know." She said goodbye to the man lying on the floor.

"God bless you." He held up his envelope. "And thank you."

Tillie walked with the soldier across the farmyard. In the distance, musketry rattled and crackled. She stopped. "Is that in Gettysburg?"

"No." He turned toward town and appeared to listen. "There's been sporadic fighting all morning at a place called Culp's Hill."

"That's less than a mile from my home."

"Oh." The soldier seemed uncomfortable with another reference to her status as guest, and instead, showed her the cannon, east of the road leading into the farmyard. "General Sykes believes the Rebels will try to reach the Taneytown Road like yesterday. If so, we'll see hard fighting right here. If you remain, you'll be in the midst of flying bullets and shell fire."

She smiled. How would that be different from yesterday? "We've been in the midst of flying bullets and shell fire since yesterday."

His face colored. "Yes, miss."

They reached the carriages. The soldier tipped his hat and walked away.

Tillie raised her foot to climb into the carriage as an artillery shell screamed overhead. She shrieked, pushed off the step with her foot, and hurled herself into the barn. She landed in a heap, arms over her head, waiting for death to strike.

No explosion. As she timidly lifted her head, the soldiers erupted with laughter.

Tillie picked herself up and dusted off her filthy dress. Flying artillery shells weren't funny.

A man lying near her spoke for them. "My child, if that hit you, you wouldn't have had time to jump."

It occurred to her how ridiculous she must have appeared, coming from nowhere to land in an undignified pile in the straw. A snort of laughter escaped as she squared her shoulders, stuck her nose in the air, and sniffed in mock offense. "Sound logic indeed." She flicked her skirt, giggled, and spun on her heel before marching outside, their laughter ringing in her ears.

In the field across the road, dust and ash settled, indicating the shell landed, harmless, in what remained of Mr. Weikert's burned-out wheat field.

Chapter 20

They headed south on Taneytown Road. The horses clip-clopped along at a steady pace until they met up with soldiers drawn up in a line held in reserve. There, Mr. Weikert stopped the buggy. "Where are you boys from?"

"Sixth Corps." The sergeant pointed in the direction they came from. "What's going on up ahead?"

Mr. Weikert laced the reins over the brake as though to begin a lengthy conversation.

The commanding officer rode up. "Move along, sir. You don't want to stay out here."

Mr. Weikert gave the officer a baleful glare, but picked up his reins and slapped them. They drove about a mile before turning left and cutting across a connector road to Baltimore Pike.

Tillie leaned forward and spoke into Mrs. Weikert's ear. "Where are we going?"

"Two Taverns."

The small town lay six miles south of Gettysburg with only a few homes and, as the name implied, two taverns. Would Father punish her for going into a tavern? She had no choice.

They passed through a strip of woods. Dead men, horses, and destroyed caissons forced them to slow and work their way around the obstructions.

She shook her head at the sight. Did these men have families? What kind of lives did they lead before the war? Did they have wives and children? Such waste. She took a handkerchief from the pocket of her skirt, which she held to her nose and mouth. Away from the overwhelming odor of gunpowder, the cloying stench of death invaded her nostrils. She kept her head down and her eyes closed, trying to breathe through the cloth.

About a mile down the road, they left the carnage behind, and she breathed in fresh air again and put away her handkerchief.

Two infantrymen ambled toward them.

"What's going on?" Mr. Weikert called out, halting the conveyance. "Are we headed into danger going this way?"

The two privates stopped. "No." The one who spoke scratched his head. "A cavalry battle took place about an hour ago, but I think you're safe." He touched his hat to the women and moved on, but his companion stayed. In his hand was a strange biscuit, which he raised to his mouth. His eyes fell on Tillie, who stared at him.

"What are you eating?" She indicated the pale, thick, cracker-type biscuit, ignoring the saliva pouring from her cheeks. Her stomach growled.

"This? Hardtack. You can break a tooth on one of these." He held it out to her, chuckling at his own joke.

She took a bite, closing her eyes and chewing with slow motions, enjoying the cracker, which tasted like flour and water mixed into a paste and baked. It needed salt.

The private chuckled and reached into his haversack. He pulled out another to give her.

She ate fast. "They're rather good." She put a hand to her mouth to stop a crumb from falling. Mother would chastise her for talking with a mouthful of food. She swallowed. "Thank you."

He grinned. "When you've eaten your fill, they aren't quite so wonderful."

Mr. Weikert made an impatient noise and gestured, drawing the soldier's attention back to more important matters. "Young man, will we be running into battle if we go this way?" He wrapped the reins around the brake handle.

"No, sir." The soldier waved in the direction the family traveled. "All fighting ceased behind us. We've been called forward to strengthen the lines along Cemetery Ridge." The boy slung his rifle off his shoulder. He set the butt on the ground and leaned on the muzzle as he would on a fence to chat with a neighbor. "Where're you folks off to?"

"We're going to Two Taverns. They said the rebels would be coming straight over our farm."

He nodded. "You should be able to travel in relative safety. I haven't heard of any clashes in that general area. We came through last night as a matter of fact."

Beckie leaned forward and smiled at him. "Such an interesting accent, private. Where are you from?"

He blushed, tipping his cap. "Miss," he greeted her. "I'm with the Sixteenth Vermont, under General Stannard."

"My thanks to you." Mr. Weikert slipped the reins off the brake handle.

"Best of luck to you, folks." The private touched his fingers to his cap, lifted his rifle, and dropped the strap across his shoulder before heading toward the Weikerts' farm.

They continued through the woods. At a small clearing, a group of Confederate soldiers sat on the ground, guarded by Union soldiers. Tillie drew in a sharp breath, and her hand flew to her throat. Dirty Beard sat among the captives, knees tucked to his chest, and his chin on his arms. She searched for Lady, but there were no horses.

Mrs. Schriver reached across her sister and touched Tillie's arm. "Are you all right?" Concern shone in her eyes. "You look as though you've seen a ghost."

"I'm fine," Tillie choked out, pointing to the captive. "That man stole my horse last week." A single tear slid down her cheek. Her heart thumped with a sudden rush of wrath. "She's dead." Dread filled her. She didn't need evidence of Lady's corpse to know she'd never see her horse again.

* * * *

As they approached the village of Two Taverns, a man stood on the side of the road and waved them down. "Are you fleeing the unpleasantness?"

"We are." Mr. Weikert rested his elbows on his knees. "We must."

"Then come and join us. We've become something of a refugee stop for those in flight." The man indicated at least twenty-five families milling about, chatting. "Please, I insist." He grasped the carriage, as though willing them to turn into the drive. "My wife and daughters are indoors preparing a picnic luncheon. Other neighbors brought food as well."

Mr. Weikert shrugged at his wife. "Why not?" He guided the buggy into the yard and hopped down.

Tillie descended and wandered around the outskirts, self-conscious. The property owner walked over.

"Please, make yourself comfortable. My name is Mr. Jones."

"Tillie Pierce." She bobbed a curtsy as her parents taught her when meeting someone for the first time. "How do you do?" She drew her arms in across her body, stopping short of crossing them. Did he smell her? What must he think of her, clothes torn and dirt stained, covered with blood? Her hand brushed the front of her dress.

"Pierce, Pierce." He wrinkled his brow. "I know a James Pierce, a butcher, in Gettysburg."

"He's my father." She smiled bright, clapping her hands together.

"A fine man." He gestured toward the tables under the oak tree. "Please come and eat. My wife and daughters are putting the food out now."

Thanking him, she joined refugees as disheveled and dirty, though not as blood covered as her. She relaxed as she filled a plate with fried chicken, coleslaw, bread, and other delicious dishes. She found herself a place and sat to give single-minded concentration to filling her stomach. While she ate, she listened to the stories of woe the others told. Warfare raged all around and inside the town, surrounding and beleaguering the residents. Many voiced the opinion the fray felt like a tipping point between winning the war and losing.

After her meal, she relaxed on the porch swing, stomach full and eyelids heavy. She took notice of where the Weikerts were in case they decided to go home. She didn't want to be left behind.

The Weikerts sat talking under the shade of an oak tree. Mrs. Schriver took the girls inside. Dan remained at the picnic tables, flirting with one of Jones's daughters.

She scanned the yard for Beckie but didn't find her. Beckie's behavior still baffled her, but she refused to be a peacemaker. Mother would insist she be the bigger person, but not this time. She crossed her arms and scowled, determined not to be the first to apologize and unable to find a justifiable cause for Beckie's anger. She'd been hateful and rude since day one. Beckie should apologize to her.

Tillie slipped her hand into her apron pocket, her fingers bumping against the Bible the captain gave her. She withdrew the book from her pocket and opened it. Psalms. They read like poetry. She loved to listen to Father read them. She sighed and fought off a wave of homesickness.

Flipping the book closed, she touched the cover, feeling the embedded calligraphy on the leather. She recalled a time when Belle confided she often opened the Bible at random places and found a Scripture to fit her mood. Tillie mentioned it at dinner that night, earning a lecture.

"The Scriptures are the sacred word of God, Tillie. Not a horoscope or cure-all/catchall for whatever ails you." His words accompanied the same stern glare he always gave her when she displeased him.

Nevertheless, she wanted to discover if Belle's theory worked. She reopened the Bible. It again fell open to Psalm 53. "The fool hath said in his heart, there is no God. Corrupt are they, and have done abominable iniquity." Drawing in a sudden breath, she shot her head up and stared straight ahead, unseeing. She was the fool. She said there is no God. Oh, Lord, I'm so sorry. Forgive me, please. She turned back to the book. "There is none that doeth good, no, not one." She drew in a deep, fearful breath; her words to the captain came back to her—if there even is a God. If.

Her father's words echoed in her mind. "The wages of sin is death, Tillie. There is none who seeks after God." With shaking hands and a pounding heart, she flipped to Romans, scanning chapters one and two, and, finding what she sought, read chapter three, verse twelve. "They are all gone out of the way, they are together become unprofitable; there is none that doeth good, no, not one." Verse twenty-three, in black and white, just for her. "For all have sinned and come short of the glory of God." Her breath came in short, hard gasps, as though someone punched her in the gut. "Oh, that's me!" she whispered, gripping the book so tight, her knuckles pressed white. I fall short of the glory of God. That's what the captain tried to tell me. That's what Father and

Mother tried to say my whole life, and I wouldn't listen. How could I be so stupid? Heart pounding, she wanted to drop to her knees in prayerful repentance, but the people around her made her hold back. Instead, she closed her eyes tight and prayed with all her heart. Oh, Father in Heaven, please listen now and forgive me my selfishness, my foolishness. Thank you for General Weed, for the captain, for my family, for your Word. Forgive me, Lord. Please forgive me.

As she prayed, a weight fell off her shoulders. Her heart broke as she gave herself over to repentance. Tears poured down her face and landed on her hands. The sheer joy of forgiveness lightened her spirit, and she felt a profound sense of freedom from disbelief and doubt, and the fear of death and damnation.

My child. The words resounded in her head. Her Savior spoke.

She squeezed her eyes tighter. I'm here, Lord. I'm here.

"My child." This time a light touch lingered on her shoulder. When she jerked her head up, an elderly man smiled down at her. His eyes were the deep blue of a winter's day but with all the warmth of summer. Laugh lines traced their sides. Deep creases formed around his mouth, and his gray beard fell to his chest. He dressed in black pants, a white shirt, and a black coat. On his head, he wore a black, wide-brimmed hat.

"I am sorry to disturb your prayers—don't be ashamed." He waved his hands, as she wiped her eyes and tried to cover her face.

"My prayers and petitions often bring me to tears. It's good we should weep over our sins and disobedience." He tapped her Bible. "Might we partake of the Word together or would you prefer to be alone with your God? I can hear the fury from your town. I thought some time with the Lord Jesus would calm my soul."

Six miles north the battle raged, but sounded as if right in front of them. Curious. At the farm, much of the fight went unheard, yet here the pandemonium was loud and clear.

She scooted over and patted the empty seat on the swing. "Please."

"What passages are you reading?" He sat.

"I started with Psalms because my father always likes to read the Psalms." In an instant, her face burned with the lie. "Actually, I opened the book and came to Psalm Fifty-Three, so I started to read. This summer I've been struggling with myself because I can't help think God can't exist. If he did, we wouldn't have such a terrible war and men wouldn't die like this. Just yesterday, talking with a captain, I told him I decided God didn't exist." She held up the Bible, her finger stuck in the Psalms to hold her place. "He gave me this Bible and told me to read. I opened it now to Psalm Fifty-Three, which says, 'The fool hath said in his heart, there is no God.' The rest of the passage made me think of Romans, so I turned there." She flipped the book open. "My father always tells me the wages of sin is death. I usually nod my head and wait for the lecture to end. Today, I don't know why, or how, but I see what the text means. I truly understand." She heard the wonder in her voice and stifled an urge to giggle from the intensity of her emotions. She sniffed. "I'm so sorry I said God didn't exist."

The man chuckled. "I understand. The Lord, in His infinite grace and mercy, often keeps us in the dark for His perfect reason and timing. When the timing is right with Him, He removes the scales from our eyes and the stoppers from our ears."

She nodded as she blinked back more tears. In the distance, the waves of battle pounded her ears, sometimes smashing against her eardrums, and other times rolling toward her like distant thunder, which gave her a new idea.

"The wages of sin is death," she said again. "Those men who are being killed right now, their wages are death?"

He inclined his head toward one shoulder. "Well, it depends." He half turned in his seat to face her. "Not death as you and I understand it. You see, if we are children of Christ, then on this earth, our only death is the physical death of our bodies. Our souls will live forever with Christ in heaven. If you live outside of Christ, as I'm certain some of those boys do, our sin condemns us to eternity in hell. That is true death. The wages of sin."

"Can I ask another question?"

"You just did." He shot her a mischievous grin.

She jerked surprised eyes to him and grinned. "My father says that." She grew serious and stared at her knees. "What I mean is: why does God allow evil to exist in the world? I don't understand. I'm told he loves us, but He lets bad things happen." She stopped, unable to find the vocabulary to voice her fears.

"An excellent question." He patted her knee. "If I may offer my humble opinion, I believe God allows evil because He is more glorified by redemption than by creation. Bad things happen to draw us closer to Him, and in turn, He redeems us, if we ask."

Her eyebrows drew together into a tight pucker. Awe filled her heart. She turned wide eyes to him. "I never thought of that." Her eyes shot to her Bible, as if to read the words on the front cover. She glanced at him through her eyelashes. "You're very smart."

"I hope so for my congregation's sake. I'm a Quaker minister."

She laughed. "Father always says when the moment is right the Lord supplies the needed instructor." She grew serious as a new thought struck her. More tears spilled down her cheeks, and she let them, unashamed of her emotions. "I have so much to ask his forgiveness for."

"My dear, ask his forgiveness, but your Father has forgiven you."

"No, I meant—"

"I know what you meant." He rose. "Now if you'll forgive me, I must speak to our wonderful hosts and thank them for their hospitality." He took her hand in his. "Thank you for sharing with me. You refreshed my soul." He kissed her hand and walked away.

Tillie watched him go, the Bible in her lap. So much to ponder. She settled herself more comfortably on the swing and gazed about her. She picked up her Bible and began to read, soaking up the words on the page as though she couldn't absorb them fast enough.

* * * *

The battle continued to rage, though not with the same intensity. Tillie caught snatches of conversation as people contemplated what they'd find when they returned home. How much more devastation could they endure?

Toward four o'clock in the afternoon, the roar of combat lessened, and by five, all grew quiet. Still, no one made a move to leave, as though they didn't want to go back, couldn't bear to witness the carnage.

Rising from his place under the oak tree, Mr. Weikert walked to the road. He stared north. Several folks joined him, casting wary glances toward town.

She put the Bible back in her pocket.

"Come everyone," Mr. Weikert called out as the sun slanted toward the western horizon. "I think it's time to go home."

Tillie searched for the Quaker minister to say goodbye, but couldn't find him. She went inside the house to say goodbye to her hosts, and asked them to tell the minister goodbye and thank you. They assured her they would. The clock chimed six times.

They rode home in silence. Tillie imagined them out for a lovely ride in the countryside on a hot and muggy evening. The closer they got to the farm, the more evidence of confusion and ferocity prevailed. Fences scattered the ground, knapsacks, blankets, and many other articles discarded along the side of the road.

"What is that sound?" Mrs. Schriver cocked her ear toward a curious humming, perplexing them and adding to their anxiety.

A mile from home what they at first took for bundles of blankets on the ground took on the shape of dead men.

Beckie choked and gasped. She covered her face with her hands and refused to open her eyes.

Tillie stared at the devastation as they passed by, her brain unwilling to comprehend.

Stopping at the house, Mr. Weikert had no choice but to leave the carriage in the road. Wounded, dead, and dying filled the approach to his farm.

"Oh my." Mrs. Weikert put her hand over heart. "Oh my," she said again, shaking her head and sniffing back emotion.

The strange humming now morphed into groans and cries. The acrid odor of smoke and gunpowder stung their noses, adding to the stench of blood, flies, and death in the motionless, humid air. Swallowing hard to keep her gorge from rising, Tillie lifted her apron and covered her nose and mouth. Her gaze drifted past her immediate surroundings to the destruction beyond the house and grounds. Wounded men of the blue and the gray lay like a writhing carpet in the farmyard and into the fields beyond. What did they do to each other? When would all this end?

The family exited the carriage, compelled to pick their steps as they approached the house, sometimes wedging their feet in between men to avoid stepping on them.

Confederates outnumbered Union almost three to one. She couldn't muster animosity toward them as, with great care, she made her way to the basement door where the rest of the family waited for the orderlies to move hundreds of men around, to make room for them.

"Well, baking bread will do these men no good." Mrs. Weikert placed her hands on her hips. "Come, girls. Let's go in search of things we can turn into bandages."

Mike, the orderly, was back at his post, stirring a pot of broth. He spotted Tillie and beckoned her. She approached him while Mrs. Weikert, Mrs. Schriver, and Beckie went upstairs. The orderly leaned close and whispered, "Go get the bucket and some more water. These boys are in a bad way."

She nodded, left, and returned carrying a bucket of water. She dipped a cloth and moved among the men, wiping their faces and hands, and giving them small sips from her tin cup.

The women came back down carrying all the linen and muslin they could find. They sat wherever and tore up their clothing, bedding, curtains, and rolled them into bandages.

Tillie moved around giving water to men well enough to drink. As she put the cup to one man's lips, he sipped and grinned up at her. Blood dribbled from the corner of his mouth. "We did it," he croaked.

Tillie's lips barely twitched a smile as she put the cup to his lips again, only half-listening.

He took another sip. "We did it." Triumph gleamed in his eyes. "We beat the Rebs for sure today."

She focused on him. "How do you know?"

He coughed, and blood splattered her. She jerked back and faced away, swallowing hard. Then she arranged her features into a calm expression, put a smile on her face, and turned back to him.

He drew in a breath and managed two words. "I know." He lay back down.

"Congratulations." She laid her palm over his clammy brow. "I'm glad."

Following the prostrate men up the stairs and into the hall outside the dining room, she offered water and a cool cloth.

"You, girl."

Tillie jolted at the sound of the surgeon's voice, hoping he called another girl.

Doctor Billings stood behind the dining room table, visible from the bloody waist up. He held a bone saw in one hand and gestured at her with his other bloodstained hand. "Come here."

Tillie's dream flashed before her eyes. She resisted an impulse to run. Instead, she put down her cup and entered the dining room trying not to stare at the man waiting for the surgeon. She kept her gaze fixed on the doctor. "Yes, sir."

"I need your help. Can you tie on a bandage?"

She shook her head.

He motioned to an orderly, who showed her with quick, practiced motions.

"Wait, do that again, but slower."

He showed her again. "I need you to bandage these men so I can assist Doctor Billings with the amputations. Can you do that?"

"I can try." Her hands shook as she took the cloths.

The medic jammed a cattle horn down over a wounded man's nose. As soon as he appeared unconscious, the surgeon cut large strips of skin and folded them back. He picked up his saw and gave it a swipe across his blood-soaked apron, before placing the instrument about two inches below the skin flaps. He got down to the gruesome task of amputation.

As often happened, the soldier was still conscious, and several strong men needed to hold him down while the doctor cut fast, through bone and flesh.

The semiconscious solider screamed and fought, spraying blood and bone everywhere.

Tillie cowered with her hands over her ears, desperate to shut out the man's screams. The limb thumped to the floor.

She ran, but got no further than the hall where her vomit splashed several poor unfortunates.

She didn't want to go back in, but the strident call, "you, girl. Come back in here!" forced her into obedience. Tillie put her apron over her face, choked back sobs, and returned.

The surgeon removed bullet and bone fragments. Then he folded the flaps of skin over the amputation and sewed them together. Another medic stood by with a cauterizing iron, which he slapped on the wound.

The soldier screamed, cried, and begged for mercy. The medic removed the iron, and two more men lifted the boy by his shoulders and hips and plunked him in front of Tillie, who couldn't see through her tears to bandage the stump.

"Hurry up, lass." The medic scowled. "We han't got all day. There're more poor divils waitin'. More than we can shake a stick at, that's fer sher."

Once she tied the wrappings on, the same two men took the soldier away.

At first, she was too aware of the horrible sight and stench of cut off limbs, blood, and burnt flesh. Her hands shook so badly she struggled to wrap the wounds and received several scoldings for being too slow.

When she stopped seeing the wounds, and even the men, she worked with the same swift efficiency as the medics and doctors. The work reminded her of the rhythm of the butcher shop after a fall butchering, when she, Mother, and Maggie wrapped endless pieces of meat.

Tillie tied the bandage to the stump of an arm and stood back. The medics took the man away. She glanced up when they didn't replace him with another. In the parlor across the hall, the grandfather clock struck two o'clock. When did it get dark? Who brought in the lamps?

"I think we're done here." Doctor Billings swiped his forearm across his face, mopping the sweat away. "I didn't think that possible."

Tillie gave him a dull stare, too tired to muster a response.

He inclined his head in her direction. “What’s your name, girl?”

She opened her mouth and croaked, “Tillie.”

He tapped his chest with a beefy finger. “Doc Billings.”

She yawned. She learned his name the day before. This was the first time he asked hers.

He waved a hand at her. “Go to bed. I’ll see you in the morning.”

“Yes, sir. Good night.”

As she walked through the silent house, the blue glow of the moon lit her path. She stopped at the front window to gaze at the white orb. How could the moon and sun go on rising and setting, oblivious to the machinations beneath them? A movement caught her eye, and she focused on the barn. The yellow glow of lamps within illuminated the white fence in the front yard, bordering the road. Piled against the fence and almost over topping it, rose a mound of discarded limbs. A man flung an arm on the heap and went back inside without waiting to see where it landed. The arm landed on the pile and rolled down the side. Tillie shuddered, but at least, its former owner stood a chance at survival.

PART 3

THE AFTERMATH

Chapter 21

Rain hammered the roof and slashed at the windowpanes while thunder rolled overhead. Tillie stretched and smiled, recalling those days before the battle when she pretended the peals sounded like cannon fire. What a ninny. A blinding flash of lightning, followed seconds later by a crack and boom rattled the windows. "They sound nothing like each other."

"Hmm." Beckie rolled over and grabbed for the blanket.

Tillie threw the covers aside and slipped out of bed. She sat on the edge of the bed and stretched again, digging her toes into the braided rug. She'd gone to bed only a few hours ago, but awoke refreshed and wide-awake. Besides, she didn't want to miss breakfast again.

Beckie shifted. Tillie watched her sleep and scowled, seeing she donned a clean nightgown the night before.

Dirty and uncomfortable, she reached up and used her fingers to try to detangle the knots in her hair. She winced when her fingers found a thick knot. She must look a fright with that rat's nest, but she couldn't help it. As she lowered her arm, she caught a whiff of her body odor. She jerked her face away and grimaced.

She feared picking up the lice crawling on the men. Thinking of the jumping vermin, she shuddered and scratched her head.

Thunder rumbled again. Would there be more fighting? Despite the thunderstorm, something was different today. She couldn't shake the feeling yesterday's ferocity brought a climax.

Tillie approached the washbasin and sluiced her face. She grabbed her shoes and tiptoed out of the bedroom.

Mr. and Mrs. Weikert, Dan, and Mrs. Schriver sat at the table, sipping coffee. Tillie stepped over and around convalescing men. She lifted her skirts to avoid hitting any of them in the face and picked her way across the room. Beyond the basement window, Confederates lay in the barnyard under the drenching rain, trying in vain to shield themselves from the downpour. Her heart went out to them.

The greeting Tillie meant to give died on her lips. A pensive air permeated the room, as if everyone sensed a change and didn't trust it. Pouring herself some coffee, she found a seat. As she lifted her cup, her gaze met Mrs. Schriver's sad eyes.

Her neighbor stared hard at her. Tillie's smile disappeared. Now what? She squirmed under the scrutiny. "Is something wrong, Mrs. Schriver?" A clear challenge rang in her voice.

Her neighbor gave her a sad glance. "I was thinking you should be home, safe, but instead, I dragged you here. When your parents find out what you've been through, I'm certain they're going to be quite angry with me."

Tillie flopped back in her chair as she released her breath. "No, they won't." She shook her head with a rueful chuckle as she waved her cup around. "How could you know this was going to happen?" She sipped her coffee. "I'm safe and alive, and Mother would say 'all's well that ends well.'"

Mrs. Schriver burst into tears. Mrs. Weikert leaned close and slipped an arm around her daughter's shoulders. Mrs. Schriver covered her face and crumpled in her mother's arms.

Tillie turned away, wrinkling her nose and making a face. "What is that smell?" She glanced around as if trying to spot the source. "It stinks like dead skunk in the rain, only a hundred times worse."

"I'm not surprised." A soldier lying nearby lifted his hand and waved it in front of his face. "What you smell is rotting flesh—animal and human."

Tillie's mouth dropped open, and she gaped at him. "How come I didn't notice it before?"

"Because the odor of gunpowder covered it, but it's been present since day one. Most of those men have been outside in the hot sun all this time. Wet weather always intensifies the stink. I found that in other battles."

Tillie didn't know what to say. Instead, she sipped her coffee and tried to swallow the lump in her throat. So much happened in the past three days. Events blurred and jumbled together in her mind.

"Do you hear that?" Dan turned toward the door.

Mr. Weikert opened the kitchen door. Through the hiss of the rain, cheering atop Little Roundtop traveled like a wave rolling toward Cemetery Ridge and on to Culp's Hill on their right.

"What does it mean?" Sadie wailed, blue eyes big and round. "Oh, what does it mean?" She threw her hands over her ears and looked around for an opening between the adults to scoot back under the table.

Mrs. Schriver held her arms out, and the child ran to her.

"No need to fret, child," one man said. "Them's our boys. It's over." A smile lit his face. "The fighting's over." He reached over and shook the shoulder of the man lying next to him. His grin faded as he gazed into the soldier's lifeless eyes. He clenched the dead man's collar, and then let go and lay back down. He covered his face with his hands. His words muffled behind his hands, "Praise God."

Dan raised his coffee cup in a toast. "Happy Fourth of July, everyone."

Those at the table lifted their cups. The men followed suit with empty hands as though holding a cup. "Happy Fourth of July," they chimed in unison.

"May the heart of this fair Nation be forever inclined unto wisdom, so we may never fall into the folly of another war." Another man, lying near the stairs, wiped tears from his face.

"Hear, hear," echoed a chorus.

The doctors arrived for another day of gruesome work. It broke the spell, and Tillie and the others put away their breakfast dishes and set about spending their Fourth of July nursing and tending the hundreds of men in the house, on the grounds, and in the barn.

****

The early morning storm moved on, Mother Nature having done her best to wash the earth clean. Throughout the day, the sky remained gray and overcast, heavy with the promise of more thunderstorms. Tillie performed her duties, oblivious to the weather. Late in the afternoon, the light dimmed. Out of the corner of her eye, she saw a finger of lightning streak through the clouds, followed by a resounding crack of thunder that made her jump.

"God is angry with the carnage." The soldier she nursed lay on the floor waiting his turn at the surgeon's table. His comment seemed directed at no one in particular.

Tillie smiled but didn't respond. She wound a bandage around his mangled leg with mechanical motions.

Two orderlies came in and dropped another man on the floor near the dining room door. A line of men waited from the table out the door and into the hallway. Tillie finished wrapping and bandaging. She drew in a deep breath and let it out, stifling a yawn. She patted her patient on the chest and moved on to the next. Before bending to her task, she rolled her head from one shoulder to the other to relieve the ache in her neck and shoulders.

Doc Billings came to stand beside her. He unwrapped the bandage and, using his fingers, pulled open the wound to inspect the bone. He sighed. "I have to take off the leg."

"No! No!" The soldier shrieked and grabbed hold of the doctor's arm. "Please, God, don't take off my leg. How will I work my farm when I go home?"

Doctor Billings put his hands on the man's arms. "Now calm down." He eased the man down and talked to him until he quieted. "I must. The bone is shattered, and there is nothing I can do to save your leg." He held the soldier's eye until the man settled. When he accepted his fate, he nodded and lay back.

Doctor Billings spoke to Tillie, but his eyes slid beyond her to the door. He straightened. "You there, little girl."

Tillie turned as Mollie shrank away from the door.

With a bloody hand, Doc Billings gestured her forward. Blood dripped off his fingers. "Come here, young lady." His voice softened. "Come and give this man a drink of water so I can take off his leg."

Tillie grabbed the scissors and cut his trousers.

Mollie inched forward. She picked up a cup next to a water bucket and dipped it in, then came close and held it, too frightened to move. Panting from severe pain, the soldier gave her a thankful smile and took the mug. After he drank, he handed it back. She took it and, crying, ran from the room.

* * * *

As the day wore on, the rains passed over Gettysburg. The gray skies remained. But by early evening, the sun managed to find a chink in the clouds, and slim rays of sunlight filtered down, warming the wet earth. Steam rose from the ground, lending a spectral aspect as thin wisps formed around lifeless men. Tillie imagined the grim reaper walking through the field, rejoicing over his fine harvest.

Despite the number of men treated, and those they didn't get to in time, the queue of waiting men never ended. Tillie began to think a procession of men stretched from Gettysburg to Baltimore waiting for help.

Finally, the time came for the family, doctors, and nurses to sit down to supper. The Weikerts used up their supplies feeding the soldiers since the fighting started three days before. In return, the army provided small fare, but they accepted the food with some grace. Her mouth watered when she remembered their meal from their first day. A rueful smile crossed her face. If they knew, they might have been more sparing. As she sipped her coffee, she glanced at the doctor. Dark shadows circled his eyes. He gave a prodigious yawn and rubbed a weary hand over his face and hair. Tillie's heart went out to him. He hadn't rested in days.

"You look exhausted, Dr. Billings." She touched his arm. "Won't you take even an hour to rest?"

He looked through her as though she were transparent. "I'll be all right," he said. "These poor men don't get a rest, so I don't either." He took a bite of his bread. He eyed her as he chewed. "You've been a great help to me these past two days."

"Thank you." She straightened her shoulders and sat tall, grateful for his praise. Hearing she mattered made her heart skip a beat.

After the meal ended, she helped clean up, and then stepped outside to use the outhouse. As she walked back across the yard, the stench of putrefaction and death assaulted her senses. Not only could she smell it, but the odor lingered on her tongue. She clamped her teeth together and tried to seal her nostrils closed, but she couldn't suppress a gag. With considerable effort, she fought the desire to leave her meal in the yard. She took shallow breaths while reaching into her pocket for a handkerchief, which she pressed hard to her nose and mouth. She stopped to take in the damage done on Little Roundtop. It was difficult to comprehend that the day before yesterday, a vicious fight occurred there. Trees, in full, green splendor the week before, now stood, stripped of their leaves. Branches reached out from the trunks as if in supplication. Some once large healthy trees now so riddled with bullets they toppled over. Others appeared chopped down on purpose. One word kept reverberating through Tillie's mind—shameful.

A movement caught her eye, and she shifted her gaze to the field below the summit of the hill. She recalled their flight to Two Taverns and the devastation that greeted them when they returned. The soldiers told her they called yesterday's fight Pickett's Charge, for the Confederate general who led the attack. Now, several men moved about the battlefield. Occasionally they knelt down, lifted men, and carried them away. At other times, they knelt, rose, and moved on. Must be looking for more wounded. No doubt, they'd be arriving here soon. Lord knows where they'd put them.

She sighed, and her body drooped. Since they were the closest hospital, they had to come here. She remembered what Dr. Billings said about her being a help. She peered at her hands, caked with grime. Dirt and dried blood packed thick underneath her fingernails. Her skin, chapped and raw from so much water, nevertheless was stained rust brown. She wiped her palms down her apron, to find it also covered in grime. She caught a whiff of herself. A sudden urge to cry overcame her. She wanted to go home and get a hot bath, a change of clothes, and wash and brush her hair. She didn't want to be around all this ruin anymore. Tillie drew in a deep ragged breath. She wanted her mother.

Standing in the yard, surrounded by wounded and dead men, she covered her face with her hands and released huge sobs. Tillie allowed herself a few moments of despair before regaining control. She sucked in huge gulps of air and pushed her sobs down, not wanting these men to witness her distress when they bore their suffering with so much bravery. Someone tapped her shoulder.

Tillie swiped at her face, blinked, and turned. A man smiled down at her. She sniffed and stared back at him. She was supposed to recognize him, but her brain didn't make a connection.

His expression changed from happiness to embarrassment as he realized she didn't recall who he was. He removed his cap and nodded a greeting. "Do you not remember me?" His eyebrows raised as he asked the hopeful question. "Do you not recollect the man who got you on a wagon on the first day?"

Tillie gasped, thrilled that a man stood in front of her, unhurt and standing on his own two feet. Renewed tears filled her eyes. She wanted to throw her arms around his neck and give him a great big kiss. She restrained herself. What would he think of her?

"Why are you crying?"

"Corporal Townsend! Forgive me please." She wiped her eyes and nose with her handkerchief. "I'm just so glad to see you well. You escaped the battle unharmed."

The corporal's smile faded a bit. "Yes, well that's not hard to do when you're attached to a general's staff." His eyes surveyed the wounded men lying close by, unease in his gaze.

"Please allow me to thank you once again for getting me here," she said. "I do appreciate the service you provided."

"There's no need for thanks," he brushed off her comment. They stared at each other. Corporal Townsend shifted his feet. He glanced about at the battered men again, and a strange expression crossed his face.

"I'm with General Sykes's staff." A derisive note edged his words. "He and my father are great friends, and it is as a favor to him I'm so situated. If I had my way, I would be among these men doing more noble work than running messages back and forth."

"But, corporal, consider." Tillie smiled. "Had you been with the men, I would not now be where I am."

Townsend looked at her, surprised, and then he laughed. "You have me there."

"How did you know where to find us?"

"The woman with you said you were trying to get to a farm a mile or so down the road. This is a mile or so down the road. I thought if this weren't the right place, I'd just continue until I found you. Tell me, how are the little girls? Are they well? I thought about those darling children all week."

"Oh, yes, they're fine. They're all inside if you would like to come in."

"I'm sorry. I can't stay long. I must say, I was pleasantly surprised when I turned in and saw you standing and staring at Little Roundtop. What were you looking at?"

Tillie pointed toward the field and the men still moving around and picking up soldiers. "See those men?" She swung her arm to indicate the men walking through the battle zone. "I was thinking that soon those men will arrive here and we'll need to help them. I must confess there's no place left to put them."

"Well, you needn't worry. Those men are gathering in the dead."

Tillie foundered for something to say. Her heart gave a painful lurch.

"Why aren't they picking up all the bodies?" Her brow furrowed. "I see them sometimes kneel down and then move on."

Corporal Townsend shrugged in a nonchalant fashion. "They're Rebs."

Tillie stared at him before turning toward the field.

"Well." He dismissed the activity on the hill. "As I said, I can't stay. I asked General Sykes for a few minutes to come here and find out what became of you. I'm glad you came through the fight unharmed as well." He waved and took his leave.

"Oh." He turned back, as if remembering something important. "I brought a gift for you." He slipped his hand into his pocket and removed an object. He offered her a token of a silver button still attached to a scrap of gray cloth.

"I cut this from a Confederate coat," he told her. "I wanted to give you something to remember me by."

She held out her hand, and he laid the scrap in her palm. "Thank you," she breathed. "I shall treasure it always." She closed her hand over the prize before putting it in her pocket. She kissed Corporal Townsend on the cheek. He blushed, stammered some words, and took his leave.

Tillie watched him walk away, her spirits lifted by his visit. She went back into the house to tell Mrs. Schriver he remembered them.

* * * *

The sun sank behind the Roundtops before Tillie, the doctors, and orderlies entered the basement kitchen for dinner. The captain who ministered to General Weed sat at the table, a cup of coffee in his hand. He stood and bowed to her.

"I must apologize to you, Miss Pierce." He removed his hat and bobbed his head. "I'm a day late in returning from my task of securing your message to your parents. The circumstances of yesterday's battle prevented me from getting here any sooner."

Tillie took his hands. "That's all right, captain. I understand the delay. Besides," she shrugged in a quick, conciliatory gesture. "You wouldn't have found us here. We decided to skedaddle ourselves. We ran to Two Taverns for safety's sake." She crossed the kitchen and used the washbasin to clean her hands and splash water on her face. She grabbed a towel to dry her face and moved to the table.

"Did you find my home?" She took a plate of food from Mrs. Weikert and sat herself down across from the captain.

"I did."

"Well, how many linden trees are outside my home?" She smiled, wanting reassurance he'd gone to the right house.

"Never mind that." He waved away her question. "I don't care how many trees are in front of your house. To prove it, I'll tell you, your mother told me about how the Rebs stole your horse. She also told me to inform you that Jenny Wade was killed while baking bread at her sister's house. She said you would want to know."

Everyone fell silent. The women exchanged glances, realizing their good fortune. Sam's words came back to her. She's a traitor, and I hope she gets what she deserves. No, no one deserved that, not even Ginny. With how much Tillie disliked Ginny, she knew Mother imparted the information as a reminder of Christ's edict to love your neighbor as yourself and to pray for your enemy, because at any time the Lord might call you to account for your deeds.

"Ginny," Tillie said.

"I beg your pardon?"

"Her name wasn't Jenny. It was Ginny. Virginia." She lowered her eyes to her plate. "Ginny Wade, and yes, Mother would want me to know that."

"Your parents were relieved to hear you are safe and unharmed. Your sister, Maggie, sends her love."

Tillie's eyes filled with tears at the thought of her family. Her heart lightened knowing they weathered the conflict and now knew she survived as well. She didn't realize the weight of the fear she lived under until now.

"Thank you," she said. "I can't tell you how relieved you made me."

The captain placed a hand over hers. Then he kissed her hand. "I'm glad I could help you in return. Now, I must get back to my unit. It's been my great pleasure making your acquaintance, Miss Pierce." He rose and headed for the door.

"Take care of yourself, captain."

He nodded and reached for the doorknob.

"Oh, captain?"

He turned at her voice.

"Thank you for the Bible. It's been of huge comfort to me."

He saluted and took his leave. After he disappeared, she realized she never asked his name.

* * * *

The clock chimed one o'clock in the morning when she dropped into an exhausted slumber. She no sooner closed her eyes, than someone shook her awake. Her body did not want to rouse enough to acknowledge the person depriving her of rest. Opening her eyes, she discovered Doc Billings standing over her holding a candle and whispering to her to get up.

"What's the matter?"

"I need you, Miss Tillie. You need to get up." He shook her again.

"What time is it?" She sat up, her brain still fuzzy.

"Somewhere around two in the morning."

"Do you never sleep?"

"I am sorry to rouse you so soon after sending you to bed. But I have a patient who's taken a turn, and he's asking for you. Please come."

Tillie flung back the covers and jumped, fully dressed, out of bed. She groped around for her shoes but couldn't find them. Instead, she went in her stocking feet toward the door.

Doc Billings followed. "Wait," he whispered. He grabbed Beckie's petticoat lying on the bed. "I need bandages. Do you think she'll mind?"

Tillie suspected she would a great deal, but didn't say so. She shrugged. "I'll tell her in the morning," she assured him.

They entered the dining room together. A private lay on the operating table. She remembered assisting Dr. Billings while he amputated the boy's right arm earlier in the day. She shook her head. No, not today, yesterday.

She approached, smelling the sweet, cloying odor of decay. One reason for removing a damaged limb was to prevent infection, though it often happened despite their best efforts.

"Miss Tillie." The boy's voice rasped her name. He extended his left hand to her. "I knew you'd come. I asked them to get you."

Tillie took his hot hand in one of hers and placed her other on his brow. In the candlelight, his eyes were glassy.

"How are you feeling, David?"

"Oh, I'm much better now you're here."

"I'm glad." She forced a smile and turned away, fussing with his bandages to hide her emotions. He was dying, and she didn't want him to see she knew.

"What can I do to help?" she asked to gain control of herself and the situation.

"You can start by tearing that up." Dr. Billings indicated the petticoat. "We'll need plenty of clean wraps for him."

Tillie squeezed David's hand before picking up the garment. After they cleaned him and changed his bandages, David drifted to sleep. Tillie went back to the bedroom for the Bible lying on the end table. She returned to the dining room and sat next to his pallet.

"Where did you go?" His voice was groggy.

"To get this." She indicated the book.

"I like Hebrews." He closed his eyes.

Tillie opened the book and read.

"Read that again?"

"Which?"

"Chapter two. Start at verse ten and go to the end," David said. "It's my favorite."

She cleared her throat and began. "'For it became him, for whom are all things, and by whom are all things, in bringing many sons unto glory, to make the captain of their salvation perfect through sufferings.'" She glanced at him and saw his smile as though drinking in the words.

"'For both he that sanctifieth and they who are sanctified are all of one: for which cause he is not ashamed to call them brethren, saying I will declare thy name unto my brethren, in the midst of the church will I sing praise unto thee. And again, I will put my trust in him. And again, Behold I and the children which God hath given me, forasmuch then as the children are partakers of flesh and blood, he also himself likewise took part of the same; that through death he might destroy him that had the power of death, that is, the devil.'" Tillie looked up to find him sleeping. She closed the book and placed it next to her. She laid her palm over his forehead again. Heat radiated off him.

She got up and, grabbing the bucket, slipped out of the room. She returned moments later and dipped a piece of the torn petticoat into the water. She wiped his face and hand, then opened his shirt and ran the cool cloth over his neck and chest, wishing she could do more. More than once her tears dropped on him, and she wiped them away.

As she worked over him, the words she read came back to her. A merciful and faithful high priest in things pertaining to God. Make reconciliation for the sins of the people. That through death he might destroy him that had the power of death, that is, the devil.

Tillie ministered to the boy whose life drifted away. He would be in Paradise soon. She understood that he did not fear death because, for him, death had been defeated. She recalled the sermon Reverend Bergstrasser gave the Sunday before the battle. Matthew 10 in which he said, though the enemy could destroy our bodies, he could not destroy our souls if we were one with Christ.

Tillie drew in a deep breath and pulled herself under control. No longer would she mourn for David, for he would be going to a place denied to her until two days ago. She would see him again in Paradise. She would recognize him, and he her. Her heart burst for joy.

During the night, she held his hand or wiped his brow with a cool cloth as he veered between wakefulness and sleep, delirium and lucidity. Just as the sun broke free of the heights to pour its rays through the window and across the sleeping boy, the young soldier opened his eyes. Tillie changed his bandages and smiled down at him. "Good morning." She lay her cool palm on his hot forehead.

"Maureen." His unfocused eyes met Tillie's concerned ones. "Tell Mama I don't feel good." The light left his eyes, and the breath left his body.

Sobs rose in her throat. She cried for all the men who died despite their best efforts. She cried because she would never get the opportunity to know them beyond the few minutes or hours given to her.

She hid her face in the crook of her elbow while his blood dripped from her fingers. Regaining her composure, she leaned over and kissed his brow. Her tears fell onto his face. She would never get used to seeing a man die.

Chapter 22

Doctor Billings cradled Tillie in his arm when they entered the kitchen. He spoke quiet words of comfort. She sniffed and nodded at intervals while she wiped her reddened eyes and moist nose. She leaned on him as he guided her to a chair and sat her down. The surgeon brought her a cup of coffee and some bread and gave her shoulder a gentle squeeze. Tillie laid her arms on the table and dropped her head on them.

Beckie barged in and tripped over a wounded man. He cried out, but she ignored him. Her skirts filled his face. "Has anyone seen my petticoat?" She glared around the room. "I got up and discovered my best petticoat missing. Tillie, are you wearing it?" She balled her fists and put them on her hips, shifting her stance.

Tillie raised her head and gave Beckie a dull stare. "Why on earth would I wear your petticoat?"

"Oh, I don't know." Beckie cocked her head, her voice heavy with sarcasm. "Perhaps because you're jealous because I have a clean one and you don't. I just wondered if you decided to put it on, that's all."

"Rebecca!" Mrs. Schriver started, but Tillie jumped to her feet.

"No, Beckie, I'm not wearing your petticoat." Her hands shook as she raised them to her bodice buttons. "Do you wish me to undress and prove it?" Unreasoning fury overtook her as she yanked the buttons, one by one.

"Miss Tillie doesn't have it, Miss Beckie." Doctor Billings stepped forward. He half turned to Tillie and gestured to her to stop. He regarded Beckie. "I took the garment early this morning. I woke Miss Tillie to help me with a patient, and I took your petticoat for bandages."

"You took it." Beckie crossed her arms and adopted a superior tone. "You slipped into my room while I was sleeping and stole my best petticoat from off my bed."

Doctor Billings flushed, but remained silent. He straightened, clenching and unclenching his fists. His expression indicated he would not dignify her accusation with a response.

"Rebecca Weikert!" Tillie slammed her fists on the table. "How dare you say such things? What is the matter with you? It's. A. Petticoat!" She almost screamed those last three words, when she recalled Mrs. Weikert's reaction to her petticoat the day they ran to the Bushmans' farm. Her rage soared. "You have several and it wasn't your best, you told me so. How selfish can you be?" She stamped her foot. "And step away from that poor man before you kill him!"

Beckie glanced down, as if aware for the first time her skirts choked the soldier on the floor. She took one large step forward. The man gasped in air.

Doctor Billings moved to check him.

Tillie drew in a ragged breath. Mother always told her when she felt about to lose control, to count to ten and take deep, slow breaths. She held her hands out to Beckie in a gesture of reconciliation and softened her tone. She sat back down. "I'm sorry I yelled. We used your petticoat to help a man. We tried to save his life, but he died anyway. Since the garment meant so much to you, I'll buy you a new one as soon as I can."

"There's no need for that," Mr. Weikert spoke up. "I'm sure Beckie didn't mean what she said."

Beckie's face colored a dull red. Her mouth worked, but nothing came out. She rubbed her arms. Then she shrugged. "You don't need to replace it. You're right. It's not my best. I'm sorry, Doctor Billings, for having snapped at you. How shameful of me."

"No harm done, Miss Weikert." He sounded calm, but he concentrated on his patient and refused to meet her eye.

Mrs. Weikert put slices of bread and a pitcher of water on the table. "Come, everyone." She waved a hand at the table. "Let's eat. I'm sure we'll all feel better after a meal."

****

They ate in silence, apparently embarrassed by the scene between the girls. Tillie took small bites and chewed with slow, deliberate motions. She swallowed and sipped water.

Someone knocked on the kitchen door. Dan rose and opened it. "Yes." Impatience laced the word. Another man in a Yankee uniform needing care?

The soldier removed his cap. "Have I changed so much, you don't recognize me, Dan Weikert?"

Beckie shrieked and ran to him. She threw her arms around his neck and knocked the young man back a couple of paces. His breath left him in a soft "oof". He laughed and, putting his hands on her waist, set her to her feet.

Mr. Weikert's face darkened at his daughter's behavior, but when she pulled away, he recognized her beau, George Kitzmiller. The family rushed to him with loud shouts of greeting.

Beckie and Mrs. Schriver took his hands and led him to the table. Mrs. Weikert placed some bread and a glass of water in front of him. He sat down, laughing.

They bombarded him with questions, and George turned this way and that trying to respond to them all. "Hold it. Hold it. One at a time. I can't answer you all at the same time."

"Was James involved in the battle?" Tillie leaned forward in her seat. "When the Reserves came through I tried to find him, but couldn't."

"I'm the one who turned when you called out. I'm only telling you because I got the impression you didn't know."

She wriggled in her seat. "I saw you turn, but I didn't recognize you. Oh, George, I'm so glad it was you, but where was James?"

"So am I." George smiled, but it was perfunctory. He grew serious. "I am sorry to tell you, Miss Tillie, but James got sick in the Peninsular Campaign."

She jumped from her chair. "What? Oh no!"

"Not to worry." He rushed to reassure her and helped her to sit back down. "He had a serious case of pneumonia and was hospitalized in Washington."

"Oh my." Tillie put her hands over her mouth. She studied George's face seeing the truth in his eyes. She dropped her hands. "I'm sorry he was taken ill. I'm glad to know he's alive. At least now I can tell Mother why he hasn't written for so long."

"I'm sure it will put her mind at ease." He patted her hand. "You can also tell her, the last I heard, he was mending well."

"Thank you, George." She squeezed his hand. Their eyes locked in a moment of sympathetic communication until Beckie slipped her arm through his and leaned against him. She glared at Tillie. That broke their eye contact. Tillie took a sip of water.

George turned in his chair and addressed Beckie's father. "Mr. Weikert, may I take these two ladies on a tour of the battlefield?"

"Are you sure that's wise?" Mr. Weikert frowned. "I'm concerned about what the girls might see. I'm not sure a tour is a good idea."

"It's perfectly safe, sir," George assured him. "Most of the Rebs left yesterday, and our men are working hard cleaning up the battlefield. We've been in something of a race against the hogs and the carrion birds."

Mrs. Schriver and Mrs. Weikert made sounds of disgust. Tillie shuddered.

"We'll be all right, Papa," Beckie took George's arm in both of hers and squeezed tight. "George will be with us, and I'm sure he will steer us away from the more gruesome sights and places."

"You can be sure of that, sir." George raised his eyebrows in a hopeful glance.

Mr. Weikert studied George's face then glanced at his daughter. He addressed his wife. "What do you think, Sarah?"

She shrugged. "Well, if you say no harm will come."

Tillie raised her eyebrows at Doctor Billings in question. He smiled and nodded.

* * * *

Stepping outside, Tillie lifted her face to the sun, the first rush of warmth a soothing comfort.

"Well, where do you want to go first?" George took a position between her and Beckie and offered an arm to each of them.

"Wherever you would like to take us, George," Beckie cooed. She slipped her arm into his and pressed it against her bosom. She gazed with loving eyes into his face. A besotted George smiled down at her.

Tillie rolled her eyes and looked away. Her gaze fell on Little Roundtop.

"Might we go up there?" She indicated the area of destruction of a few days past.

"I thought you'd never ask!" George said. "That's where we fought, and I did so want to show you where yours truly comported himself so bravely."

Laughing, the three young people set off in the direction of Little Roundtop. George Kitzmiller, acting as tour guide, explained the actions of the afternoon of July the second. Beckie and George clung to each other, and Tillie, feeling like an unwanted third wheel, lagged behind and wandered off some paces to give them some privacy.

"After we raced across the farm, we were placed in reserve up here." George slid his eyes to Tillie as he talked, doing his best to include her in the outing. They reached the top, coming out on the other side to a rocky, boulder-strewn hillside, long known as The Devil's Den. In the past week, the location earned its nickname, for the scene below them seemed culled out of hell.

"Those rocks down there," George nodded to some glacial boulder formations ten to twelve feet high and forming a series of boxlike enclosures, "the men call, The Slaughter Pen." His arm swept off to his right, indicating the grassy slope beyond. "That's now The Valley of Death." They stood on the crest of Little Roundtop and stared into the once beautiful Plum Run Valley.

Tillie gazed at the destruction, thinking the name appropriate. Valley of Death. Everywhere one turned, dead bodies—men and horses—bloated in the heat. Shattered caissons and cannon, scattered everywhere, some aimed at the sky as though the next attack might come from heaven itself. Others still aimed at points distant, showing the direction from which they expected the enemy. Around those silent sentinels lay more dead men, killed while operating their guns. The ground remained littered with rifles, knapsacks, hats, and all kinds of accouterments of war.

"So many," Beckie choked out. "How is it possible? Are any men left alive?"

"Those dead are principally the Confederates."

"What will happen to them?" Tillie suppressed an urge to run and check for survivors.

"If the Rebs want their men back, they are welcome to come and get them." A deep voice lifted behind them.

George, Tillie, and Beckie turned to find a man walking toward them. He wore a Union uniform and on the back of his cap, a deer's tail swung back and forth. "Corporal Wilson, 149th Pennsylvania." He approached, and snapping his right hand up, palm out, he saluted George.

"Lieutenant Kitzmiller, Company K, First Pennsylvania Reserves." George returned the gesture. "Allow me to present the Misses Weikert and Pierce."

The corporal touched his fingers to his hat brim in greeting, and the girls each said hello.

"Oh, I've heard of the 149th," Tillie said. "You boys come from up north in the mountain regions. You're called the Buck-tails."

"Yes, ma'am, we do." His voice rumbled in a rich deep baritone. "I myself am from Wilkes-Barre. Pleased to make your acquaintance."

Tillie tried to catch sight of the buck tail pinned to the back of his hat. Corporal Wilson grinned, removed his cap, and offered it to her.

"You know." His eyes sparkled. "You can't get into the 149th unless you've plucked a tail off a buck to hang on the back of your cap."

"Really?" Tillie gaped.

George and Beckie laughed. Wilson laughed and winked.

"Oh, I see." Tillie joined in the laughter, but a twinge of embarrassment shot through her. She handed him his cap, which he slipped back on his head.

To change the subject, she gestured to the corpses lying below the summit of Little Roundtop. "What did you mean when you said if the Confederates want their men back they should come and get them?" She scowled. "Surely you don't want the Rebs to return, do you? Do you think we should leave them unburied? That wouldn't be Christian."

Corporal Wilson didn't reply. He shrugged and turned to stare down the Plum Run Valley.

"We did a lot of our fighting out on the railroad cut north of town on the first day," he told them. "Them bas—uh, those men did some of the hardest fighting I ever seen." He fell silent. His eyes hardened. "They sure are some d—uh—good fighters. We beat them off. They come back so we beat them off again, and again they come back. We began to think there was an endless supply of them boys, but we drove 'em off for good. Not before losing our commanding officer, Colonel Stone, and our second in command, Lieutenant Colonel Dwight. Good men."

Corporal Wilson's eyes fixed on a point down the valley, and Tillie turned. She scanned the destruction below her. Pointing to the Valley of Death, she marveled. "Look how they all lie in a row like corn or wheat."

"They lay as they fell," George said.

Tillie nodded, acknowledging the remark. She tried to picture these men—alive, advancing side by side—cut down, side by side. Her brow creased again. The extreme bravery the men required to move forward, knowing they might die, and go anyway. She became aware of an almost reverential silence, broken only by their quiet voices, the soft breeze moving through the trees, and the sound of her own heartbeat.

The words of James, chapter four came back to her. "Whereas ye know not what shall be on the morrow. For what is your life?"

What was her life? No answer came to her.

"Well, lieutenant"—Corporal Wilson's deep baritone brought Tillie out of her reverie—"I've tarried long enough. I must be on my way." He saluted George and again touched his fingers to his hat brim. "Ladies, a pleasure."

Tillie and Beckie murmured goodbyes as he strode down the hill and into the Valley of Death, whistling "Dixie".

Beckie let out her breath. "There goes a strange fellow."

Why must Beckie always do that? Must she always dismiss people out of hand, rather than try to figure them out? Tillie pushed the thought away. "After what he's been through I suspect he has the right to be whatever he wishes."

Beckie glared at her. Tillie met her gaze, refusing to back down.

"Come." George broke the tension. "I want to show you where some of the bravest men I know did some of the fiercest fighting."

Beckie broke eye contact first. She allowed George to turn her around and lead them back the way they came, crossing the rocks and plunging into the woods of Little Roundtop. George followed a line of rocks and fallen timber standing like an ancient stone wall in severe disrepair. Tillie tried not to glance down the slope of the hill because she knew what would meet her eye.

As soon as the thought came to her, she looked. Row upon row of dead men, some lay with their heads toward the stone wall, which told her they had been shot while coming up the hill. Others sprawled on the ground facing the opposite way, arms above their heads, one leg crooked as though shot in the act of running away.

The breeze rustled through the trees, silent sentinels of the dead. In their mottled shade, stillness prevailed, affecting the three as they sauntered about. Their normal speaking voices lowered until they almost whispered. The reverence of the place awed Tillie.

Below the summit of the hill lay more dead bodies clad in gray. She averted her face.

They continued to move along parallel to the hastily erected wall extending deeper into the woods. When they came to a certain spot, George stopped and addressed to the two women. Though he stood surrounded by trees, the sun still shone bright on him. Tillie glanced up. The tops of the trees shattered, the branches, denuded of their summertime leaves, stretched their arms out in dismay.

"They look like horror-struck witnesses." Tillie twisted this way and that. "If trees could feel, these would be screaming in agony."

Beckie smiled at her, but Tillie saw her roll her eyes when she looked at George.

"This is where the 20th Maine boys held off Colonel Oates's Alabamians and helped us win the day on July the second. If they hadn't been here, the Rebs would have swarmed over this hill and come charging down the other side, taking us from behind. In fact, the Rebs would have been in your backyard. Even when the Maine boys ran out of ammunition, they still kept fighting. Instead of backing off they charged the Alabamians and chased them back down the hill."

Tillie tried to picture the scene George painted. She gazed about her. "I remember cannonading so loud we couldn't even talk to each other. Even shouting into one another's ear, you still couldn't hear. We were terrified." The simple way she explained didn't do the situation justice, but she couldn't conjure the words to describe the experience.

George strolled to a tree, and using a jackknife, pried loose a bullet lodged deep in the trunk of a once mighty oak. He brought the mangled slug to Beckie, and removing his cap, held it out to her. She smiled and put it in her pocket.

Wanting to be anywhere but here, Tillie walked a few paces away and pretended to examine an oak, felled by bullets, while the couple exchanged an intimate moment.

They started back late in the afternoon. On the way, George picked out a few more spots where fighting had been fierce. Mr. Sherfy's peach orchard and the adjoining wheat field now yielded a crop of dead bodies. He didn't take them over, merely pointed them out as they walked home. Tillie remembered being on the roof and asking why those men were so far forward. Now she saw, from a distance, the horrible result of their mistake.

As they walked into the yard, it was clear neither George nor Beckie wanted his visit to end. "Won't you stay and eat supper with us, George?" Beckie tilted her head and ran her hand up and down his sleeve.

"Thank you, no." George removed his cap and wiped his brow. He gave her a look of regret. "I promised Ma I'd take supper with them. I must return to my unit by eight o'clock this evening, so I won't be back again. I'm not sure when I'll get another chance to come home."

"I understand." Beckie pouted, and then flashed him a brilliant smile. A look of fury flashed in her eyes, but she covered it with a shrug and cast her gaze to the ground. When she looked back at him, her smile was sugary sweet. She held her body rigid, and Tillie could tell she did not understand and was miffed at his refusal.

"Thank you, George, for including me in your tour. I had a good time." Tillie extended her hand. "But if you'll excuse me, I'll go see if Doctor Billings needs me. We've been gone all afternoon." On impulse, she leaned in and gave George a quick peck on the cheek. She trotted inside, leaving them alone to say goodbye. She enjoyed their walk, but she wanted to be alone, discomfited and anxious by the sights. Though she lived through the fighting, now two days past, she never imagined the scale on which human beings imparted such violence upon one another, and still called themselves human beings.

Instead of going in search of Doctor Billings, she headed to the bedroom and retrieved her now precious Bible. She clasped the book to her breast then sank to her knees beside the bed, needing to pray. The sight of so many men left out in the weather, to rot like so much refuse unsettled her. It was one thing to observe from a distance, quite another to stare down into the blackened, bloated face of a once vibrant man. She knelt by the side of the bed for a long time, trying to clear her mind, but she didn't know what to pray for. The men in the field were dead. Their need for prayer ended. She offered up a grateful word of thanks for James's life, though ill, and asked the Lord to heal him.

She let go and cried. She cried for all the wounded men who still needed so much care. She cried for the dead men still left on the field. She cried for those men who emerged physically unscathed but bore unseen scars. Most of all, Tillie cried for herself, overwhelmed by her circumstance. As she wept into the quilt, warmth overtook her, as if someone dropped a blanket over her shoulders. A soft voice spoke in her ear, "Be still."

Tillie jerked her head off the bed. Her gaze roamed around the room, and she raised the blankets and glanced under the bed. Did someone sneak in to play tricks on her? She wiped her tears and studied the room. She was alone. Tillie shook her head. She was being silly. Her emotions ran away with her. The words of the young captain came back to her, "Because God meant it for good." She rose to her feet and laid herself across the bed. Then she opened her Bible and began to read.

Chapter 23

A rumor sped through the Fifth Corps, about a hospital camp established on York Road, a mile outside of town. Ambulances dispatched across the battlefield, gathered up the wounded. So far, no one had collected the poor souls from the Weikerts', much to Mr. Weikert's consternation. As the battle faded further into the past, Mr. Weikert wandered his lands and house bemoaning his fate to all. His anger often exploded without warning. Even Mollie and Sadie tried to avoid him, not knowing what would set him off.

His wife and daughters paid no mind to his bitter complaints as they continued to work. The more he complained, the less people listened. Even the men feigned sleep to escape him. The doctors took to calling him "The Mean Dutchman", though never to his face.

Mrs. Weikert closed the cupboard door, but didn't bother locking it. "We're out of flour and sugar." She faced her husband. "Do you suppose the army might give us some?"

"How should I know? What am I? The flour and sugar man?"

Everyone gaped at his savage tone.

"Jacob, please don't shout at me. I'm simply trying to tell you our circumstances." Mrs. Weikert grabbed her apron in her hands and squeezed the fabric in spasmodic motions. Emotion choked her voice.

He stomped to the kitchen door, flinging it wide. "You want circumstances, woman, I'll give you circumstances! Look outside." The door slammed against the wall and rebounded back. Mr. Weikert caught it in a white-knuckled grip. He flung his other hand out toward his farmyard. "The pigs escaped the first day when the army tore down my fences for firewood. Those that didn't escape, they carted off. Any cows not killed in the fighting either went dry, or again, the army got them." He slammed the door with a resounding bang. The frame swayed with the impact. "I know our circumstances!" He flung the words at her, while his face blotched purplish red and the vein in his forehead throbbed fast.

Mrs. Weikert shrunk in the face of his fury. She tucked her lips between her teeth, stared at a point on the floor, and did not utter another word.

Dan concentrated on making coffins. Beckie and her sister did their best to create biscuits with the few supplies left.

Tillie cared for the wounded, trying to move around in an unobtrusive manner. He counted her among the mouths to feed, though he didn't come out and say so. Perhaps if they hadn't eaten so well on the first day, they wouldn't be in the predicament they were in now. Recalling that first meal the day she arrived made her mouth water. Now they ate bread with water. Coffee was long gone.

When could she go home and not be a burden anymore? The battle ended six days ago. Why wait any longer? Since no one discussed her leaving, she didn't ask, even though the Confederates left Saturday morning and today was Tuesday. Most of the Union departed Monday in hot pursuit. She picked off pieces of her bread and chewed. While she ate, she pulled her Bible from her apron pocket to read.

"Miss Tillie, join me in the surgery room when you've finished." Doctor Billings walked out of the room.

She glanced up from her book in acknowledgment. After her meal, she washed her dishes. At the top of the stairs, she remembered she left the Bible on the table. Tillie went back to the kitchen. Halfway down, voices drifted up to her. Deep in discussion, they did not hear her return. She froze, trying to decide if she should continue down or go back up, but Mr. Weikert's words held her.

"We're gonna starve come winter, Sarah. You mark my words."

Tillie peered over the railing. Mr. Weikert stood at the door staring out at his destroyed farm. He faced his wife when she didn't answer. "I can't repair these fields, not this summer. My livestock is gone. It's too late in the season to do more than put in a winter garden, but a garden won't grow without water."

Mrs. Weikert sighed, a tired, resigned breath of air. “Jacob, we’ll get by.” She made a lame gesture with her hands. “I don’t know how, but we’ll get by. Stop fretting. You’ll worry the children.”

Tillie made a noise on the stair and bounded down the remainder of the steps. “Oh, there it is.” She gestured toward the table. “I thought I left it here.”

Mr. Weikert glared at her. Mrs. Weikert waited in polite silence for her to leave. Tillie fingered the book. Dare she speak? “My father likes to read from Matthew. One verse in particular goes like this: ‘Therefore, I say unto you, take no thought for your life, what ye shall eat or what ye shall drink; nor yet for your body what ye shall put on. Is not the life more than meat, and the body than raiment? Behold, the fowl of the air for they sow not, neither do they reap, nor gather into barns; yet your heavenly Father feedeth them. Are ye not much better than they?’” Her eyes traveled from one adult to the other. They didn’t respond. She shrugged, a quick gesture, and smiled. Slipping the book into her apron pocket, she headed upstairs.

****

“Tillie, we leave after breakfast,” Mrs. Schriver announced the minute Tillie entered the basement kitchen.

“Yes, ma’am.” Tillie nodded. “I’ll be ready.” She didn’t want to sound pleased over the prospect of going home, but she was homesick and wanted to be away from this place.

Remembering her manners, she smiled at Mr. and Mrs. Weikert, who sat holding hands at the table. “Thank you for sheltering me. I hope I didn’t cause too much trouble or inconvenience to you.”

“Oh, child, not at all.” Mrs. Weikert returned her smile. She let go her husband’s hand, moved hers to her lap, and back to the table. “We just wish you came to us under better circumstances. Don’t we, dear?”

He glared at the table. Did he think her insolent for quoting the Bible? She didn’t want him to despair over his farm. Even so, she got the distinct feeling, in some odd way Mr. Weikert equated the devastation of his property with her presence.

After a quick meal, Mrs. Schriver gathered up her daughters and Tillie, and after saying their goodbyes, they headed home.

"I hope I still have a home to go to," Mrs. Schriver said as they trudged up what was left of Taneytown Road. A hard rain saturated the ground during the night. Their feet sunk deep in mud, as thick and gooey as when they arrived. Mrs. Schriver, Tillie, and the girls struggled along as the slime squished under their shoes and sucked at their feet. Muddy water once again drenched the hems of their dresses. Only today, they didn't have to battle an army marching in the opposite direction.

The stench of rotting horseflesh, as well as the flesh of those men laying on the battlefield, still lay thick in the heavy summer air. Tillie put her arm over her nose and mouth and tried to breathe into the fabric of her dress.

She took a new grasp on Sadie's hand and continued walking. Several times, they detoured around horses, bloated to double their size, blocking their way. They took wide berths around groups of dead men lying in rows as they fell.

"Why are their clothes all torn up?" Mollie stared at the corpses, their garments in disarray on their decomposing frames, as though someone had rifled their bodies.

"Don't look at them," Mrs. Schriver commanded, jerking the child forward.

"Mr. Kitzmiller told us the other day." Tillie also studied the bodies. "The soldiers often did that to themselves, looking for their wounds. He told us they knew if they were gut-shot they'd die."

"I don't want to hear any more about soldiers dying or their wounds!" Mrs. Schriver shrieked. "I want to go home!"

The girls fell silent as they continued walking. Hopping over puddles of blood and body parts still lying in the fields, and around ruined accouterments of battle. Inured to the destruction around them, they no longer reacted to it.

Nothing compared to the flies. Black masses of bluebottle, blowflies, and horseflies flew about at ground level. Their little group walked along, disturbing large clouds of the pests that rose up and settled back over their feasts as soon as the women strode by.

They came to Mrs. Leicester's home. General Meade made his headquarters here. Tillie's heart sank at the sight of the property. Widow Leicester lived in her two-room home with her son, surviving hand to mouth. Reverend Bergstrasser often took up offerings to help the poor in town and frequently bestowed the help upon Mrs. Leicester. Her small farm, all she owned in the world, now destroyed. Maggot-infested horses decomposed in the yard. Soldiers lay where they died, her fences gone. Shells struck the house several times. A shell destroyed the steps leading to the front door where Tillie sat and rested the day they went to the Weikerts'.

"Oh, poor Mrs. Leicester. What will she do now?" Tillie stared at the devastation.

"I don't know. Her son won't be able to do much to make repairs. I hope the men in town can help. Poor woman." Mrs. Schriver eyed her girls. "Well come on. We might as well see what's in store for us."

They started to walk away, but Tillie couldn't pull her eyes away from Mrs. Leicester's house. Pillars holding up the front porch roof were gone, and one corner of the roof sprawled on the boards below.

Someone jerry-rigged poles to hold up the part of the roof still attached to the house, allowing the soldiers to come and go without fear of the structure falling on them. Beyond this mess, a huge hole gaped in the roof where a cannonball made a point of entry. The chimney was a heap of smashed bricks. Shattered caissons were left scattered about the yard, some still hitched to their dead horses.

"I feel as though I stepped into a strange and blighted land," Mrs. Schriver said in a low frightened whisper.

The destruction cast a pall over the landscape, causing them to speak in quiet, respectful tones. Tillie nodded, unable to find words to describe her emotions. Her throat tightened. Surely if she tried to speak, she would dissolve into uncontrollable tears.

They entered the cemetery, compelled to pick their steps. Even so, once or twice, they tripped over broken blocks of headstones, and here too, dead men and horses littered the ground.

Something was missing, but Tillie couldn't discern what. For the first time in her life, she was uncomfortable and a little frightened to be outside.

"It's so quiet." Mollie stared about her with huge blue eyes, voicing Tillie's subconscious thoughts. The child's words dropped an unsettling piece of the puzzle into place. Aside from the horrific destruction, a terrible silence surrounded them. She recalled before the battle—for that was how she thought of things now—walking through the cemetery and listening to the birds as they sang or the wind as it sighed through the trees. The absence of these sounds unsettled her.

Passing through the shattered archway of the once beautiful entrance gate, Mrs. Schriver stepped on a wooden sign. Tillie picked it up, recognizing it as the sign that always hung outside the cemetery gate. She read aloud. "'The use of firearms within the boundaries of this cemetery will be prosecuted to the fullest extent of the law.'" Someone drew a huge X through the words and underneath scrawled, "Order rescinded until further notice." She laughed, cringing at the sound.

They emerged on Baltimore Street, but when they reached the Garlachs' home, a barricade blocked their way. All kinds of material, piled against the wall of the Garlachs' home, stretched across the street to the wall of the Winebrenners'.

"My table!" Mrs. Schriver shrieked, throwing her hands to her face. "What is my table doing in this heap of mess?" Sobbing, she clawed through the tangled mass. Her efforts growing frantic as she uncovered other belongings. Enraged, she tried to untangle the pile in search of more treasured items incorporated into it. Mrs. Schriver discovered her parlor sofa lying on its side, riddled with bullet holes. She fell upon the sofa, cradled her head in her arms, and wailed harder.

"Mrs. Schriver, this does no good." Tillie tried to be of some comfort, but the woman ignored her and wept over her belongings. After a few minutes, Mrs. Schriver, in a fury, began to yank and pry in another futile attempt to free some of her furniture. Tillie stepped back and waited. Couldn't the woman see they were just things? Her life—her daughter's lives were more important. When Mr. Schriver came home from the war, they could always buy a new sofa. Tillie took Mollie and Sadie by the hand. While Mrs. Schriver sobbed and tugged at the barricade, Tillie studied the pile, looking for places to climb over it.

Finally, Mrs. Schriver gave up trying to reclaim her furniture. Whoever made the barricade knew how to construct an impenetrable wall, and she couldn't budge it. She threw her head back and screamed invectives at those responsible for abusing her belongings.

Tillie placed her hands on Mrs. Schriver's arm. "Please don't cry, Mrs. Schriver. It's hard to see your furniture like this, but stop and think. You're alive. The girls are well. Please don't cry."

While Mrs. Schriver swallowed her sobs, sniffed, and wiped her face, Tillie showed her where she thought they could climb the barricade. Mrs. Schriver went first. Tillie helped the girls climb the stack and handed them over. Then Tillie climbed over the top of the pile and picked her way down. They exchanged silent hugs. She waited while the others went up the steps and disappeared inside without as much as a backward glance. She curbed the urge to run and forced herself to adopt a sedate walk home.

As she approached the vacant lot next door, she discovered several holes and chips in the bricks on the south side of the house. Tillie lingered to count the bullet holes, quitting at seventeen. She didn't need to count them all. Fear pricked her heart. Were they safe and unharmed or did someone die like Ginny?

What if someone lay hurt or dying and the lieutenant chose not to tell her? Tillie rushed up the stairs and hurried into the house. Once inside she stopped short. Huge bundles lay strewn throughout the hallway. Did the Army force them to leave? She peered into the parlor. A bloodstain spoiled the couch. Someone's been hurt! Did they die here? Was one of her family hurt, dying? "Stop!" she scolded, unwilling to raise her voice above a whisper. "Just stop."

In the sitting room, bundles of cloth and bowls cluttered every inch of the table. Some of the bowls half filled with water, others with cloth bandages hung over the edge. She tiptoed inside and ran a finger around one of the bowls, pushing the cloth back in. Bending down, she righted a chair, and then another she pushed back into place.

The silence made her heart pound and her hands shake. She tried to make as little noise as possible. She carried a bowl into the kitchen, which was also in complete disarray. The food shelf stood empty. Someone left pots and pans unwashed in the sink, crumbs and empty crock jars on the table.

The chairs here were also in disorder. Mother always pushed the chairs in at the table in a neat square when not in use.

Fear pricked Tillie's heart. Mother would never leave her kitchen in such a state. Something happened.

A floorboard creaked over her head. Her eyes went to the ceiling, and she listened. Another footstep, coming from the room above her, at the top of the stairway. William's bedroom. Tillie walked to the hallway and jogged up the stairs. At the landing between the first and second floor, she heard Mother say something in a quiet voice and Maggie respond.

Tillie entered the bedroom. Mother sat on the edge of the bed, with her back to the door. Maggie sat on the other side, dipping a bandage into a basin of water. They concentrated on the soldier moaning between them. The sickening sweet smell in the room told her his wound festered.

Tillie opened her mouth to say hello when Mother rose from the bed. She turned to stretch her back and saw Tillie standing in the doorway. Mother froze and her eyes widened.

"Am I so changed, Mother, you don't even recognize me?" Tillie's laugh sounded forced.

"Oh, my dear child, is that you?" Mother held out her arms, and Tillie threw herself into her warm embrace. "I'm so glad you're home again. No harm has befallen you?"

Tillie tightened her grip on her mother as sudden sobs jerked her body. Mother's embrace deepened as she rocked and crooned into Tillie's ear. Maggie's arm slid around her back, and Tillie released one of hers and embraced Maggie as well. The three women hugged and cried. After several moments, they pulled apart, and Tillie smiled at them. "I must look a sight. You didn't even recognize me when I came in." She swept a hand down her dress. "I confess I am filthy."

"For a moment I thought you were some ragamuffin orphan looking for a home." Mother sniffled and wiped tears from her cheeks. "Your clothes are still in the basement. Why don't you go down and get yourself a bath." She put her arm around Tillie and guided her out the door and back down the stairs all the while keeping up a commentary. "Father went to the church to find a doctor for that poor man." She gestured toward the bedroom. "He took a turn for the worse in the night. Sam went home for a few days. I trust the captain told you about Ginny?"

"He did." The smile disappeared from Tillie's face. Deep circles lurked under Mother's eyes, and her hair needed brushing. Her skin appeared sallow and her cheeks sunken, but all things considered, they came through pretty well. The soldier moaned again. Mother glanced back upstairs.

"You go ahead, Mother. I can get my own bath ready and change, and come up to help you if you need me. If not, I'll be happy to clean up downstairs."

Mother brushed her knuckles along Tillie's cheek. Tillie closed her eyes and leaned into Mother's hand. Mother kissed the spot where her hand touched. "Welcome home, my dear. I'm so glad you're back, safe and sound."

"I'm glad to be home." Tillie smiled. "I missed you all so much." Her voice choked, and water filled her eyes. She cleared her throat and blinked fast several times.

Mother returned upstairs. Tillie watched her go then went down to clean up.

Chapter 24

Tillie bounded up the cellar stairs and closed the door before stepping into the kitchen. She bumped into Father as he entered from the backyard.

He grabbed her in a fierce embrace, startling her as his tears wet her shoulder. She patted his back with soft, uncertain strokes. Father held her so tight, her ribs hurt and she struggled to breathe. Nevertheless, she wrapped her arms around him and squeezed him tight.

"Oh my dear, sweet child. Please forgive me for sending you away." Her wet hair muffled his words.

"Father." Tillie hugged him tighter. "There's nothing to forgive." She kissed his cheek and smiled. Her tears mingled with his, and her heart swelled.

He cupped her cheeks in his palms and stared deep into her eyes, before snugging her back into his embrace. "I sent you from the frying pan straight into the fire."

"You did what you thought best. I'm not angry." She leaned back in his arms. "Besides, all's well that ends well."

At dinner, which consisted of bread—without jam or apple butter—and water, they exchanged stories. While they ate, she told them of her experiences—about General Weed, of the Army forcing them from the house, and of their desperate flight to Two Taverns. At several points, she hesitated. How much of what she witnessed should she share? She picked her words, not wanting to upset her parents. They expressed their guilt many times already. As she finished, she shrugged as though to say, oh well, I'm safe and unharmed.

Taking Father's hand, she glanced around the table. "I do have one good thing to tell you as a result of my experiences." A sudden stab of self-consciousness overcame her as heat rose up her neck and into her face. She gave them a shy smile. "You and Mother will be pleased."

"Do tell." He squeezed her hand.

"When I sat with the captain caring for the general, he gave me his Bible. We talked a great deal. Then we evacuated. I found a lot of time to read and… I can't explain it, but I understood what you and Mother tried to tell me all these years. A man came over and helped me work through the passages. Turns out he's a minister." Looking around at her family's bemused faces, she smiled a big happy grin. "Well, I guess what I'm trying to say is I've given my life to Christ. I don't want to sound like I'm bragging, but it's true."

Father stood and tugged Tillie to her feet. He held her close. He wiped the moisture from his eyes. "My child! So long we waited for you to say those words." His tears wet her cheeks when he kissed her.

Mother turned her from Father's embrace and engulfed her in a soft and gentle hug. "I'm so happy, my dear. We've prayed over your soul."

Tillie cried. "Yes, I know. I'm so sorry for the anguish and the hurt I caused. I'm a terrible sinner, and I hope you can forgive me." Maggie joined in the family embrace. They hugged, kissed, and cried before, sniffling and smiling, they returned to their seats.

"We shouldn't be sitting here like dolls, we should be thanking God!" Tillie smacked her hand down on the table. "We're safe, we're alive, and James, at least, is still among the living." She grabbed Father's hand. "Tell me what happened to you."

"Yes." Mother grinned, a conspiratorial tone in her voice. "Tell her about your harrowing experiences."

"You can also tell her how you captured confederate prisoners with an empty musket!" Maggie added, with a sly wink toward her sister.

"What's this?" Tillie grinned. "Father, do tell!"

He held up his hands in a gesture of surrender. "All right, all right! Margaret, do we have any coffee? This is going to be a long night of storytelling."

"A little, James." Mother's tone said she didn't think they should waste it in such a way.

"Make some." He decided.

Mother rose and went to the stove. The conversation continued while she prepared a pot of coffee. When ready, she set out a cup for everyone, including Tillie.

"Thank you." She smiled at Mother, who never allowed her to drink coffee before.

"So, Father, tell me what happened to you." Tillie sipped from her cup.

"Well." He fiddled with his wedding ring. "First things first. Soon after you left, the battle started in earnest. Reverend Bergstrasser stopped over to say they brought the wounded to the warehouses by the railroad station. He asked if I wanted to go along and offer our services, so I decided to go."

Father sipped his coffee. He placed the cup back on the saucer and began to twist his wedding ring.

Tillie sat up straight.

"We found several of our boys badly hurt and begging for whiskey to deaden their pain." He laid his hand over Tillie's. "Remember when you asked me why on earth they would want such a thing?"

A frown shadowed her face. Memories of soldiers crying for booze, or a bullet, to end their agony assaulted her, making her swallow hard and shift in her seat to rid herself of the vision.

"Well, now we can understand why. The suppliers moved most of the alcohol out of town, but I told them I'd try to get some from private homes. I went door to door, but couldn't find any. Our soldiers began running through the streets. I shouted at one to stop, but he kept going. Another stopped long enough to tell me the army was retreating toward the cemetery. Then he too, ran off. I left your mother and sister alone with Sam, so I rushed back as fast as possible. Within a block of our house, a Rebel soldier appeared from behind Winebrenners'." Father sipped his coffee.

"What happened?"

He set his cup down with a deep breath. "Well, he hallooed, and then shouted, 'Hey, what are you doing with a gun in your hand?' I assure you, my dear, I wasn't armed. I put my hands in the air and said, 'I have no gun!' That made no difference. The man raised his rifle and aimed at me. I threw myself upon the ground as he fired. I can still hear the whistle as the bullet passed over my head. He apparently thought he hit me, making one Yankee the less before going on his way, because he didn't wait to discover if he killed me."

Tillie gasped, "Oh, Father, no!"

Maggie held up one finger. "It gets better."

Tillie's gaze slid from her sister to her father.

Father chuckled. "After he disappeared, I got up." He leaned in close. "No sooner did I do so, when I found myself surrounded by no less than five Confederate soldiers who came from Breckenridge Street. By way of greeting, they said to me, 'Old man, why ain't you in your house?' When I replied I was trying to do so, they told me to fall in, which I did, and walked with them to the steps. When I reached the front door, I said, 'Now, boys, I'm home and I am most certainly going to stay here.' I hoped they would let me go inside, but one of them demanded to search the house for Union soldiers. Not knowing better, I assured him they wouldn't find any, just two women and a young boy." Father narrowed his eyes at Mother in a mock glare and wagged a finger at her.

Tillie swiveled her head from one parent to the other. "What happened?" Her voice rose with excitement.

Mother and Maggie exchanged a glance and laughed.

Tillie spread her hands out. "What?"

"Well," he resumed his story. "Those men believed me and moved on. With a huge sigh of relief, I went up the steps, but another squad of Rebels arrived and also insisted on searching the house. They threatened to break in the door, but I convinced them to desist, insisting we had no soldiers. Besides, I said, breaking into private homes was against the rules of war, which seemed to decide them. One of them asked me to give my word, so I did, and another of them said, 'Boys, I take this gentleman's word.' Another asked me, 'By the way, what are your proclivities?'" Father sat up straight and puffed out his chest like a proud peacock. "I told them, 'I am an unconditional Union man and a whole-souled one.'"

Tillie gasped and covered her mouth. Her eyes widened as she stared at him.

"They said to me, 'Well, we like you all the better for that. We hate the milk-and-water Unionists.' They told me to get inside saying they wouldn't shoot me, but somebody would. Most likely our own men, as the Yankee sharpshooters out by the cemetery started sending their bullets in this direction."

"I saw bullet holes on the side of the house when I came home," Tillie interrupted. "Seventeen of them."

Father nodded. "There are more on the back of the house as well."

She waved her hand at this turn of conversation. They could discuss bullet holes later. "What happened next, Father?"

He sat back. "Well, I went up the front steps only to find the door barred against me. I pounded, but no one answered. I went to the back, hoping to get in through the kitchen door—also locked. I banged on the door and shouted for all I was worth for someone to let me in. Still no answer. Thinking I might be shot for trying to get into my own home, I began to wonder what to do. Then I remembered the outside cellar door, discovered it unlocked, and got in the house." He put a hand on Tillie's arm. "Imagine my surprise." He chuckled again. "I got in and found no less than five," he held up a hand, all five fingers spread, "wounded Union soldiers hiding in the basement with your mother, sister, and Sam. Two captains, one corporal, and the other two privates. They stayed for the three days of fighting. They had to as we were behind Confederate lines. Mother and Maggie dressed their wounds."

"Is the man upstairs one of them?"

"No." Mother flicked a hand toward the ceiling. "His name is Colonel Colvill of the First Minnesota. A few days after the fighting ended, some of his men came to the house and asked if we would take him in. He seemed in such a bad way. I thought what if James or William needed help? I would want someone to nurse them in my absence, so I told them to put him in William's room."

"We've been caring for him ever since." Maggie's voice held a note of tenderness.

"What happened to the five men?"

"A day or two after, a group of soldiers with a cart came and took them to Camp Letterman." Maggie told her.

"To where?"

"To Camp Letterman. A hospital camp the Army set up on York Road about a mile outside of town."

"I knew about the camp." Tillie nodded. "I didn't know it had a name."

"During the day," Maggie went on, "we stayed in the basement. Only at night, after the shooting stopped, did we come upstairs and go to bed. I assure you, I did not sleep a wink for three nights."

Mother and Father murmured their agreement.

"One night," Mother picked up the thread of the story, "late in the night I heard voices outside and noises in the house. I feared they would find the men, so I got up and peeked out the window. Father told me to get back in bed, but I needed to see."

She took a deep breath. "Confederate soldiers came out of the basement and crossed Breckenridge Street, their arms full of the food we hid. They sat themselves down on the curb and enjoyed a little picnic." Her voice choked, and her face hardened.

Maggie put her hand on Mother's arm.

"How did they get in?" Tillie eyed Mother then Maggie.

"Through the outside basement door." Father shook his head. "It now has a lock on it, but it feels a bit like closing the barn door after the horse has escaped. I never thought anyone would take such advantage as they did."

"So much for our efforts," Tillie said. "How naïve to think a simple curtain would keep away hungry hordes of men."

She turned to Father. "Tell me how you captured Rebels with an empty musket. I want to hear about that."

"Well." He held out his coffee cup in a silent request for more. Mother refilled everyone's cup.

"The day after the fighting stopped, I went outside to see what might be going on. I found a musket lying on the road and picked it up. As soon as I did, I saw a Rebel running behind Mrs. Schriver's house. I held up the gun and shouted, 'Halt!'"

Tillie gasped.

"He threw up his hands and hollered, 'I'm a deserter, I'm a deserter,' and I said, yes, and a fine specimen you are. Fall in!" He placed his hand on top of Tillie's. "I started marching him toward the Diamond, when two more Rebs appeared out of nowhere. I called to them, and they also fell in." Father sipped his coffee. "Then some Union soldiers appeared, and I handed them off. But I decided I was having so much fun, I went in the direction of Cemetery Hill to see if I could find more Rebs. To get around the barricade, I went toward Washington Street, and on that corner, I found another Reb. When he saw me, he put down his gun and raised his hands. Two of his companions appeared, and I marched them back toward the Diamond until I came across more Union men to hand those Rebs over too." He lifted his cup for another sip then grinned. "I decided at that point, not to push my luck too much and came home. When I arrived, I checked the gun and found it empty of bullets." He threw his head back, and his laughter rang through the room.

Tillie laughed with him. "Oh, Father, that must have been quite a shock. Oh my."

After a few moments, they calmed down, and everyone fell silent. Then Maggie picked up the thread.

"One of the five soldiers, hiding here, Corporal O'Brien," Maggie straightened in her chair, "told me about his frightening encounter with the Rebs. We put the wounded in all the spare bedrooms, including yours, so the corporal stayed on the sofa in the parlor. In the morning, as I dressed his wounds, he told me the Rebs came upstairs. He crawled off the couch as quietly as possible and hid. They wandered from room to room. One speculated whether we harbored Yankees in the house. Another replied, seeing they were in Yankee territory, the house harbored nothing but Yankees, just not prisoner types. The corporal hoped the darkness would hide him, biting his tongue to keep from laughing and giving himself away. The Rebel soldiers passed right by him and went back downstairs."

"My." Tillie's heart lurched. "At the Weikerts', the Union Army surrounded us. We only encountered wounded Rebs. I'm so thankful you came through unharmed."

****

They sat at the kitchen table and talked until midnight, catching up and enjoying each other's company before retiring. Then for the first time in eight nights, Tillie climbed into her own bed. She sank into her mattress, uttered a deep sigh of contentment, and fell fast asleep.

She awoke before sunrise. Used to rising early while at the Weikerts', and forgetting she was home, she got up. Half-dressed, she froze and gazed around her bedroom before bursting out laughing. "I could have stayed in bed a while longer. I'm home now." She chuckled at herself and finished dressing. She washed her hands and face, then combed her hair one hundred strokes before braiding it, and offered a word of thanks to the Lord for simple things like clean clothes and hairbrushes.

She made her way down the hallway, arriving in time to see Father disappear up to the attic. Curious, she followed him. He stood at the south window, staring out toward Cemetery Hill. He turned at her approach and held out an arm.

She crossed to him and laid her head on his chest. He held her close, kissing the top of her head.

"What are you doing up here, Father?"

"Oh, just looking. During the battle I came up here to watch what went on." He took her elbow, moving her in front of him.

"You put yourself in danger." She peeked at him over her shoulder.

"Look." He pointed toward Mrs. Schriver's house.

Tillie sighted down the length of his arm as if down the barrel of a gun. She peered into her garret. Someone punched several holes through the wall on either side of the window. On the floor, under the window, was a large, dried pool of blood. Tillie frowned. "I'm looking, but I'm not sure what you're showing me."

"Do you see those holes in the wall?"

She nodded.

"The first night I came up here. In the small hours of the night the sound of our boys, chopping, shoveling, pickaxing—preparing their breastworks for the next day's fight—carried in the cool air. Afterward I came up here during the lulls. Sometimes the wounded boys joined me." He draped his arm over Tillie's shoulder. "Confederate soldiers took up a position in Mrs. Schriver's garret. They're the ones who made the holes in the wall, like portholes. They used her garret as a sharpshooters' nest. Many of our boys wished they were still armed so they could take care of them." He shrugged at her horrified expression. "Once the boys on Cemetery Hill figured out where the firing came from, they let loose a volley this way. I still marvel that the Yanks didn't send a shell or two toward us. One of the sharpshooters threw his arms up and fell backward. A mad scramble ensued, and they dragged the man off to the side. After dark they carried his body out the back door and into her garden."

Tillie turned around and hugged him. Father responded with a gentle squeeze across her shoulders.

"At the Weikerts'." Her voice sounded muffled against his shirt. "On the second day, some soldiers came to the house and asked to go up on the roof. Mrs. Weikert told me to show them the way, so I did. They allowed me to join them. One of them even gave me his field glasses!" She grinned, recalling her fascination with the glasses. "At the time, I didn't understand what they showed me, but General Sickles had moved his men into Mr. Sherfy's orchard. Way out ahead of the rest of the Union line." She refrained from bragging and sharing how she had discovered, and asked, what he was doing, bringing it to their attention.

"A terrible fight," he agreed. "The man in your brother's bed led the charge to drive the rebels from there." He shook his head. "One of his nurses told us of the two hundred sixty-two men Colonel Colvill led into the Peach Orchard, only forty-six came out alive, including him—barely."

"Poor man." Tillie frowned. "I hope he gets better."

"As do we all." Father resumed his story. "At night they would leave the garret and come over here. They entered the cellar, took our food, and went out to the curb on Breckenridge to eat. Now, there's nothing left stored for winter. It will be a hungry time for many in town, including us. So, I come up here, look over at where our boys fought with such valor, and wonder what's to become of us."

Tillie studied her father. He never shared his doubts with her. Now uncertainty quavered in his voice, and fear reflected in the crease of his brow and set of his jaw.

"We'll be all right, Father. You always tell us to wait on the Lord and he will provide. Do you still believe that?"

"Yes, I do. Perhaps, with everything that's happened these past days, I forgot. Thank you for the reminder." He smiled down at her and hugged her close.

Tillie leaned against him, savoring his embrace. She inhaled, and this time, the metallic scent of animal blood no longer made her want to gag. It was part of Father, like his warm brown eyes and graying temples. A pang of regret hit her for all the times she hurt him by avoiding his embrace. "Come." She tugged his arm. "Let's go downstairs and see what Mother made for breakfast. She always puts something on the table for us."

When she smiled up at her father in complete confidence, he leaned down and kissed her forehead. Arm in arm, they left the garret and went down to breakfast.

As Tillie cleaned up from their meager breakfast, her gaze fell on a round hole in the wall, behind the cook stove. Curious, she bent for a closer look.

"That happened during the third day." Maggie entered the house from the kitchen door, clean sheets draped over her arm. "Some Rebs—deserters we think—came and told Mother to go upstairs and cook them some food. I don't know how she managed to be so brave, but she told them no. She wouldn't cook for her own family just then, and she surely wouldn't cook for them. A short time later, a volley of fire came this way, and after the fighting ceased, we came up here and found that hole. Sam found the bullet on the floor by the sitting room door." Maggie gestured toward the doorway. "If Mother complied, she would have been killed."

"So you were in danger." Tillie pushed down a wave of emotion.

Maggie shrugged. "No worse than you, or anyone else around here, and besides, we all survived."

****

While Mother and Maggie continued to care for the colonel, who mended slowly, Tillie spent her time downstairs cleaning and restoring the house to its former condition. One afternoon, she headed to the basement to find something for dinner. Stopping in front of the shelf Sam and Father made, she stared at the empty space.

"How gullible to think a simple curtain would protect our food." Pursing her lips, she twisted her apron in her hands. Sighing, she turned from the bare shelf. As she ascended the stairs, she prayed. The passage she read to Mr. Weikert popped into her head, and she relaxed and thanked the Lord.

Tillie worked in the kitchen, using the cleaning to think what to do. Behind her, the door opened. Assuming Father returned home, she didn't turn until she felt a tap on her shoulder.

"Sam!" Tillie threw her arms around his neck in a sisterly hug.

Seemingly taken aback by her affectionate outburst, he did not reciprocate her hug.

"Sam, I'm so sorry about Ginny."

He ducked his head. "Thank you." His eyes darted around the room.

Tillie didn't know what to say or do to help or make him feel better. Worse, her burst of emotion embarrassed him. "Are you back for good?"

"Not yet. I came for two reasons. First, I came to welcome you home. Second, I wanted to tell your folks I'll be back in a week or two. My mother is devastated by—by everything. Mr. Garlach made a coffin for us. The funeral is tomorrow."

"We'll be there."

Sam sniffed and glanced around the room again. "Uh, some wagons are coming through town from York Road. They're from the Sanitary Commission." He jerked his thumb toward the door. "The Christian Commission is also coming. Mr. Fahenstock says they'll be using his store as a supply depot. If you have soldiers in your house, you can get medical supplies."

"What about food? We need food."

"I don't know. I'm sure if you go down, they can help you."

"Thank you." Tillie selected a basket off the shelf and tugged her bonnet from its peg. "Do you want to walk with me?"

They exited through the back gate and headed toward the Diamond. They walked in awkward silence, and Tillie's heart ached at the change in him. Sam, always a quiet, thoughtful boy, now seemed pensive and brooding. A pinched and haunted look shadowed his eyes. An air of sadness surrounded him, seeming to go deeper than the loss of his sister.

"Did you hear about Wesley Culp?" She tried to peer into his downturned face.

"Yeah."

Tillie waited, but Sam remained quiet. Never, in the time he lived with them, did Tillie feel a wall between them, but now he was a stranger. She couldn't think of what to say or do.

"They say he died on his father's land." Sam spoke into the silence.

"I heard that too."

"Johnston Skelly's dead too."

Tillie's heart skipped a beat. "Oh, Sam, no. Didn't Johnston begin courting Ginny after Wesley's family refused their marriage plans?"

"He did." Sam smiled a sad smile. "I'd pick Johnny over Wes any day."

"Did Johnny fight here?" Tillie touched his arm.

Sam drew away. "He didn't. He got wounded in one of those fights the armies engaged in on their way up here. There's a story going around that Wes and Johnny met and talked awhile. Johnny asked Wes to deliver a message to Ginny, but Wes got killed. Then Ginny died." Sam gestured toward Fahenstock's store.

Ahead, hundreds of wagons stretched down the road and around the corner at Middle Street, each waiting their turn to unload provisions.

"Oh my." The words rushed out on a breath of air. She suppressed the urge to run to Fahenstock's, forgetting Sam for the moment in her relief.

"Tillie?" Emotion choked Sam's voice.

She turned and watched his face. He seemed to struggle with something.

"I didn't mean what I said—when I called Ginny a filthy traitor and I hoped she got what she deserved—I didn't mean it. I was mad." The words came in a rush. He kept his eyes focused on the ground and scuffled one foot along the pavement. He lifted his left index finger and swiped at his nose. Tears splashed on his shoe tops, but his shoulders slumped and his body relaxed as though he'd been carrying that burden around with him since Ginny's death.

"Oh, Sam." Tillie placed a gentle hand on his shoulder. "Of course not." Despite his reluctance to be touched, she kissed his temple.

Sam sniffed. "Do you suppose Ginny, Johnston, and Wes are in heaven now?"

Tillie cringed. She never paid enough attention when these discussions came up. Now he asked questions she couldn't answer. She cast about in her mind for the answer Father or Reverend Bergstrasser would give, but decided on the truth. "I don't know, Sam, but I don't think so. The reverend says you must give your soul to Christ. Did they do so?" Tillie fumbled for words, stopped, and cast him an apologetic glance. "Perhaps you should ask Father or Reverend Bergstrasser this question. I'm not answering well, I fear."

"No, you did. I don't think my sister ever did, and Wesley went off and fought for the other side. Not sure that counts though." Sam stared at Tillie and shrugged a shoulder as if the question no longer mattered to him. "Well, wherever they are, I'm sure their messages are being delivered and received."

Tillie laughed. "You are a practical soul, aren't you, Sam?"

Sam laughed too, and Tillie took his arm, their friendship restored. He didn't pull away this time. Together they reached Fahenstock Brothers.

Chapter 25

The following day, the army doctor Father requested arrived to examine the colonel. Tillie brought him upstairs.

Mother rose when they entered. Maggie stepped back. The two men waited on either side of the head of the bed, almost as though they meant to protect their commanding officer from a sawbones.

The gray-haired doctor stooped over as though he'd spent far too many hours hunched over an amputation table. He examined the ankle and back, none too gentle in his ministrations, turning him this way and that, smelling his breath, and inspecting his bandages, all while ignoring his patient's exclamations of pain. He removed the dressing covering his shoulder blade, scowled, and muttered incoherent words.

Mother inhaled through her nose and straightened her shoulders, but remained silent.

He took the colonel's pulse, sat him up, and pushed him forward so his head almost rested on his knees.

Colonel Colvill gritted his teeth to keep from crying out, but his hands grabbed the blankets and twisted.

The doctor plucked a probe out of his shirt pocket and began to dig deep into the wound.

The patient cried out and begged for mercy, but the doctor ignored him. When through, he laid him back down and patted his good shoulder.

The colonel lay back, panting. Sweat dripped off his forehead.

Doctor Wilson turned to the women. "The bullet lodged near his spine and must be extracted if he's to make a full recovery. It's not doing damage now, but may shift and cause paralysis. Also, the metal is causing infection, which needs a good cleaning." He contemplated each one of them. "Who among you ladies can assist me?"

Maggie made a choked sound and ran from the room, one hand over her mouth, the other clutching her abdomen.

"Okay, not her." He watched her depart, his smile wry and amused.

Mother swallowed hard several times.

"I will." Tillie half raised her hand. "I helped at the Weikerts'. I can assist you," she repeated, as though trying to convince herself as much as them.

"Good." Wilson rose from the bed and rolled up his shirtsleeves. "Please." He came and stood in front of Mother. "Get me some warm water so I can wash up and sterilize my instruments."

She murmured assent and took her leave.

He refocused his attention on his patient who had passed out. "I think I can remove the bullet and clean the infection to prevent spreading." He stretched his arms and flexed his fingers. "The ankle wound is healing well." He glared at Tillie. "You sure you know what you're doing?"

Startled by his abrupt manner, she opened her mouth to speak, but he cut her off.

"You boys." He indicated Walt and Milt. "I'll need you to keep the good colonel calm. In case he gets uppity during the surgery."

"Yes, sir." They spoke in unison.

"Got any whiskey?" Not waiting for an answer, he turned to Tillie, eyebrows raised, awaiting her response.

She almost forgot the question. "Oh. Uh, yes, sir. I–I helped out at–at Mr. Weikert's." Heat crept up her face, and she took a step backward.

"Good." He pointed toward the washstand as Mother entered with a basin of steaming water and a clean towel draped over her arm. "Put it there. Thank you, kindly." He escorted Mother out of the room and closed the door.

"Well." He clapped his hands together and went to the washbasin. "Let's get started, shall we?"

* * * *

Tillie assessed the instruments while Dr. Wilson gave the two men a signal to roll the colonel onto his stomach and hold him down.

They clamped down as he picked up a scalpel and widened the opening.

Colonel Colvill screamed.

"Hang tight, boys." He cut the wound deeper and took the clamp she held ready for him.

The poor colonel struggled and fought, but couldn't escape the two holding him down with ease. He begged for mercy, cried out, swore, and wept as with quick, savage movements, the physician probed for the bullet. Finally, the colonel passed out.

"That'll keep him quiet." Doctor Wilson pushed the instrument deeper into the gap and manipulated it. "I'm almost finished…almost…there." He twisted his wrist one more time and extracted a mangled bloody object, which he dropped into a pan Tillie held out for him. He set down the tool and observed as she, with tender, gentle movements, cleaned and bandaged the wound.

"You do good work."

Despite her fury over his callous disregard for his patient's well-being, she smiled at the compliment, hearing gruff approval in his voice. "I assisted Dr. Billings, who was posted at the Weikerts'."

"John Billings?"

"Yes, sir." She packed the area a little more and, with help from Walt and Milt, wrapped a bandage around the colonel's rib cage.

"A good man and a fine doctor."

She grinned. "Yes, sir."

* * * *

Tillie carried a basin of steaming hot water, preparing to go up the stairs without tripping over her skirts or spilling water. Mother followed with clean bandages, soap, and a towel. The colonel's male nurses were going to give him a bath. The doorknocker clattered against the door. Tillie froze. Did she try to go upstairs or answer the door?

"I'll answer the door." Mother turned Tillie back to the stairs. "You take the water up."

Dr. Wilson returned to check his patient's progress. He came with another wounded man lying on a litter. Mother let them in.

"His name is Private Kline." He gestured to the young man carried up the stairs. "With such an accomplished nurse in the house, I decided to bring him here. He needs special care, and I don't have enough people to help with him."

"Of course." Mother nodded. "We'll look after him. Tillie in particular will see to him. Don't worry."

For three weeks, Private Kline recuperated in James's bed, becoming Tillie's most trying patient. A bullet shattered his left elbow. His forearm and hand now hung limp and useless.

"They might as well cut the stupid thing off, for all the good it'll do me," he bemoaned, for what seemed to Tillie, the thousandth time.

"So why didn't they amputate your arm when they had the chance?"

He glared at her. "No one will touch me with a saw. I'd rather leave the blasted thing hanging dead and useless than amputated."

She shook her head. "I don't understand. You said—"

"I know what I said," he snarled. "But I couldn't stand the idea of them cutting off my arm. I'm so worthless now without both arms. Why didn't I just die?"

"Don't talk nonsense." She scowled at him. As much as she disliked his incessant whining, she recognized most men did not handle their wounds well. So she swallowed her impatience and remained kind and calm. Sometimes, though, her lack of good grace escaped her before she could stop herself. She tried a new tack and put mock ferocity in her voice. She gave him another stern glare as she tucked in his sheets. "I'll not accept such talk, Mr. Kline. If you don't cease and desist, I'll tell Father to turn you out of the house."

"You will not." He turned away from her and stared out the window, self-pity and anger burning in his face.

Tillie wanted to smack him. "Don't tempt me." She sat in a chair next to the bed and took his left hand into her right one. "Try to squeeze my hand." Using her best helping tone, she almost willed a sign of movement. They stared at his offending limb. "Don't worry, Barney. Perhaps you need time."

"No, Miss Tillie. You can see the muscles are shrinking. My left arm is smaller than my right and shorter too. The doc said the elbow is shattered and won't work no more."

Laying the appendage down, she pulled the blanket up. No sense trying to force things. "I'm sorry, Barney."

"It's all right." His eyes traveled to the window. "Ain't your fault."

She pursed her lips and tried to think of something comforting. "I'll let you rest now." She rose and left the room easing the door shut behind her. She let out a long, slow breath and leaned her back against the door. She closed her eyes. "Heavenly Father, please be with Barney. Let him feel Your presence. He's hurting so, not just physically, but in his heart. Heal him, Lord, and give me the wisdom to deal with him. Help me be kind and comforting. Amen."

Tillie entered the sitting room, and found where her Bible lay next to Maggie's chair. She sat and picked it up.

Private Reed, one of Colonel Colvill's attendants, wandered in.

She put the Book down and started to rise. "Can I get something for you, private?"

"No, no. Sit down, please." He waved her into her seat. He dropped onto the sofa and rested his hands on his knees. His fingers drummed on his pants, index finger to pinkie, nonstop. He opened his mouth to speak, stopped, and for some reason, his face flushed.

What was the matter with him? Tillie bit her lip to keep from smiling.

"Uh." He ran his hand through his red hair. "The colonel is resting, and your mother and sister are such devoted caregivers. I decided to come down and see if you needed any assistance."

A flirty sounding giggle escaped her. She clamped her lips shut, her face heating faster than a cook stove. "I could have used your help when I first got home, but now it doesn't take much time to clean up down here. Father spends most of his time out at the butcher shop with Sam, and everyone else remains upstairs."

Private Reed nodded. He looked about him, still drumming his fingers on his knees. "This is a nice house."

"Thank you." She rose. "I think I'll make tea. Would you like some?"

"Yes, please. Tea would be wonderful." He spoke fast and started to rise, but she waved him back down.

Returning a few minutes later, she carried a tray. He left the sofa and joined her.

Tillie placed a cup and saucer in front of him, set the creamer and sugar bowl near his hand, along with a plate of gingerbread baked earlier in the morning. She poured steaming brown liquid. "May I ask you a question, private?" She took a seat to his left and balanced her teacup in both hands.

"Please, call me Walter—Walt."

She smiled. "May I ask a question, Walt?"

At his inviting glance, she told him about Barney. "I don't know how to reach him. His life isn't over because he can't use his arm, but he thinks so. Of course, I don't know how one feels when they lose a limb or are in so much pain. I'm afraid I'm not being sympathetic, and I want to be."

"Give him time. I'm sure he'll come around. My mother likes to say the Lord's grace is sufficient for today. If Christ lays a trial at our feet, He will lead us on the path to get through. I think that's true. What does your Good Book say?" He inclined his head to her Bible on the side table.

"I'm reading Ephesians. The passage from 4:29 to 5:2. However, I don't think throwing verses at him is the answer right now. Still, I pray them for myself before I tend to him, so I don't say something unkind or reflect his bitterness back at him."

"I can't think of a better passage. You're right, of course. Spouting verses at him is not a good idea. Reflecting Christ's words is."

He smiled at her, his even, white teeth shining out of a freckled face both boyish and charming. He pushed a shock of red hair from his face, but it fell back across his forehead. He gave a small, unconscious shake of his head. His deep green eyes, though now resting on her, seemed interested in everything going on around him.

Tillie started and turned her attention to her hands wrapped around her cup. He caught her staring, and she prayed he didn't think less of her. Reaching for the teapot, she refilled her teacup as though it might save her from drowning in his presence. "Where are you from, Walt?" She liked saying his name. Tillie held the pot out, offering him more.

"Hamline, Minnesota. Milt and I joined up together." He pushed his cup closer to her.

"You two have been friends a long time?"

"More than friends. He's my cousin. His mother is my mother's sister."

"That explains why you two get along so well."

Walt laughed, and his green eyes sparkled. "Well, most of the time we do." He lifted his teacup and took a sip, then put it down. "What about you and Miss Maggie? You two seem to get on well, too."

Tillie giggled. She gave him a sidelong glance and let a coquettish smile curve her lips. "Well, most of the time we do."

They both laughed.

* * * *

That afternoon began a new routine for Walt and Tillie. Claiming they didn't need him upstairs, Walt helped Tillie. He chopped wood and brought water, and together they planted and tended a winter garden. After completing those chores, they enjoyed tea before he rejoined those upstairs.

"How is your patient in the room next door?" Walt sat at the table in the sitting room while Tillie poured for both.

She set the teapot down. "He can still get sulky about his arm, but most of the time, I don't allow him to. We've talked a great deal about occupations he might do without his wound interfering, so I think he's making progress."

"Good news." Walt's voice sounded vague and uncertain. He drummed his fingers.

She eyed his nervous gesture. Did she say or do something inappropriate? Trying to think, she handed him the cup and saucer.

The cup rattled in his hand. Tea splashed the front of his uniform. Grabbing a napkin, he mopped up the hot liquid and swiped at his coat, muttering the entire time.

She stared at him, mouth agape. "Are you all right?"

"Yes, yes. I'm fine." Again, his voice sounded vague and unfocused. He scowled at his uniform and dabbed at his chest again. His eyes darted about the room as though he wanted to be anywhere but there.

"Are you sure?"

"Hmm, what?" He blinked seeming to come back to reality.

A flash of insight hit her so hard she almost couldn't breathe. He came to tell her he loved Maggie and wouldn't be sharing tea with her anymore. Tillie made a small noise in her throat as she struggled to suppress the jolt of pain like a bayonet to the heart. She blinked fast several times and gripped her teacup until her knuckles whitened. "Walt? Is something wrong with Colonel Colvill?"

"No. He's fine. He's mending so well, in fact, they don't need me here." He sat, refilled his cup, and sipped.

That explained his nervous behavior. Either he mustered back into the army, or he was going home. She drew in a slow, deep breath and exhaled.

"Tillie, would your father object if I asked you to go walking with me in the evenings?"

Her mouth dropped open. "What? I mean—what?" Gentlemen asked Maggie to go walking. They didn't ask her. They chucked her under the chin and called her a sweet child. Her knees went weak, and she would have swooned if she weren't sitting down. "I—well, I don't know what Father will say." Heat crept up her neck and infused her face. She kept her eyes fixed on the table.

When she put the teacup down, Walt clasped her hand. "Would you object if I asked him?"

Tillie clamped her lips together to hold back a wild urge to laugh. She needed a moment to regain her composure. "No. I wouldn't object." She squeezed his hand and beamed.

* * * *

Walking up Baltimore Street to Fahenstock's Store, her basket dangling on her arm, Tillie started to raise her face to the warm sun, but sighted a dense, black smoke billowing in the northwest sky. They scheduled today to burn the last of the animal carcasses. She forgot, or she would have put off her errands until tomorrow. The prevailing winds carried the plume away from town, but the knowledge of the activity threw a pall over the beautiful late-summer weather. Tillie squared her shoulders and hurried about her business. As she bustled along, further reminders of July's fighting rumbled past her in the form of a cart, driven by Mr. Weaver. Piled high with corpses in various stages of advanced decomposition, the wagon rattled and jolted along the road, making the corpses seem to dance a macabre sort of jig.

Tillie, long inured to the smell of death, found herself unprepared for the grotesque sight. She clamped a cloth over her mouth, closed her eyes, and gagged, though nothing came up.

The group of colored men, calling themselves reapers, finished the job of gathering and interring those bodies left out in the open. Now, Mr. Weaver, Mr. Biesecker, and their crew took on the more gruesome task of locating the graves of those killed in the heat of battle and disinterring them, to rebury them in the new Soldier's Cemetery.

Gettysburg paid the men well to dig up, catalog, and prepare the bodies for burial. Any Confederate soldiers they found they put into coffins and sent by train to Richmond.

Praying for a quick end to the cleanup made Tillie wonder how the new cemetery was coming along. A committee formed in mid-August, and since some of the desired land included Father's orchard on Taneytown Road, he joined.

Mr. Wills, the chairman, wanted a big, fancy, dedication ceremony. He picked a day in late October, now only a few weeks away, but Father thought it foolish. Too much work still needed doing. A springtime ceremony would be wiser. But Mr. Wills, always a determined man, got his way.

She entered Fahenstock's to complete her errands.

"Good morning, Mrs. Fahenstock. Good morning, Mrs. Eyster." Tillie greeted her teacher with warm affection. "I've been meaning to stop by and visit. But we've been busy tending wounded, and there doesn't seem enough time in the day."

"Not to worry, my dear. I'm in no fit condition to entertain." The teacher put her hand on Tillie's arm. "Did you hear? A cannonball went right through my roof! Thank goodness, I don't sleep in that room. Still, I've never been so frightened in my life."

"I'm so glad you weren't hurt."

"No. The Lord protected me on July the second. Since then, I've had a house full of wounded men, and my neighbors have been so kind. The men came over straightaway after the fighting and repaired my roof. Why, Mr. Hollinger built the cannonball into the wall next to the window while he made the necessary repairs." She shook her head, as if she couldn't imagine why she would want such a reminder incorporated into her house. "I'm afraid school is closed for a long while if ever again." A long doleful sigh escaped her. "They took my books off the shelves and used them for pillows, and they became so saturated with blood, I had to throw out almost my entire collection of texts." Tears sprang in the teacher's eyes.

On impulse, Tillie embraced her. "I'm so sorry. Can I do something to help?"

Mrs. Eyster sniffed and offered a grateful smile. "What can you do?" She lifted her shoulders in a despairing shrug. "What can any of us do?" She touched Tillie's cheek and bid Mrs. Fahenstock a good day before leaving the store.

"That woman." The storeowner huffed as she moved around the counter to help Tillie. "She'll tell the same story to anyone willing to listen."

Tillie's eyes remained on the door. "I guess that's what happens when there's no one you can share your troubles with." She turned a haughty glare on Mrs. Fahenstock as new respect bloomed in her heart for the lonely widow who was her teacher.

* * * *

Since returning from Fahenstock's, Tillie cleaned the kitchen, swept the floors, and dusted the sitting room and parlor. Now, with her chores complete, she didn't know what to do. Mother and Maggie remained above stairs, Father and Sam in the butcher shop. She didn't want to read so she went up and checked on Barney. He slept. Tillie closed the door with a soft click and went back downstairs.

She took a seat in Maggie's rocker and picked up her Bible, turning it over and studying the gold embossing. As she ran gentle fingers over the lettering, visions of General Weed and the captain filled her mind. She kicked herself for not asking his name. Tillie closed her eyes and said a prayer for his safety, trusting the Lord knew him, even if she didn't. She smiled as she examined her Bible, now dog-eared from use. She flipped the book open to her place marker and settled in to read, when someone knocked on the front door. Tillie sighed, laid aside her Book, and answered the summons.

A young woman stood on the doorstep. Worry and anxiety etched her face. In one hand, she held a valise. Her other hand clasped a white handkerchief, which she pressed over her nose and mouth.

"My name is Eliza Colvill." The woman lowered the cloth to introduce herself. "I understand my brother, William, is at this house."

"He is. Please come inside." Tillie swung the door open.

Their guest stepped into the hallway and waved the kerchief in front of her face. "My word." She put her hand over her heart. "What an odor!"

"Yes, I know. We've had to keep the windows closed against the smell. I assure you, it's not usually like this."

"I suppose not." The young woman, not much older than Maggie, set her valise on the floor beside her foot.

Tillie berated herself. Such a stupid comment. Miss Colvill must think her a ninny. They stared at each other.

Eliza raised her eyebrows. "May I see my brother?"

"Of course!" Tillie picked up the carpetbag. "Come with me."

Mother sat on the bed, wiping a cool cloth over the colonel's brow while Maggie tied a fresh bandage around his ankle. Walt cleansed the wound in his shoulder. He winked at Tillie when she walked in. Private Bevans gathered up the dirty bandages.

"Mother, this is Miss Eliza Colvill." Tillie made the rounds of introductions before taking the bowl Private Bevans held.

Eliza's eyes grew round as she sighted her brother.

Mother rose and took the young woman's arm. "Do not fret, my dear. He's mending well, albeit slowly."

Miss Colvill shifted her gaze to Mother then back to the bed. The colonel still wavered in and out of consciousness. Occasional moans escaped his lips and a pasty pallor discolored his cheeks, but he lived.

"Will he know me?"

"Of course he will. Come." Mother invited her to sit.

Miss Colvill lowered herself and grasped her brother's hand. "Billy?" When he didn't respond, she cast a fearful eye back to Mother, who nodded encouragement.

She tried again. Shifting to make herself more comfortable on the mattress, she spoke louder. "Billy, it's me, Eliza. I'm here to help care for you. Father sent me." She stroked the back of his hand looking for some sign of recognition. His eyes moved underneath his lids, and he moaned. A triumphant smile curved her lips as tears flowed down her cheeks. "I know. I understand," she crooned. "You'll be all right, Billy. I'm here, and I'll help care for you. You'll be all right."

Tillie glanced at her mother and sister. She couldn't see past her tears. She left the room with the valise, which she took to her bedroom. She trudged downstairs to wash bandages and prepare supper.

Chapter 26

In the months since the fighting ended, Gettysburg endured a second kind of invasion. Thousands of people came from every Northern state, looking for loved ones to bring home and nurse back to health in the comfort of their own beds or to bury in the family plot. The townsfolk again found themselves taxed beyond their means. Even Camp Letterman filled to capacity. Soldiers still obtained care in homes, churches, and schools. Attendants from Camp Letterman came around again to Tillie's home to check on Colonel Colvill and Private Kline. The colonel remained with the Pierces, as did his sister, but Private Kline, improved in body and spirit, asked to go to the hospital camp, to Tillie's relief.

She and Maggie cleaned the room and bedding so Miss Colvill could sleep nearer her brother.

They wrangled the mattress down the stairs and into the backyard where they emptied and washed the cover. Now, they struggled to hang it to dry.

"Maggie, may I ask you a question?"

"Of course. What's on your mind?"

"Well, I was wondering. When George wanted to court you, what did he do? What did he say?"

The smile faded, and a pain as fresh as the day he died glimmered in her eyes.

"I'm sorry." Tillie squeezed her hand. "Forget I asked. I didn't mean to cause more grief."

"No, I'm happy to answer your question." Maggie gave a few more jerks to straighten the mattress cover. "Well, the first time, I was shopping for Christmas presents, and he came in the store. He walked over and said hello." Her face softened. "I didn't think anything of it. He was always polite. A few days later, I was walking home from school, and he asked if he might escort me. That's when he inquired if he might seek Father's permission to court me."

Tillie's brows creased. "Do all men do that?"

"They should. Whom do you have in mind?" Maggie glanced sidelong at her. "Private Kline perhaps? Or Private Bevans?"

Tillie laughed. "Private Kline departed us, thank goodness." She tugged on the mattress cover. "And a certain young private is loath to leave your side." She pointed up at the bedroom window where Colonel Colvill lay. "In fact, he seems to be waiting for you."

Maggie turned in time to see him pull back, as though fearful of being caught staring. Maggie tsked and shook her head. "I told you, I'm done with soldiers."

"I know, but I think you need inform Private Bevans."

"I have, but it doesn't seem to be getting through." Maggie raised her face to the autumn sun and took a deep breath. "Mmmm. What a beautiful day. I haven't gotten outside in a long time."

"It is a beautiful day."

"You still didn't tell me who he is." She gave Tillie a teasing nudge.

Tillie's face grew hot, and she fussed over the mattress cover. Suddenly, she didn't want Maggie to know who showed an interest in her.

"Tillie, Miss Maggie." Walt approached. "Your mother is wondering when you're coming back in to finish cleaning the room."

"Tell Mother we'll be right in," Tillie called back. "Thank you, Walt." She couldn't suppress a pleased smile.

Walt waved and strode to the house.

She peeked at Maggie, who stared at her, mouth agape. "Him?" Maggie drew the word out in one long, incredulous syllable.

Tillie's smile disappeared. She scowled. "Why not?"

"He's much too old for you. He must be at least twenty-five, that's why not."

Tillie said nothing for a moment, and then whispered, "I know. But he likes me."

* * * *

One evening after supper, while Tillie cleaned up, Walt remained in the kitchen. "I'm afraid with all the people in the room, I'm going to be flattened against a wall, unable to move," he joked.

"I think you'll manage." She didn't know what sort of response he expected. She grabbed the broom and swept the floor while water boiled on the stove. She emptied the pot into the basin and gathered up the dishes.

Walt continued to sit at the table.

Tillie watched him through her lashes, the way Maggie did with George. She poured water into a pot and put it on the heat for tea. As she washed dishes, she peeked over her shoulder.

His eyes on her made her uncomfortable. She brought him a plate of gingerbread. "So how is our patient doing?" She ventured a conversation.

"I think he'll pull through. The shoulder wound is closing up and doesn't appear as though he'll have residual damage, though I can't say for sure. The foot may be another matter. It's healing well, but we don't know if he'll ever be able to walk on it again. He might need crutches for the rest of his life."

"I hope not." Tillie soaped and scrubbed.

"So do I. He's always been an active and energetic man. Crutches would slow him down." Walt shifted in his seat. He picked a piece of gingerbread to crumbs in his plate, but didn't eat it. "He is a God-fearing and faithful man who always accepts that, whatever tests the Lord sends him, they are for his good. I must say, I've never seen him discouraged in his faith. I wish I was more like him…." He drummed his fingers on the table.

She tried to ignore the drumming and wash the dishes. Something bothered him. Should she ask the cause? No. If he wanted to tell her, he would. She smiled and turned to him. "I guess I'm so new in my own faith I haven't experienced discouragement." As soon as the words left her lips, she regretted them.

Walt rose from his seat. He gave her a long, sad look. "You will." He threw the crumbs away. "Rest time is over. I should get back to work." He turned his back on her and left the kitchen.

Mouth agape Tillie stared after him as the teakettle began to whistle.

* * * *

On a cool, crisp day, about a week after Miss Colvill's arrival, Tillie answered a knock at the front door. A woman around Mother's age stood on the doorstep, a valise in one hand and a piece of paper in the other.

"Good morning. May I help you?" Tillie prayed she didn't want accommodations. They had so little room left.

The woman's kind features arranged in a worried frown. Beneath her bonnet, gray hair framed her heart-shaped face with friendly, yet apprehensive, blue eyes. Deep crow's feet revealed a woman who smiled and laughed often. Right now, though, her face registered surprise, as though she never expected a warm reception.

"Yes." Her eyes darted past Tillie into the house. "My name is Abigail Greenly. Is this the Pierce residence?"

"Yes. I'm Tillie Pierce. How can I help you?"

"I've come from the railroad depot. I came to Gettysburg to be near my son at Camp Letterman. I went to every hotel, but they say there's no room at the inn, so to speak. None of the rooming houses have any vacancies either. I returned to the station because I didn't know what to do. I prayed for help, and a man came over and gave me this piece of paper with your name and address. He said you might have room for me. The man who wrote this note, Mr."—she consulted the sheet then looked back at Tillie—"Mr. McCurdy said I might find a room here."

"Uncle Robert!" Tillie stepped aside to let her in. "Please come in. My mother is upstairs. If you'll excuse me, I'll go and get her." She took Mrs. Greenly's cloak and hung it up, then excused herself and jogged up the stairs. Moments later Mother came down, with Tillie at her heels.

"Mrs. Greenly." Mother held out a hand in greeting. "I'm Mrs. Pierce. How do you do?"

"Mrs. Pierce." Mrs. Greenly took Mother's hand. "I was told I might find accommodation with you." She showed Mother the slip of paper and explained her predicament and how she came by their address. "I won't be much trouble. I promise you that. Every waking moment I intend to spend at my son's bedside. I just need a place to lay my head at night." She drew in a deep breath and crinkled the paper in her palm.

Mother gave a soft smile and squeezed the woman's hands. "Of course you may stay with us. My brother did the right thing in sending you. No need to fret." She led her into the parlor. "You must be tired. Tillie will take your things upstairs to Miss Colvill's room." She sat on one end of the sofa and Mrs. Greenly on the other. "We have other guests, but there's plenty of room for one more."

Tillie took Mrs. Greenly's bag and ascended the stairs. Did Mother plan to take in any more strangers? How were they to accommodate one more? Where were they going to get the food? She did a mental check of all the people under their roof. First, Sam returned the Monday after Ginny's funeral, Miss Colvill, the colonel, Private Bevans, Walt, Maggie, Mother, Father, herself, and now Mrs. Greenly. Too many people to feed. Tillie needed to speak with Father. Maybe he'd stop Mother from taking in any more strays.

* * * *

Tillie stood in the kitchen doorway peering across the yard. Father worked in the butcher shop after supper. Darkness approached early now, and he and Sam sharpened knives and cleaned the shop under lighted lamps. They spent most of their time out there nowadays. Lifting her chin, she crossed to the shop and rapped an anxious tap on the door. "Father, may I have a word with you?"

He smiled at her. "Tillie, what are you doing in here? I thought you hated this place."

"I'm used to butchery." She grinned. Instant heat infused her face at the wry note in her voice. She grew serious. "Can I speak to you—alone?"

He wiped his brow with his forearm. "Of course. Sam, we're pretty much finished, and I believe Mrs. Pierce set out more lessons for you."

"Yes, sir." Sam sighed, lowered his head, and shuffled off toward the house.

When he disappeared, she stepped inside. "Father, shouldn't you speak to Mother about allowing another boarder? We don't have enough to feed everyone and now Mrs. Greenly. I don't know how we're going to manage. Shouldn't you say something? Ask Mrs. Greenly to leave?"

As soon as the words left her mouth, Tillie sensed trouble headed straight for her. She shrank within herself and waited for the storm of Father's wrath to break over her head. Instead, he shook his head and gazed at her with sad eyes. "The Lord still needs to work on that selfish streak of yours, daughter."

"I'm not being selfish, Father. I'm trying to stretch our resources so we can all eat."

"It is selfishness, but I won't debate you." He sat at his bench and held his arms out to her. Without hesitation she went to him and perched herself on his lap. He closed his arms around her with a quick squeeze.

"I'm not going to send Mrs. Greenly away for the simple reason that to do so would be cruel. Perhaps there isn't much more space, and if another person comes to the house, we might all need to sleep standing up to accommodate. The Lord sent her to us and to turn her away would be to turn Him away. Remember, Tillie, 'As you do to the least of my brothers, you do to unto me.' Mrs. Greenly is our sister, and it comforts Mother to board her. It also helps Mrs. Greenly, and if we run out of food, the Lord will provide us some more, don't you think?"

"Yes, Father." Her face flamed. She wanted to go back inside and pretend this conversation never happened.

He seemed to read her thoughts and tightened his arms around her. "Being born in faith, Tillie, is a lot like being born in life. We don't come into the world knowing everything we need to live. Someone has to teach us. That's why we send you to school and impart our morals and values. In the same way, the Lord will lead you to lessons of faith to help you to grow as a believer."

An unexpected wave of emotion washed over her, filling her eyes. "Thank you, Father." She wrapped her arms around his neck and hugged him tight. She kissed his cheek. "I love you."

Father patted her back and cleared his throat.

She got up off his lap and started for the door.

"There is one more thing I want to discuss with you, Tillie."

"Yes, Father?" Something in his expression sent her guard up.

He rose and pulled on his waistcoat. "Private Reed approached me earlier this week asking if he could take you out walking in the evenings. I don't like this flirtation with Mr. Reed. It must stop. I told him no."

"It's not a flirtation, Father. We're just friends."

"You may pretend it's a friendship, young lady. But I have eyes in my head, and so does your mother. He's a soldier. A soldier who will leave us when the colonel is well enough to depart. I want it to stop, Matilda. Do you understand me?"

When he called her Matilda, Tillie knew better than to argue. Still several responses came to mind, and she hoped the darkening room hid her flaming cheeks and balled fists. She clamped her lips between her teeth and, through dint of will, remained silent.

Father dropped his hand on her shoulder. His deep brown eyes bore into hers. "Do you understand me?"

She looked down, cowed. "Yes, Father. I understand."

"Good." He stroked her cheek. "It's for the best."

"May I ask you a question?"

"You may."

"Is this because of George?" She recalled her conversation with Maggie. Did she have something to do with Father's denial?

Father cupped her chin. "I would be a liar if I said no, but it's not the only reason. I don't wish to be harsh on you. I love you and want the best for you. You're only fifteen years old. In another year or two, if this war is over—please God—and if a young man comes along more suited to you, I'd be happy to welcome him into my home. But not yet, my dear. Not yet."

"Yes, Father." To show she didn't mean any disrespect, she gave him a hug and turned back toward the house, sorry she came out to talk to him.

****

Over the next few weeks, Tillie found Mrs. Greenly remained true to her word and did her best not to burden the family. She arose each morning before dawn, dressed, and set out for Camp Letterman before the sun broke the peaks of the surrounding hillsides. To lighten her burden on the family, she took her meals at the camp and did not return until late at night.

One night, Tillie waited up. She wanted to talk to her about starting work at the camp. Ever since her conversation with Father, Walt remained above stairs caring for Colonel Colvill.

He came down for his meals, never met Tillie's eye anymore, and when finished eating, went back upstairs.

She struggled to eat at each meal. Heartbreak over Father's refusal killed her appetite. Her mind screamed for Walt to look at her, just once, so he would know she wasn't at fault, but he didn't. As the days passed, she wanted to escape Walt's presence. Even though he remained upstairs, she felt his presence in every fiber of her being. Working at the hospital might be the perfect solution.

As the hallway clock chimed ten, Mrs. Greenly entered the house and closed the door with a quiet snick. Tillie stepped into the hallway and whispered a good evening.

"My goodness, Tillie. What are you doing up so late?"

"I wanted to speak with you."

"Dear me, what could be so important that you should wait up until all hours of the night to speak with me?" Mrs. Greenly smiled. "Should we go into the sitting room to talk or is this more of a parlor type conversation?"

"Oh, no, we can go into the sitting room." Tillie led her into the room. "I've made some tea."

"Then let's have some tea and conversation." Mrs. Greenly took off her wrap, hung it up, and entered the sitting room. She poured tea for herself and Tillie, and sat in Mother's rocker.

Tillie settled herself in Maggie's chair. Not sure how to begin, she shared her experiences at the Weikerts', and the days following.

Mrs. Greenly listened and sipped her tea.

When Tillie finished her tale, she waited for Mrs. Greenly's response.

"My husband died in '59." Mrs. Greenly twisted her teacup in her hands.

Tillie's brow creased. She raised her cup to her lips, trying to figure out the turn in the conversation. She took another swallow and waited, a polite smile curving her lips.

Mrs. Greenly gave her a weak smile. "What you did at the farm was God's work." She ran a finger around the rim of her cup, and then put it down. She sat back and folded her hands in her lap. "My oldest son, Isaac, was killed at Fredericksburg. My middle son, Matthew, at Malvern Hill. He didn't die right away.

He lay in a hospital for about three weeks before he succumbed. I didn't go down to help care for him, of course, Malvern Hill being in Virginia." Mrs. Greenly's eyes, fixed on a spot in the hallway, became distant, as though she saw her son, dying alone. Her voice grew faint. "I should have. I should have gone to him somehow, some way." She shifted her gaze to her lap while her hands clasped and unclasped. Her last words sounding like an indictment against her as a mother.

"I'm so sorry." Tillie cringed, wanting something more comforting and profound to say, lost at this sudden and sorrowful turn. She leaned over and squeezed the woman's arm. "I'm so sorry. I wish…" She didn't know what she wished.

Mrs. Greenly laid her hand atop Tillie's. Tillie clasped her hand and met Mrs. Greenly's gaze.

"Joseph must survive." Mrs. Greenly's words and expression grew fierce and determined. "He must survive. He's my only remaining child." In a sudden, excited shift, she smiled at Tillie. "Come with me tomorrow. Meet Joseph. It would be a comfort if the two of us pray for him."

Tillie's eyes widened. This was what she wanted—and dreaded. "Do you think I should? I've wanted to go. That's why I stayed up to talk to you, but aren't there enough people to help?"

"Oh, gracious, I daresay not. Almost four thousand men are in the most desperate need of companionship. Oh, they have nurses and doctors enough to do the difficult and gruesome work. What the boys need is people willing to keep them company while they recuperate. If they saw your pretty face, I know it would speed their recovery. Besides, I think it would benefit you a great deal to get out of the house a little. Come with me in the morning. Please."

Tillie contemplated the idea of reading to the soldiers and talking to them, not changing bandages or having to assist amputations. She doubted the pretty face remark, but she smiled. "I'd love to." She squeezed Mrs. Greenly's arm again. "I must confess I feared they'd make me do the gruesome work, as you put it, and I can't bear the thought." Tillie repressed a shudder as memories assailed her.

Mrs. Greenly patted her hand. "I'm so glad I thought to say something." The woman rose and picked up their teacups. She carried them into the kitchen where she washed and put them away. When she came back to the sitting room, she led Tillie upstairs. "We must get a good night's sleep. Dawn comes pretty early each morning, as the late Mr. Greenly liked to say."

"Yes it does."

At Mrs. Greenly's bedroom door, Tillie wished her a good night. She slid into bed, excited by the prospect of helping at Camp Letterman.

****

In the chill late-September morning, Tillie shivered under her cloak as they walked the three miles down York Street to Camp Letterman. Their conversation ranged over numerous subjects. She liked Mrs. Greenly very much, happy to discover that, despite their ages, she made a friend.

"Father refused permission to Private Reed." She confessed her disappointment, confident Mrs. Greenly understood and wouldn't mock or tease her. "It's a bit like running away, I guess, but I can't tolerate the avoidance any more. That's why I wanted to accompany you to…" Tillie's mouth fell open as they reached the entrance gate.

Mrs. Greenly watched Tillie's face, her grin wide. "I felt the same way my first day. I couldn't imagine where I would find Joseph in this tent city." She pointed out landmarks to Tillie, who listened in stunned silence. The camp, an impressive testament to Union military might and resources, occupied almost every square acre of old Mr. Wolf's eighty acre farm. Laid out in orderly fashion, a main thoroughfare ran through the center. Streets branched off on both sides and acted as the dividing line between the Union and Confederate sides. The lanes between the tents spanned wide enough to accommodate two people, walking abreast, to pass in either direction without bumping into each other.

Row upon row of white canvas stood in straight even lines, arranged in blocks throughout the meadow. Six avenue-sized blocks held twenty-four tents per avenue. Groups of four made up a ward. Inside each tent, twelve to sixteen patients awaited care.

A spring used to run from the woods through the meadow, making a lovely place to come on a hot summer day. Someone, the Army Corps of Engineers no doubt, had diverted the spring. Now, tents popped up there, planted in the ground like crops. As she took in the scene, her only thought was that Mr. Wolf must be turning in his grave.

She couldn't see the military value of placing Camp Letterman in such a spot, but the Army chose the site well. The property had a good mix of woods and open space and, with the spring, an excellent supply of fresh water. Railroad tracks less than five hundred feet from the camp's edge made it ideal.

Near the woods to the southwest and close to the road, smoke billowed from the chimney of a wood and canvas constructed edifice. Mrs. Greenly said it was the cookhouse. Tillie thought of the two orderlies who made beef soup at Mr. Weikert's and wondered if they were here. She made a mental note to stop by and check.

Beyond the cookhouse and close against the woods, another wood and canvas building stood dark and silent. A sign above the door read Dead House. Tillie swallowed hard. On the other side of the main tent area, to the northeast, the officer's quarters separated from the enlisted quarters, by a looming graveyard marked with a sign indicating the Union and Confederate sections. Other sections of the camp, set apart for their own mysterious purposes, remained dark, unused, and sinister. She gazed around at a vast tent city, intimidated by the prospects.

"Over there is the surgery." Mrs. Greenly pointed to a large half wood, half tent construction near the woods. "And over here," she gestured to a row of tents, "is where Joseph waits for me. Come, Tillie." She took Tillie by the elbow and proceeded into the camp. The guard on duty said good morning. "I'll take you to Joseph's tent and introduce you to his tent mates."

Tillie followed like a docile sheep, intimidated by the camp's size and complexity. As they passed the tents, she took surreptitious peeks inside the open flaps. The early morning light had not yet penetrated the canvas tops, so she saw nothing but a dark, cavernous hole. A garland of evergreen boughs shaped in a circle hung above each entrance, with more evergreen boughs twisted into the shape of a five-pointed star within the circle. She wondered why, but decided to ask later. As they passed another, she peered inside. A lantern lit within showed men sleeping.

Others stared outside. Still others thrashed in their agonies or cried out in pain—a sound Tillie hoped never to hear again, and she tried to shut her ears to their suffering. "Do they do nothing for these men?"

"Of course they do, dear." Mrs. Greenly tucked her arm around Tillie's shoulder. "But no matter what they do, some still suffer, and some are on the edge of their eternal rest." She turned a corner and entered the second tent on the left side of the lane. Tillie followed and stood at the foot of the cot as Mrs. Greenly sat in the campstool and took the young boy's hand. She kissed his hand then pressed his palm to her cheek. She laid her other hand on the boy's forehead and stroked his hair, her action filled with love and longing. "Joseph," she sing-songed. "Mother's here."

Joseph groaned.

Hope shone in Mrs. Greenly's bright blue eyes. "See? He knows I'm here. He'll be well soon."

Tillie couldn't meet her gaze. She recognized a dying man when she saw one, and estimated it would take a matter of days before he passed. She couldn't bring herself to say so. Instead, she nodded and struggled to push down a wave of grief. She couldn't bear for Mrs. Greenly to see her face so she made a point of studying the other men. Tillie cleared her throat and smiled. "You promised to introduce me to these fine boys," she choked.

Chapter 27

It didn't take long for Tillie to establish a rapport with the men, some of whom she nursed at the Weikerts'. She enjoyed spending time with them.

Camp policy required that the orderlies sweep, empty the chamber pots, and change the linen daily. Many of them scoffed at what they considered not only women's work, but also a silly directive. However, it made a profound difference to the convalescents' health. Despite the efforts at cleanliness, though, the odor of twelve to sixteen men confined in a tent lingered. She didn't need to ask about the evergreen boughs.

Mrs. Greenly spoke true. There were nurses and doctors aplenty, and no one asked for Tillie's assistance in surgical procedures, which allowed her to develop a routine.

Each morning, she sat with Joseph and Mrs. Greenly. He lay unconscious on his cot while Tillie and his mother prayed. Afterward, Mrs. Greenly seemed content to sit by his side talking to him in quiet tones while stroking his forehead and squeezing his hands.

Tillie visited the other men. "Good morning." She sat next to a man in a cot three down from Joseph. "I'm Tillie. Can I do anything for you?" She smoothed his blankets to have something to do with her hands.

"You come in every morning and sit with that poor boy. I was kinda wondering when you would come and pray over me like you do him." He sat up a little.

Tillie folded her hands in prayer. "We can pray now if you like. What's your name?"

"Jones, Private Jones."

"It's a pleasure to meet you, private." She cocked her head and smiled. "I must call you something other than Private. What's your first name?" She took her Bible out of her apron pocket.

"Michael."

"Hello, Michael." Tillie offered her hand to shake. They talked a few minutes, becoming acquainted. "Shall we pray?"

"Please." He settled himself and bowed his head. They prayed for the next quarter hour. "Where are you from, Michael?"

"Hartford, Connecticut."

"I've never been to Hartford. Is it a nice city?"

"Nice enough, but not so pretty as the land here." He nudged her arm. "I hated the idea of fighting here. It's too pretty to tear up."

Tillie beamed. "It is pretty here." They sat in silence for a few seconds. Tillie resisted the urge to readjust his blankets again. "Um, how long have you been in the army?"

"I joined up in '61." He shrugged. "My girl said she would be proud to marry a soldier." He chuckled. "I heard she married a businessman."

Tillie shot up straight in her chair. "She didn't!"

"Yeah, she did. My mother confirmed so in one of her letters. You see, I've been wounded before, at Second Bull Run, and apparently Melissa—that's her name—thought I died, so she married someone else."

Tillie stared at him, mouth ajar. "Forgive me for saying so, but you don't seem very broken hearted."

He laughed. "Well, I'll admit to a few bad days when I first found out, but then I thought her rather prudent to find a fella whose life wasn't in danger all the time."

Tillie laughed. "I like your attitude."

* * * *

The camp administrator, Dr. Janes, ran Camp Letterman in true military style. Guards refused admittance to the civilian volunteers until seven thirty in the morning, after the patients received their breakfast and had their bedding and clothes changed.

After her morning prayer time with Joseph and Mrs. Greenly, Tillie went to the cot, once occupied by Private Jones, but now held Private Markham. She settled into her camp chair. "Good morning, Private Markham. How are you feeling today?"

"Oh, I'm fine, Miss Tillie. I feel a chill this morning. Is there frost on the ground?"

"Not yet. A heavy dew, but no frost. It is only late September."

"Perhaps the Good Lord is holding off the severe weather until we're all well enough to move. Who knows?" Private Markham pulled his shortened arms from under the blanket and rested his stumps on the top of the coverlet. He indicated the side table with his chin. "The mailman left a letter for me. I think it may be from my ma. Would you mind reading it for me?"

"Of course." Tillie picked up the envelope and removed the letter. She read in a low voice, conscious of those around them. She finished and put the letter back into its envelope and set it on the table. "They're just picking apples now? We picked our apples weeks ago."

"In Vermont, where I'm from, you don't pick apples until a hard frost. That's when they're best."

"Doesn't that ruin the fruit?"

"Certainly not!" He reacted with mock outrage. "A hard frost does something to the apple. I can't say why, but the skin snaps when you bite in and the apple is tart and tasty. Makes for the best cider too." He sighed, and a dreamy expression crossed his face. His expression changed again as his brow creased, and a frown pulled at his lips. "I'll never pick an apple again." He held up both arms, his right arm amputated at the wrist and the left at the elbow, before dropping them at his sides.

"That won't mean the end of your life though." Tillie phrased her words with care remembering Barney Kline.

"No." He looked her in the eye. "No, but every once in a while I look down at my hands, or lack of hands, and I think, I won't be able to pick apples again or tie my shoes or button my coat. It comes to me in little ways."

Tillie pursed her lips, casting about in her mind for some way to comfort him. As always, inadequacy stabbed her.

"There is one good thing I can think of." His voice grew hopeful.

"What's that?"

"Well, I never wanted to be a farmer. Now I can do what I always dreamed of."

"Which is?" She tried to think of a profession that didn't include the use of one's hands, but couldn't.

"A dry goods store. I always wanted to own a store and our town could use one. I thought maybe I'll take my army pension and open up a dry goods store."

"How does owning a dry goods store change things? Wouldn't you still need your hands?"

"The things I can't do with my hands, I can hire someone to do for me." He grinned at her.

Tillie straightened his bedding. "What a wonderful idea."

* * * *

Tillie walked to the cookhouse to discover if Mike and Bill, the two men who cooked at the Weikerts', were cooking here. No one knew who they were, so she left, a little disappointed that they were gone. She saw Nellie Auginbaugh speaking to the guard at the front gate. Tillie veered off to greet her.

Nellie came to Camp Letterman to offer her services. She was twenty-two, so Tillie never knew the woman well, but as their paths crossed more and more, they grew friendly. Mrs. Greenly, in typical fashion, took an instant liking to Nellie and invited the young woman to share lunch with her and Tillie.

"So, Nellie, tell me of your experience. Tillie shared with me what happened to her. I'd like to hear your story." Mrs. Greenly spooned her soup.

"I work at Mrs. Martin's." Nellie used her napkin to clean her spoon before eating. "Mrs. Martin owns a millinery shop on Carlisle Street." She looked at Mrs. Greenly. "I'm an apprentice."

Nellie spooned her soup and swallowed. "When the Yankees came, I was working on a new hat. Mrs. Martin is such an exacting task master, I didn't pay attention to the goings-on outside until Mr. Martin told me the Yankees had arrived and it looked as though the Rebs came out to meet them. He thought I should go home. We were so close to the fighting that Mr. Martin kept going outside to watch. I paid him no mind because Mrs. Martin said the hat needed to be done for Mrs. McCreary by the next day, and she wouldn't pay me if I didn't finish. I told Mr. Martin I would go home at my usual time and no sooner."

"Nellie!" Tillie appraised her new friend. "How brave. Weren't you in danger?"

"I didn't think so at first. Mr. Martin kept pacing in and out of the store and telling me I ought to go home, but I continued to object. All of a sudden, a bullet hit the brick of the building. Mr. Martin grabbed my arm and yelled at me, 'Hat be hanged, girl, get home now!' I'm glad he threw me out when he did, because just as I got out on the street, Yankee soldiers came streaming by me, running for their lives, hollering at me to get inside as fast as I could."

Her blue eyes took on a faraway look. The spoon dangled in her hand as though she forgot she held it. She shook her head and blinked. "When I got home, a dead Union soldier lay in front of our house. My father knelt over him and wrapped a blanket around him. Pa saw me, stopped, and took me inside. After the fighting ended that first day, he went back outside to see about the dead soldier. Someone took the blanket so Father got another and wrapped him up again. He tried to find someone to take the man away, but couldn't find anyone. The Rebs swarmed everywhere so he left the body lying on the pavement. The poor boy lay on the pavement for almost a week and a half before someone took his body away. Horrible, so horrible." Tears filled Nellie's eyes. She dropped her spoon and pushed her plate away. She crossed her arms, rested them on the table, and stared out the tent door.

Memories flooded Tillie's mind. The faces of the boys they couldn't save continued to haunt her.

Mrs. Greenly continued to eat her soup, as though unaware of the emotions she unleashed in her two companions.

"Excuse me, ladies."

The three of them turned to the orderly standing at their table, hat in hand. "The surgeon would like to see Mrs. Greenly. It's about your son." He gave them a nod and disappeared.

"Oh no! I knew I shouldn't have left his side." Mrs. Greenly jumped from her seat, fear and panic showing in the strained, tight muscles of her face. "Tillie, please come with me," Mrs. Greenly whispered. "I don't wish to go alone."

"Of course I will, but let's not overreact. Perhaps he's awake and asking for you." Tillie rose. They excused themselves and hurried back to Joseph's tent.

The surgeon sat in the chair next to Joseph's cot. He rose when they entered. "Mrs. Greenly, I consulted with my colleagues, and we agree the best thing for your son is to amputate his arm."

Mrs. Greenly rocked back as though he struck her. "But without his arm, he won't be able to do the farm work. How will he milk cows, bring in the corn, and do the other things needing two arms?"

"Mrs. Greenly." He placed a gentle hand on her shoulder. "Do you wish your son to survive? We need to reverse the infection, and the best way to do that is to amputate."

Tillie touched Mrs. Greenly's arm while the woman gazed at her dear son.

"I've seen this done many times, Mrs. Greenly. Joseph does stand a better chance of survival if they amputate. They saved many soldiers at the Weikerts' in just this way."

Tears filled Mrs. Greenly's eyes as she saw, perhaps for the first time, Joseph's sad state. His face, ashen gray, with sweat coating his forehead and sunken cheeks was a death mask. He shivered and clasped his blanket close about him as he groaned and muttered in delirium. Mrs. Greenly covered her face with her hands and nodded, then wept. Tillie stepped close and put her arms around her friend's shoulders while the woman struggled to regain her composure.

The doctors jumped into action. They took the boy, placed him on a litter, and took him to the surgery tent. Tillie and Mrs. Greenly sat on his cot waiting. Joseph returned three hours later, though it seemed an eternity, minus his left arm above the elbow. The bandages had a greenish smear amidst the blood. Tillie prayed they caught the gangrene in time. If they did, he may survive. If not…She refused to consider the alternative. Mrs. Greenly fussed over him, tucking him in and speaking soft gentle words to her unconscious son.

Tillie slid to her knees beside the cot. "Heavenly Father, not our will, but Your will be done for poor Joseph. It would mean so much to his mother if he survives. He is the last of her sons. She'll be alone after this. Please be with this young man today and help him recover. If that is not Your plan, then be with dear Mrs. Greenly. Be her aid and comfort. I pray these things in the name of Your Son, Jesus Christ. Amen." Tillie rose and went to find a soldier who might need some company. She wanted someone to talk to who could make her feel less sad.

* * * *

Darkness came early, and the September nights held a nip in the air. Tillie returned to Joseph's cot and found Mrs. Greenly still at his side, stroking his hair, speaking to him in soft tones and holding his remaining hand, tears sliding unnoticed down her cheeks, landing on the boy's blanket.

Tillie perched on the other side of his cot, not wanting to disturb the woman's grief. She waited a few minutes before touching her arm. Many mothers and fathers grieved for their sons, but the depth of Mrs. Greenly's grief pierced Tillie's heart.

Joseph's eyes flew open, and he stared up at her. "Mother?" he croaked. "Dear Mother."

"Yes, son, I'm here. Mother's here!" Mrs. Greenly clasped Joseph's hand to her bosom. "I'm here. Mother's here."

Joseph swallowed hard and seemed to stare with sightless eyes, still in his delirium. He blinked a long slow blink as recognition shone in his eyes. He smiled at her and mouthed the words I love you. Then he took a deep breath. "Good bye, Mother," he whispered. "Good…bye." The light left his eyes, and a smile traced his lips as if he found peace.

Mrs. Greenly collapsed over her son's body, weeping as though her heart would break. "Joseph! Joseph!"

Tillie rose and took Mrs. Greenly by the shoulders. She lifted the woman from the bed and held her while they cried. When they were exhausted, they walked home.

* * * *

Tillie and her family stood in the hallway by the front door. Mrs. Greenly had announced the night before that it was time to go home. Now, they gathered to see her off.

"You won't reconsider?" Father held Mrs. Greenly's cloak while she tied her bonnet. She turned around, and he laid the cloak over her shoulders.

"Such a lovely offer, and I'm honored and humbled you would want my son buried in the Soldier's Cemetery." Mrs. Greenly took the basket Mother handed her. "However, I wouldn't be able to visit him here. I want him nearby, next to his father and two brothers. He has an infant sister buried there as well. I do hope you understand."

Father nodded and squeezed her hand. "Of course, we do."

"When I go…" Mrs. Greenly smiled at Mother and Father. "We shall all be together once again."

"We quite understand." Mother hugged her. "Please know you're welcome to come and visit any time. We shall miss you so much."

"I shall miss you all. Especially you, Miss Tillie." Mrs. Greenly wrapped her arms around Tillie in a long hug before kissing her cheek.

"I'll miss you, too." Tillie sniffed into Mrs. Greenly's shoulder. They hugged each other tighter.

"I like to think if my daughter had lived, she would have been much like you," Mrs. Greenly whispered in Tillie's ear.

Tillie kissed her cheek.

They broke apart, sniffing.

Father held the front door open.

Mrs. Greenly went down the front steps as the Pierces gathered on the stoop. She blew them a kiss, faced forward, and adjusted her cloak and bonnet. Hanging the basket on her arm, she put on her gloves. She signaled to the wagon driver, waved to the Pierces one more time, and walked to the train station behind the wagon carrying her son's coffin.

Chapter 28

In the days following Mrs. Greenly's departure, Tillie continued visiting Camp Letterman. She did so now with a renewed heart, as though she wanted to honor her memory of Mrs. Greenly and Joseph by doing her best for those still left. Her work became less strenuous, as each day more men received discharges from the hospital, back either to their units or to the Invalid Corps to complete their convalescence. By mid-October, around two thousand soldiers of the original four remained, many of them Confederates still awaiting transport to prison camps.

Every day she went about her duties talking with the boys, writing letters, reading books, and bringing some of their favorite foods. As they recovered and departed, Tillie was sad to see them go, but happy they were well enough to leave the hospital camp. Once or twice, she met soldiers who, in some way or other, substituted for her own brothers.

As the Union side thinned out and men left, workers struck the tents and sent them to the newest battlefield site. The southern side, however, remained unchanged. None of the soldiers departed. In fact, very little activity occurred on that side.

The main thoroughfare acted as the dividing line, and the visitors behaved as if no one crossed it. Only those caring for the Southern boys ventured into "enemy territory," all clad in blue.

Tillie searched for someone to grant her permission to help. Heart pounding, she stepped across the lane. Her knees knocked, as a sudden sense of having stepped into forbidden territory washed over her. Why was she so nervous? She wasn't going into the Confederacy itself, for goodness sake.

She straightened her shoulders, pushed away her ridiculous thoughts, and walked with a halting gait up the row of tents. Their flaps, closed against the late-October chill, didn't encourage her. She didn't dare push open a tent flap and barge in. Her breath constricted in her throat. She started to go back to the other side when a man's voice stopped her.

"Hello. Can I help you find something?"

Tillie spun around. "Hello." Her voice trembled, and her legs wobbled. "I've been coming here to help our boys. No one comes to visit these boys, so I thought perhaps I might offer my services." Heat infused her face, but she couldn't help it. "If I'm not allowed over here, then I apologize." She searched his face for some sign of what to do. When she didn't get one, she made a lame gesture. "I'll go back." She started to leave.

"Well thank God." His words stopped her. "I hoped someone would pity these boys. It's all hustle and bustle over there, and a graveyard over here." He took her by the arm and dragged her three tents down. "Come with me."

"There are some boys in here. Once they get used to you, they'll be friendly enough. At least, I hope so."

"Are they unfriendly?" She never considered they might be hostile.

"Well of course, they're not friendly. They think of us as the enemy. These men are in need of companionship beyond what I and my limited staff can do for them, but I think you'll win them over." He gestured to her. "I've seen you around here. You have a way about you I think these men will respond to. At first, they'll refuse to be friendly, but in the end, they'll be grateful for a pretty girl giving them attention." He walked away, leaving her standing like an idiot in front of the tent.

"Well, Matilda Jane Pierce, you made your bed." She peered over her shoulder, hoping no one heard her talking to herself, squared her shoulders, and went inside.

She stood at the entrance, feet stuck to the ground. She couldn't move another inch if someone pushed her. The flap fell down and brushed her skirts. She glanced at it, and then faced the men. She said nothing, letting her eyes adjust to the dim interior.

Several men sat up in their cots bracing themselves on elbows. Others raised their heads and stared back with sullen glares. Some flopped down and turned their backs on her.

This wasn't going to be easy. She forced herself to move further inside.

"Good morning." She gazed at the men in their cots. "My name is Tillie. I live in Gettysburg." What a stupid thing to say. She chuckled. "Of course I live in Gettysburg. Where else would I live? I came in to say hello. If you gentlemen need anything, I'd like to help." She studied each of the men.

They lay on army cots, each man with a heavy woolen blanket, yet they shivered in the cold morning air. The woodstove at the far end of the tent gave off no heat because no one had bothered to light it. As on the Union side, many of these men were missing arms or legs. Some were in the delirium of fading life, others fought for their recovery. Without thinking about it, Tillie moved toward the woodstove. "I didn't come prepared today, but I can bring some fruit with me tomorrow or some other foods if you wish. I can read aloud or write letters for you."

No one responded, but she refused to give up so easily.

"What's your name?" she asked soldier after soldier, none of whom answered. Most turned their backs as she approached. One boy, not much older than her and missing his left foot, glared. Something about his ginger hair and blue eyes seemed familiar, but Tillie couldn't place him.

"What's your name?"

He didn't answer. Tillie wondered if here, at least, would be a start. She pursed her lips, bowing her head, as if accepting defeat. She reached the woodstove and put her hand on it. As she suspected, it was cold.

"Well." She gave a self-deprecating shrug. "I can't do anything for you today. My decision to come over here spontaneous, to say the least. Tomorrow I shall bring a book of poetry if you like. Oh! How about a copy of Mr. Thoreau's newest work and some home-cooked food? Also, I'll bring a pencil and some paper in case you want to compose letters. I'll post them for you later."

She didn't receive a response and didn't expect one. Feeling like a fool, she left to find the doctor.

"I have to go back now. It's almost dark, and I must get home. I'll come back tomorrow. Can you tell me what kind of food I can bring the boys?"

The doctor gave her a hard, penetrating stare. "If you do, I'll let you know."

"What does that mean? Of course, I will. I said I would."

"The same as many others. If you decide to return, I'll tell you what you may fix for their recuperation. If not, well, no harm done." He clicked his heels, pivoted, and marched away.

"I'll see you tomorrow," she called. He disappeared into another tent, and with a tread as heavy as her heart, she walked away.

* * * *

Tillie worked in the kitchen after supper, preparing a basket of bread, cheese, and some apples for the Colvills to take on their trip back to Minnesota. Maggie and Mother cried over his departure.

"Tillie?" Walt stood inside the sitting room door, holding a pistol and bayonet in his hands. Ever since Father's refusal, he took pains not to be alone with her.

Lost in her musings, she jumped at the sound of his voice. Her face and ears warmed. She shoved her thoughts into a far corner of her mind. "Hello, Walt. I'm preparing a basket for Colonel and Miss Eliza. Can I pack something for you and Milt?"

"No thank you. I wanted to come in and say goodbye." He took another step closer. "I'd like to give you something, if you think your father won't object. A token to remember me by."

"I don't think Father would object." She wasn't sure that was true.

Walt extended his arms, offering the gun and bayonet. "I want you to take these. I'm mustering out, so there's no reason for me to keep them. If anyone comes to take the pistol from you, tell them I bought it with my own money." He turned the gun over and showed her his initials, W.S.R. PVT carved into the handle. "See? That's proof she belongs to me." He placed the weapon in her hand. "Don't worry. It's not loaded." He laughed. He laid the bayonet across his palms as an offering. "I want you to keep this as well."

"Walt," she breathed. "These are lovely. Are you sure you want to part with them?" The beautiful workmanship of the steel glinted as it rested across his palms.

"I want you to keep them." He stepped forward. "As a token of my esteem and to say how sorry I am about the way things happened. I didn't want to get you into any trouble, and I do hope we can remain friends." Earnest green eyes pierced her heart.

"I'd like nothing better. I'll treasure these items forever. Thank you." She accepted the bayonet.

He bowed and left the kitchen.

She held the blade close to the lantern and read the inscription down its length: To our beloved son, Private Walter S. Reed, Co. G, First Minnesota.

Tillie clasped it to her breast and said the words aloud. Then she grasped the pistol and carried them to her room where she put them in her armoire.

On her way back downstairs, she stopped in the doorway of the colonel's room. "Good evening. So, tomorrow is All Hallow's Eve, and you leave us."

"We do." Eliza extended her hand. "Though with much sadness. Billy and I feel as though we're leaving our family."

"We do too, I assure you." She clasped Eliza's hand. "Mother says your brother reminds her of William." Her eyes darted to Walt and back. "In fact, we've grown quite fond of all of you." As she spoke, her eyes again darted to him.

He turned his back, but Miss Colvill's glance passed between the two. Sympathy glowed in her eyes.

"Well, Miss Tillie." Colonel Colvill held a hand out to her. "I couldn't find myself in more loving hands than those of you and your mother and sister."

"I didn't do so much." Tillie protested, folding his hand in hers.

"You took care of things that needed taking care of so your mother and Maggie might tend to me. I must say, I have the greatest respect and admiration for my companions, but female nursing is much tenderer than male nursing. Women are more caring and sensitive." He stretched his right arm in a wide circle. His shoulder moved well, though he would always experience stiffness and less mobility. "I shall forever be grateful to your family."

"As shall I." Miss Colvill slipped her arm around his waist and leaned her head on his shoulder.

Tillie choked up. "It's as if I'm saying goodbye to another brother and sister. I'm going downstairs before I burst into weepy tears."

They laughed at her frankness.

Tillie kissed them each on the cheek. She left, blowing her nose and wiping her eyes.

* * * *

Tillie exited the house early in the morning, having said her goodbyes the night before. She presented herself to the doctor caring for the Confederates.

"Well, I must say." He didn't smile, but the hard glint in his eyes softened a bit. "Come with me." He turned his back on her and led her to the same tent she'd entered yesterday. "These boys need the most help. I'd like you to stay with them for a while."

Tillie nodded and opened her mouth to ask what she should do, but found herself staring at his back as he walked away.

* * * *

She arrived home at four in the afternoon, darkness almost upon her. A letter sat on a table inside the front door.

"Thank goodness you're home." Maggie greeted Tillie at the door, her voice full of excitement as her hands pulled at Tillie's cloak. "We've been waiting for you. Mr. Buehler stopped by this morning and delivered this." Maggie pointed to the table.

Tillie lifted the envelope. "William!" She beamed at Maggie. "At last."

"Hurry and get settled. Father's been waiting for you to come home so we can have dinner and then William's letter. I'm on pins and needles."

Tillie rushed into the kitchen, found her seat, and listened as Father read the Bible story of the prodigal son. When he finished, Mother passed around the food. Any other night they would all converse, but tonight, they concentrated on finishing their meal.

"We can clean up after Father reads William's letter, girls." Mother kept her eyes on Father as she spoke. "Just this once."

He nodded his agreement.

"Thank you, Mother." Maggie grinned and rose from the table.

* * * *

Tillie sat on the settee. A few weeks before she started learning how to knit using a set of Mother's old needles. She brought her yarn and needles to the settee, close to the lamp.

Sam sat at the table, his grammar book open, but ignored as Father took the letter from the envelope.

"It's dated July 25," Father said, a note of disappointed surprise in his voice. His brows furrowed as he flipped the page over in his hand and glanced at the empty back. "So, he was in good health as of July 25. That's a blessing, I suppose."

"James, please, read his letter." Mother sat in her rocker, knitting needles flashing in her hands.

"I'm sorry, dear. Of course." Father cleared his throat. "'Dear family, I'm writing these few lines to let you know all is well. I'm sorry for not having written sooner, previous commitments preventing.'" He snorted. "No doubt lack of ambition being one of them."

"James." Mother shot him a reproachful glance.

He reddened. "Yes, well." He scanned the page. "Let's see. 'I fought and survived Antietam without a scratch even though I was only one of a handful of men from my unit to do so. Please do not worry for me, Mother, I assure you I am in the best of health, as I pray you all are."

"That's a relief," Maggie sighed. She too held knitting needles and worked on a sweater for him.

Father continued, "'Sadly, two of my tent mates and best friends, did not. We were sent back to Washington for a few months. I am sorry to tell you James is in a hospital in Washington with a bad case of pneumonia but is mending well.'" He lifted smiling eyes to Tillie. "Of course, we already knew."

Tillie blew him a kiss.

He read on, "'What was left of my regiment afterward, they reformed and posted in Kentucky. When we arrived, we heard about the battle at home. I asked permission to go home, but was denied. So, I am sending this letter in hopes you are all safe and well. Praise God Vicksburg also fell on July four. I can't explain why, but I feel we've passed through the crucible and the war will end soon, and in our favor. Please the Lord Almighty the war end soon. Dear family, write back to me as soon as you can, so I know you are unharmed and in good health. Your loving son, William H. Pierce.'" He folded the sheet and placed it back into its envelope.

Tillie bowed her head and gave thanks to the Lord for word on both of her brothers and for the fact they visited each other in Washington. Even though his news was months old, having his letter boosted her spirits. "So, William is well. James is recuperating from his bout with pneumonia." She wiped tears from her face. "The news is old, but I'm glad. I think they're going to be all right."

* * * *

Tillie fixed a rice pudding dish her mother always made for her when sick. She cut up some apples and added them to the pudding. She prepared spoon bread, and for a treat, a pan of gingerbread. Northern boys loved gingerbread. She hoped the Southern boys would as well. She stopped calling them Rebs a long time ago. To her, they were Confederates, wounded boys who wanted to go home, but would go to prison instead.

Tillie pulled the pan from the oven.

Mother stopped short and gazed about in dismay. "Good heavens, Tillie. Did the Rebs come marching through here?"

"I'll clean up. I promise." Tillie scratched an itch on her cheek leaving a smudge of flour.

Mother grabbed a rag and wiped up the flour and sugar scattered on the table. She seized the broom and swept the floor. "Who is all this food for?" She kept her gaze on her task.

"For the Southern boys at Camp Letterman."

"I see."

Tillie cocked her head, brows creased. She put the hot pan down. "You don't think I should? Do you think me wrong for wanting to help them?"

Mother created a neat pile of dirt. She wouldn't meet Tillie's eye as she arranged the pile with her broom.

"No," she lengthened the word and tapped the broom around the dirt pile she created. "I don't think you're wrong." She glanced at Tillie. "But you never did this much baking for our own boys."

Tillie said nothing for a moment. "You yourself said, whatever these boys think they are, they're still Americans. Do you still believe that?"

Mother swept the dirt into a dustpan. "I'm not sure. After what they put us through, they didn't seem to want to be part of this government, this country, anymore."

"President Lincoln says we're still one country. Where can they go? They can't physically leave. That's what he says anyway." Tillie shrugged. "Besides, plenty of women cook for the Union boys. No one cooks for the Confederates." She took a knife and cut the bread into small squares then put it down and studied her mother. "Do you want me to stop helping them?"

Mother pursed her lips. She carried the pan to the back door. When she returned, she replaced broom and pan, crossed to the table, and sat. "Why do you ask?"

"Because, ever since I told you what I'm doing, I get the feeling you and Father aren't pleased." Tillie wrapped the cut-up bread in a moist cloth and placed it in the basket. "So, I'm asking if you disapprove."

Mother leaned against the table. "We don't disapprove as such. We're concerned with what will happen when others in town find out you're helping men who created such devastation here. We're concerned things may not go well for you."

For a split second, she considered telling Mother, but decided not to. She nodded, acknowledging her concern. "Didn't our Lord's sacrifice on the Cross give me eternal life? If I can show people His sacrifice through a little sacrifice of my own, then perhaps they will remember His love and find some comfort. Maybe my work will teach them. This is something I must do. Jesus is calling me, regardless of what people will think."

Mother reached for Tillie's hand. "Very well. Your father and I will stand behind you and help you in any way we can." She kissed Tillie's cheek. "You've grown up. Become a fine, God-fearing, young woman, and I'm proud of you." Then she squeezed her hand and left the kitchen.

Tillie perched the basket on the corner of the table and finished cleaning the kitchen. Mother gave her a lot to think about, but it wouldn't change her resolve any. While at the

Weikerts', she cared for Union and Confederate alike and saw little difference in the suffering of either side. Blood was blood, and death afflicted them both. In the end, no matter what side they were on, when they died, they cried for their mothers. She'd determined to give kindness to these men, who caused so much destruction in her world. She couldn't explain to her family what she endured there, and they didn't or wouldn't understand. When she finished cleaning up, she took the lamp and headed for the stairs. She went to bed and prayed for her new boys.

* * * *

Tillie returned with her basket laden with food, books, and implements to write letters. Her feet crunched the frosted grass, and she did her best to avoid the icy puddles in the road. Her breath produced small clouds of steam. She hoped the boys were warm enough last night.

Tillie arrived, a bright, cheery good morning on her lips. Few responded. Most shivered under their blankets. She crossed to the stove and put her hand on the cold metal. "I thought so." She glared at their only heat source. "I brought some wood." She knelt, pulled out books and food, placing them with care. She took sticks of wood, enough to start a fire, and arranged them in the bottom of the stove. "Why didn't someone come in and build a fire for you last night?"

The boys laughed in derision. No one answered.

"Oh." She wanted to disappear every time she said something that displayed the gulf between them. Instead, she busied herself with building the fire. She used some of her precious writing paper and a match from a tin thrown to her. When she got a small flame going, she added more sticks then larger pieces.

"I got these from my father's orchard. They tore down our trees for the soldier's cemetery. I love the smell of apple wood. Mr. Everett is coming to dedicate the cemetery." She talked while she worked to build up the fire. "The ceremony is set for November nineteenth. Two weeks from today. Mr. Lincoln might come!" She grinned at the men.

Their glares and mutterings struck a deathblow to her enthusiasm. She licked her lips. "Uh, I'll go find some wood to keep this fire going." She set the food to warm and beat a hasty retreat.

A short time later, she returned, arms laden with wood. She tended the stove until she got a good fire. She laid more wood on and shut the door before turning to the men. "There are fewer of you than yesterday."

"They're starting to move us out." A soldier ventured to tell her. "We're going to a place called David's Island in New York." He sat up.

"I've never heard of it before." She passed the food around to the boys.

Stopping in front of the boy with the ginger colored hair, she studied his face. "I remember you. I told you I would." She waited, giving him a chance to respond, but he stared at her, silent. "You were outside our house after church, tying your shoe, a day or so before the fighting started. I was rude to you." She offered him some gingerbread, but he didn't move. She set it on a stand next to his cot. "I'm sorry about that." She remembered his smile, the way his cheeks dimpled, his salute cocky and full of superior confidence.

She eased herself down. "My name is Tillie. What's yours?"

He turned his face away.

"Aw go on, talk to her," someone challenged. "She ain't gonna bite ya."

The boy remained silent.

"You were tying your shoe when we walked by. You gave me a salute and went on your way." She put her hand on his arm.

He withdrew his arm. Still he said nothing.

About to give up trying, she started to rise when another thought struck her. "Listen." She stood, clasping her hands in front of her. "You're angry and I understand." She didn't expect a response, but his face blotched almost purple. He glared at her.

"You understand?" he sneered in a thick, Southern accent. "You understand what it's like to lose everything, do you?" He lifted his leg minus his foot, which he dropped back on the cot. "You people took everything from me and more, so don't tell me you understand. I don't want your understanding or your pity!" He snatched up the gingerbread and flung it at her. "Go away and leave me be!"

She blinked a slow, deliberate blink and unclenched her jaw. She folded her lips under her teeth and squeezed, wanting to slap him. Instead, she bent and gathered the crumbs. "You haven't lost everything." Her tone remained friendly, but now held an edge. Rather than meet his eye, she brushed bits of gingerbread from her skirt. Her shoulders drew back, and she stared down at him. "You lost your foot."

She walked away.

* * * *

Tillie walked toward the dining hall. An orderly brought the men their lunch, which reminded her it had been hours since breakfast. Hungry, she headed to the mess tent, but she couldn't get the boy with the ginger colored hair off her mind. How to reach through his hostility and pain?

Her knees knocked together as she approached. Last week, someone threw food at her, splatting the floor in front of her. The harassment began when she started helping on the other side. She understood what the doctor meant when he doubted she would come back, and because of his sarcasm, she refused to quit.

Now, most everyone ignored her. She couldn't decide which was worse. She stepped into line with a pounding heart and sweaty palms. Her hands shook as she grabbed a plate. She made her selections and walked down the rows of tables, looking for a place to sit. Two weeks ago, people invited her to sit with them, but now, they turned away or blocked her from sitting down. She couldn't help feel she ran a gauntlet every lunchtime, but remained convinced she was doing the right thing.

Spying Nellie Auginbaugh at a table talking with her cousin and a couple of civilian doctors, Tillie walked over. "May I sit with you?"

Nellie's cousin snorted. The doctors concentrated on eating. Nellie stared. "Of course." She grabbed her plate, rising to her feet. "We were just going. We have to get back to our boys."

Tillie sat with a heavy sigh and ignored the doctors across from her. She closed her eyes to pray over her food, but hot tears squeezed between her lashes. Oh, Lord, am I wrong? What should I do? She opened her eyes, sniffed, and forced herself to eat, even though her appetite disappeared. She chewed and swallowed without tasting, keeping her eyes on her plate. Her head jerked up when a warm hand covered hers.

"No need for tears, Miss Tillie." A soft Irish lilt fell on her ears like comforting musical notes. The chaplain settled across from her.

She touched her face. Her fingers came away wet. Her fork clattered to the plate as she covered her face and wept. She dropped her hands, sniffing. "I'm so confused. Did I get it wrong?"

"Get what wrong?" He cocked his head and chewed.

"I thought God wanted me to go over to the Confederate side and help those boys. They have no one. So many people serve our Union boys, but those boys are alone. At the Weikerts', I cared for Union and Confederate alike, and no one seemed to think that wrong. Now I'm a pariah." Every ounce of her misery she poured out in her speech. "I thought God wanted me to go over and help them."

"Oh, but we must be careful not to presume to know what God wants for us, don't we now." He wagged a finger at her. "Still, I see the good you're doing. I care for the spiritual needs of those boys. They speak highly of you."

Despite her tears, she smiled.

"Pride goeth before the fall, my dear." He rolled the R when he said pride. Frowning, he scooped another forkful of food.

Her brow creased. "What do you mean?"

He swallowed. "You smiled when I said they speak well of you. I understand you feel complimented, to be sure, but we must be careful of letting the devil get a foothold, by the pride in being so well thought of."

"More like, I'm glad someone appreciates what I'm doing. Do you think I'm presuming what God wants for me? I wondered about it last night, so I went to the Bible. Second Corinthians seemed to make things clear. 'All things are of God, who hath reconciled us to himself by Jesus Christ and hath given to us the ministry of reconciliation.' So I thought I did the right thing."

"Well, who am I to argue with Second Corinthians?" He sipped his coffee and put his cup down. A gold cross, pinned to his lapel, caught the light. A soft smile touched her lips. Always a teacher when she needed one. Thank you, Lord.

"You rather put me in mind of 'Love your neighbor as yourself and pray for your enemies.'" He offered a smile.

"Reverend Bergstrasser would say our neighbors are our brothers and sisters in Christ, not the Confederates who happen to be in the area or the man who lives next door."

The chaplain nodded, looking thoughtful. "That would be true. But are you certain you don't have neighbors, brothers in Christ, in those Confederate tents?"

"No."

"Don't you think you should go find out?" He winked at her, pulled out a pocket watch, and clicked the top. "Well I must run. I'm late." He snapped the timepiece shut and slipped it back into his pocket. "I enjoyed our conversation and look forward to seeing you around."

"Thank you, sir." Tillie picked up her fork. "Thank you for everything."

Chapter 29

Reading aloud from Shakespeare's Sonnets with Private Johnson, Tillie glanced at Tommy, the ginger-haired boy, who lay on his cot, across the aisle, whittling. Sam often whittled when he needed to sort things out within himself. Her voice drifted away as an idea began to take shape.

"You know what, Miss Tillie." Johnson pushed the book down to her lap, bringing her back to reality. "I'm kinda tired. I think I want to rest a bit, and after, write a letter to my sweetheart. You don't mind, do you?"

"Of course not." She took some paper out of her basket, along with a pen and some ink. "I'll leave you now." She rose and crossed to the ginger-haired boy. He chipped away with vicious hacks. "I can bring you more wood, if you want some. My father's apprentice whittles a lot. Sometimes, he even makes something worth looking at." She chuckled.

The boy turned the stick in his hands and returned to gouging out chunks and letting the chips fly.

She sighed and walked away.

* * * *

As soon as the sun edged toward the peaks of Big Roundtop and the clouds began to turn purple, Tillie started for home. Mother made her promise to be home before dark, but she stayed a bit longer to finish some things before going home. Now she walked fast. A chill November breeze touched her skin. Her cheeks tingled, and her breath puffed out in white billows. Would Mr. Garlach give her some spare pieces of dressed wood? Perhaps if she asked in a circumspect way, he may be willing.

She approached the outskirts of town, and as she passed Racehorse Alley, something hard hit her right arm. She spun around in the gathering darkness trying to identify the culprit.

"Traitor!" a man shouted, but she didn't recognize the voice.

Her scalp prickled as feet pounded down the alley. She picked up the rock. People disapproved of what she did, she knew, but she never thought her neighbors would turn vicious. She was one of them. She stared down the lane. The darkening passage and looming buildings menaced her now, as though hiding monsters. She dropped the stone, grabbed her skirts, and ran home.

As she entered the house, her stomach growled at the smell of dinner. She took off her cloak and bonnet and hung them up. Holding out the cuff of her sleeve, she examined it for tears. She didn't find any, only a dirt mark where the rock hit her.

Father stepped into the hallway. "You're home. Good. I'm getting ready to read. Hurry and wash up."

"Yes, Father." She breezed into the kitchen and poured water into the washbasin. After a quick cleansing, she dropped into her seat with a sigh, relieved to be home, safe and secure, around people who loved her.

Father opened the Bible to the Book of Matthew.

She listened, and when he finished, she passed food around the table, eating her meal in silence and partially listening to the general conversation.

"Are you well, dear?" Mother placed her palm on Tillie's forehead.

"I'm fine. I'm tired." Tillie smiled, then turned her eyes to her plate and continued to eat.

"Well, go to bed early. You spend far too much time at Camp Letterman, if you ask me."

"I like what I do." She forked another bite of food and chewed.

Father tapped her arm. "Join your mother and me in the parlor after supper."

His expression said they wanted to discuss something important. Her heart skipped a beat. Did she do something wrong? "Of course, Father." She saw no point in pursuing the subject at the table. He wouldn't speak in front of the others.

After helping Maggie clean the dishes, Tillie sat on the parlor sofa. She folded her hands in her lap and waited for her parents, sitting together on the settee, to begin.

"What's wrong, my dear?" Mother asked.

"Why do you think something is wrong?" She studied first one parent, then the other. Did someone tell them of the harassment?

"My love." Mother tilted her head and gave her a gentle smile. "You are my child, and I love you. Do you think I can't tell when something troubles you? Is that boy still giving you a hard time?"

"Well, yes, but I don't worry about him. Mostly he ignores me. I think I found a way to get through to him. Father, do you think Mr. Garlach would give me a piece of surplus dressed wood? Something he can whittle. After my confrontation with the boy, whose name is Tommy, the others started to open up." She rearranged her skirts, trying to put her thoughts in order. "I ate lunch with a chaplain today. I'm having a little trouble with people in town who seem to think I've forgotten who I am and what those Southern boys are."

Her parents exchanged a knowing glance.

Tillie noticed but went on. "We spoke for some time about reconciliation and finding out if there are brothers in Christ among those Confederates." She sighed and beat back a wave of sadness. "I feel a little like this past summer. People say things that make sense at the time, but then I'm not sure what we talked about or if I heard right."

"Heard what right?" Father's brow creased. He sat forward.

"Well, Chaplain Combs and I spoke of Second Corinthians. Tonight, you read blessed are the merciful and blessed are the peacemakers for they shall be called children of God. I know my heart is not pure at all, and I'm wondering if I'm doing this for God's glory or my own." She uttered a heavy, worried sigh. After a few moments of fiddling with a pleat in her skirt, she glanced at her parents.

"Why do you worry about whose glory you do this for?" Mother tilted her head.

"Because." Tillie shrugged and kept her eyes on her lap. "Because people at the camp hate me for what I'm doing. Someone threw a rock and hit me in the arm as I walked home tonight." She wiped a tear away, hating to tell them of the incident. "I don't like it when people dislike me. My first instinct is to behave contrary to them."

"Who threw a rock at you?" Father demanded, but Mother placed a calming hand over his arm.

"She's obviously unharmed, James, and we can get to that later."

Tillie smiled. "Mother's right. It doesn't matter who threw the rock, and I didn't see them anyway. It came flying out of Racehorse Alley and hit me on the arm."

Father drew a deep breath and let it out. "I'm glad you're telling us this. It's the reason we wanted to talk to you." He clasped Mother's hand. "You speak true when you say they don't like what you're doing. I've been told outright people think you're providing aid and comfort to the enemy. The Lord tells us to pray for our enemies. But I did read tonight that He also wants us to be reconciled to our enemies and to be peacemakers. Some people are not ready yet. In the meantime, you'll need to fill yourself with an enormous amount of grace." He rose and went to her. Kneeling down, he placed his hands on her knees. "I'm proud of you, Tillie. You are working out your faith well. Tomorrow, I shall walk you to Camp Letterman, and I'll pick you up at four o'clock. Perhaps if people realize your mother and I sanction your actions, they'll reconsider before throwing anything else at you. I'll go to Mr. Garlach and ask for some wood."

"All right. Thank you, Father." She slipped her arms around his neck. "Oh, by the way." She pulled back to see into his face. "Can we stop at Mr. Buehler's first thing? The boys want me to post letters for them."

Father pushed her away and stared hard at her, his mouth agape.

She fidgeted. "Is something wrong?"

"You can't mail letters to the South. That's treason. They won't be delivered."

"I'm not committing treason. I know what's in the letters. I helped write most of them. I'm not sending military secrets. Just notes to their families telling them they're all right."

He rose to his feet. "The contents aren't important. Sending letters south is considered a treasonous act." He glared at her. "I'm not going to let you send them. It's too dangerous. I forbid it." He held out his hand. "Give them to me."

Tillie's face fell. She considered arguing with him, but changed her mind. Treason was a frightening word. She went into the hallway, returning with a small packet, which she gave to him.

Mother rose and put her hands on Tillie's shoulders. "We worry about you, Tillie. Father and I don't disapprove of what you're doing for the Confederate boys, but people in town do. We only ask—be discreet."

"I will be discreet. I am being discreet. This is silly and narrow-minded. They're not the hated 'Rebs' we talked about all summer. They're poor boys who are hurt and far away from home. Wouldn't you want some woman to care for James or William the same way? Wouldn't any mother here?"

"Tillie, it's not so simple. Of course, I'd want someone to care for your brothers if necessary, but we're not discussing them. We're talking about your safety and standing in this town. You have a future to consider."

"I beg your pardon?"

"Yes, you heard me right. Soon, those boys will be sent off to whatever prison camp they're assigned to, gone for good. You, on the other hand, will be here for a long time to come. Care for them. Lord knows they need some kindness. Perhaps, after the war, your actions will go a long way toward mending fences, but don't burn your bridges in the process."

Tillie studied her parents. "Do you feel the same way, Father?"

"I do." He put the packet of letters into his breast pocket. "It may sound selfish and self-serving, but Mother's right. Your future is here. Theirs is not. You must think long term. You don't want to damage your standing."

She stared at Mother, who met her eyes with a steady gaze.

Tillie nodded. "I understand what you're saying, and I will try to adjust my behavior accordingly." She exhaled. "If you don't mind, I'm exhausted. I'd like to go to bed now." She gave her parents a hug and kiss and trudged upstairs.

* * * *

Rising early the next morning, Tillie dressed and ate a quick breakfast. She stepped into the hallway and donned her cloak and bonnet. As she buttoned up, Father joined her at the front door, pulling on his coat and hat.

They walked toward the center of town. Their conversation the night before left her disgruntled. She'd lain awake a good portion of the night. She didn't know how to broach the subject or how to interpret his silence. By the time they reached the Diamond, she couldn't take it any longer. "Are you keeping something from me? You don't want me doing this work?" She turned puppy-dog eyes to her father. Would they stop her or would they trust her?

He checked each road entering the Diamond, waiting for an opportunity to cross. When the intersection cleared enough, he grasped her elbow, and they trotted across. Upon reaching the other side, he released her and walked with his head down, hands in his pockets. He gave her a sidelong glance. "I'm only trying to protect you. That's all your mother and I are trying to do. That's my job."

"Protect me from what? Angry people?" She snorted. "There are some things you can protect me from and some you can't."

Father bobbed his head and raised one eyebrow in open acknowledgment.

"You and Mother talked last night about mending fences without burning bridges. Do you disapprove of my helping the boys?"

"No, we don't." He raised his face and stared down the street, as though reluctant to meet her gaze. "You're right—they're not soldiers anymore, just wounded men who need some Christian charity. Some people can't get past the fact those boys fought against this country and wrought so much havoc here. I can't blame them for reacting the way they do. Still, word is, Camp Letterman is to be disbanded soon, so I don't see the harm in helping."

Tillie gaped at him. "You 'don't see the harm in helping,'" she repeated, unable to keep the sarcasm at bay.

"Listen." He held up a hand to forestall her words. "Your mother and I understand you believe the Lord led you to take this stand. We can't gainsay you. This is between you and Him. We can't make this journey with you. That's not to say we're not concerned with how others will treat you, but you must see we haven't stopped you from going either."

"Why not? If you're so upset about the way I'm treated?"

"Because your situation puts me in mind of a similar one for me about two years ago. Do you recall right after William left for the Army, and I needed someone to work in the butcher shop?"

Tillie nodded. "You and Mother talked about a number of boys to apprentice."

"Yes, we did, and in the end, we chose a young man who never even applied for the job."

"Sam."

"Yes, Sam. We picked him because we believed, with his father in prison and his poor mother overwhelmed by her circumstances, we needed to get him out of that havoc and into a Christian home. I took a lot of guff from people who thought me mad. Everyone said he would murder us in our sleep or rob me blind. Mr. Garlach, in particular, warned me time and again, trash is trash and I should leave it alone."

"Mr. Garlach said such a thing about Sam? I'm surprised. He treats him so well."

"He does now, but in the beginning he disliked and mistrusted him, as did many in this town. The sins of the father visited on the son, I suppose. We can't deny his father is a disagreeable black spot on our town's character. My point is, we did what we knew in our hearts was right. Right for us and right for Sam. We were led to choose him, and while we didn't get half as much heartache as you, we can and do understand your position."

Approaching the front gate of Camp Letterman, Father let out a low whistle.

Tillie laughed. "This is nothing compared to August. You should've seen it then. It's about a quarter the size now." She took his hand. "Thank you, Father, for telling me about Sam." Rising on her tiptoes, she kissed his cheek before walking away, chirruping a good morning to the guard, who smiled and returned the greeting.

* * * *

Tillie entered the tent and went straight to Tommy's cot. He rolled over, presenting his back to her. She ignored the rebuff. "I brought something for you, Tommy." She put her basket on his blanket and reached into the bottom. Out came a beautiful piece of maple. Laid in her hand the block fit the length of her palm to her fingertips. The wood, sanded smooth and soft so the user wouldn't pick up splinters.

He refused to acknowledge her.

Tillie used the wood to nudge him in the back, hoping to provoke him.

"Go away." He waved his arm in her direction, a feeble gesture of dismissal. "Leave me alone."

"I'll not." She pushed him again. "You whittled the other day. I talked to my father, and he went to my neighbor, who gave me this piece of wood." She laid the block on his hip, on top of his blanket. "This is my way of saying I'm going to make your life miserable until you decide to stop feeling sorry for yourself. If that doesn't work, I'll read Bible verses to you all day about the sin of self-absorption."

The other boys laughed.

"Give him Hades, Miss Tillie," Private Jones heckled.

"Give up the fight, boy," Sergeant Davis hollered over. "She's got you in her sights. You don't want to be in the way when her cannons go off, do you?"

From where she stood, she saw Tommy's face turn a deep scarlet. "Let him alone, boys. I think he gets the general idea." She held her hands out, pleading for silence. "Let him be."

Tillie left his cot and set about building a warming fire in the stove. She ignored Tommy for the rest of the morning.

* * * *

The orderly brought their noontime meal, so Tillie went to the dining hall. For the hundredth time, she wondered she if did the right thing, baiting Tommy. But kind and gentle sympathy didn't seem to work, and she couldn't think of another way. She started praying, an unformed prayer, unsure what she wanted to ask. With the boy bound for prison camp, she knew enough to understand he had a slim chance of surviving, even under the best of conditions. As she walked and prayed, a sense of peace filled her soul. The same as she'd had in Beckie's bedroom after returning from the battlefield.

Near the dining hall, Nellie emerged from a tent, almost colliding with Tillie. "Nellie!" Tillie's hands shot out in a reflex to stop the collision.

With a startled "oh," Nellie jumped back, as though to avoid touching Tillie. "I do beg your pardon." Her tone formal and stiff.

"That's all right." Tillie shrugged. "I hope you weren't hurt."

Nellie didn't answer and, without another word, strode away, quickening her step to put distance between them.

Tillie's heart pounded, and hot tears scorched her eyes.

Nellie glanced back and walked faster. She too, headed for the dining hall.

Tillie walked slow enough to ensure she did not catch up with the older woman. Why didn't people try to understand? Why did they judge? "Judge not, lest ye be judged," she snarled under her breath, then closed her eyes, took a deep breath and repented.

Be still. The words echoed in her mind.

After her meal, she returned to the tent determined not to let her neighbors' actions affect her attitude with the boys. But, when Tommy shoved something under his blanket before turning his back to her, something in her snapped. She marched up to the foot of his cot and dropped her hands on her hips the way Mother did when annoyed. "You know, when I first saw you that day after church, I honestly felt sorry for you. You looked so hungry and a bit silly in your outfit several sizes too big, but mostly, you were hungry. I wanted to invite you in for lunch, that's how much pity I had for you. But you're nothing but a selfish, spineless whiner. I should have saved my pity for someone far more worth the energy." By the time she finished, her voice shook from the emotions surging through her.

He met her diatribe in complete silence, though his blue eyes rounded big as saucers.

Tillie stared hard at him, willing him to say something, anything, but he didn't.

"Oh, fine. Be that way, you spoiled, selfish, rotten…little boy!" She waved an angry hand and stormed out of the tent. For the first time since she started working, she went home early. She didn't even care if they had wood for the night.

* * * *

Tillie returned the following morning and stood inside the entrance of the convalescent tent. Her eyes traveled over the boys huddled beneath their blankets and stopped at Tommy. She approached his cot with a slow, contrite step. "I wish to apologize to all of you, but especially you, Tommy, for my behavior yesterday. My outburst happened because of something else, not you. I unleashed my frustrations on you, which was wrong. Will you forgive me?"

"Miss Tillie." Private Johnson sat up and smiled at her. "We may spend almost all of our time in this tent, but we're not ignorant to what goes on around here. We see how your people treat you for taking care of us. We see it in the way we don't get wood at night, in the way you fight for us to get even small luxuries. They talk about you when you're not here. Yes, they talk about you, and no, it's not worth repeating the things they say. They're the ones without Christian charity. There is one thing we've been wondering though."

Tillie's throat tightened, and she blinked back tears. "What's that?"

He grinned and glanced around at his comrades, including them in his joke. They snickered.

"What took you so long?" All the men burst out laughing, except Tommy.

It took a minute for Tillie to realize they laughed in sympathy and understanding. She joined in, sniffing back tears.

A blue-clad soldier came in, carrying wood, and Tillie gave him a little dig. "I'm sorry." She grew serious. "I don't understand why you never get wood at night. I ask every night to make sure you get some, and they always assure me you will."

"Well then, you're naïve if you think they're gonna give us wood." Private Wilson put his hands behind his head.

The Yankee soldier opened his arms, dumped the wood, stormed out.

"Thank you, ever so much," Tillie called as he snapped back the tent flap and left.

They laughed at his retreating footsteps.

"She's stupid," Tommy blurted out. "You're a dumb, know-it-all, stupid woman."

The laughter abruptly ceased.

Tillie stared at him. "He speaks!"

"Tommy, leave her alone." Private Bacon lowered the book Tillie gave him the day before. He scowled at Tommy from his cot next to the ginger-haired boy. "She's been nothing but kind and generous, and that's rare around here. We can all go to prison camp and take with us the memory of her kindness."

Tommy turned his face away and muttered under his breath.

"Besides," Bacon continued, returning to his book, "she's right, and I, for one, am sick and tired of your attitude."

Again, the men laughed.

Tillie used the diversion to kneel and arrange the kindling. After she lit a match, the flames gathered strength while she organized her thoughts. She put wood on the flames and shut the stove door, holding her hands out to feel the heat radiate.

Satisfied, she rose and stalked to Tommy's cot. "I thought about you all night last night. I want to tell you a story. On the Yankee side, I cared for a man who lost both his hands. A farmer in civilian life. Imagine trying to farm without hands." If she thought Tommy would respond, she was in for disappointment.

He kept his eyes averted and pulled his blanket over his head.

"Tommy, look at me. Your life isn't over. Do you want me to tell you about the boy without his hands?"

"No." Tommy's muffled voice came from under the cover. "Leave me be."

"I won't leave you be. I don't believe in allowing people to wallow in self-pity. It's sinful. The boy who lost his hands had more reason than you to despair, but he doesn't. He's decided he`ll go home and open a dry goods store. He said there would be things he can do and things he can't, but those he can't, he'd find people who can. He's not going to let his circumstance stop him. I can't imagine why you would let the loss of one foot stop you. Get up out of the wallow. Stop feeling sorry for yourself. You're going to go to prison camp soon. You'll need every ounce of fight left in you to survive." She glared at him, breathing hard. "My point is you can find something else to do with your life, but only if you're willing to survive and go home."

"I don't need you telling me what I can and can't do. Why don't you go away?"

Tillie shook her head and walked away. She sat next to Private Wilson, smoothed his blankets, and helped him to sit up.

He patted her hand. "You did fine, Miss Tillie. He needed to hear it. We been saying the same thing, but he needed to hear it all the same."

"I hope so."

* * * *

Two days later, Tillie arrived at Camp Letterman to discover the entire Confederate side empty. Soldiers worked, striking the last few tents.

She ran back to the gate. "Guard!"

"Yes, miss?"

"What happened to the boys? My boys? Where are they?"

"Well, miss, the prison transport train came for them last night. We loaded them up and sent them to a brand-new prison camp in Illinois called Rock Island." He put his fingers to his hat brim. "Please excuse me now, miss." He walked away.

Her heart sank, and she bit back bitter tears. Why didn't they tell her? Give her a chance to say goodbye? She stared at the dead earth where sixteen men lived for a short time. She would never lay eyes on them again. "Why didn't you let me say goodbye?" She screamed at the place where the tent once stood. People milling around stopped and stared at the crazy girl screaming by the gate. Then they went back to business.

* * * *

She walked to the dining hall, not expecting anyone to join her at mealtimes anymore. Today she didn't care. She wanted to be alone.

Dr. Janes, the camp administrator, entered the dining hall and stood on a chair. The hall grew quiet.

"Ladies and gentleman." He put out his hands in an unnecessary gesture for silence. "Ladies and gentleman, I wish to make an announcement." He made a show of sliding on spectacles and withdrawing a piece of paper from his coat pocket. He unfolded the sheet and held it at arm's length. "By order of President Lincoln, General Halleck, and Dr. Letterman this camp is to be disbanded by the close of business on or before the twenty-second of November, in the year of our Lord, eighteen hundred and sixty three." He lifted his eyes from the paper and glanced around the hall. "Thank you." He stepped off the chair and left.

Silence greeted his announcement. After he disappeared, the general buzz of conversation picked up again. One week from tomorrow. Today would be her last day. She saw no point in coming back. These boys didn't need her. She returned to her meal. One good thing about people refusing to speak to her: it left her with plenty of time for prayer and meditation.

"Miss Tillie, may I join you?" The chaplain smiled down at her. He held his hands behind his back.

"Chaplain Combs. Your company is most welcome."

Reverend Combs sat across from her and set down a wooden horse, carved in the act of running, tail and mane caught by the wind and flowing behind the animal. She bore strong legs with muscle definition carved into the thighs, the hooves chiseled to precision. The horse's arched neck displayed fierce pride, yet the eyes showed a calm, gentle demeanor.

For the first time in months, Tillie thought of Lady, and her heart lurched. Her hand shook as she picked up the carving. "Where did you get this? It's lovely." She ran her finger down the length of the horse's side. She could almost feel the muscles flex with movement. She touched the muzzle and imagined the soft snout. Tears filled her eyes. "Oh, she's so beautiful."

"The boy, Tommy, asked me to give this to you. No explanation, just 'See Miss Tillie gets this and tell her I'm sorry.'"

Tillie clutched the carving to her breast, tears spilling down her cheeks.

"I take it you found a brother or two in that tent."

"It seems I did."

Chapter 30

Whoever said nothing ever happened in Gettysburg? Tillie waited on the front step for the rest of the family. They were going to the dedication ceremony, but so far, everyone else seemed to take their time coming out. She didn't want to miss a thing.

She glanced at the door, braced her hands on the railing, and hoisted herself up. She peered toward the Diamond.

A crowd milled about, and the buzz of hundreds of voices carried to her ears. She couldn't see the telltale sign of Mr. Lincoln's tall hat. Dropping back to her feet, she pushed open the door. Where did everyone go? "Hurry! They're coming. You'll miss it." She slammed the door.

Leaning out over the railing again, she glimpsed people, but no sign they were starting toward the cemetery. Tillie skipped down the steps and out to the curb, stopping in the center of the empty street, and waited. She looked at the closed door, drew in a deep breath, and went back to the front step.

President Lincoln's arrival at the train station yesterday touched off an impromptu celebration lasting late into the night as townspeople wandered the streets serenading the Executive, Mr. Seward, and even Mr. Everett, the main speaker. Now, the party continued as they made their way down Baltimore Street.

A tall man, wearing a high, black stovepipe hat, a black coat and pants rode a calm and gentle brown horse. Two men flanked him. Mr. Seward on the President's left and Mr. Wills on his right, but Tillie only had eyes for Mr. Lincoln.

She clutched her hands to her breast and bounced on the balls of her feet. They approached Middle Street. If the rest of her family didn't come soon, they'd miss out! The President of the United States riding a horse down her street. She pushed the door open again. "The President's coming. Hurry!" She slammed the door a second time and spun around.

Music drifted to her ears. Somewhere near the back of the line, a flute tootled out the tune "The Flag Of Columbia." The three men at the head of the column approached West High Street. Almost oblivious to the massive crowd gathered about them, the riders came abreast of her.

Tillie straightened her shoulders and put on her most solemn face. She mustn't smile at the President. What would he think of her?

Lincoln and his companions passed, deep in conversation. The President turned to speak to Mr. Wills, his gaze straying past the lawyer's shoulder, resting on her.

Not knowing the proper protocol, Tillie wanted to be dignified. A grin split her face, and she sank into a clumsy half curtsey. Rubbery knees failed to support her, and she lost her balance. Her hand whipped out and caught the railing in time to prevent an undignified spill on the front stoop. She straightened.

President Lincoln didn't smile, but his expression softened and the corners of his mouth lifted a little. He raised his fingers to his hat brim and nodded at her, as though they shared a private joke.

Mr. Wills turned to find out who caught his guest's attention, and he too, bowed his head and touched his hat to Tillie.

A military entourage clattered along behind the President.

The front door opened, and the rest of her family joined her on the step.

"You missed it! The President just rode by, and you missed it!"

"Well, we got out here as fast as possible before you pulled the door off its hinges." Mother adjusted her bonnet.

An open carriage drove by with Mr. Everett, the key speaker, inside. A young woman sat next to him, fussing over the old man. Though a mild day for mid-November, he wore a heavy blanket like a shawl around his shoulders. The woman tucked another warm covering about his hips, using her body to shield him from the wind.

"Is he Mr. Everett?" Sam's voice held a mix of awe and disappointment. In honor of the orator's visit, Mother made him read a series of Mr. Everett's old speeches and lectures. "He's so old."

"He's eight-six." Father put his hat on his head. "He has a right to look old. He's an extremely sick man. He shouldn't be out here."

Mother and Maggie murmured sounds of pity for Mr. Everett.

Tillie studied his appearance. The old man did appear uncomfortable in his greatcoat and blanket over his shoulders and one about his legs. The woman did her best to tuck blankets around him and use her body to shield him from the wind.

"She must be his daughter." Mother's eyes rested on her. "I understand he travels nowhere without her."

"Why didn't they provide a closed carriage for him?" Maggie gazed with sympathy as they rode by. "The poor man."

Once the conveyance passed, the parade swept the Pierces in. At the back, martial music now played "Marching Along".

Tillie bounced on her toes to the lively tune. She sang the last of the refrain. "For God and for country, we are marching along."

Sam picked up the tune and joined in, "Marching along, we are marching along. Gird on the armor, and be marching along. Lincoln's"—he substituted the President's name for the original, McClellan—"our leader, he's gallant and strong. For God and for country, we are marching along."

Tillie grinned at him, surprised by his clear tenor. She'd never heard him sing before. She only sang when certain the music would drown out her voice.

He grinned back.

After crossing Washington Street, they entered the still incomplete, wrought-iron gates of the new National Soldier's Cemetery. Even unfinished, a grand design took shape.

They laid the cemetery on a hexagonal plot of land, in a D-shaped pattern. Each Northern state, allotted a block of graves, lay within the semicircle. Handwritten signs on sticks indicated the location of each state.

They entered the gates. Mounds of dirt, still smelling of disturbed earth lay beside open pits waiting for their recipient, and markers indicated graves not yet dug, and would have to wait until spring.

"Still a lot of work to do." Maggie scanned the area.

A new wrought-iron fence separating Evergreen Cemetery from the National Soldier's Cemetery stood half-complete.

Maggie indicated a couple standing near the Pennsylvania marker. "There are the Sandoes. I think I'll go over and speak to them." She left, wending her way through the crowd.

"There's President Lincoln with Governor Curtin and Mr. Seward." Tillie shielded her eyes from the weak sun and gazed at the platform on which the dignitaries seated themselves, laughing and talking with each other.

She grabbed her father's arm and smiled up at him, eyes shining. "Mr. Lincoln tipped his hat to me when they passed the house!"

Father squeezed her shoulder. "Good for you."

She scanned the program in her hand. "At least seventeen governors are here, as well as many senators and congressmen."

On the podium, Secretary Seward spoke to the President as he made himself comfortable.

Around the cemetery, strangers searched for their beloved's gravesite. Tillie focused on one woman, whose physical appearance reminded her of Mrs. Greenly. When the woman found a grave, she dropped to her knees in grief, while her husband stood by in silence. Many others turned away, devastated, when they did not find what they sought.

"Those poor, poor mothers and wives." Mother shook her head. "It's enough to break one's heart. I wonder how Mrs. Greenly is faring."

The band played "The Battle Hymn Of The Republic", its up-tempo sweeping the crowd as people wept over the mounds of earth.

"Come." Father took Mother's elbow and put his other hand on Tillie's back, between her shoulder blades. "Let's look around, shall we?" He directed his family away from the sight of so many people mourning their loved ones.

The "Battle Hymn Of The Republic" ended with a flourish, and the band played a more solemn tune, "May God Save the Union".

The mood of the tune grabbed her, and Tillie sang along.

"May God save the Union! God grant it may stand,
The pride of our people, the boast of our land;

Still, still 'mid the storm may our banner float free,
Unrent and unriven o'er earth and o'er sea."

The coronets and trumpets took over the sad tune. Tillie let the music fill her.

"May God save the Union! The Red, White and Blue,
Our States keep united the dreary day through;
Let the stars tell the tale of the glorious past,
And bind us in Union forever to last."

The crowd picked up the tune, and before the third verse, even those on the podium sang. At the final verse, the crowd raised their voices and almost shouted the words.

"May God save the Union! Still, still may it stand
upheld by the strength of the patriot hand,
to cement it our Fathers ensanguined the sod,
to keep it we kneel to a merciful God."

The last notes drifted away on the breeze as the crowd hushed and migrated toward the platform.

Reverend Stockton rose and began his invocation. He raised his hands over his head calling upon the presence of the Lord. "Oh, God our Father," he intoned, "For the sake of the Son, our Savior, inspire us with thy spirit and sanctify us to the right fulfillment of the duties of this occasion..."

Tillie stopped on a small rise of land where she could see between the shoulders of two tall men in front of her. She clasped her hands together beneath her cloak and an excited shiver ran down her body. Reverend Stockton's deep baritone carried over the crowd, fitting the occasion. "...Looking back to the dark days of fear and of trembling, and the rapture of relief that came after, we multiply our thanksgivings and confess our obligations to renew and perfect our personal and social consecration to thy service and glory..."

Heads bowed in supplication. Every man present had removed his cap as the reverend's voice carried over the silent, respectful crowd. Feeling a bit like her old self, Tillie lowered her head and closed her eyes as she let Reverend Stockton's voice flow over her and fill her soul.

"...Oh, Lord, our God, bless us. Oh our Father, bless the bereaved, whether absent or present. Bless our sick and wounded soldiers and sailors. Bless all our rulers and people. Bless our army and navy. Bless the efforts to suppress this rebellion and bless all the associations of this day, and place, and scene forever. As the trees are not dead, though their foliage is gone, so our heroes are not dead though their forms have fallen. In their proper personality they are all with thee…"

The sun found a chink in the clouds and shone on the platform, seeming to illuminate Reverend Stockton with ethereal light as if God himself listened and approved.

A murmur rippled through the crowd as the reverend finished and sat down.

The marine band played through a quick tune as Edward Everett rose and shuffled to the podium. He took his time getting his notes out of his coat pocket and putting his spectacles on his nose before turning to the bandleader and nodding. The music stopped.

Tillie clapped as hard as everyone else did. She exchanged excited grins with Sam.

When ready, Mr. Everett took hold of the lapels of his coat and surveyed the crowd and grounds. A hushed silence fell over the listeners.

Tillie's heart pounded, and she clasped her hands together, waiting for his words to fall on her ears. Mr. Everett tipped his face to the shaft of sunlight, as though peering through the clouds, seeking divine assistance. He lowered his face and began:

"Standing beneath this serene sky, overlooking these broad fields now reposing from the labors of the waning year, the mighty Alleghenies dimly towering before us, the graves of our brethren beneath our feet, it is with hesitation that I raise my poor voice to break the eloquent silence of God and nature. But the duty to which you called me must be performed; grant me, I pray you, your indulgence and your sympathy." Even at the age of eight-six, and though sickly, his strong orator's voice resonated, carrying to the mass of people waiting, as if to receive manna from heaven.

A shiver of excitement shot through Tillie. She too read his speeches in honor of his visit.

He began speaking of funeral rites and customs of ancient Greece, expounding on a battle in ancient Athens. Tillie's brow creased, and she tilted her head, trying to keep up with his logic. What did ancient Greece have to do with what happened here? She and Sam glanced at each other.

"What in the world?" Sam mouthed.

Tillie shrugged. "He's just getting started. I'm sure it'll get better," she whispered in Sam's ear. She crossed her arms, shifted her weight, and turned back to Mr. Everett.

As his speech continued, he brought the battle of ancient Athens into sharp relief, and again, she thrilled to the excitement of his oration.

"…That battlefield where Persia's victim hoard first bowed beneath the brunt of Hellas' sword."

So caught up in his oration, Tillie could almost imagine the blade sliding between her rib cage. She breathed in deep.

"We have assembled, friends, fellow citizens, at the invitation of the Executive of the great central State of Pennsylvania, seconded by the Governors of seventeen other loyal States of the Union, to pay the last tribute of respect to the brave men who, in the hard fought battles of the first, second and third days of July last, laid down their lives for the country on these hillsides and the plains before us, and whose remains have been gathered into the cemetery which we consecrate this day."

Tillie nodded in unconscious agreement. Men fought and died here, and they should honor them.

She scanned the crowd and saw a woman pull a handkerchief out of her reticule and dab at her eyes. A man slipped an arm around her shoulder and kissed her temple.

Mr. Everett talked about the days of Secession, addressing the issues surrounding secession, and brought the crowd forward to July. Tillie leaned forward, eyes locked on him, mouth open slightly. He told her things she didn't know before, or never took the time to put into the grander scheme of the war. He came to June thirtieth.

Such an exciting day, the day the soldiers came to town. In her mind's eye, the river of blue flowed up Washington Street and through town. She reached over and clasped Sam's hand. He squeezed and let go.

"And now the momentous day, a day to be forever remembered in the annals of the country, arrived. Early in the morning on the first of July the conflict began. I need not say that it would be impossible for me to comprise, within the limits of the hour, such a narrative as would do anything like full justice to the all-important events of those three great days, or to the merit of the brave officers and men of every rank, of every arm of the service and of every loyal State, who bore their part in the tremendous struggle."

Mr. Everett went on to describe the fighting on the second and third days as well. Sweeping his arm across the fields of Gettysburg, he let his voice ring out over the crowd. She thrilled to the cadence and rhythm of his words.

He turned to the crux of the war, and once again, she found herself learning something. He spoke of the Constitution, explaining how the South did not have the Constitutional right to secede. He explained the power of the Federal Government, established by the People of the United States. Not by individual states, but the people. He spoke of the rightness and justice of putting the rebellion down.

"And now, friends, fellow-citizens of Gettysburg and Pennsylvania, and you from remoter States, let me again, as we part, invoke a benediction on these honored graves…You feel that it was greatly auspicious for the cause of the country, that the men of the East and the men of the West, the men of the nineteen sister States, stood side by side, on the perilous ridges of the battle…God bless the Union; it is dearer to us for the blood of brave men which has been shed in its defense."

Too bad she didn't have a handkerchief to wipe her wet eyes. Instead, she used a corner of her cloak cuff. As she tilted her head to wipe her face, her gaze caught Father using a handkerchief to wipe his eyes.

Mr. Everett's speech lasted two hours, though the time flew past. A moment of hushed silence greeted its end. Then the crowd broke into wild applause. Mr. Everett bowed his head, acknowledging them, before shuffling back to his seat. His daughter rose and helped him to sit.

The military band played through a quick rendition of "Lincoln And Liberty". The last notes drifted away on the breeze as Mr. Lincoln rose, extending his hand to Mr. Everett, who half rose and shook the President's hand.

Mr. Lincoln towered over the podium. With his left hand, he reached into his coat pocket for his speech while holding his spectacles in his right hand. Then he reached up and removed his hat. With his hat in his hand, he couldn't unfold his speech. He started to put his hat back on, but seemed to change his mind. The wind picked up and almost snapped his speech out of his hand. He half turned first to the right and then to the left.

People around Tillie snickered. Men shook their heads. "Our fearless leader," the man next to her spoke in a low voice to his companion. They laughed.

Tillie glared at him, but he didn't glance in her direction.

Mr. Seward rose and took the President's hat saying something as he did so. The President smiled and answered. Mr. Seward sat back down, crossed his legs, plopped the top hat on his lap, and folded his arms.

Again, President Lincoln surveyed his audience. In his high tenor voice, he began to speak. "Four score and seven years ago, our forefathers brought forth upon this continent a new nation: conceived in liberty, and dedicated to the proposition that all men are created equal."

"What is this claptrap?" a man muttered, taking swift notes. A card in his hat brim identified him as a reporter.

Tillie's brow creased.

"Now—" The President's voice sailed over the crowd. "We are engaged in a great civil war, testing whether that nation, or any nation so conceived, can long endure. We are met on a great battlefield of that war. We have come to dedicate a portion of that field as a final resting place for those who here gave their lives that that nation might live. It is altogether fitting and proper that we should do this."

"The man's a fool," the reporter next to her muttered, but he didn't stop his writing.

His companion shook his head. "Of course it's fitting and proper. That's why we're here."

They laughed together.

Tillie scowled and sidled closer to Father. He put his arm around her and squeezed, as though to say, don't worry, they're the fools. She laid her head on his arm, grateful he understood her.

"But in a larger sense, we cannot dedicate, we cannot consecrate, we cannot hallow this ground. The brave men, living and dead, who struggled here, have consecrated it, far above our poor powers to add or detract. The world will little note, nor long remember what we say here, but it can never forget what they did here. It is for us the living, rather, to be dedicated here to the unfinished work, which they who fought here have thus far so nobly advanced. It is rather for us to be here dedicated to the great task remaining before us. That from these honored dead we take increased devotion to that cause for which they gave the last full measure of devotion. That we here highly resolve that these dead shall not have died in vain. That this nation, under God, shall have a new birth of freedom and that the Government of the people," Mr. Lincoln stressed the last line of his speech.

"By the people, and for the people, shall not perish from the earth."

He turned to sit back down to a smattering of applause.

Tillie raised her hands to clap. Was he done? Mr. Everett went on for two hours. Mr. Lincoln only two minutes.

"Mr. Lincoln certainly doesn't mince words, does he?" Father said a chuckle in his voice. "I believe I just heard the shortest speech ever from a politician."

"James, don't be disrespectful." Mother frowned at him, though her eyes sparkled. "Although, I must say, after Mr. Everett, I expected a bit more."

"Looks like Mr. Seward is going to speak now." Sam pointed to the podium.

Mr. Seward jumped to his feet, as though he realized, as the President seemed not to, the crowd anticipated more. He pulled his notes from his pocket and began speaking, but people drifted away.

With a sense of anticlimax, Tillie walked beside Father. They went to the Pennsylvania section of graves and looked at the wooden markers naming the men lying beneath.

Many people wandered the gravesites of the various other states, perhaps looking for loved ones, perhaps just looking. Would this be their one and only trip to Gettysburg? Their only chance to say goodbye to a dear one? She didn't know, but as her gaze roamed the field, she spied Mrs. Schriver, holding her daughter's hands and talking to Beckie at the far end of the Pennsylvania section. Sadie waved at Tillie. Tillie smiled and waved back.

Their terrible row over the petticoat and her many angry and unkind thoughts toward Beckie pricked her conscience. She never apologized for her part in their argument.

"Would you all excuse me a moment? Beckie is over talking to Mrs. Schriver, and I need to speak with her."

They promised to wait for her by the front gate, and Tillie waved an acknowledging hand as she headed toward Beckie and Mrs. Schriver.

Beckie scowled at Tillie's approach and affected to turn away.

Tillie halted, uncertain of the rightness of her decision. No. Better to apologize than not. She steeled herself and resumed her pace. "Hello, Mrs. Schriver. Hello, Beckie."

"How are you, Tillie?" Mrs. Schriver smiled. "It's been a long time."

"Yes." Tillie's hand found the top of Mollie's head. "I am sorry for that." She smiled down at the child, who stared up with enormous blue eyes. "Hello, Mollie."

"I hear you've been working hard at the former camp hospital." Mrs. Schriver kept the conversation going.

"I did. No nursing duties, but I tried to give the boys some comfort."

"Aid and comfort—to the enemy I heard—traitor," Beckie spat, her hate-filled eyes roamed over Tillie. "Traitor."

"Rebecca!" Mrs. Schriver scowled. "What a nerve."

"That's all right, Mrs. Schriver." Tillie held out a hand palm out to quiet the woman. Tillie stared at her former friend, challenging her with her eyes. "I came over to say I owe you an apology. I said terrible things to you. You have a right to be angry with me."

"Yes you did, and yes I do."

"You both said some terrible things to each other." Mrs. Schriver nudged her sister's shoulder.

"That doesn't matter." Tillie's voice softened as she addressed Mrs. Schriver. "What matters is I gave in to my anger.

I'm sorry. Can you forgive me?" She extended her right hand for a truce handshake.

Beckie glared at her, refusing to shake her hand.

A surge of sadness swept over Tillie. She dropped her hand to her side. "I hollered at you over a silly petticoat. What I didn't understand, as I do now, is they were destroying your home and your father's livelihood right before his eyes. I should have understood, and I didn't, so I judged you. I was wrong. Please forgive me."

Mrs. Schriver gaze bounced between the two of them. "Rebecca," she prompted again when Beckie didn't answer.

Beckie's shoulders shot up and down in a quick, indifferent shrug. "Fine." She walked away.

Pursing her lips, Mrs. Schriver's face showed her sympathy before she followed her younger sister. She caught up, grabbed Beckie's shoulder, and turned her around. Mrs. Schriver said something with force and gestured back toward Tillie. Beckie glanced her way, shook her head, and continued to walk away. Mrs. Schriver let her go, following.

Tillie watched them leave, sending up a prayer for Beckie and her family before rejoining her own by the cemetery gate.

"Well, have you made things new?" Mother wrapped an arm around Tillie when she joined them.

"I tried to." She inclined her head and shrugged to show her lack of success.

"Do you want me to talk to her?" Maggie scanned the crowd, looking for Beckie.

"No." Tillie stopped her. "She needs to make up her mind. Either way, I'll pray for her and will always consider her a friend, even if she doesn't consider me one." She smiled. "A captain I met while at the Weikerts' said this is a terrible war, but God will use it for good." She locked eyes with each member of her family. "No," she shook her head, "it'll be all right. Everything is going to be fine, not as before, I don't want that, but new and better." A surge of love for her family welled up, and she smiled a happy, contented smile. "Come on." Her voice grew stronger as she wrapped her arm around her sister's waist and laid her head on her shoulder in a quick hug. "Let's go home."

Epilogue

"Did you ever make it right with Beckie, Ma?" Annie leaned close in the growing darkness.

"No. Unfortunately, Beckie was never willing to meet me halfway, ever again." A small, sad, half-smile curved her lips. "Beckie married her Mr. Kitzmiller after the war, and I understand they still live in Gettysburg."

As always happened when Tillie told the story, she remembered with fondness and longing those she loved.

After his apprenticeship, Sam left town to begin his own business. Tillie never heard from him again. She tried searching for him to no avail.

James and William both survived the war. James stayed in Washington, D.C. and worked as a government clerk. He had a lovely family.

Poor William didn't fare so well. He came home and took over the butcher shop after Father, but though William married a wonderful Gettysburg woman and seemed to be settling in raising his family, he never shook the demons of his war experience. He lived well, until three years ago when Father died. Without warning, he left everything—including his family. His wife discovered him in a rooming house in Philadelphia, and having given himself over to the ravages of drink, he sent her away. Tillie no longer knew if he was alive or not.

A deep hole of grief lingered in her heart still for her beloved sister, Maggie, who died in 1867, when an epidemic of tuberculosis swept through town. Tillie could never think of her without choking back tears.

Though Gettysburg worked hard to prevent disease, the tuberculosis epidemic claimed many lives, including Mollie and Sadie Schriver. Having contracted the disease, Mollie died in 1872, shortly after Tillie married Horace. Two years later, Sadie succumbed. Both women died at the age of twenty-two.

Mother went to her rest in 1881, and Father followed her eight years later. Now, all those she knew and loved in those days were gone forever.

A tap on her shoulder jolted Tillie.

Horace leaned in, studying her face in the growing dark. "Are you all right, my love?"

She squeezed his hand and kissed his cheek. "I'm fine. I was just remembering." Emotion choked her voice.

Horace drew her into an embrace and kissed the top of her head.

"I still can't believe you met President Lincoln." Harry spoke into the growing darkness. "What was he like?"

"I didn't meet Mr. Lincoln. I just saw him. He tipped his hat to me, and I heard his speech. That's all. Don't exaggerate the situation."

Harry chuckled and lay back down. "Yes, ma'am." He exaggerated his response, but a note of humor lightened his voice, so Tillie chose not to take offense.

"You know…" She jerked a thumb toward her husband. "You would do well to ask your father some questions. He was a soldier."

Horace chuckled around the pipe clenched in his teeth. "Oh, my dear, I was just a lowly private marching hither and yon. Your story is much more interesting, I assure you." He removed his pipe and tapped the bowl against his palm. "We best get a move on." He rose. "We want to get to the park before the fireworks start. We don't want to miss that, do we?"

The children jumped up. Mary brushed grass and leaves off her skirts. Annie, in imitation of her adored sister, adjusted her skirts, while Harry jogged inside for his coat and hat. He reemerged with his father's garments in his hand as well.

While Tillie and Horace strolled, the children disappeared into the park ahead of them. Crowds formed as people, laughing and talking, gathered for the fireworks show.

"I know when you think of those days, they always bring sadness. I'm sorry for that, but I think it important for the children to learn what this," he swept his hand around the park to indicate the celebration, "is really all about."

Tillie smiled. “I agree.” She leaned her head on his shoulder. “Speaking of my experiences does, sometimes, make me sad, especially when I think of the people I loved then.” She turned to him and laid her palms on his cheeks. “But I wouldn’t change my experiences for anything. Those days made me the woman, wife, and mother that I am.”

A whistling sounded to the left, and a small boom reverberated through the air. For a split second, she heard the cannon chasing her from the Weikert house. Colored lights lit their faces. Horace’s eyes glowed with the love that made her feel so safe and secure. She exhaled, and then gazed at the fireworks flashing and decorating the sky. They were supposed to represent those days when the nation was born, but they would always remind her of her girlhood when the nation, rent by growing pains, emerged like her—stronger, wiser, and full of faith and hope.

The End

HISTORICAL NOTES

First, this is a work of fiction. I discovered Tillie's story while traveling in Gettysburg. Though they don't know it, I'm deeply indebted to the Schriver House Museum for first introducing me to the story of the town of Gettysburg and Hettie Schriver in particular. It was while on a tour through that wonderful museum that the tour guide patiently answered my many questions, and after the tour, gave me several books to read. Almost as a throw-away, he also gave me Tillie's memoir.

I also owe a huge debt of gratitude to the Adams County Historical Society for their in-depth knowledge and willingness to share that knowledge. They have a fantastic library of first person accounts and I'm not ashamed to say I spent countless hours in there reading almost every one. Many of their comments and situations made it into my story, most particularly, Salome Myers recounting of hiding their maid and Nellie Auginbaugh's story. The episode of Dr. Billings telling Mollie to come and give the man a drink of water so he could take off his leg, also came from a first person account. Though not Mollie's experience, touched by the memory, I had to use it.

In school, we learn about the movement of the soldiers and the progression of the battle, as though the town itself and the people living there did not exist. I don't ever recall learning how the townspeople coped with this tragedy. I know I never learned what happened to the African-American community. When I read Tillie's memoir, At Gettysburg: Or What a Girl Saw and Heard of the Battle, I just knew I had to tell the entire story.

George Sandoe was the first civilian/soldier to die at Gettysburg. He was a married man in real life, but I wanted to honor him and I needed a way to do that. So in my story, George became Maggie's unmarried beau. He was on his way to Carlisle when killed by Confederate skirmishers, who surprised him and his two companions, who managed to escape.

Maggie died in 1867. I couldn't find anything that told me her cause of death, but a tuberculosis epidemic swept through the area, around that time, so it seemed natural that she should succumb to that disease.

Hettie Schriver's husband, George, never came home from the war. Captured after Christmas 1863, he was sent to the infamous Andersonville prison in South Carolina where he perished, along with so many other soldiers. Hettie eventually remarried and left Gettysburg.

Tillie did nurse soldiers at the Weikert farm and at Camp Letterman. She did not record in her memoir if she ever nursed the Confederate soldiers, but from what I learned of her through my research, I decided she was the kind of person who would have. She saw so much horror for a young woman of fifteen and I consider myself honored to have gotten to know her as well as I did. Out of necessity much of her life that she didn't record in her memoir I invented. I tried to stay true to the Tillie Pierce that I came to know through years of study and I hope my readers feel I accomplished that goal. Tillie died in 1914 at the age of 66, just days after her birthday.

ABOUT THE AUTHOR

Angela Moody lives in Vermont with her husband, Jim, her daughter, Alison and their two cats. She also has a son, Stephen, and his wife, Amanda.

Angela has been writing short stories and novels from an early age, always in the historic fiction genre where she feels she shines.

One of her passions is crochet. From the time she learned the craft, she was “hooked”. She loves reading, writing stories and spending time with her family. One of the items on her bucket list is to visit every civil war battlefield site at the time of year each battle took place.

No Safe Haven is her first Christian novel and she has plans for two other historical fiction novels as part of a three book set entitled “Young American Heroines.”

Angela is a member of American Christian Fiction Writers.

Connect with me online:
Facebook: http://facebook.com/AuthorAngelaMoody
Amazon.com/Angela Moody

Did you like this book? Please go to Amazon.com and leave a review.

31352279R00201

Made in the USA
Middletown, DE
27 April 2016